Praise for

Look for Me

"Shawgo's writing captivates both the medical and nonmedical reader. A compelling story. I look forward to the sequel!"

—*Michael Cacciatore, MD, OB/GYN*

"I found the book engaging and difficult to put down. I felt like I was actually there."

—*Melanie Reis, CNM, ARNP*

"A deep display of the enduring strength and compassion that inspires caregivers. I recommend this book; it is a true lesson and embracing story."

—*Caren J. Bock, BSN-RN, CPN, Author of* Wings: A Story of Transformation

Wait for Me

"I found this book very informative and entertaining. It provides an insightful look at a facet of our military history that has too often been overlooked. The author has a great future ahead that is well deserved."

—*Donald L. Finch, Captain, United States Navy (Ret.)*

"I find Janet's writing style very compelling, leaving the reader to wonder what will be found just around the corner. This is a tribute to all females who sacrifice their lives in the service to others."

—*Christine Leblond, Colonel, United States Army (Ret.)*

"*Wait for Me* catches your attention from the very beginning. Janet has shown the courage of women during a time of war. They answered the call to serve their country and went where the need was greatest."

—*Pamela L. Little, Captain, United States Air Force, North Carolina*

Find Me Again

"I have read and enjoyed all of Janet's books, and after reading the first few pages of *Find Me Again*, I know I'm in for another great ride. Janet writes strong and wonderfully self-sufficient women, and she captivates her readers with powerful story lines that flow without friction. I am a huge fan, and will continue to be for years to come. Bravo, Janet!"

—*Neeley Bratcher, Author of The Victoria Childs series*

"Janet has done it again—a wonderful story from the first to last paragraph."

—*Michael Cacciatore, MD OB/GYN*

"Wonderful story of the continued journey of two families brought together once more inspired by courage and faith. The strong spirit of family has built bridges between the generations by preserving and sharing their histories and keepsakes. Experiences shape us and instill within us values that give direction and meaning to our lives, allowing the bonds of family to always be strong."

—*Rosemarie Masetta, RN, BSN*

"Janet does it again with the final book in the *Look for Me* trilogy. Set aside plenty of time to read, as you will not want to put this one down. There is a larger sense of the paranormal element in *Find Me Again* than in the others. The love story was brought to a wonderful ending with a great lead into a spin-off series. I can't wait to see what else is in store for us from this wonderful indie author!"

—*Stephanie Shaw, Steph's Book Club*

FIND ME AGAIN

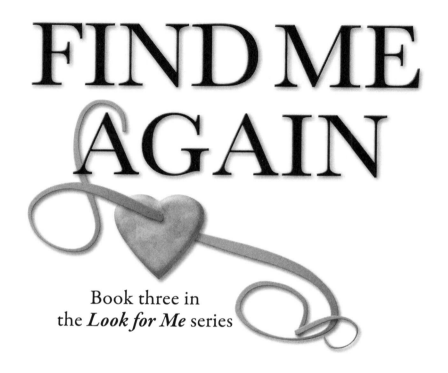

Book three in
the *Look for Me* series

JANET K. SHAWGO

Two Harbors Press
322 First Avenue N, 5th floor
Minneapolis, MN 55401
612.455.2293
www.TwoHarborsPress.com

ISBN-13: 978-1-62652-614-3
LCCN: 2014901653

Distributed by Itasca Books

Book Design by James Arneson

Printed in the United States of America

Titles by Janet Shawgo

Look for Me

Awards

Winner Romance Division 2012 International Book Awards

Winner Historical Fiction 2012 Chanticleer Book Review

Finalist Historical Fiction Division 2012 International Book Awards

Finalist Romance Division 2012 Next Indie Generation Book Awards

Finalist Mainstream 2012 Chanticleer Book Review

Finalist Historical Fiction 2012 Chanticleer Book Review

Finalist Historical Fiction 2013 Laramie Awards Chanticleer Book Review

Finalist Romance Division 2013 USA Best Book Awards

Wait for Me

Awards

Finalist Romance Division 2013 Next Indie Generation Book Awards

Finalist Best Design Fiction Division 2013 Next Indie Generation Book Awards

Finalist Romance Division 2013 International Book Awards

Finalist Historical Fiction Division 2013 Chanticleer Book Review

Finalist Romance 2013 Chatelaine Awards Chanticleer Book Review

To Mom and Dad, thanks for watching over us.
I love and miss you both every day.

Acknowledgments

Over the past few years putting this series together I have had the wonderful opportunity to reconnect with so many of the people that have touched my life over the last twenty years as a travel nurse. My book tour across several states introduced me to new readers, allowed me time with family and to spend a precious moment that will not come again. The smiles and support of everyone has kept me going on the path to finish. My family has been there pushing and encouraging me. My sister, Joan, reminded me to keep my readers interested and most of all happy. To my readers, you never cease to amaze me. The wonderful comments and passion about your favorite part of each book down to the smallest detail lets me know the late nights and rewrites were worth the time. I have been fortunate to win numerous awards, be associated with Dunn Brothers' Coffee & Books program, and have the continued smiles and support of my publisher, Two Harbors Press: thank you.

This series may be finished but I am not. There are more books in the mill, and I hope to keep you interested in each one. Open your mind, read a book, any book by any author, and escape for an afternoon with a cup of coffee, tea, or a glass of wine.

WHITE FAMILY TREE

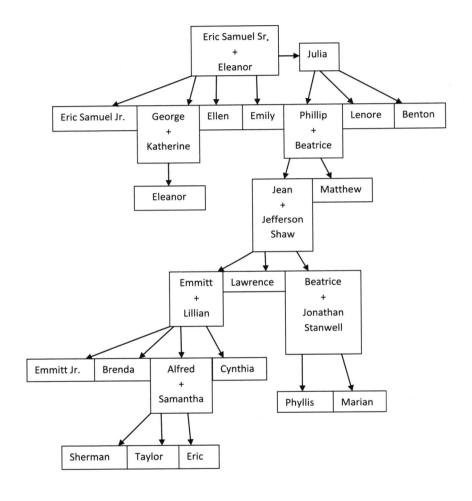

BOWEN FAMILY TREE

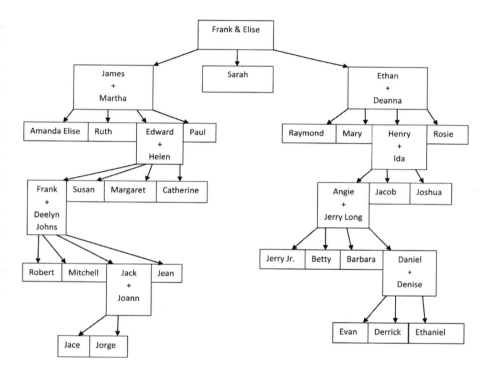

KEENS FAMILY TREE ~ MISSISSIPPI

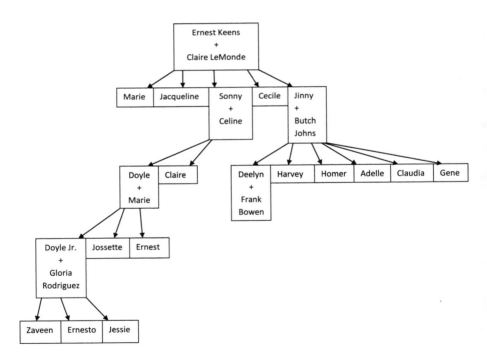

Duncin Keens
+
Maudie Sandifer

| Duncin Jr. | John | Ezekiel | Abraha | Luke | Mark | Matthew | Martha Ann Catherine + James Bowen |

KEENS FAMILY TREE ~ LOUISIANA

Ernest Keens
+
Claire LeMonde

Marie | Jacqueline | Sonny + Celine | Cecile | Jinny + Butch Johns

Doyle + Marie | Claire

Deelyn + Frank Bowen | Harvey | Homer | Adelle | Claudia | Gene

Doyle Jr. + Gloria Rodriguez | Jossette | Ernest

Zaveen | Ernesto | Jessie

Benjamin Family Tree

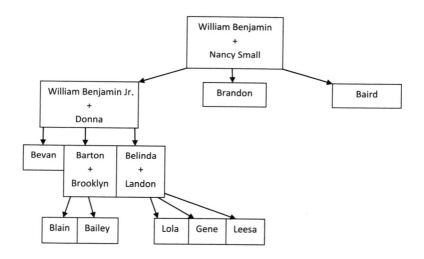

Prologue 🙠

Beatrice Shaw-Stanwell sat in her office at the *White Daily Journal*. She looked around the office and could not believe so much time had passed. It seemed like yesterday she was a child pestering her two older brothers, Emmitt and Larry. Beatrice never intended to work or manage the newspaper. She had been pushed into the business against her will by her mother. "It's your duty to the White-Shaw family," she had told Beatrice. A duty she fought but later came to like, enjoy, and eventually love. She had been at the *Journal* since six-thirty this morning checking on the morning edition and finances, and now it was time to deal with personal business. The papers on her desk would transfer management to her great-nephew Sherman Shaw. Beatrice looked up at the photograph of her three great-nephews on her desk. Sherman, the oldest, was very much like her late brother Emmitt, driven financially and technologically. He had always been interested in the workings of the paper, even as a child. He paid his dues working long hours even throughout college. His computer skills had brought the paper online and secured a future for the *Journal.*

Beatrice had hoped that Taylor, the middle nephew, would be the one to run the paper, but his life had taken the same path Larry had traveled. She thought about her brother, Larry: his life as a war correspondent and his work after the war living in Hawaii. Beatrice remembered how quickly Taylor had left New York right out of college. He told the family, "It has been far too long since our family reported the news." His writing style was like that of Larry and an ancestor named Samuel White. When stories from all three were placed next to one another it was as if there had been one author. Taylor's decision to be an independent reporter had taken him to Africa. Beatrice knew he would eventually report for the *Journal*, but first he wanted to prove he didn't need Shaw money.

Eric, the youngest, had not finished high school, and his interest was basketball and girls at this moment in his young life. Beatrice's own daughters had no desire to run the family business, nor did her grandchildren. According to the last will and testament of Phillip Alfred White, the *White Daily Journal* would be passed onto "family that would continue the newspaper."

"Mrs. Stanwell," her secretary said.

"Yes."

"There is a man here to see you."

"I'm not expecting anyone this morning," Beatrice stated.

"He said his name is Bentwood Milton, attorney for your late brother."

Beatrice was perturbed this man had arrived without an appointment, but this was something Larry would have arranged to irritate her even in death. Larry had died two months ago and this visit would be about his estate.

"Show him in."

Bentwood Milton had taken a chance with his unscheduled arrival at the newspaper. Beatrice Stanwell was not a woman to be seen without an appointment, but he was following the instructions left by his client and good friend, Larry White-Shaw. Bentwood's phone calls this morning had paid off, and he felt what he had to tell her in regards to Larry's will would be better received here in the office.

"Mr. Milton," the secretary addressed him.

"Yes."

"Mrs. Stanwell will see you now."

Bentwood took a deep breath and walked into a large office. He observed the numerous awards that hung on the wall to his left, and then turned his attention to the photographs on the right. These were photographs of the Shaw family with presidents, senators, and dignitaries from around the world. Bentwood then focused on the commanding presence of the matriarch of the White-Shaw family, who sat behind an Asian rosewood desk. "Thank you for seeing me without an appointment, Mrs. Stanwell," Bentwood said and shook her hand.

"Please sit down. I assume this concerns my brother's estate in Hawaii."

"Yes it does," Bentwood said.

"Larry never did hold to the standards of brotherly courtesy, so your unexpected visit today does not come as a surprise." She smiled. "What does my late brother have to say in his will?"

Bentwood cleared his throat. "Do you know a family by the name of Bowen?"

❦

Two hours later, Beatrice watched as Bentwood left her office. She had heard the story of Samuel White and Sarah Bowen from her grandfather. A love lost due to war, and now it had repeated itself: Larry had lost the love of his life during WWII. Her name was Susan, Susan Bowen. She was a relative of Sarah Bowen. Their two families had been connected for over a century. Beatrice leaned back into her soft leather chair, looked at the clock on her desk, and then reached for the bottom drawer. She took out her favorite bottle of bourbon and poured two fingers into a crystal glass. *Larry, what the hell were you thinking?* she thought, and drank the bourbon in one swallow. Her brother had left a daunting task to his great nephew, Taylor, and his instructions were clear. Larry's estate in Hawaii, all his wealth, and his part of the *Journal* would be Taylor's

once he finished the story of the Bowens and Whites. The items—
a necklace, note, and journal belonging to Sarah Bowen—must be
returned to her heirs along with all proceeds from the book once it
was published. This responsibility would be Taylor's to complete.
Larry left another twist to this task: Taylor is to find an heir that is
presently a nurse. This person will be the liaison between the Bowen
and White families. Taylor must make the trip to Waynesboro that
Larry never made and then pay his respects at the Bowen cemetery,
to Susan.

To make matters more complicated, Beatrice had no way to contact Taylor due to his unknown location at this time and no definite
return date to New York. She turned and opened the antique safe
that had remained in use for over a hundred years at the paper. She
took the first edition of *The Women Who Travel in War* out of the
safe. Beatrice knew this should be at the museum, but there was an
emotional attachment. She ran her hand across the book, written
by her ancestor so many years ago, about the Civil War and the
nurses that had traveled during the war to heal. She opened the
box Bentwood had given her and placed the book and instructions
in it. Beatrice felt this might help Taylor, give him a starting point
for his research. All the handwritten notes and personal items of
Samuel White had been given to her favorite museum for preservation and safety. Taylor would have access to these at his leisure
should he need further information. She turned back and reached
for the phone on her desk.

"Miss Wise," Beatrice said.

"Yes."

"Would you contact Sherman at his home?"

"Right away."

"Tell him I need to see him here at the office as soon as possible.
Then please contact the attorneys for the paper and ask them to
come, too."

"Anything else, Mrs. Stanwell?"

"No, that will be all for now, thank you," Beatrice said as she
poured another two fingers in her glass.

Beatrice must now tell Sherman what had been left to his brother. She did not look forward to this conversation. Sherman and Taylor had been fiercely competitive over the years—academics, sports, women; the list of arguments went on and on. Larry's controlling interest in the newspaper was something he had never flaunted or enforced over the years. This turn of events would increase tensions between the two brothers. Sherman's obsession over the *Journal* would now intensify. The legacy he had expected, counted on since Larry's death, now belonged to Taylor.

Chapter One 🐾

LOUISIANA STATE UNIVERSITY
BATON ROUGE, LOUISIANA
FRIDAY, MAY 19, 2000
7:00 P.M.

Zack stood with classmates and waited to be called to the stage to receive the diploma for all her hard work over the past four years. The political science degree with a minor in mid-Eastern languages was a personal goal set and now attained. The language courses had been grueling but, as she now realized, worth the hard work. Zack had gone to the university under a full scholarship and maintained the grade point average to keep it. Zack's family back home just didn't have the kind of money it took for a four-year degree. Before college, she had worked for her uncle as a pilot dusting crops and as a guide for gun and bow hunters on their land back home. All this had helped to open a bank account for emergencies that might arise while at the university, but additional jobs on campus also helped.

"Zaveen Adelle Catherine Keens." The speaker called her name.

Zack could hear her family's hoots and hollers, which made the smile on her face even wider. She walked to the stage, received her cords for academic achievement, and shook hands with the chancellor; then she held her paper high and left the stage. She let out a huge sigh of relief and was just a little sad that her "cousin," Jace, had not been able to attend her graduation. They would get together later to talk and maybe Jace could help her decide on the next step to take—masters and then possibly a PhD?

Zack's family was not the only party interested in her graduation. Bevan Benjamin had been at LSU for several weeks talking with counselors and faculty about a small number of students. He opened his file on Zaveen. She had become of interest to the company when she enrolled in a specific foreign-language class. He looked at her history: born January 1, 1978, in Morgan City, Louisiana; mother, Gloria Rodriguez; father, Doyle Keens Jr.; and two younger brothers. She was proficient with gun and bow, a licensed pilot, and spoke three foreign languages fluently. Zaveen had graduated early from high school, and taken accelerated classes that had given her college credits, which allowed her to enter LSU as a sophomore. What impressed Bevan was her family history; she was related to Deelyn Bowen, who had been a Jedburgh in World War II, information not known to Zaveen or the public. She was small at five foot three inches, had brown skin, black hair and eyes to match, was physically fit, and now spoke Arabic. Bevan had spent time with Zaveen's language professor and had received confirmation that she would be able to tackle Farsi and Kurdish with no difficulty. She was single, with no immediate attachments other than family. He took an envelope from her file, left his seat, and walked toward the family and friends that had just acknowledged Zaveen's accomplishment. He would now see if she would answer the call of her country and follow him to Washington. Zaveen was perfect, a perfect candidate as a field agent with the CIA. . . .

Commencement completed, Zack now looked for her family and prepared for the endless photos, hugs, and conversing between English, French, and Spanish.

"Excuse me, Zaveen Keens?" a stranger asked.

Zaveen turned around to look up at the stranger. She recognized this man; he had been on campus for a month in the common areas.

"Yes, can I help you?" Zack responded and held out her hand.

As she shook his hand the flood of information began even though she tried to stop it. *Why did this always happen at the wrong time? Damn gift!* she thought. He was older, with graying temples;

handsome; slight Southern accent. She also picked up on anxious-
ness—perhaps he couldn't wait to get back to the hotel so he could
take his evening run? Single (no ring or tan line on his left ring
finger) . . . but there was someone in his life; Armani suit and tie,
shoes that cost three hundred dollars when he bought them new a
year ago. Finally, the light scent of Gio. He worked for the government and now she was curious how he knew her by sight and name.

"I believe you can. My name is Bevan Benjamin and I have something for you." Bevan took the envelope and handed it to Zack. "I'll
be here until Wednesday and would like to talk with you about your
future plans. What I offer pays well—good benefits, retirement, and
travel."

Zack was surprised with this offer. She hadn't even thought
about a job. Right now all she wanted was to go home, be with her
family, fly, and spend some time out in nature.

"I assume your contact information is in this envelope?"

"Yes, and the address for an interview, if you're interested," Bevan
answered.

"Zaveen, Zaveen," a female voice called.

Zaveen turned and heard her mother congratulating her in
Spanish, followed by her father in French. She smiled and turned
back to ask another question of Mr. Benjamin but he was gone.
Zaveen looked at the envelope with her name on it and decided to
open it later, after family had left and she could be alone with her
own thoughts.

Bevan Benjamin's hotel
Baton Rouge
Wednesday, May 24, 2000
5:00 p.m.

Bevan had finished his last scheduled interview. Out of the
ten invitations he had given out at graduation, five had made

appointments and two had just shown up. Three had not responded, and Zaveen was one of those. Bevan felt he couldn't have been that wrong about her. His flight back to Washington was at nine that night so he would need to leave around seven. Bevan decided to eat, have a drink, and think about the three candidates he felt would be company material. He packed, took his files with him, and went down to the hotel restaurant and bar.

"What can I get you?" the female bartender asked.

"Grey Goose dirty martini and a menu, please," Bevan responded.

Bevan took the menu from the bartender and watched her start his drink. As he looked at the menu he realized he hadn't eaten all day and the surf and turf sounded wonderful.

"Here you go: one dirty martini. Ready to order?"

"Surf and turf—" Bevan was interrupted before he could finish his order.

"Medium rare on the steak, baked potato—plain—butter and sour cream on the side, steamed carrots, soup of the day, Irish coffee, and crème brûlée after dinner," Zaveen finished ordering for Bevan.

The bartender looked at Bevan and he nodded his head.

"Am I that easy to read?" Bevan asked and looked at the young woman standing in jeans, LSU T-shirt, and purple and gold high-tops.

"Not really, I have this ability," Zaveen answered.

"I see that, and you were correct about my order."

"My grandma, maw on my father's side, called it an inner sight. She always told me it was a gift from God . . ." Zaveen hesitated.

"But?" Bevan tried to encourage her.

"But it's difficult at times to always know more than you should about people, even if they have just left a room."

"I don't understand," Bevan said.

"Most people don't realize they leave a part of themselves wherever they go. Not just physical things like hairs or fibers but thoughts and feelings," she responded.

"Is this ability something you can control?"

"Sometimes . . . but the stronger the emotions the faster the information comes at me like a dam breaking and water flowing fast.

It can be overwhelming." She stopped and focused on why she had come. "I apologize for interrupting your dinner but the clerk at the desk said you were here."

"It's fine, Zaveen, I didn't think my profile of you had been wrong." Bevan looked at the bartender. "We're going to move to the corner table."

Zaveen followed Bevan and sat down as he pulled out her chair.

"Thank you. My family didn't leave until today. My parents felt they needed to help pack my apartment and all my clothes. This outfit is all that was left in my room. They're anxious for me to come home."

"You look fine and I understand. What can I do for you?" Bevan said.

"If it isn't too late I would like to talk with you about your job offer with the CIA."

Bevan smiled and took out his cell phone to reschedule his flight.

Chapter Two &

Jace Bowen-Kindle sat on the tailgate of her dark green, 1998 Toyota pickup, alongside the road just outside of Chinle, waiting for the moon to rise. She had spent the entire day in Gallop, New Mexico, going through the shops, and had wished at times she still had a home. The Native American artwork was beautiful—paintings, rugs, carvings, jewelry; no detail escaped the artists' eyes. She had allowed herself to buy a few items like a coyote fetish, a dream catcher with several strands of cedar beads, sage, and something special for Zaveen: a raven fetish. Jace was so proud of her distant relative for finishing college. They wrote to one another often since the death of Jace's grandmother Deelyn. Jace thought how strange it was that death always brought families together instead of gathering to celebrate the living. When Jace first met Zaveen, "Zack,"they talked like they had known each other for years instead of only a few minutes. Their friendship had continued to grow since the funeral. Jace regretted not attending Zaveen's graduation but knew she understood. They would find time later to talk and share the changes in their lives.

Jace thought about the conversation earlier today with several Navajo women about plants and herbs growing locally in the wild. She made notes in a small journal on remedies, specifically to remember new plants she had not used in the past. Jace was excited about the possibility of adding to her growing collection of medicinal herbs. She had always grown or collected herbs, plants, and flowers to make teas, creams, and oils for natural healing. She had been fortunate enough to graduate from a college where there was a holistic program, which allowed her to later pass a certification exam. Holistic healing was her calling; she felt pulled toward the type of care that treated the whole person.

She moved a few bags in the back of the truck and found the large box her mother had sent just before she left her last assignment. Jace pulled out a pocket knife and opened it. The first thing Jace saw was a letter from her attorney. There was still enough sunlight left for her to read over the papers that stated she was no longer married and could take back her maiden name of Bowen. Jace took a deep breath. *Nice birthday gift.* Kind of like the gift her husband gave when he announced that he didn't want to wait to start a family any longer; so he started one with another woman. That was almost two years ago. She closed her eyes and rubbed her head, feeling the rise of what could be nuisance. Jace reached in her backpack, took out a bottle of lavender, and then put some on her temples and the base of her neck, knowing this had always worked to stop a headache in the past. It would take time now to change her name back to Bowen on credit cards, her nursing license . . . a lot of busy work. She knew at twenty-six she had plenty of time for a family, but her career was important to her at this point in her life. Jace came from a long line of nurses and healers; at least that's what she had been told. She knew about a great-aunt that had gone overseas in World War II as a nurse and had been killed by a Nazi spy. The family never talked about Aunt Susan's death, no matter how many times she had asked. Her grandfather refused to discuss her or much about the war. The only thing he would ever say was the war gave him his wife. Grandfather would look at her and tell her that she had Susan's eyes, sweet smile, and love of nature.

Over the past year as a traveling nurse, Jace had taken two assignments and found that she loved being able to fill the needs of the hospitals. What she had really enjoyed was going to new places and experiencing all there was to see and do there, from the largest city to the smallest town. Jace's thoughts were interrupted when she heard the cries of the crows and distant call of coyotes. The rest of the items in the box would have to wait until later. She took out her CD player, placed the ear phones in her ears, lit the sage smug stick, and listened to the drums of the Navajo as the full moon sat on top of the mesa and filled the valley below in white light.

AMERICAN AIRLINES 757
NEW YORK-BOUND FLIGHT
10:45 P.M.

Taylor Shaw was on the final leg of a two-day flight home to New York. He sat in first class, rubbed his head, and reread the telegram he had received just three days earlier:

> *Aunt Beatrice is dead, heart attack, you have responsibilities at home.*
>
> *Sherman*

Taylor shook his head. Sherman was arrogant, thoughtless, and selfish. This telegram saddened him. He had hoped his absence would calm the waters between the two of them: obviously not. He didn't relish the thought of the necessary reading of will and business of the paper. He was thankful he had no interest or part of the family business, other than reporting the news. Taylor looked forward to seeing Eric. His younger brother had dropped out of college to work on his photography career. He hoped to talk him back into the classroom to finish his degree. Eric was a free spirit, enjoyed freelancing and the quick money that came with it, but he had a genuine passion and innate ability to see what others could not—and capture it on film. Taylor had seen that ability only one other time.

"Mr. Shaw, would you mind signing this?" the flight attendant asked.

Taylor looked up, took the magazine, and saw it had his photograph and article about Africa. He took a deep breath, as this was the last article he had done with his photographer Heather. She was Korean, orphaned at birth, but had been adopted and brought to the States at the age of six months. She used a camera like it was part of her. Heather had been able to keep up with him in the field; she had never faltered or backed away. Her photographs helped him win several awards. He had not intended to fall in love with her, but he proposed under a hail of bullets and bombs. They had agreed to marry once this story was printed. All journalists know the dangers when they enter into battles on foreign lands; death always seems far away, until it happens in front of you. Heather had been shot by a stray bullet intended for someone else in another part of the world—a "casualty." She died in his arms. It had been six months ago when he stood at her gravesite, and now another funeral. Death comes in threes, or so he had been told as a young child. Old wives' tale, he had hoped. Taylor signed the magazine and handed it back to the attendant.

"Thank you. Did anyone ever tell you that you have the most unusual green eyes, almost haunting?"

Taylor smiled. "Yes, I hear that quite often, thank you."

"We'll be landing at La Guardia soon. Can I get you anything?"

"Yes, I could use something for a headache, if you have it," Taylor answered.

As he swallowed the tablets he leaned back and looked out the window to the welcoming lights of home.

JACE'S HOTEL ROOM IN CANYON DE CHELLY
CHINLE, ARIZONA
9:00 P.M.

Jace fumbled with the key to her room. Once the door opened she dropped the box and backpack on the bed, then rolled her suitcase to the corner. She looked around the room and wrinkled her nose. She opened her backpack and took out a small oil burner and tea light, then poured several drops of eucalyptus oil in the top of the burner. She lit the tea light and sniffed the air. "Now that's better."

She was tired but needed to get things ready for tomorrow. There was a full day planned, so she took her hiking boots out, oiled them, and laid out clothing for her walk down to White House Ruins. She then picked up the brochure on helicopter rides over the Grand Canyon. This would be a birthday gift to herself, and she would enjoy every minute of it before heading to her assignment in Flagstaff. Jace was hungry but wanted to shower. She reached for the menu and made her choice, ordered room service, and headed toward the bathroom. Timing was everything. Once showered, Jace put on her favorite pair of worn-out blue scrubs just as she heard the knock on the door—dinner was served. Once the last French fry was gone, she turned on the TV and started to comb out the tangles in her blonde hair. She pulled the box over and dumped everything out on the bed. There were cards from family and another box that had an old bible and pouch of some kind. Jace looked for the letter from her mother; inside she found a check for ten thousand dollars. She smiled, as this was her part of the Bowen trust; the money came from the sale of a large part of land in Waynesboro, Georgia. She had fond memories of the farm and family trips there as a child. Jace could remember going to the Bowen cemetery to help tidy up the grounds and pay respects to loved ones. She looked at the check; it was a blessing but would not cover all the debt she had at the moment. The divorce had left her with little reserve and her now ex-husband had not sent the money for his half of the house. Jace's lawyer had told her last week he would push harder on that money—money she would need to start life over. She looked at the bible; it belonged to Martha Keens Bowen. Then she looked at the pouch, which belonged to Sarah Bowen—ancestor, healer, and Civil War nurse. According to her mother's letter there was a journal that Sarah had kept during the Civil War. Jace's great-aunt Susan had taken it overseas during World War II and it had been lost. Jace opened the pouch and found a bell, some old rags, and a book that had been written in the 1860s titled *The Women Who Travel in War.* There was another book on healing, written in 1835, and a handwritten manual about the usage and preservation of herbs, by Elise and Sarah Bowen. The pages were soft but the edges were beginning to become brittle and tear. She was concerned this book would disintegrate if she didn't take appropriate measures to preserve it—and soon. She would call her friends in Galveston and see if they knew of a place to preserve this history somewhere in the Houston area. Jace was saddened about Sarah's journal that had been lost; what stories it must have held. She opened the published book and read the dedication to Sarah. The room suddenly filled with the scent of lilacs, overpowering the burner and causing a sudden chill to run down her back. She opened her cell phone to make a call home but there was no signal.

"Damn it," Jace said out loud.

She picked up the phone in the room and made a long-distance call home to San Antonio. Jace was glad to hear her mother's voice.

"Mom, can you tell me about the items in this box?" Jace asked.

"Jace, the items in the box had been kept by your relative Angie Long. They were to be passed on to the next nurse in our family. There hasn't been another nurse since your aunt Susan and Angie."

"Mom, I don't understand," Jace said.

"Jace, honey, this is our family history and you are now its keeper."

Chapter Three 🙦

WHITE DAILY JOURNAL OFFICE
MANHATTAN
FRIDAY, JUNE 2, 2000
12:30 A.M.

Sherman now claimed the chair and desk that once belonged to Aunt Beatrice. He waited for Taylor—five years he had waited for this moment, five years he had not been able to control or make the changes he wanted at the newspaper. Now he couldn't make any of these decisions because Uncle Larry had given it all to Taylor! He had talked with the attorneys at the paper; their only suggestion was to buy Taylor out. Sherman had worked at the *Journal* since he was fourteen, and now at thirty-one, he felt this business belonged to him—he deserved it. He would have the *Journal*, whatever the cost.

"Mr. Shaw, your brother is arriving," the security officer announced over the intercom.

"Thank you."

Sherman turned to open the safe. "Piece of junk!" He intended to rid himself of this very soon. Sherman took out the box, letter, and the final will and testament of Lawrence Samuel White Shaw. He swiveled back as he heard the door open.

"Nice touch, Sherman; first-class ticket home and now sending the limo for me. You know how I feel about such things."

Sherman smiled and pushed everything toward Taylor.

"What is this, Sherman? I'm tired and not in the mood."

"It's something our dear late uncle left you."

"Larry?" Taylor asked.

"Yes."

"What the hell is it? I'm tired of your fucking mind games, Sherman!"

"You really don't know, do you?"

"Know what?" Taylor asked.

"That Uncle Larry left you his part of the *Journal* . . . the controlling part."

The shock on Taylor's face answered Sherman's last statement.

Taylor sat down, and then opened the letter addressed to him from Bentwood Milton.

Sherman rose, walked over to the bar, and poured a drink. "You really didn't know, did you? Scotch?"

"You know I don't drink Scotch and, no, I had no idea," Taylor said and continued to read over the letter. He then opened the envelope that contained the will and began to scan it quickly.

Sherman took out his aunt's favorite bottle of bourbon and poured Taylor a drink.

"I'll take a rum and coke since you're pouring, brother," Eric said as he entered the room.

Taylor stood up, shook hands, and then hugged his baby brother. "Are you old enough to drink? When did you get so tall?"

"Twenty-two. My last birthday, which you missed. Welcome home. I see Sherman has given you the good news," Eric said and laughed.

"I'm glad you think this is funny," Sherman said.

"I think anything that irritates the shit out of you is funny. This is what you get for being the manipulative jerk you've always been. Thank God Uncle Larry knew what you were like and chose not to give in like Aunt Beatrice," Eric said.

"You weren't left anything, Eric—that should tell you what the family thinks of you," Sherman said.

Eric's voice began to grow in intensity. "I will choose what to do with my life—not you. I'm not going to let you control me. Keep the damn family money for all I care. I'll survive, Sherman!"

"Enough of this bickering! It accomplishes nothing," Taylor said. "Sherman, what do you want from me?"

"I want to buy you out."

"Have you read this?" Taylor said and handed Sherman the will.

"No," Sherman said and took the will and began to read. The crease between his eyes became deeper and his face and neck turned red.

"Careful, Sherman, or you might explode," Eric said. "It looks to me like there's more good news in those pages."

"That bastard! What the hell was wrong with him?" Sherman said and threw the will on his desk. Aunt Beatrice had failed to go into details about the will. She had only told him Taylor had been willed the controlling interest in the paper. Old bitch held out on him just like Larry.

Eric picked up the will and began to read. "Oh, this is great. I love an adventure."

"I need to make copies for you and the paper's attorneys. But it's very clear that until I fulfill the terms laid down in the will I cannot do anything with my controlling interest," Taylor said and looked at Eric.

Sherman wished he had shredded everything now, but Bentwood Milton called every month to check on Taylor. He knew there were other copies. "Alright, how long do you think this little adventure is going to take you?"

"Sherman, I'm going to need to look through all this information, read the manuscript, journal, and the first edition of *The Women Who Travel in War*. If you need or want an answer right now it's not going to happen," Taylor said.

"Well, I will be happy to help you since I'm not busy at the moment," Eric said.

"Wasting your life while your inheritance sits in the bank," Sherman replied.

"Taylor, what do you need to start this project?" Eric asked, ignoring Sherman.

"Well, once we have paid our respects to Aunt Beatrice, I think there were personal papers given to the museum that belonged to

Samuel. They need to be looked at and then we need to make notes from them," Taylor said.

"I can do that," Eric said.

"I'll get a few private investigators started on this for you and see if we can speed things up," Sherman said.

"No, didn't you read the will? I have to do this myself. I don't believe there is a time limit. Sherman, I have never cared about the politics of the paper but since I do have controlling interest, I will carry out Uncle Larry's wishes. You can continue to run the paper. Once I have fulfilled this we can sit down and discuss a buyout."

"Where do you need to go?" Eric asked.

"Hawaii. I need to contact the newspaper where Uncle Larry worked; maybe there is still someone alive that knew him and can give me information."

"Awesome, road trip!" Eric said.

"Who said you could come along?" Taylor said and smiled.

"I won't interfere and I can run errands, be an extra hand for you," Eric said.

"You will want to talk with his attorney and good luck with his old apartment," Sherman said and laughed to himself, thinking about the shoe box his uncle lived in there in Hawaii. He then thought about his brother's attempt to make a holy quest out of this situation. A simple phone call could finish this in a week's time. He would give Taylor space but he would not wait forever and intended to speed things up if at all possible, regardless of what Larry's will stated.

"Eric, I want to go home. I'm tired, need a shower, and a suit for the funeral," Taylor said.

"I had several sent to the house from my tailor," Sherman said.

"Of course you did," Taylor responded.

"You can't be seen in a suit off the rack. For God's sake, Taylor, you're a Shaw," Sherman chastised his brother.

"Come on bro, we have plans to make and plane tickets to buy," Eric said.

Sherman watched his brothers leave his office. He walked to the window and watched them get into a taxi instead of the limo.

Sherman's frustration and anger began to grow again. He walked back to the desk and picked up the phone. The top button was pushed and he waited.

"This is Sherman Shaw; I have another job for you." He then hung up the phone and faxed a copy of the will to an unlisted number.

❦

SHAW FAMILY PENTHOUSE
MADISON AVE.
2:00 A.M.

Taylor walked out of the bathroom—towel wrapped around his tall, tanned body—and looked at the ten suits Sherman had brought to the apartment when one would have sufficed. He turned as the door opened, knowing it was Eric.

"Whoa, I didn't think there were gyms where you were at in Africa," Eric said. Just then he knew Taylor was upset. "What's wrong?"

"Do you realize that the cost of these ten suits would feed an entire village in Africa for a year or more and add another building to the hospital in Cameroon?" Taylor said. "And as far as the muscles go, it's from helping with hundred-pound bags of food for refugees, building temporary housing, and carrying water for pregnant women."

"Sorry, I didn't know," Eric apologized.

Taylor looked at his brother. "It's okay. How could you know? I wasn't the best at writing to you. Tell me what's been happening here."

"Things haven't been the best here since you left. Taylor, you know what Sherman is like—his love of money and power has no boundary."

"Yes, I do know and I intend to make this a lesson in humility and patience; something he has never possessed in his adult life.

23

Mother, Father, and Aunt Beatrice bowed to his every whim, but not this time. This time he will have to wait."

"He's not going to like it," Eric said and smiled.

"It's time he learned not everything revolves around him," Taylor said. He grabbed a pair of sweat bottoms and put them on.

"Well, while you were showering the dust off I made reservations for us."

"I hope you gave us enough time to look at Samuel's papers?"

"I did, and I got a hell of a deal. We leave July Fourth, that gives us almost a month; and the seats are business class. I hope that is acceptable," Eric said.

"Fine," Taylor said.

"Uncle Larry was a surfer, wasn't he?" Eric asked.

"Yes, and an avid swimmer, but his chain smoking killed him," Taylor answered. "I need to call Mr. Milton tomorrow and let him know when we'll be arriving."

"You know Sherman intends to throw the antique safe out," Eric said.

"Damn it! That has been in the family forever. One more thing I need to save. Any ideas?" Taylor asked.

"Maybe the museum. I'll ask when I copy Samuel's papers. One of mother's friends is a docent," Eric said.

"I have a lot of reading to do," Taylor said. He was actually happy to have something to help keep his mind off the past six months of his life.

"It's good to have you home," Eric said and hugged Taylor.

"Yeah, I just wish it was for another reason; I hate funerals."

"See you in a few hours," Eric said.

Taylor watched Eric leave and then sat down on the bed and opened the box. He took the letter addressed to him personally from Uncle Larry and opened it. A heart necklace with pink stone and a note fell out onto the bed. Taylor looked at the note. "I promise . . . Sarah." Taylor picked the heart up and held it in his hand. The room filled with the scent of lilacs. He looked up to see there were no flowers in his room and felt a chill run down the back of his arms and neck. Taylor looked at the letter.

Taylor,

As I sit here knowing that I do not have much time, there is a story I need to tell you. What you are about to read could be considered the ravings of a mad man but I will ask that you read this letter with the open mind I know you have. Tell Sherman nothing of this letter or of the contents of the manuscript.

My story begins one morning talking to Grandfather Phillip White . . .

Taylor finished the letter and looked at the necklace. He wasn't sure what to make of the letter he had just read. Uncle Larry was right: this did sound like the ravings of a crazy man, but it intrigued him. Was it possible for love to conquer death? Was it possible for two souls to continue to search for each other? Questions with no answers at this time, and possibly he would never find an answer, but it would not stop him from searching. He would honor his uncle's last wishes: carry this necklace with him and keep it close to his heart always, no matter where he went from this moment forward. Taylor placed everything back in the box. His uncle had left him a huge task but he would honor his last wishes. The footwork would be the hard part. He smiled and thought, *Well, life is an adventure.* Taylor had always enjoyed a mystery, and this was definitely a mystery to solve. Maybe there would be another book to write. He walked over to the TV and turned it on to the channel that played forties music. Frank Sinatra sang, "This Love of Mine."

Taylor had always enjoyed Big Band music and tunes with haunting melodies. He crawled onto a soft bed and laid the necklace on the bedside table. As Taylor drifted off to sleep he could swear he smelled lilacs again.

White Daily Journal Office
5:00 a.m.

Sherman sat at his desk, drank Scotch, and waited. All of this was unacceptable. He had a paper to run; he was responsible for the employees, to the readers . . . and he had plans for the future: Mayor Sherman Shaw. This was just not going to work—all this waiting. He grabbed the phone as the top light lit up.

"Where the hell have you been!"

"Shaw, I looked at the paperwork you sent over. This is a simple job. Why are you calling me?" the male voice asked.

"Because I don't intend to wait another five years! I may need your special talents," Sherman said.

There was a long pause. "Transfer my fee. I'll be in touch."

"Done," Sherman said and hung up the phone. He stood up, walked over to the window, and watched the sun rise. His plans on hold once more, he downed his Scotch and threw the glass across the room; it shattered as it hit the wall.

"Fuck you, Uncle Larry!"

Chapter Four ❧

Taylor stood in his room, looked at the suitcase he had yet to pack and the papers lying all around, and wondered how he thought a month would've been enough time to prepare for the task Uncle Larry had left him. His worst deadline did not compare to all that was still ahead of him. Even Eric had begun to complain about all the work Taylor kept finding for him to do that was within the parameters of the will. He looked at his watch and realized he'd been up over two hours trying to finish the last of his thoughts before they left for Hawaii. The book on Northern and Southern nurses had been interesting, and so were Samuel's personal notes. Sarah's journal had been very informative and touching, as it gave a face to the war. Personal feelings written from the heart for the men she healed, the women she taught, and the man she loved all showed her humanity. He was sure the heart made of blue checkered gingham had blood on it. Whose blood? He bet it was Samuel's. Taylor was interested in the Confederate spy named the Night Walker that Sarah had mentioned. He wasn't sure but thought this young man was her friend. The only name he could find was Mack.

The unfinished manuscript simply needed a dedication and some information about Susan's family. Then the dying man's only other request had been for Taylor to pay his final respects at Susan

Bowen's grave. All of this was something his uncle could have done, but he left it to him to finish. Taylor believed his uncle wanted him to complete the story of the Whites and Bowens all along. Taylor wasn't sure how or if he would be able to do this, but if he could find the right Bowen it would be possible. Taylor thought about the need for photographs to complete the family histories. He would have Eric read the manuscript once they arrived in Hawaii. Taylor had no idea of how deep Larry's involvement had been in WWII. He was positive no one in the family knew, but he was very proud of his uncle at this moment.

"Taylor, how long have you been up?" Eric said as he walked out with coffee and breakfast. "Wow, what a beautiful morning."

"Early, and thanks for bringing breakfast. I had to finish some things before we leave. I had the manuscript scanned and transferred to my computer for easier transport. You need to read it at some point," Taylor said.

"What about the journal?" Eric asked.

"It's going with me," Taylor answered.

"Any idea how long the Whites and Bowens have known each other?"

"As far as I can tell, at least before the Civil War," Taylor answered.

"Well, I'm about packed and ready to see what lies ahead in Hawaii," Eric said.

"I still need to pack," Taylor said. "What about the safe?"

"Being picked up tonight around eight. We're to meet Mrs. Barnes there at nine," Eric said.

"Why?"

"She said she has papers for us to sign," Eric answered.

MUSEUM OF THE CITY OF NEW YORK
9:00 P.M.

Taylor and Eric watched as the movers placed the antique safe from the *Journal* into a spot in a back storage room of the museum. Both men knew it would be cared for, displayed, and appreciated here. A part of White history was now preserved as it should be for all to enjoy.

"The library is most grateful to have another donation from the Shaw family," Mrs. Barnes told them.

"We're happy you could take it," Taylor responded, and then he signed the papers she had given him.

"Taylor, we need to go, our flight's early," Eric said.

"Before you go, I have something I need to give you. It was found when Samuel's possessions were given to the museum."

Taylor and Eric watched as Mrs. Barnes opened another safe and took out a small satin bag and handed it to Taylor.

"I believe this belonged to someone named Sarah," Mrs. Barnes said.

Taylor took the small satin bag and opened it. A silver band with a pink heart in the center tumbled out into his hand. Taylor picked the ring up and looked at the inscription: *To my Sarah, Love Samuel.*

"Where did you find this?" Taylor asked.

"When your ancestor's personal belongings were given to the museum, the pouch that he carried his papers, pens, and ink bottles in were also given to us. One of the employees found a side pocket deep in the pouch. We feel this was where he kept money and other valuables safe."

"It worked well," Eric said.

"Yes it did. It belongs to your family, and if you will sign this release you may take it. We would love to keep it, but it doesn't feel right for some reason."

"Thank you, and I'll see it gets to the rightful owner one day," Taylor said.

As both men left the museum, Eric stopped and looked at his brother. "Taylor, how are you going to get that to the rightful owner? She's dead."

"Yes, Eric, she's dead but not her heirs. This belongs with the rest of Sarah's possessions and should be returned, don't you agree?"

"I guess," Eric said.

"Good, ready to go?" Taylor said.

"Hawaii here we come!" Eric said.

NATIONAL SECURITY AGENCY
FT. MEADE, MARYLAND
10:00 P.M.

Bevan sat in his office and stared at the stack of folders and phone messages on his desk. His mind was on the upcoming cadet class. He had pushed to get Zaveen through and was worried time would run out. He had looked at the application she had returned with copies of family bibles. Bevan had trouble believing people still relied on such things when it was possible to find almost anything on the internet.

"Boss, whatcha still doing here? Didn't anyone tell you it's a holiday?" E. asked.

Bevan looked up to see his right-hand computer geek standing in the doorway. Ethaniel Long, "E.," was twenty-two and had been hired almost out of high school. He was brilliant, and his computer skills were far and above those that were writing code for companies intended for the general public. He had written numerous programs for the company and spent as much time in his secured office as Bevan.

"I could say the same for you," Bevan said and smiled.

"Oh, don't worry about me. DeAnna Kingston has plenty of things planned for me tomorrow," E. said.

"How is her clothing line coming?"

"Fine. she flies to New York at the end of the week to finalize all details and prepare for her debut," E. said.

"Are you going?" Bevan already knew the answer.

"Yeah, right. I would be as comfortable there as she would be in here."

"You know you can take anytime off you need, you have enough saved," Bevan said.

"Thanks, but I'm taking her to Ireland, Scotland, and then we're going to Japan for a week the middle of next month. Don't you remember? You had to approve all that time off."

"That's right. I'm going to need you to get a couple of files ready for me before you leave—priority status," Bevan said.

"Your brother's son, Blain, and Zaveen Keens, right?"

"Yes," Bevan answered.

"Almost done, just have a few more things to check. Their files will be on your desk early next week."

"Remind me to put you in for a raise."

"You already did," E. said and walked off back to his office.

Chapter Five ❦

Jace thought about how time had passed since she started the assignment in Flagstaff. She drank coffee and looked at the mountains on the early drive to Sedona with her new friend, Jessica. They had met the first night she worked at the hospital and found they had many things in common, like their love of nature. Jessica was a traveler and had invited her to spend the day hiking and exploring the beauty of Arizona. Jace had accepted the invitation.

"Jessica, I hear this place is very spiritual," Jace said.

"There is supposed to be a vortex in one area. I have our day pretty much mapped out; and call me Jess. I brought my tent and sleeping bags just in case we decide to spend the night."

"You know, I'd really enjoy that," Jace answered.

"Then camping it is; we'll stop at a store and get more supplies." Jess looked at the envelope in her friend's hands. "Are you ever going to open that letter from your lawyer?"

"I need to but worried that I'll be angry about the amount, and I don't want to ruin our day," Jace said.

"Well, if it isn't what you agreed on make your attorney do his job."

Jace opened the envelope and began to smile.

"I guess it's what you wanted."

"More. Now I can buy into the bed and breakfast with my friends in Galveston," Jace said.

"Awesome, count me so there! I love B&Bs," Jess said.

"Now I can relax and really enjoy our day."

"Jace, tell me more about being a holistic nurse. It sounds interesting."

"Let's save that conversation for this evening."

Keens Farm
Morgan City, Louisiana
7:00 a.m.

Zack stood on the back porch step enjoying the warmth of the sun on her face, watching bees collect pollen from the honeysuckle, and listening to the sounds and absorbing the scents she had missed over the past four years. The smell of breakfast her mother was cooking, brothers arguing in the yard, her father singing in French, the dog barking at the cat: these were simple things, but they touched her heart. It was good to be home, sleeping in her bed with fresh sheets that had been dried outside.

"Zaveen, come here," her father called from his work shop,

"Coming, papa," she answered.

"I had your bow restrung last week. You'll need to shoot before we go hunt."

Her brothers and parents had tried to make her return home an easy transition. Zack was not used to resting or having extra time, so she had filled it with flying and would be leaving in the morning to go hunting with her father and brothers on family land.

"Ernesto! Jessie! Mamma needs you in the house," Zack told her brothers and messed their hair as she walked by them. "Don't argue, just go, okay?"

Both boys headed inside to help. She had gone to church, said rosary with her mother, finally got her short hair cut right, but all she could think about now was the conversation she had had with Bevan Benjamin. She knew it would take some time to complete the background check. The application was extensive and she had used family bibles to complete some of the information on distant relatives. She knew her cousin Deelyn had been a WASP, but most of the information had been classified. Deelyn never spoke of her time during the war. Mr. Benjamin had not given much detail about what type of job she had applied for, but Zack knew her background and language abilities would make her an asset in several parts of the world.

"Papa, do you know anything about Deelyn Bowen?" Zack asked and picked up her bow to test it.

"Not much, my college graduate, why?" he returned the question.

"Just curious," she answered and tried to think of what she would be able to tell her parents should she be accepted. Zack tried to come to terms with the possibility she would have to lie to them about her job.

"Is there something you need to tell me?" he asked.

"After you and mamma left to come home, I had a job offer," Zack said.

"Was that the paperwork from the government?" Doyle asked.

"Oui," she said.

"Do you wish to talk about it?"

She smiled when her mother called in Spanish from the back door that breakfast was ready.

"Our conversation will have to wait; your mother has made eggs and chorizo with fresh tortillas."

"Oui, it will wait," Zaveen said as they headed toward the house. "Papa, please don't say anything to mamma just yet."

BLUE WATER CONDOS
HONOLULU, HAWAII
3:00 P.M.

The flight had been long and both men were ready to relax and settle in at Larry's apartment. Taylor hoped that it was in a decent living condition. The cab stopped in front of a building with a sign that read "Newly Remodeled Condos for sale." Taylor paid the driver and they got out.

"Taylor, are you sure this is the right address?" Eric asked.

"According to the will it is . . . ? We need to find Harry Hawthorne."

"Thank you, Uncle Larry!" Eric screamed and raised both his fists into the air. "I hope it faces the beach. I don't remember, I was just a kid the last time we were all here."

Taylor turned and looked at his brother and shook his head. "Can you bring it down? There is no telling what shape the condo is in, and I'm sure no one kept it maintained over the years. As I remember, his apartment did face the water." Taylor tried to calm his brother's excitement.

"Whatever, it can be 1980s teal and peach with a brass chandelier; Hollywood lighting in the bathroom. I can even deal with black and white TV. All I care about is an ocean view."

Taylor rang the superintendant bell. A man in his early seventies answered the door.

"Mr. Hawthorne, I am—"

"My God, you have the same eyes as Larry."

"Taylor Shaw, and this is my brother, Eric," he finished.

"Just a minute, I'll get the keys. It'll be nice to have someone in Larry's apartment—I mean, condo. You'll have to excuse the odor the painters left today. They just had a couple of places that needed a touch-up. Damn movers can't seem to bring up furniture these days without screwing up the paint," Mr. Hawthorne rambled on.

"I'm sorry, what painters, furniture?" Taylor asked. "It's a holiday."

"Oh, when I found out your arrival date from Mr. Milton the orders your uncle left were to paint, then update the décor and furniture to match the year. I hired a decorator to come in and make the correct choices and, boy, she did a bang-up job."

"Shit, Taylor! This is going to cost us a fortune," Eric said.

"No, no—all paid for upfront, before your uncle died." Mr. Hawthorne put a key in the top lock on the elevator and took them to the penthouse. "After the Korean War the owners of this building decided to sell. Larry and several investors jumped on the opportunity. Your uncle was a major financer in the building and was therefore given the option to reserve the penthouse. Once the laws changed the building turned all apartments into condos, allowing tenants the option to own. Larry sold his original unit for a substantial profit, then moved into the penthouse. He was only there the last five years of his life. I hope you guys will be happy here; and if you are unhappy with the decorator's choices, all you have to do is call this number and they'll be very happy to accommodate you, both of you." Mr. Hawthorne handed the decorator's business card to Taylor.

Harry took a moment to think of the last time he saw his good friend, Larry, here in the penthouse; he brushed a tear away, then pushed both doors open to the main room. The smell of fresh paint was ignored when both men stood stunned at the sight before them. Taylor and Eric dropped their bags and walked directly to the open balcony to the full view of the blue ocean; the sun glistened off the water and caused their eyes to focus on the lush green mountains. A breeze carrying the scent of plumeria swept over both men. They stood and steadied themselves at the railing.

"There's three bedrooms and three baths," Harry told them.

Taylor looked at Eric, who seemed to be interested in the surfers and bikini-clad women at the beach. He walked back inside and began to explore the penthouse, trying to make sense of everything, but he just couldn't at the moment. Taylor looked at the artwork and realized it was one of his favorite artists. *How could he possibly have known?* he thought. Taylor looked at Mr. Hawthorne. "It's perfect."

"Cable, telephone, and internet all paid in advance for the next five years, all the dues for services here in the building, too. Yes, sir, your uncle knew how to take care of business. Bar, pantry, and fridge all stocked as of yesterday. Welcome to Honolulu."

Mr. Hawthorne handed Taylor two sets of keys. "You can stop by in the morning to sign some papers, preliminary of course. Bentwood will have the rest in his office for you."

"What is this other set of keys for?" Taylor asked.

"The garage."

Mr. Hawthorne took Taylor and Eric to the basement and walked them to the farthest end, where they stopped in front of a door that was oversized.

"Taylor, what do you think is in here?" Eric whispered.

Taylor looked at Mr. Hawthorne. "You know, don't you?"

Harry smiled. "Yes, but if I tell you it'd spoil the surprise."

Taylor took the key, placed it in the lock, turned it, and watched the door rise as multiple lights brightened the darkness.

"Shit! I thought the balcony view was awesome, but I was mistaken," Eric said.

Both men walked inside and began to look at what Uncle Larry had also invested his money in, starting with the large number of surfboards. Taylor was sure they were worth a fortune. He then walked over to the solid black, custom-made 1963 Harley-Davidson FL Duo-Glide, sitting next to a red 1966, 911S Porsche.

"The Harley and Porsche were maintained monthly after your uncle passed. He had the Harley custom-painted, didn't like the orange. The surfboards are all classics and signed by their designers. A lot of them were your uncle's friends. If you two don't know already, Larry was a good man; he gave a lot of money to charity and helped to rebuild the city after the war. Larry never married—said he lost his only love during the war. He invested his money well. You know he only drove the Porsche once or twice; mostly he took public transportation." Mr. Hawthorne took out a handkerchief and blew his nose. "I hope you'll be happy here."

Taylor turned around to see Eric standing in front of the Porsche, wiping tears away.

"Really Eric?"

❧

JACE AND JESSICA'S CAMPSITE
SEDONA, ARIZONA
10:00 P.M.

Jace and Jess sat around the small campfire and talked and laughed about the events of the day. Jace had never climbed, and felt accomplished and satisfied at the end by following Jess's instructions.

"Jess, hold still and let me put this on you," Jace had told her friend.

"I can't believe I tripped after all the climbing and hiking I've done over the years. Thanks for not laughing at me. I feel like a klutz."

"You might not have tripped if you hadn't been staring at the guys in front of us," Jace said.

"What you really mean is I shouldn't have been staring at their butts," Jess said. "What are you putting on me?"

"Lavender oil on the bruise, a marigold cream and tea tree oil for the road rash. I brought some chamomile for a tea later; it will help you sleep."

"I don't think I will need the tea. I'm exhausted," Jessica said.

Both women looked up at the stars.

"I'm so glad we did this," Jess said.

"Me too. I want to experience all that I can while I'm traveling. Did I tell you about my trip to the Redwood Forest?" Jace asked.

"Tell me; I want to go. Is it worth the trip?" Jess asked.

"Worth every mile. I drove in one morning and found a place where I could pull off the main road. I got out and headed into the forest. I walked up and stood at the base of one tree that was almost three car lengths in width. When I looked up I couldn't see the top, and I stood on pine needles so deep you could sleep on them. The scent—clean and fresh—surrounds you like a blanket, and the silence, the peacefulness, makes you feel like this must be where God lives. I stayed for several hours and as I returned to the truck it was difficult to think of the ones that were cut down."

"Maybe I need to take an extra week off and go. I have reservations to take a hot air balloon over the vineyards. One of the other travelers told me about it—I can't wait," Jess said. "So much to see and do."

"I know Fisherman's Wharf in San Francisco, Disneyland, Hollywood, Huntington Beach, and the Santa Monica Pier. I love being a tourist," Jace responded.

"Now tell me about being a holistic nurse."

"Jess, holistic nursing is my calling. I believe in caring for the entire person—body, mind, and spirit. As a child I was always taking care of stray cats or puppies, injured birds, and I made all my medicines out of flowers. The neighborhood kids called me the flower nurse." Jace laughed.

"That's funny."

"In nursing school, I began to meditate before exams. I used music and aromatherapy to relax."

"Did it help?" Jess asked.

"Yes, especially with the stress of finals and state board exams. I studied holistic classes and obtained my certification," Jace said. "I believe conventional and alternative systems of care can and do work together."

"Such as?" Jess asked.

"Reiki, healing touch, nutrition, massage, spiritual and emotional counseling—but one of my favorites is laughter. These are just a few; there are many more that can be integrated into everyday care, care for the whole person."

"You use a lot of aromatherapy. I've seen your collection of oils," Jess said.

"Yes, but I do like to integrate massage, too. You might be interested in going with me to a workshop or convention. I believe you'll get the answers you need," Jace finished.

"I may take you up on that one day."

Taylor stood at the railing and looked at the magnificent view before him. Boats, ships, yachts all decorated with colorful lights, and fireworks so close you could reach out and grab them. His body told him it was tired but his mind was spinning.

"Beer?"

"Yeah, thanks," Taylor said. "Eric, I don't understand all of this ... and I'm quite sure Sherman has no idea either."

"Well don't look at me! I have no intention of saying anything, trust me. I died and went to heaven the moment I saw the Porsche," Eric said and smiled.

"I remember Uncle Larry as a simple man. I mean, he had a decent place, not overstated; he was always generous to us boys, but all this really seems over the top to me. Larry was an award-winning reporter and his two books after the war were on the New York Times Best Seller list for weeks. He left me a huge task, and from the letter I read, it has a deeper meaning than any of the family realizes," Taylor said.

"What letter?" Eric asked. "You didn't tell me about another letter."

"I have something you need to read. I see no harm since Sherman is the only one I was told not to let see it," Taylor said and left the balcony for a moment.

Eric sat down and waited for his brother to return. He smiled when the refrigerator door opened, as he was ready for another beer. He reached up and took the beer from Taylor.

"Taylor, is this place really going to be yours once the provisions of the will have been fulfilled?" Eric asked.

"I guess. I knew Uncle Larry had money but he never bragged about it, it wasn't his way," Taylor said as he handed the envelope to his brother. "Eric, when you read this, I want you to keep an open mind." Taylor sat down and waited for his brother to finish the letter. "I hope Mr. Milton will be able to answer some of the questions I have about the will."

Eric folded the letter and put it back into the envelope. "Taylor, you don't really believe this, do you?"

"You tell me," Taylor said and took the heart necklace out of his pocket.

"What?" Eric said.

"Wait," Taylor said. Within moments the air around them filled with the scent of lilacs.

"What the hell, Taylor?" Eric asked.

Taylor replaced the necklace in his pocket and the scent subsided. "I'm not sure. I'm curious about Samuel and Sarah, friends, maybe lovers, and the ring proves he intended to marry her, but both are definitely tied to one another in a promise of some type involving this necklace."

"It seems Uncle Larry was unable to get all the answers he needed before he died," Eric said.

"Exactly. And according to this letter, there are a lot of loose ends that need to be tied together. Uncle Larry and Susan Bowen were descendants from the White and Bowen lines back to Samuel and Sarah."

"How weird is that? Taylor, are you thinking that history repeated itself, only this time Susan died instead of Uncle Larry?"

"Possibly . . . the manuscript is informative, well written, and I expect it to be a best seller once published," Taylor said and then paused.

"But . . . ?"

"But it is a ruse. There isn't that much to finish. The things left could have been done easily. This letter to me was written to pique my journalistic curiosity. Uncle Larry sent Milton to keep Sherman or anyone else from prying into his affairs. The stage was set and now all the players are present," Taylor said. "The real task ahead of us is to find Sarah and Susan's heir, to pull the family histories together."

"Alright, I'll bite. Whatever you need me to do within the parameters of the will I'll do," Eric said.

"I've made a list of things to get started. The attorney, newspaper, read Sarah's journal again . . . oh, and we'll need to make a trip to Waynesboro. I need to talk with the family and go to the cemetery," Taylor said.

"What do you expect to find there?" Eric asked.

"I'm not sure, but it's part of the will so there must be some information I need there. Plus, I need to pay Larry's final respects to Susan and her family."

"What do you want me to do?" Eric asked.

"Keep the fridge and bar stocked—we have a lot of work ahead of us."

"That, I can do," Eric said. "Anything else?"

"Yes, I want you to consider going back to college. I've seen your work and it's good. No, that's not correct—your work is outstanding. A degree would only add to your resumé and you would get the inheritance you deserve," Taylor said.

"Thanks for the concern, big brother, but I have no intentions of going back. College is not for me. Besides I'm getting by for now, and not having a degree irritates the shit out of Sherman. That alone is worth the price of my inheritance," Eric said and laughed.

"I think the provisions of Grandfather's will shouldn't have been so strict about our inheritance. A career is a career regardless how you obtain it," Taylor said.

"Sherman loves holding it above my head, but it sticks in his throat because I don't really need the money. I'll get the big picture one day and be set for life—hopefully here. I hate the winters in New York."

Taylor picked up a remote and hit the play button. His Bing Crosby CD began to play "When you wish upon a star."

"You're kidding, right?" Eric said.

"Just deal with it and listen; right now you and I are the two luckiest guys in the world," Taylor said. The two men clinked beer bottles.

"To Uncle Larry," Eric said.

"To Uncle Larry," Taylor repeated.

"Oh, happy birthday. You're what—thirty now?" Eric said and laughed.

"Twenty-eight, butthead," Taylor said.

Chapter Six ❧

Jace stood and watched the sun change the gray of night to the brilliant colors of Arizona—terra-cottas, sand, brown, and red brick—across the mountains. She closed her eyes and took a deep breath of the fresh morning air.

"Can you believe the beauty of the morning?" Jess asked and handed Jace a cup of coffee.

"God's handiwork," Jace replied. "How many weeks do you have left on your contract?"

"About three, you have what—six?"

"Yeah, I took a shorter contract this time," Jace said.

"Where're you headed?" Jess asked.

"Galveston to sign papers, pick out my bedroom, and acquaint myself with my new home base."

"How big is this place?"

"My friends had it built and if I remember right it's either six or seven bedrooms on a street named Jolly Roger on the west end of Jamaica Beach," Jace said.

"You're kidding, right?"

"Nope, it's all true. The streets are named after pirates, islands, and ships. There is a sunset view to die for, I'm told. My friends said it's on a canal, direct launch for a boat, kayak, Jet Ski, or a swim. You'll be welcome as my guest anytime," Jace said.

"Thanks! I love B&Bs. I will definitely come and visit," Jess said.

"Where are you headed?" Jace asked.

"I'm going to San Francisco for an eight-week contract. I plan to do as much sightseeing as possible. I'm going to then head to the Boulder area for a while. You'll have to come see me and we can go to Estes Park and stay at the Stanley Hotel. We can rent one of the haunted rooms."

"I understand Stephen King was inspired to write the *Shining* when he stayed at the Stanley," Jace said.

"I love a good ghost story, don't you?" Jess said.

Bentwood Milton's Office
Honolulu
10:00 a.m.

Bentwood had been at his office since seven preparing all the preliminary paperwork for Taylor to sign. He had paid all the bills for the remodeling and décor. He was sure Taylor had no idea the true inheritance Larry had left him. The penthouse and toys in the garage were a small percentage of what Larry had accumulated through his investments and book sales. The government had been more than generous after the war for Larry's voluntary involvement. Larry never spoke about his time overseas—not to anyone. Bentwood was curious about the last manuscript, and he assumed it covered what had happened to Larry during the war. Bentwood would have to wait and read it along with the rest of the world. The final totals would be given to Taylor only after the terms of the will were fulfilled.

"Mr. Milton, Taylor and Eric Shaw are here to see you," his secretary announced.

"Send them in."

Taylor wasn't sure what to expect from this attorney. From what they had seen so far, a lot of money was involved. He was curious to see if this man could be trusted.

"Mr. Milton," Taylor said and shook hands.

Eric reached out and shook hands, too.

"Gentlemen, please sit down and call me Bentwood. How was your trip?"

"Good," Eric answered.

"I guess you have some questions about all of this here in Honolulu," Bentwood said. "Coffee?"

"Yes, please," Eric said.

"Yes, thank you. All of this has been somewhat overwhelming since the death of Aunt Beatrice. This mystery and search with the reward has been a little concerning but has piqued my curiosity. The fact that I now have controlling interest in the newspaper is causing an issue for Sherman," Taylor said.

"Taylor, Sherman can just deal with it," Eric said.

"Both of us remember Uncle Larry as a simple man, so you must understand our shock at the accommodations we found," Taylor said.

Bentwood smiled. "Did you talk with Harry?"

"Harry did most of the talking, we just listened," Eric said.

"That's Harry, but if you want information on your uncle, Harry's the man to talk to, especially when it comes to Larry's life after he returned from the war. Harry was a mail clerk at the newspaper and Larry got him the job at the apartments later. Everyone else is dead or gone from the island. There is family on the Bowen farm named Long and Benjamin. You'll want to contact them. They may have information you could use."

"What about you?" Taylor asked. "How did you come to know our uncle? You are obviously a close and trusted friend."

Bentwood smiled and leaned back into his chair. "Larry worked for my uncle, Richard Milton, at the newspaper. I was a young, unguided teenager headed for trouble. When your uncle returned from the war, he took an interest in me. He helped me to focus, first as a surfer, then with my academics, and later law school. I owe what I am today to your uncle," Bentwood told them.

"Do we owe you anything for all that you've done over the years? Legal fees, money for the condo . . . ?" Taylor asked.

"Your uncle gave me more than money could ever buy. If it weren't for him, I would be rotting in a prison somewhere. I'll be forever grateful to Larry. Shortly before Larry passed away, he left to me all the things you were given, for safe-keeping; plus, he left a substantial fee for my services. No, you owe me nothing."

"I understand there are papers for me to sign," Taylor said.

"Preliminary right now, but once you fulfill the requests in the will permanent papers will be filed and all monies and properties will be yours. You do understand the terms of the will?" Bentwood said and then looked at Eric.

"I'm just the secretary. I'm working for food and beer," Eric said.

Bentwood laughed. "Taylor, the majority of the work must be done by you."

"Understood. I do have a question. Is there anything in the will that keeps me from selling things and donating the money to charity?" Taylor asked

"Once all provisions of the will are met you can do whatever you wish," Bentwood said.

Taylor looked at his brother's shocked face. "Suck it up, Eric."

Penthouse
Honolulu
1:00 p.m.

Taylor sat in the main room looking over the papers Bentwood had given him. He made notes on the places they needed to go and people to contact. Eric was in the kitchen concocting something for lunch. Taylor could hear his Harry Connick, Jr. CD in the sound system. His voice encapsulated the image of men from the forties. He thought about the record collection his uncle had and made a note to look for those albums later. The meeting this morning with Bentwood had confirmed what he had hoped to be the case and that he was someone they'd be able to trust.

"Eric, what are you cooking?"

"My special chicken enchilada ring. Very simple, and it's really good warmed up the next day," Eric answered. "Oh, and my awesome *pico*."

Taylor laughed. "I guess you can stay then."

"Did you find anything in Samuel's book, like personal notes about Sarah?" Eric asked.

"No," Taylor said.

"I find it hard to believe that he didn't write anything about the woman he intended to marry," Eric said.

"The book's dedication is pretty straightforward. He detailed what both Northern and Southern nurses were exposed to during the battles, namely the elements and dealing with little or no supplies. There are interviews with Sarah and the women she traveled with and his personal observations. A couple of chapters are very graphic: like his description of a young boy he had met before one battle found later 'stacked with the dead like cord wood,'" Taylor said.

"I wonder if during that time period you kept feelings to yourself. Perhaps what was spoken between them was just that, between them," Eric said.

"Very insightful for a college dropout," Taylor said.

"Thanks, I do have my moments."

"Samuel may have been that way but Sarah did put her feelings down in the journal. She talked about the women she travelled with—particularly the injured men and women they cared for—her love for Samuel, and her friendship with someone named Mack."

"What can I do to help?" Eric asked.

"I need you to start calling appraisers and get the surfboards and the Porsche appraised. You can ride the Harley for now, if you must," Taylor said.

"You aren't really going to sell them, are you?"

"Yes, I am. Neither you nor I need them. The boards probably belong where avid surfers can view them, but the money they might bring in could help so many in need. The Porsche goes, too. Uncle

Larry bought the Porsche, I'm sure, for an investment; but you heard Harry, he rarely drove it. I have no desire to own it and, once again, the money will help others," Taylor told him.

"I figured as much, but I appreciate the use of the Harley for now," Eric said.

"Eric, you know how I have always felt about the vulgarity and misuse of wealth. We have an opportunity here to do the right thing and help a lot of people. I do, however, prefer to live where it is warmer; maybe we can stay," Taylor said and smiled.

Both men heard the timer go off.

"Lunch is served," Eric said.

Chapter Seven 🖋

NATIONAL SECURITY AGENCY
FT. MEADE, MARYLAND
MONDAY, LABOR DAY, SEPTEMBER 4, 2000
6:00 A.M.

Bevan yawned as he entered the main doors and headed toward his office. The lights in his office were on and he could hear his secretary, Darlene, on the phone taking messages for him. This was not what he had planned for this morning. His computer alarm had notified him to come to work immediately. The reports he would need were already on his desk. As he stood and glanced over them, he took the last drink of his Starbucks and he knew the day would belong to the company. Bevan closed his eyes, rubbed his forehead, and walked back outside. He stood and hesitated before he opened his cell phone. Bevan sighed and hit number one.

"Laura, don't wait on me."

"Bevan, not again," she said.

"You knew there was a chance I couldn't be there."

"I know. Come by later, if you can."

"I'll try," Bevan said. He turned off his cell phone and returned to his office. Bevan thought about Laura Edwards and wondered why she put up with him and the company. She was a self-sufficient woman, an attorney, and partner in a large firm. The one thing they had in common was their love of running. He thought of that memorable October morning when he had decided to take a different running path. It had been difficult to ignore the tall slender figure with long auburn hair pulled back in a bright green ribbon and her expensive running outfit that hugged in all the right places when she passed him. At the end of his run he was happy to see the flat tire on her Lexus when he lagged in behind her. He changed her tire and was pleased when she suggested dinner as payment for his time. That had been almost a year ago; now the only problem between them was that he was never around. Laura had once told him, "I'll take what time you can give me; just don't ask me to marry you." He would make this weekend up to her. He would find a bed and breakfast away from D.C., maybe in Key West, for Christmas. Bevan opened his desk drawer and removed the blue box that held an engagement ring. She didn't have to marry him; he just didn't want her to look elsewhere.

Bevan returned to the work on his desk and began to look through the reports. He recognized a name that increasingly continued to show up in his intel reports on investigations into ARC out of New York. Bevan looked at the calendar and knew E. wouldn't be back for at least another week to ten days. He would have to gather what information he could and forward it to E. in a to-do file for him to take up upon his return. Bevan then picked up his phone and made a call to an old friend.

"Ron. Bevan here. I need you to do some checking on an Aaron Reece Caydon; he owns ARC Investigations. His office is located in one of the twin towers. Oh, and Ron, I need it yesterday."

Bevan hung up the phone and pulled Aaron's military file on his computer. This was not the first time he had read over Aaron's file. Bevan and Aaron were not strangers to one another. This man had been in the Special Forces, black ops; he had completed numerous missions with positive results; he had been decorated for bravery and honorably discharged. The company offered a position and Aaron had accepted. His work with the company had lasted only three years. Then he left and started his own business. What appeared on the computer screen was generalized. Bevan needed something else not available on a computer. He walked out to his secretary's desk and handed her a note.

"Your private files?" Darlene asked.

"Yes."

"All of them?" she inquired.

"No. Just the one marked Special Interest," Bevan said. He returned to his desk. The FBI had sent over information on Caydon and his involvement in possible illegal arms sales with insurgents in Iran. Nothing concrete, and the FBI informant disappeared before any formal charges could be filed. Bevan leaned back in his chair. *This man is going to be a problem.*

❦

CAUSEWAY
GALVESTON ISLAND, TEXAS
10:00 A.M.

Jace put the CD in the truck player and turned up the volume. The voice of Glen Campbell began to sing "Galveston." She smiled and drove over the bridge. To her right she could see the pyramids of Moody Gardens; a few minutes later she was at the Sixty-First Street exit. Glen finished as she came to the sea wall and turned right where the sign said, "Jamaica Beach eleven miles." She was excited about a home here on an island. Jace knew about the history of the 1900 hurricane and that extreme weather would always be a concern living here. She would place all her important papers and personal items centrally where they could be moved quickly for evacuation. Jace passed Pirates Beach, then the state park where campers and tents were located for the holiday weekend. The one light ahead was Jamaica Beach. Jace turned right on Buccaneer and drove straight to Jolly Roger; one more right and she followed the curve around to the address she had been given. The large home had a circle drive where Jace parked her truck. She opened her door to a heat that could only be described as oppressive.

"I hope you have your bikini ready," Candi said.

"It'll cool down, promise," Casie said in an identical voice.

The forty-year-old twins hugged their friend and partner. Candi and Casie had lived down the street from Jace and her ex-husband in San Antonio. Candi's husband had been a paramedic and was killed on a call in crossfire between gang members. The sad part was that he had been attempting to save a young girl who had also been shot. Financially, Candi was set for life. Casie divorced husband number three and had been living with Candi while she was waiting for her settlement on property when both came up with the idea of a B&B. Jace had sat with them and looked at the house plans and made the comment, "I would love a simple life in Galveston." Both women never forgot that comment, and when Jace's marriage fell apart, her two friends called. At that time there wasn't the money she needed to be a partner, but now she would be part owner of the home before her and hopefully have a little peace of mind.

Both women were tanned and had lost weight since leaving San Antonio. Their short blonde hair had almost turned white in the coastal sun. Candi was the money wizard and Casie an awesome cook. The combination worked well. They had a great website, and they figured the money they had put on its design should bring more business. Jace knew there would always be bedrooms to clean, linens to wash, et cetera, and she was excited to help. She didn't cook, and hopefully Candi could give her financial advice. The twins also knew she would not always be there, that her first love was nursing and caring for others.

"Welcome to the Jolly Roger B&B," Candi said.

Jace smiled. "I hope there's not a pirate waiting for me inside."

"No, just a cold drink and food, if you're hungry," Casie said.

"What about guests?" Jace asked.

"Up and gone to the beach for the day. Come on in. Time to get acquainted with your new home," Candi said.

"We have three rooms that we haven't used, since we wanted you to have your choice," Casie said.

The three went inside and welcomed the cool blast of air. Jace was surprised at the simple island décor the women had chosen. The rooms were eye-pleasing and the furniture comfortable. The music was, of course, Jimmy Buffett, and the outside view to the canal, lovely.

"There are two rooms on the top floor and one on the main floor," Candi said.

Jace looked at all three and chose the larger room on the top floor with an individual deck facing the canal.

"Good choice. If you want to repaint we have a handyman that can do it in a day or so," Casie said.

"No, actually this terra-cotta is perfect," Jace answered.

"Great, go get your swimsuit and we'll help you unpack later," Candi said.

Jace walked out and got her suit and the box from her mother. She needed to get the handwritten book preserved before any more deterioration happened. Jace looked at the house and was concerned about the B&B since only two rooms were rented over a busy holiday.

Casie handed her a glass of white sangria when she returned downstairs to the kitchen. "You're going to love this, it's my own recipe."

"Ladies, how's business?"

The twins laughed. "Honey, now that you have your room, we can answer all the holds. The B&B is booked every weekend starting next week through the first of the year," Casie said.

"Wow, that's great," Jace said and let out a sigh of relief.

"You're going to love it here," Candi said.

"Welcome home, welcome home," a strange voice called.

"What is that?" Jace asked.

"That's Happy Hour, our Moluccan cockatoo," Candi said.

"He's a hit with the guests and a very loving bird," Casie said.

Jace walked over and Happy Hour laid his head down for her to rub. She laughed, and then started back upstairs to change into her swimsuit and find some sunscreen for an afternoon of talk and relaxation.

"Jace, the lawyer sent the papers for you to sign—you'll have a third of the ownership of the business. We'll go over it after the party tonight," Casie said.

"What party?" Jace called from the stairs.

"Jamaica Beach has a Labor Day cookout every year—food, booze, and music. Money goes to the community," Candi said.

"One more question; what's the golf cart for?" Jace asked.

Both women laughed.

"Island transportation."

ॐ

OFFICE OF ARC INVESTIGATIONS
TWIN TOWERS, NORTH
NEW YORK
12:30 P.M.

ARC Investigations didn't usually have meetings on a holiday but there was just too much money at risk not to accept this last-minute gathering. The information being purchased could be considered questionable and would be of concern to the FBI or NSA, but less important than the heavy-handed dealings he was usually involved with. He was happy to charge a lot for little this time.

"Thank you, gentlemen," Aaron said and took the two briefcases full of money.

"Our people thank you. It is an honor to do business with a man who understands our cause," the first man said.

"Of course," Aaron said, then handed the man a folder with the information that had been requested.

"Next year the world will see and know," the third man said.

"A year you say?" Aaron said.

"A year and seven days," the second man said.

The men finished their coffee, rose, and left the office.

Aaron turned and looked out the window.

"I should schedule a vacation for 9/11."

ॐ

Jace sat on the backseat of the golf cart and listened to the twins talking. The party had been fun and she was impressed with the closeness of the community in Jamaica Beach. Now she was tired and ready to just sit on her deck and look at the sky.

"Home sweet home," Candi said as she parked the cart.

"How about a nightcap?" Casie asked.

"Sounds good. Meet you two in my room," Jace said and headed upstairs. She opened the sliding door and sat down in the lounger. The evening had cooled, just as she had been told it would, the coastal breeze light and inviting like a lover's touch and so quiet the splash of small fish could be heard below in the canal. Jace reached toward the sky, as the stars seemed so close. This was the most relaxed she had been in over a year. It only took a divorce and traveling across the country to obtain it, but at this moment it had been worth it.

"Here you go. One more sangria?" Casie asked.

"Thanks. Where's Candi?"

"She's getting the originals for you to sign and checking on reservations," Casie answered.

"I have something I need to show both of you when Candi gets up here."

"I'm here! Whatcha got?" Candi asked.

Jace went inside and brought back the pouch and handwritten book. Both women were sitting on the railing when she returned to the deck. "Mom sent this to me on my birthday. She said it belongs to me, my family history."

Both women looked over the book on herbs and the first edition on Civil War nurses.

"Well, you are right about needing to get this preserved—and soon. I know someone in Friendswood that can help us. I'll call in the morning," Candi said.

"You realize these items need to be in a museum, don't you?" Casie asked.

"Yes, but for some reason I feel a duty to keep them for a while," Jace responded.

"Let's get it preserved properly and then make that decision later," Candi said.

"Ever since I started going through all this information I've been thinking about Waynesboro, a lot. How weird is that?" Jace said.

"Well, who knows, maybe your ancestors have unfinished business that only the living can complete," Casie said.

"Do you really believe that?" Jace asked.

Both women looked at each other and laughed.

"Oh, most certainly," Candi said.

"Get some rest. You can get settled in tomorrow," Casie said.

Jace watched as both women left. She had heard about the special connection twins had, and her friends seemed to prove the theories. They finished each other's sentences and seemed to know when they were needed to help each other; it was a little spooky at times. Jace had enough money to take a month off. She knew there would be money from the B&B as income but not for a while. She would check to see if there was work in the area through a local agency before taking another assignment away from her new home. Jace finished her drink and headed inside. She could not shake the need to go to Waynesboro. Jace knew someone that might help her with all these questions and feelings. She smiled and grabbed her cell phone.

"Zack, sorry to call so late. How would you like a few days in Galveston, at this awesome B&B?"

Chapter Eight 🙚

BUSH AIRPORT
HOUSTON, TEXAS
MONDAY, SEPTEMBER 11, 2000
8:00 A.M.

Aaron sat in first class, drinking Baileys and coffee while waiting for the rest of the passengers to board the 757 to Hawaii; he was taking the first flight out of Houston to Honolulu. The flight from New York to Houston the day before had been uneventful. He would have preferred his own jet but the mechanic at the airport informed him the plane had been tagged. Today he had used one of his many aliases to stay under the government radar. Since he had left the military most of his work had been legal, but there was not a lot of money on those jobs. The jobs that called for his special abilities had paid extremely well. His last job had possibly placed him on a watch list with NSA and the FBI. He still had friends that kept him informed about the inner workings of both agencies. If it had not been for those connections the FBI would have ended his career. Aaron's contacts and friends would continue to enjoy the many perks he could offer as long as the information remained correct and arrived in a timely manner.

"Miss," he said.

"Yes, sir, what can I get you?" the stewardess asked.

"Another Baileys, please."

"Right away."

Aaron watched as the tall brunette walked away. He wondered if she would be available once the plane landed. He would further that line of thought the closer the flight came to Honolulu. A free place to stay and pleasant company would be preferable to the prying eyes of cameras in a hotel. He returned to the files he had obtained, complete with financial reports and photographs of the Shaw family. Sherman was financially set, his assets solid, but there were a couple of questionable accounts outside the country. Taylor was living a simple life, no extras; his inheritance had been used for his education, and the rest had been donated to charities. Taylor lived on his money alone—none of the Shaw wealth. Aaron grinned when he looked at the financial status of Eric. The youngest brother was barely getting by financially, in debt, but he too had not drawn money from the Shaw finances. Aaron noted that Eric had not accessed any of his education money.

He had been unable to get any financial statement on Larry Shaw, which irritated him. This man's information should have been easily accessed. Aaron looked at the military document marked "sensitive material World War II, Jedburghs." This information was interesting since Larry's life after the war had been simple. His work at the newspaper and the books he had written seemed to be Larry's life. Aaron realized he had read both of Larry's books on WWII and now understood how a simple war correspondent knew more than he should about the inner workings of the military. Aaron put away the files and looked out the window as the plane moved away from the gate. According to Sherman the first person he needed to talk with was Harry Hawthorne.

"Your Bailey's and coffee," the stewardess said.

"Thank you, Miss . . ."

"Lyssa."

"Lyssa, a beautiful name for a beautiful woman. Will you be returning back to Houston?" Aaron asked.

She smiled. "No, I'm off for a few days." She handed him a piece of paper and walked off.

Aaron smiled as he looked at an address and phone number.

SCHOLES AIRPORT
GALVESTON, TEXAS
NOON

Jace and Zack had filed their flight plans yesterday, after their tour at the Lone Star Flight Museum. Zack had been given a tour through the B-17 and had been allowed to sit in the Texan. Jace felt bad about dragging her away. The twins had understood what they needed to do in Waynesboro and encouraged them to go. The book on herbs had been taken to a place in Clear Lake for preservation and would be back when they returned. The week had been enjoyable; they laughed, swam, cooked out, drank sangria, spent time on the Strand spending money, ate at Rudy and Paco's, and caught up on all the changes that had happened to both of them over the past year, including Zack's job offer with the CIA. Jace looked up as Zack returned from her preflight check of the plane. They were related through marriage, but she felt their friendship would only grow as they both searched for answers about a history that seemed to be lost to both of them.

"Are we ready for takeoff?" Jace asked.

Zack returned a thumbs up. "Let's go."

Both women entered the Cherokee, belted in, and placed headphones on so they could talk during the flight. The takeoff was smooth and as they banked over the gulf, Jace felt an uneasiness. Not about the flight but what they might be headed to in Waynesboro.

"Jace, stop worrying about Waynesboro. Remember it's family, and the dead sometimes leave this earth with unfinished business," Zack said.

"You and your second sense. Do you really believe that's what all these feelings I'm having is about, unfinished business?" Jace asked.

"That and more. There's a man. I can't see him yet, but it involves a man," Zack said.

"Well, I hope he's good looking," Jace said and smiled at Zack. "I called the Longs and they will meet us at the county airport."

"If it's like my family, there will be a lot of talking and food."

"For the Bowens there isn't any other way," Jace said and both women laughed.

"Oh, and your new partners, they're upfront and honest, you don't have to worry about them or your money."

"Thanks, but that I already knew."

BURKE COUNTY AIRPORT
GEORGIA
4:30 P.M.

Daniel and Denise Long had been at the county airport for about thirty minutes when the small plane landed. Denise reached out and took her husband's hand.

"Daniel, that must be them," she said.

"Good Lord, how long has it been since we've had Bowens, Keens, and Longs together?" asked Daniel.

"Too long," Denise answered.

"Well, at least we can show them a warm welcome," Daniel said. "Did Jace say what she was looking for?"

"All she said was something about 'unfinished business.'"

Jace was glad to be out of the plane and was stretching when Zack crawled out of the Cherokee. They walked to the side hatch and took out their bags.

"Zack, that was a nice flight, long but nice."

"I love flying; it's the only place I truly feel safe and at peace."

"It shows," Jace said. She looked at the man and woman waving at them. "It looks like our welcoming committee is here."

"Then let's go meet our family," Zack said.

Both women walked over to the older couple that waited and immediately were hugged.

"Oh my goodness. Jace, you have your Aunt Susan's smile and eyes. And you have to belong to the Keens side of our family," Denise said.

"Zaveen Keens, but everyone calls me Zack. It's nice to meet both of you."

"Well let's get going! The rest of the family and a meal is waiting," Daniel said.

Jace and Zack looked at each other and smiled.

Their ride from the airport to the Long home was filled with history of how much land had belonged to the Bowens before the war, the burning of the first house, when Sherman marched across Georgia, and how as everyone moved away the land was sold and the money distributed to the heirs. There had been a trust at one time but that money no longer existed.

"The only property left that belongs to the family is the B&B and ten acres of land where the family cemetery is located," Denise said.

When the car turned on the road heading to their destination Jace noticed a medical clinic on the corner. It seemed to still be open; several cars were parked outside and lights were still on inside.

"They're keeping late hours," Jace said.

"That's Doc B's clinic. He and his wife can't make it tonight but you two are invited to dinner tomorrow night. Donna said they have information that should be passed on to the Bowen family," Denise said.

"Here we are," Daniel said.

Both women looked up at a huge house with a sign on the front that said "Long Bowe B&B." There were at least twenty cars and trucks parked everywhere and music could be heard coming from the house.

Jace looked at Zack. "Are you ready for this?"

"Absolutely," Zack said and smiled.

Hours passed as cousins, aunts, uncles, and family friends introduced themselves, each having a story they felt needed to be told.
Comfort food and drink, including local wines, were set out family
style as everyone filled their plates. The recurring comment from
everyone was how Jace resembled Susan.

After dinner, Denise walked through the large home with Jace
and Zack looking at family photos on the walls.

"Jace, here's Susan and her friends when she was overseas," Denise said.

Jace and Zack looked at a group of four women in full uniform
smiling next to a jeep; there was a castle in the background.

"England or Scotland, not sure, and there is nothing written on
the back of the photograph. She was a wandering spirit, worked all
over the place," Denise said. "So when the war broke out she saw the
chance to travel overseas."

"Sounds like you," Zack said. "You do have her smile and eyes."

"Are there any photographs of Sarah or her family?" Jace asked.

"I've never seen any pictures of the family, but I think there is a
close-up of just Sarah. I'll see if I can find it before you two leave,"
Denise said.

As family and friends began to leave, Jace and Zack walked out
and sat in the swing on the huge front porch. Jace handed Zack a
glass of red wine.

"Thanks, I don't usually drink wine but this is good—not too
dry, a little sweet," Zack said.

"This reminds me of another wine from a Texas winery, Brushy
Creek. I have some bottles back in Galveston. I'll give you one when
you head home," Jace said, and then she crossed her arms. "It's a lot
cooler here than Galveston."

"I love it. Do you feel like we've done this before?"

"I was just about to ask you the same question. Funny how family
and the ties we have can cause such strong emotions," Jace said.

Zack sat for a moment. "I think it's more than that."

Zack and Jace looked up as the screen door opened. "Ladies,
time for bed. I've opened the country cousins room for you. I hope
you'll be comfortable," Denise said.

They followed Denise upstairs to a room with two single beds covered with handmade quilts. An oil burner with the scent of lilacs was burning, and a teapot full of chamomile tea waiting.

"Breakfast will be at nine a.m. since we have all been up so late. It's nice to have you here. Good night," Denise said.

Jace and Zack quickly dressed for bed, drank their tea, and then were enveloped in down and the smell of fresh linens.

"Zack."

"I know, it feels like we're home."

Penthouse
Honolulu
10:30 a.m.

Taylor stood on the balcony enjoying the morning. They had settled into life on the island and were becoming almost too relaxed. He turned when the front door opened.

"Eric, where are the estimates on the surfboards?" Taylor asked his brother as he walked into the apartment with his surfboard. "I see you're continuing to adjust to island life."

"Taylor, I love it here. I feel better than I ever did back home. The estimates are on the table and you were correct: they are worth a small fortune. I contacted one of the designers Harry told me about and you should be very pleased with the numbers."

"Thanks, one less thing to deal with when I'm done," Taylor responded.

"Making any progress?" Eric asked as he moved his own surfboard onto the balcony.

Taylor was happy his brother had found something to keep him busy while he followed up on some leads from the manuscript. "I have a list of people to talk with if they're still alive in Waynesboro and Macon. Eric, you need to read this manuscript. Uncle Larry was at the naval airbase when Japan attacked. He was injured and said that a woman in a blue checkered dress from the Civil War era saved him. He said she smelled like lilacs." Taylor looked at Eric.

"This book is beginning to sound like a ghost story, at least it will to the public," Eric said.

"He was also involved in some activities during the war that I'm going to have cleared through military channels before this can be printed."

Eric laughed. "Really, like what—military secrets?"

"Yes, that's exactly what it is. Uncle Larry was involved in some dealings with the French resistance and it was classified. He mentions a female Jedburgh and being best man at a wedding between this Jedburgh and a B-17 pilot."

"Names?" Eric asked.

"No, but his feelings for Susan Bowen were what I thought. He intended to find and marry her after the war. Her death affected him deeper than any of us realized. He devoted several chapters to their meeting and relationship during the war."

"Does he say much about her death?"

"Yes, he also details her transformation from Susan to the woman who saved him at Pearl. This woman tells him that she found him once and he would find her again. She transforms back to Susan and dies in his arms," Taylor finished.

"Well that just sent chills down my back. You know, I remember conversations about how Uncle Larry changed when he returned from the war. Aunt Beatrice tried a number of times to introduce him to her single friends when he would visit, but Larry always backed out or excused himself for personal or health reasons," Eric said.

"Sounds like he felt he would be cheating on the dead."

"What's wrong? You have that look on your face," Eric said.

"Thinking about Heather and feeling a little guilty that I don't feel about her the way Uncle Larry felt about Susan. I want a family and someone to love me for eternity," Taylor said.

"Then I would say you haven't met the woman that touches your soul," Eric said.

Taylor looked at his brother and smiled. "What are you, my shrink?"

"Nope, your bro. You cooking tonight?"

"Steaks bought, marinating in the fridge, and I found a nice Bordeaux," Taylor responded.

"Sweet."

Chapter Nine ❧

Bevan had ended up sleeping on his couch at the office, dreaming of Laura instead of spending the holiday with her. He had an early briefing with the president and needed a quick shower and shave before the meeting. Bevan was gathering clean clothes and his personal kit when the phone rang.

"Gone? What the hell do you mean he's gone!" Bevan took a deep breath and regained his composure. "Find him!"

"Problem, boss?" E. asked.

Bevan turned and looked at his right-hand man. "You will never know how glad I am to see you. Aren't you back early?"

"A few days. DeAnna got word she was needed back in New York, something do to with shipments, wrong type of material—you know, stuff I don't want to know about—so we came back early. Sounds like there's a problem."

"Yes there's a problem, there are always problems, but right now I need you to start on the file marked ARC Investigations."

"What else do you need?" E. asked.

"I need to know where he is. The field agent assigned to watch him, lost him. E., check all commercial flights out of New York, all trains . . . hell, check the damn buses!"

"On it, boss," E. said, and then he turned around to leave.

"E., it's good to have you back."

E. waved his hand and left.

Bevan turned back to his desk and looked at the packages addressed to Zaveen in Louisiana and the other to Blain in Augusta. He picked them up, walked out of his office, and handed them to Darlene.

"These have to go out today. Overnight them."

"Right away."

Bevan headed to shower and then dress for his meeting. He stopped back in his office for his briefcase. His head was pounding due to the lack of caffeine; as he turned, Darlene was standing in the doorway with a large Starbucks.

"What would I do without you, Darlene?" Bevan said.

Long Bowe B&B
Waynesboro, Georgia
9:00 a.m.

The breakfast nook in the kitchen was a favorite spot when only a couple of people were at the B&B. It was cozy and warm, always inviting, so it seemed only natural for Zack and Jace to make their way to it for breakfast.

"Denise, I can't eat another bite, but I will have another cup of coffee," Jace said.

"Did you ladies sleep well?"

"Better than in my own bed back home in Louisiana," Zack answered.

"Is the family cemetery within walking distance?" Jace asked.

"No, but there's a jeep outside we have for guests to take and use when they're here. Daniel can draw a map since the roads still aren't marked out there. I'll pack a lunch in case you two aren't back for a while."

Jace looked at Zack as she stopped, and stared toward the back door of the kitchen. "Zack, what are you looking at?"

"Denise, is there a root cellar close?"

"Lord girl, how did you know that? There was years ago but we filled it in—too unstable, with no support," Denise said.

Jace decided it was time to leave before Denise began to ask more questions she couldn't answer or Zack would have to explain her special abilities.

"What time are we expected at Doc B's home?" Jace asked.

"Donna said to come around seven thirty."

"Hope they don't mind casual," Zack said.

"Honey, that's all there is around here," Denise said and laughed.

Zack had taken the keys and pulled the jeep around in front of the B&B when Jace walked outside.

"I guess you're driving? That's what I get for forgetting my back-pack," Jace said.

"Of course—fly, drive—can you read the directions?"

Jace made a face as the two left the B&B drive. An hour later, after two wrong turns, they arrived at the Bowen family cemetery. Both women got out and started toward the cemetery. Jace took the family bible out of her pack and handed it to Zack. She took out a legal pad and pen.

"This is not what I expected," Jace said.

"Someone has made a project to keep this cemetery manicured, pristine," Zack said.

Both stopped and looked at the sign on the gate. "Our Duty to the Dead. To all that enter this gate, please be respectful to those who came before us."

"I remember as a child we would come and pull weeds, cut the grass, and put flowers on the graves, but I was afraid with the family becoming distant it would be in ruins," Jace said.

Zack walked over and touched the headstones. "Some of these are old and some are new, but they seem to have all been treated with something to keep the weathering to a minimum." Zack said. She turned to see Jace a distance away kneeling. "What did you find?"

"Sarah's grave. Bring the bible."

Zack walked over and observed a family plot with five graves.

Jace began to read off names to Zack. The dates were faint, not easily read, but the names were deeply carved in the stone. Full names were written down on the legal pad so the bible could be corrected at a later date. "I'm afraid it may have been too late when they treated these older markers."

Zack looked at the place where Sarah was buried. "Jace, who are Elise and Frank?"

"They were the parents of Sarah. James and Ethan were Sarah's brothers. . . . Zack, can you read the dates?"

"No, but I have an idea." Zack stood up and began to look at adjoining plots. "I wonder why Deelyn and Frank weren't buried here, Jace; I found Ethan and Deanna's plot!"

"Grandmother and Grandfather made their home in San Antonio after the war; both loved it and raised their children there," Jace said and looked up as Zack walked away toward the jeep. Jace was beginning to think she should have brought paper and charcoal to make tracings.

"I hope this works," Zack said and took the lens cap off a camera.

"Nice, looks expensive," Jace said.

"Graduation gift. I put black and white film in it this morning. I'm hoping it will give us the clarity needed to pull some of these dates up," Zack said and began to take pictures.

"Zack, take pictures of every marker here. I'll be able to make a more detailed family tree with the correct information."

Zack stood adjusting her lens. "Does that say, 'I promise' on Sarah's grave?"

Jace knelt down again and touched the marker. "Yes."

"Any ideas?"

"I was hoping you might have an answer. Your special ability not picking up anything?" Jace asked.

"Not here, but I'm really drawn to Martha's grave for some reason."

The morning turned into early afternoon when both women sat in the back of the jeep eating and trying to put what they found in perspective. The "snack" Denise had sent was a picnic basket stuffed with fried chicken, potato salad, and homemade rolls. There was a jug of sweet tea Daniel had set in the cooler. Jace looked around at what grew in the nearby nature.

"Zack, this place is full of plants, flowers, and trees that have healing qualities. Sarah and her mother would have harvested what they needed for healing right here," Jace said.

"Do you have any idea what the words on Susan's headstone meant?" Zack asked.

"'Wait for me' on Susan's, 'I promise' on Sarah's, words out of place, some meaning that family either didn't pass on or was placed at someone's direction," Jace answered.

"The words mean something to somebody," Zack said.

"I feel like Sherlock Holmes. Maybe once I get more information I can put this mystery together," Jace said. "Zack, where are you going?"

"I saw some flowers that still had blooms, thought we might put them on Sarah, Susan, and Martha's graves."

Jace smiled. "Right behind you."

NSA
MARYLAND
6:00 P.M.

Bevan had finished another long day. It seemed lately they were all turning into twelve- and sixteen-hour days. The report in front of him concerned information in the Middle East.

"Sir," Darlene said as she stood in his doorway.

Bevan looked at his watch. "Can't keep a lady waiting, can I?"

"No, sir," she responded.

"Good night, Darlene. See you tomorrow," Bevan said.

"Enjoy your dinner," Darlene replied.

Bevan turned off his desk lamp, grabbed his coat, and headed toward the front door. As he reached for the handle on the door he heard his computer guru calling.

"Boss! Boss! Hold up a min."

Bevan turned around and knew by the look on E.'s face there would be no dinner or Laura this evening. "That bad?"

"Well, I don't have what you want."

"Any chance I have time for dinner?"

"This guy has just disappeared off the face of the earth. I have checked everything, including car rentals . . . dinner? Is that where you're headed?"

Sometimes Bevan wondered about his computer genius. "Can this wait or do I need to call Laura?"

"No, I'm going to stay and work on this; just wanted to let you know, he has to be using multiple aliases."

Bevan took a breath. "Fine. I'll call after dinner and check on you. If you don't find anything, I have a couple of numbers I can call, people who owe me a favor."

"Score, see you tomorrow."

"E., if you don't find something in the next couple of hours, go home. I need you fresh and on your game. We need to find this bastard."

"Deal."

Bevan got to his car and called Laura. "I'm on my way."

"Bevan, for once I'm the one running late. Please order my favorite Pinot Noir. I won't be more than twenty minutes," Laura said.

"See you soon," Bevan said.

Bevan left the parking lot and stopped for the routine security check at the gate. His mind was on Laura and his plans for a Key West Christmas, so the motorcycle that pulled out two cars later went unnoticed.

❦

Home of Bill and Donna Benjamin
Waynesboro, Georgia
7:30 p.m.

Jace and Zack drove up in front of a two-story log cabin set back in a line of trees. The smell of food enveloped both of them as they exited the jeep. The lights made the house feel warm and inviting.

"If we hadn't had directions, I never would have found this place," Jace said.

"Very nice," Zack responded.

"I hope they like the wine I picked out at the liquor store in town," Jace said and turned around to see Zack staring at the house. "What's wrong?"

"Jace, do you know the last name of this family?" Zack asked.

"No, I forgot to ask Denise," Jace said.

"It's Benjamin."

Both women walked up the stairs where Bill and Donna Benjamin waited. Once introductions were completed they welcomed both women to their home.

"Please come in, dinner is ready to be served," Donna said.

"Are these your children?" Zack asked as they walked past numerous photographs on a baby grand piano.

"Yes, Bevan is our oldest, Barton, and Belinda," Donna said with pride.

"Any grandchildren?" Jace asked.

"Five all together, two belong to Barton and three to Belinda. Blain, our oldest grandchild, will be going to Washington very soon to work," Donna said.

"Interpreter, I believe," Bill said.

The four sat down to a fabulous gourmet meal. After dinner, dessert was served along with more wine.

"Thank you for having us," Jace said.

"Nonsense, we're just sorry we couldn't have met you last night but we had a couple of emergencies," Bill said.

"Jace, thank you for the wine—very nice," Donna said.

"I became interested in wines about three years ago and decided if I was going to give them as gifts I should know more about them. I began to stop at small local wineries to educate myself on the types of grapes and fruit used to make wines. I discovered wine can also be made with honey, called mead. Once I began to feel comfortable with the different blends and tastes my choices became easier," Jace said.

"You did well. The Cabernet Sauvignon you chose was a nice complement to dinner," Bill said. "But I understand your visit here is more than just to renew family ties."

"Yes, a few months ago my mother sent me a pouch obviously from the Civil War era, bible, three books, and a bell. The only thing my mother said was that I was now the keeper of the family history. I was told that my great-aunt Susan had a journal belonging to Sarah Bowen that was lost during WWII. The reason for my visit is I believe there are things that have been left unfinished due to an untimely death. For some reason it seems I'm the one to try to see they are completed," Jace said and looked at the faces around the table. "I know all this sounds odd, but the stories here are not complete. Odd messages left on grave stones leave questions that need to be answered."

Donna looked at Bill.

"I think I might be able to give you some of the answers you're searching for or at least head you in the right direction," Bill said. "Donna, would you go get mother's scrapbook?"

"My father had been in love with your Aunt Susan but she had not felt the same. Susan joined the military and went to Europe; father was called back into service and sent to the Pacific. He almost died from malaria and was discharged early. On the trip back to Waynesboro after being discharged he discovered Susan's body was on the same train along with a young nurse. This nurse was the daughter of the physician that had covered his practice while he was away. Nancy Small and Susan Bowen became best friends while they served together as task nurses during World War II. Nancy was injured the same time Susan was killed; she was discharged and brought Susan's body home. Nancy and father later married and the rest is, well, history so to speak," Bill finished.

"I want you to look at this scrapbook," Donna said. "I have photographs and some notes here that I think may help you."

Donna showed them photos of the "Georgia Peaches," someone called B.O., and the two women that were later confirmed as Nazi spies. There were many pictures of Nancy and Susan, always smiling and their arms around each other.

"Who is this?" Zack asked, pointing to a picture of Susan and a tall man.

"That is Larry White. The man Susan fell in love with," Bill said.

"White, that's the name in the book," Jace said.

"What book?" Bill asked.

"Something about women in war, I can't remember his first name," Jace said.

"Larry White was a reporter, originally from New York but moved to Hawaii before the war," Bill said.

"Nancy told us that Susan and Larry were descendants of two other star-crossed lovers," Donna said.

"What are you talking about?" Jace asked.

"The Bowen and White families have been connected for centuries. A young reporter named Samuel White fell in love with a Civil War nurse, Sarah Bowen. He was injured and died in her arms at Gettysburg," Bill said.

"That's the name, Samuel, the one in the book about nurses during the Civil War," Jace said.

"Did your mother ever say anything about a journal?" Zack asked.

"Yes, that's how we know most of this history. Susan would read parts of the journal to her friends. Susan mailed the journal back to the States for safety," Bill said.

"Where?" Jace asked.

"New York. She was supposed to meet Larry White there after the war for a special dinner," Donna said.

"Then there is a chance the journal that belonged to Sarah Bowen is still in his possession," Jace said.

"Possible, but he passed away in 1995," Donna said.

"Then he has relatives somewhere and we now have a place to start looking," Zack said.

"Zack, it's late and we need to get back. Donna, Bill, I want to offer you both a week at a B&B in Galveston called the Jolly Roger. It will be my treat for all that you have kept safe these many years," Jace said.

"We may take you up on that offer one day," Bill said.

"I want you to have this," Donna said and handed Jace a photograph of Susan and Larry.

"Thank you, he was quite handsome . . . there's something about his eyes," Jace said.

"Haunting almost," Zack said.

Donna smiled. "Bill, will you walk the ladies out? Come back anytime, girls."

"Jace, Zack, good luck. I hope you find the answers you're looking for, and maybe the dead will finally be at peace," Bill said.

"I'm going to try," Jace answered.

Chapter Ten ❧

Aaron had been awake since four a.m. waiting for Lyssa's alarm to go off. She had a flight at eight this morning and would be gone for a week. The week had been pleasant, even though he had not made as much progress on Sherman's request as he had planned. He allowed the lovely distraction to take a small amount of his time. Now he would go back to work.

"Lyssa, it's time for you to get up," Aaron said and kissed her shoulder.

Lyssa placed her hand on his face. "Liam, I'm going to miss you. Will you be here when I get back?"

"No my love, I have appointments, but I will not forget where you live."

"You're welcome to stay while I'm gone, save on your expense account. Just leave the extra key above the door."

"I may just do that."

"Join me for a shower?" Lyssa said.

"Of course."

❧

NSA
Maryland
10:00 A.M.

Ethaniel was frustrated. He was not the type of individual to become angry or have tantrums. He felt that was a waste of time and energy, which was better spent on solving problems. He stood in the doorway of Bevan's office and looked at the floor. E. knew he didn't have the right program at this point to find Aaron. He would need to develop something new.

"Boss."

"Can't find him?" Bevan said.

"I was able to track him from New York via train to D.C. he took a red-eye to Atlanta, then a private jet to Houston . . . After that I lost him. He used two aliases and although the descriptions are dissimilar, it was him."

"Aliases and disguises . . . I should have figured that into his disappearance. He could be anywhere now." Bevan could feel a headache coming from the base of his neck and reached for a bottle of Tylenol in his desk drawer.

"Sorry, he just vanished. This is going to be difficult, but I have an idea forming up here," Ethan said and pointed to his head.

"I didn't expect this to be easy; he was trained by the best: us. What worries me is he may still have friends, friends that either share his beliefs in free enterprise or enjoy what he can offer."

"I just wanted to keep you updated but I'll keep looking. Oh, I'm going to be gone over the weekend."

Bevan smiled. "New York?"

E. sighed. "New York."

LONG BOWE B&B
GEORGIA
NOON

Denise had been up early as usual getting things ready for another day at the B&B. She had enjoyed breakfast with Jace and Zack. Denise had given them more family information from Angie's bible and had made to-go bags for both of them.

"Jace, Zack, I want both of you to come back anytime," Denise said.

"Thank you, this week has been wonderful and I now have a place to start looking for answers," Jace said.

"Yes, thank you," Zack said.

"Daniel will take you back. Have a safe flight and call to let us know you made it safely."

"I will," Jace said.

The trip back to the airport seemed shorter. Jace watched Zack go in and set the flight plan back to Galveston. The Cherokee had been brought out, and refueled, and all that was needed was the preflight check. There had been so much information given to her at the Benjamins she was still trying to digest it all.

"We're ready to go, Jace," Zack said.

"Daniel, thanks again for a wonderful visit," Jace said and hugged him.

"Like Denise said, come back anytime. Oh, I almost forgot, Denise found this and said to give it to you. It's a photograph of Sarah Bowen," Daniel said and handed Jace a brown envelope.

"Thank you."

"Safe trip, don't forget to call when you get home," he said.

"I promise," Jace said. She walked out onto the airstrip and entered the Cherokee, where Zack was waiting.

"Ready to go? What's that?" Zack asked.

"Sarah's photograph."

"Well, let's see it."

Jace opened the envelope and pulled out the picture. The only sound in the cockpit was the gasp from both women.

"Jace, it's you!"

Jace turned pale and stared at a photograph that could have been her, a hundred years ago.

❧

JOLLY ROGER B&B
TEXAS
8:00 P.M.

Zack, Candi, Casie, and Jace sat on the deck enjoying the evening and finishing a second bottle of Merlot. Jace had brought all the pictures they had been given from Waynesboro.

"I need to go make a call. I'll be right back," Jace said.

"This is unbelievable," Candi said.

"Why family resemblances can show up generations later . . ." Casie started.

". . . This close," Candi finished.

"Possibly, who are we to say?" Casie said.

"Zack, a package came for you the other day. It was a special delivery from Louisiana," Candi said.

"Duty done, call made to Daniel and Denise saying we made it safely home," Jace said as she walked outside where the others sat.

"Jace, I picked up your book and they said you got it there just in time. Another month and it would have been toast," Casie said.

"Thanks so much. What do I owe you?"

"The bill is upstairs," Candi said.

"Zack said you two were able to obtain a lot of information about this mystery of yours," Casie said.

"We did, but I still have a lot of blanks to fill in before it's finished," Jace said.

"How 'bout something to eat?" Candi asked.

"Sounds good," Jace said

Candi brought the package out to Zack. "We'll have something ready in a minute. You two chill."

Jace looked at Zack as she opened the package from home. "What is it?"

Zack held up two language boxes, Farsi and Kurdish. "The letter says I'm to report to Washington."

"When?"

"Two weeks."

"What are you going to tell your family? You can lie to them but don't try to lie to me."

"Jace, I'm not sure where I'll end up but I can't worry my mother. I'll probably tell them the same story Blain Benjamin told his parents."

"Well, guess I better give you this then," Jace said and pulled a small box out of her jean pocket. "It was for your graduation but I think now is more appropriate."

Zack took the box and opened it, then looked at her.

"It's a Zuni fetish, a raven. It's magic, a messenger of great mystery, a change in consciousness; it represents 'anything we have the courage to face, we have the power to transform.' Keep it close for luck," Jace said.

"After the couple of weeks we've had you can count on it," Zack said and hugged Jace. "You know, I need to leave tomorrow and get home. Two weeks is not going to give me a lot of time to do some prep and explain what I can to my family."

"I understand. Email me or write when it's possible; I don't want to lose touch," Jace said.

"Not a chance," Zack said.

"Can you smell that?" Jace asked.

"I think that might be more than just a snack," Zack answered and both women took their wine and went inside.

Chapter Eleven 🐦

SCHOLES AIRPORT
GALVESTON, TEXAS
SUNDAY, SEPTEMBER 17, 2000
10:00 A.M.

Jace stood and watched as Zack loaded the Cherokee with goodies from the twins for her family and two bottles of Brushy Creek wine. They hugged and promised to keep in touch; then Jace watched until Zack disappeared from sight. The past two weeks had gone by all too quickly. She got in her pickup and drove down the sea wall to The Galvez to meet the twins for Sunday brunch. Jace looked at the gun turret as she drove past the San Luis. There was so much history here and she needed to take the time to read and embrace the place she now called home. She pulled up to the valet; the walk into this beautiful building was only surpassed by the wonderful scent of food on the large buffet.

"Jace, over here," Candi said and waved.

"We've already paid for yours. Sit down and enjoy a mimosa," Casie said.

"Girl, you look good in green," Candi said.

"I bought it on the strand while Zack was here," Jace answered.

"Island dress suits you well," Casie said.

Jace sat down. "Thank you, and this is wonderful."

The waiter served a mimosa to Jace.

"A toast," Candi said, and all three raised their glasses. "To the future."

"To the future," Jace and Casie repeated.

❧

RUNWAY ON THE KEENS FARM
MORGAN CITY, LOUISIANA
11:30 A.M.

Doyle stood and watched his daughter land. He had been there for some time, thinking about the package that had arrived for Zaveen. They had never finished their conversation that day about the job offer from the government and, now, though he had hoped she would stay close to home, his second sense told him it was not to be.

"Zaveen, welcome home," Doyle said.

Zack hugged her father. "Merci, papa. Where is mamma?"

"At home, cooking."

"Of course, what was I thinking?" Zack said and smiled.

"Did you get the package? Your mamma insisted I send it since a courier brought it to the house. Do you have something you need to tell us, Zaveen?"

"Oui papa, I have much to tell everyone," Zack said.

Doyle took a deep breath and looked at his daughter, now a woman with a future ahead of her. "Then we should go and talk to your mamma."

"Papa, I don't think she is going to understand. I have been gone a long time and it may be a while before I can come back," Zack said.

"It'll be fine, my college graduate. We both knew you would fly away eventually."

"I just want to make you proud of me," Zack said.

"Oh, Zaveen, we already are, more than you know," Doyle said. "We need to go; your mamma is waiting."

Zack smiled as Doyle put his arm around his daughter and they headed home.

Chapter Twelve 🐦

Aaron had locked Lyssa's apartment and left two dozen white roses in the bedroom. He left them more out of courtesy than as a romantic gesture. He deleted all of the pictures she had taken the week they had spent together; he had cleaned her computer and sterilized the living areas. He used the same simple disguise for today as he had while following the Shaw brothers around: thicker eyebrows, gray in his hair, and a heavy moustache. He left the apartment complex through the stairwell, knowing there were no cameras there. He exited out the side of the building and waved to the taxi waiting for him at the front of the building.

"Where to?"

"Airport, main terminal," Aaron said.

Aaron had spent the week after Lyssa had left following Eric to and from the beach; Taylor had been more aloof. He had followed Taylor earlier in the week to the newspaper and was interested in the box he carried out and back to the condo. Taylor swam laps in the pool every morning at about six a.m. but he had not taken in the night life, other than an occasional dinner out with his brother. Due to the security now in place at the condos, it was impossible for him to get inside without concern over being caught on film. He had an appointment later today to talk with Harry Hawthorne about the condos that were for sale. He would see what he knew, if anything. Sherman seemed to think he had information that was important. Once he left Hawaii, he would head to a safe house in Las Vegas and call Sherman from one of the casinos to update him. His trip to Waynesboro would come later.

"Here you are, sir," the driver said.

Aaron exited the cab and left a decent tip. He walked inside and headed to the baggage area where a man holding a sign with "Williams" on it waited.

"Are you the driver?" Aaron asked.

"Yes sir, luggage?"

"Just one bag," Aaron said and handed the driver his bag. He stopped in the baggage area and looked around to make sure he hadn't been followed; force of habit and sometimes games must be played to throw off your opponent. Aaron followed the man to a waiting limo and gave him the address to the condo.

"Staying long?"

"No, just checking on some property. I will need you to wait for me," Aaron said.

"Not a problem," the driver said as he left the airport. In a short time the driver pulled up to the front door of the condo.

Harry Hawthorne looked out his window as the limo drove up. A "Danfield Williams" had called two days ago and made an appointment to see the three condos that were for sale. Harry watched as the potential tenant got out of the limo.

"Bastard thinks he can pull one over old Harry, does he? Harry may be old but he's not blind," he said out loud.

Harry had seen this man following Eric to the beach several times. He didn't know what he wanted, but he didn't intend to give it to him. Harry reached over and pressed the record button on the security cameras that had just been installed.

"Let's see if these damn things are worth all that money."

Two hours later, Aaron left with less information than he already had gathered over the past week. It seemed Harry Hawthorne was a formidable adversary. He was unable to get any additional information about the tenants or if the penthouse would be available at any time in the future.

"Back to the airport, sir?" the driver said.

"Yes, I'm done here for now," Aaron answered and looked toward the window where Harry Hawthorne stood and stared at him. "Is that old man smiling?"

"What did you say, sir?"

"Nothing."

Chapter Thirteen ❧

Bevan looked over the reports on the new recruits since their arrival on the second. In the four weeks since testing began, three students had risen above the others. He smiled at the scores between Blain and Zaveen. It seemed these two were going to be one and two out of the class. His bet would be that Zaveen would end up first. He wondered if they would be as competitive in field testing, too.

"Boss, I have something for you," E. said as he slid into Bevan's office.

"What?"

"I have a phone call from a Las Vegas casino to New York on the second that lasted five minutes."

"Where?" Bevan asked.

"The *White Daily Journal* . . . ?" E. responded.

"I think it's time we send someone to talk with Sherman Shaw. We need to see what his connection is with ARC Investigations," Bevan said.

"Boss, I finished a new program. I need you to send up the chain, and I have a request for some new equipment," E. said.

"Put it on my desk," Bevan said.

"Already there in your inbox," E. replied. He then turned around and headed back to his "cave."

Bevan picked up his phone and made a call to the FBI New York office. "Ron, it's Bevan. I need you to do some leg work this time."

"Where?"

"The *White Daily Journal*. You need to talk to a Sherman Shaw."

"Anything particular?"

"Ron, I really need you to push this man. We need to see what his involvement is with Aaron Caydon."

"National security?"

"Possibly terrorism," Bevan said.

"I'll get back to you. It may be a while; I want to catch him off guard."

"Fine, I need some answers," Bevan said.

PENTHOUSE
HONOLULU
NOON

Taylor looked over his notes on the manuscript and the information he had obtained at the newspaper. There was a contract that had been signed by the publisher of Larry's other two books for the rights to this one when finished, regardless of the date. Taylor made a note to contact the company to make sure this was still in good standing. He stood, walked out on the balcony, and thought about where he should go next. He turned as the door opened.

"Eric, we need to make some plans." Taylor turned to see Eric and Harry heading toward the kitchen.

"Hello Harry, what's going on?" Taylor inquired.

"Harry here has some interesting information and pictures of someone who was apparently following us back in September," Eric said.

"Sherman, damn it!" Taylor said.

"Mr. Shaw, this fella followed your brother to the beach several days, and I saw him outside watching you come and go," Harry told them.

"Whoa, who taught you to be so observant?" Eric asked.

"Larry told me that for the most part people are good, but there is that small percentage that ain't. I've always watched my back and now it has paid off," Harry said and handed Taylor five pictures of "Danfield Williams." "He asked a lot of questions about the tenants and about the penthouse."

"Privacy of the tenants stopped you from telling him anything, right?" Eric said.

"That and I knew he wasn't who he claimed to be, bastard," Harry said.

"I don't recognize him, do you, Taylor?" Eric asked.

Taylor looked at the pictures of a well-dressed man. "Was he tall?"

"About six foot two, two hundred pounds, but muscle not fat; seemed to be well educated and thought old Harry wouldn't see through his disguise," Harry said and laughed.

"Dark hair—black or brown?" Taylor asked.

"Black hair with some gray, grayish blue eyes, and a striking presence; he had some silly thick eyebrows and a fake moustache," Harry said.

"He has to be a private investigator of some kind. Knowing Sherman this guy is probably ex-military and good at what he does," Taylor said.

"Taylor, why is Sherman pushing so hard on this? He can't possibly know about all of this, and he is set for life financially," Eric said.

"There is a lot of money and power associated with the newspaper. I wish I could tell you for sure, but the thought of not having total control is destroying his soul," Taylor said.

"Nothing good comes from that type of thinkin,' boys," Harry said.

"What worries me now is how far Sherman is willing to go to get all that power" Taylor said.

"If this guy is ex-military and works for money, he knows Sherman has access to give him what he wants whatever the cost. I bet he has given him a copy of the will, too," Eric said.

"And that is an issue now. If he was here that means he is on the same tract looking for the same people," Taylor continued. "I don't want to do anything right now, but what would you think about Christmas in Georgia?"

"Brrrr—guess I'll have to buy a coat. Where in Georgia?" Eric asked.

"A B&B. There must be one in Waynesboro. I'm hoping they'll be able to give us directions to the Bowen farm," Taylor said.

"I'll watch over everything while you two are gone," Harry said.

"You're quite the guard dog," Eric told him.

Harry started to laugh as he headed toward the door. "Ole Harry's pretty spry for his age, and you can call me Bulldog."

Taylor looked at Eric after Harry left. "Did he say to call him Bulldog?"

"Yeah, he did."

"I think there is more in Harry's background than just being a mail clerk."

"Think we'll ever find out?"

"Probably not."

Harry walked back to his condo and shut the door. He went into his bedroom and pulled out an old scrapbook. Harry thought he had a few minutes to visit some old friends and have a drink. He sat down in his favorite chair, poured some rum into a glass, and began to turn the pages. He stopped when he came to a group photo taken many years ago. Harry was only sixteen when he joined the military. He ran his hand over the group of Jedburghs and smiled at the woman that saved him that frigid night they jumped into enemy territory. That night he earned his name, Bulldog.

"To my fellow lads and you, lass, jolly good show." Harry's accent slipped out as he toasted his comrades.

Harry was older and his health issues were becoming a problem. He was determined to live long enough to see Larry's final wishes carried out. He would have one last thing to do when Taylor succeeded. A picture needed to be passed on to Taylor and the heir of the Bowen family. Harry took a faded yellow photograph from the back of the scrapbook and held it for a moment. A wedding picture found in Sarah's journal was given to him for safekeeping. On the back the only words written were "James and Martha." Harry replaced it in his scrapbook, then stood to go make his rounds before heading to the local senior citizens afternoon bingo.

Chapter Fourteen ❧

BUSH AIRPORT
HOUSTON, TEXAS
THANKSGIVING, NOVEMBER 23, 2000
9:00 A.M.

Aaron sat in the bar drinking Irish coffee and waited for his flight
to Scotland. He dreaded the next eight to twelve hours, as he would
be flying coach. At least he had purchased two seats to have some
elbow room. He would lie low for the next three to four months and
count on his associates to obtain information on the Shaw brothers
and watch Bevan Benjamin. He would go to Georgia after the first
of the year, maybe in February. Aaron doubted Taylor would find all
the information to finish the guidelines of the will by then. Sherman
was becoming a problem, and their conversations had been less than
pleasant after he left Hawaii.

"Another one, sir?" the bartender asked.

"Bud Johnson from Muleshoe, Texas," Aaron said with a heavy
drawl and reached out to shake hands. "Make it two, I have time."
His associate in Scotland would be at the airport in Glasgow to pick
him up. Aaron turned and looked out the window at the clouds
building.

"Here you go, sir," the bartender said and sat the cups down in
front of Aaron.

"Guess I'd better drink up, pardner, it might get a bit rough,"
Aaron said.

❦

JOLLY ROGER B&B
TEXAS
NOON

Jace was coming downstairs to the smell of turkey, dressing, and pumpkin pie. The smells brought back holidays past at home or at her grandparents' home. She laughed thinking how Grandmother Deelyn was not the cook in the family, and after the third ruined turkey Grandfather did all the holiday cooking.

"Jace, can you set the table? We have three couples that will be joining, so nine places all together," Candi said.

"I'm glad to help," Jace answered.

Jace had been fortunate with the B&B to not have to work since Labor Day, but she was beginning to feel caged in and had been talking with several recruiters about jobs starting in the next thirty to sixty days.

"Jace, you've been spending a lot of time upstairs. What are you working on? You haven't even been for a walk on the beach in two weeks," Casie said.

"I'm trying to correct the family tree and figure out where I need to go from here. The book written by Samuel White is extremely interesting, a lot of information I never knew. The dedication has to mean that Sarah and Samuel were in love. I still don't have enough information, but I did some research online and found the company that bought out the publisher. I don't expect any answer until after the holidays are over."

"I checked the mail yesterday and there was a package for you; it's from Louisiana," Candi said and gave Jace a glass of wine.

Jace opened the box and a read the note from Zack's mother. *Zaveen said you might need these. Just return them when you are finished. You should come see us for Christmas; Zaveen is coming home for a few days.* Jace picked up two bibles and a photo album.

"More research?" Casie said.

"I hope more answers," Jace replied.

"If you two can stop talking, we need to get the table set. Our guests will be arriving soon," Candi said.

"Are these paying guests?" Jace asked.

"Yes, they'll be here all weekend," Candi said.

"You two made an awesome investment and I'm happy to be a part of it," Jace said.

"But you'll be leaving in the next month or so, right?" Casie asked.

"We've seen you pacing the hallways and out by the launch," Candi said.

"I need to find something for a few months," Jace said.

"Not a problem, you know that you can come and go as you please," Candi said.

Jace hugged both women. "You two are the best."

The ship's bell outside rang.

"Our guests have arrived," Candi said.

"Come in, come in, everyone's welcome here," Happy Hour sang from his perch.

White Daily Journal Office
Manhattan
2:00 p.m.

Sherman sat in the back of the limo cursing under his breath. He had left his home full of important guests, some that could possibly be future financial supporters, to meet with an impertinent agent that all but demanded he come to his office at the newspaper *now*. He probably should call the attorneys for the paper, but he really needed to get this over with quickly and return to the house. He made an excuse to his guests about an emergency at the newspaper that demanded his presence, but he would return soon and had asked for everyone there to stay and enjoy his hospitality. As Sherman entered his office he observed a man sitting at Louisa's desk with his feet up. He opened his office door as the agent stood.

"This is damn inconvenient, agent!" Sherman was loud and obnoxious.

"Edwards, Agent Ron Edwards, FBI, and I apologize for the visit, but it is of a serious matter and your name has come up in one of our investigations."

"My name! What investigation? And what could be so serious I'm dragged out of my home on Thanksgiving?" Sherman shouted. "Maybe I should call my attorney!"

"You can do that, Mr. Shaw, and have him meet us at the Federal Building on Monday morning after you have spent the entire weekend in our custody, or you can answer some simple questions about your relationship with ARC Investigations and go back home to your guests," Ron said.

Sherman calmed for a moment and realized the agent was serious. "Agent Edwards, my apology, what can I help you with?"

"A national security threat, possibly terrorism." Ron looked at Sherman.

"On American soil?" Sherman asked.

"Could you tell me how long you have known Aaron Reece Caydon, and what type of work he is doing for you?"

"Would you mind if I fixed a drink?" Sherman said and walked to the bar. "I would offer you one but I know you're on duty." Sherman wiped his forehead with a cocktail napkin.

"Mr. Shaw, I would appreciate it if you would simply answer my questions," Ron said.

"Of course. Mr. Caydon and his people are doing some background checks for me involving my great-uncle's last will and testament," Sherman said and walked back to his chair. Sweat trickled down his back.

"It must be important. Our reports show you have given this man a rather large sum of money in the past few months," Ron said.

"My late uncle's estate is complicated and he is simply helping to tie up a few loose ends," Sherman said, trying to stay calm.

"Mr. Caydon is under investigation at this moment and it would be advisable for you to seek another investigator."

"Thank you, I will. Is there anything else?" Sherman hoped he had satisfied Agent Edwards.

"That will be all for the moment, but we may have more questions later." Ron stood to leave.

Sherman stood. "Anytime, whatever I can do to help the FBI."

"Then we'll be in touch; and, please, if Mr. Caydon should contact you I expect a call," Ron said and handed Sherman his card.

Sherman's hand was shaking as he reached for the card.

"I'll find my own way out. Happy Thanksgiving," Ron said.

"You too," Sherman said and watched Agent Edwards leave his office.

Sherman waited a few minutes and then pulled out a disposable cell phone from the bottom drawer of his desk and left a very short message. "What the fuck are you involved in? The FBI just left here, you bastard!" Sherman hung up and destroyed the phone. He would receive a package now with another disposable phone and a date and time for a call. Sherman thought Aaron had always been overly cautious, but after today he would never question him again.

FBI FEDERAL PLAZA
NEW YORK
4:00 P.M.

Ron sat down at his desk and looked over his notes, mostly the reactions he caused while talking with Shaw. He didn't like this man but didn't really have anything other than his many years of gut feelings to go on at this time. Ron picked up his phone and hit a speed dial number.

"Bevan, sorry to bother you today, but I just left Sherman Shaw. I decided today would be a good time to catch him off guard, with his brownstone full of guests."

"Ron, I've always trusted your judgment. What do you think?" Bevan asked.

"I don't think he is involved in any national security issues but his dealings with Caydon are not all honest. I'd like to know more about the loose ends he is tying up for Shaw. I have a feeling they could end up in the East River," Ron said.

"I'm not sure I feel any better," Bevan said.

"I'll tell you this, Sherman Shaw will make some type of contact with Caydon after this visit, so if you need me to keep checking I have some free time," Ron said.

"Appreciate it. Let me know if you come up with anything."

"Happy Turkey Day."

"Same to you and, Ron, be careful."

Chapter Fifteen ❧

Jace had taken out her last bag and needed to make one more check before getting on the road. She had her research to take with her for down times. She was anxious to see Zack and find out how she was doing with her work for the government. Jace went back inside to the smell of muffins and fresh coffee.

"You two really didn't have to get up this early," Jace said.

"Oh, stop. We have rooms to clean and get ready for the weekend. Shopping, laundry, cooking—all the things we love," Candi said.

"I need to run upstairs and then we can have breakfast," Jace said. She made her last trip upstairs to make sure the bed was made. She took towels and linens down to the laundry room and returned to the deck off the kitchen for a look at the rising sun.

Casie walked out and handed Jace a cup of coffee. "You're going to miss us."

"Of course, but I'll be back," Jace said. She laughed thinking about the *Terminator* movies.

"Well you better get going—day light's a wasting," Casie said.

"Tell Zack and her family hello, and you have a great Christmas with them. When does your contract start again?" Candi asked.

"January eighth at a small hospital in Augusta. Thought I would do more research."

Jace and the twins walked out to her pickup. Casie handed Jace a basket to give to the Keens. Jace hugged both of them. "I'll call when I get there."

"Safe journey," Casie said.

"Ditto," Candi added.

Jace smiled and got into her pickup and drove away from the Jolly Roger. She looked into the rearview mirror and saw her friends standing watch until she rounded the corner. Jace only had a little over five-hour drive to Morgan City. Zack had promised to take Jace to New Orleans at least once while she was there. She smiled at the thought of walking down Bourbon Street. Jace took out her Otis Redding CD and put it in the player. She turned up the volume to "Sitting on the Dock of the Bay."

NSA Candidate Housing
Alexandria, Virginia
8:00 a.m.

Blain Benjamin took a break from the extra work he had been assigned due to his failure to come out in first position this session. He walked down to Zack's open door and watched as she finished packing. He was attempting to think of something nice to say. What he really wanted to do was to shove her in the duffle and throw it in a closet.

"Next time I'll be leaving early and you'll be sitting here until Christmas Eve doing extra work."

Zack smiled and looked at her classmate. "Well if you had practiced a little harder at the range you'd be the one leaving. It's obvious you didn't stay up as many nights as I did studying for exams or you would have scored higher on the sleep deprivation studies and . . . "

"Okay, okay Zack, you've made your point. You better get ready for the next classes. I don't intend to be caught eating your dust again," Blain said.

"What? The physical training? Did you forget what I did and continue to do for extra money?" Zack asked as she grabbed her bag and headed toward the front door where a taxi was waiting. "See you next year."

Blain watched his classmate leave, jealous of the extra time awarded—but she was right. Zack kicked his ass on the range and studies. He would have to work harder in the weeks ahead. Zack had a ten-point lead over his total scores right now. The small woman from Louisiana was proving to be a pain in his ass, but she would make an awesome partner one day, just not his. Zack was smart and resourceful; he was wrong to have counted her out from the beginning of training. He would also never ever play poker with her again. She seemed to know what everyone had in their hand and what they were going to bet. That was too spooky.

PENTHOUSE
HONOLULU
NOON

Eric had been waiting on Taylor for twenty minutes. He hadn't really minded as he stood on the balcony for one more view.

"Eric, let's go!" Taylor called out.

"I'm ready," Eric said and walked back inside.

"Harry called a taxi for us," Taylor said and closed the blinds to the balcony.

"I'm going to miss that view," Eric said.

"It's only a few weeks, and if I need to stay longer you can come back, agreed?"

"Deal, I have a job after the first," Eric said proudly. "Can't sponge off you forever and I need to get back to what I do best."

"It's not sponging, you're earning your keep, but I understand. I'm beginning to feel the same way. Even though I want to finish this mystery, I need to go back to reporting. I'll see what I find during this trip, then make some decisions," Taylor said.

The elevator door opened to Harry waiting. "You boys better hurry."

"We're good on time, Harry; and thanks for taking care of things while we're gone," Taylor said.

"Come back safe, and good hunting," Harry said.

Taylor and Eric got into the cab.

"Airport," Taylor said.

"We've both been busy, but did you find a B&B?" Eric asked.

"Oh yeah, I did. It's called Long Bowe."

"Like a bow and arrow?"

"No, like Long and Bowen," Taylor said and smiled.

"We're staying at the place we were going there to find?" Eric asked.

Taylor started to laugh. "Yes, it seems there are other forces at work here, and thank goodness they're on our side."

"Well this should be interesting. Is that other family there too?" Eric asked.

"Benjamin, yes, they have a clinic on the same road the B&B is on," Taylor said.

"Sweet, what are you going to tell them?"

"I haven't decided, but I'm going to just play this off as a bonding time for us and say we're history buffs tracing Civil War information in the area. I'm not ready to start asking questions just yet about their family and ours; it might make them defensive."

"We, or you, can always come back later."

"True. But I want to see what I can find without having to dig too deep into family skeletons right now. I feel we'll get more information with honey and pretense of ignorance."

"You lead and I'll attempt to follow."

Chapter Sixteen ❧

Jace sat in the den reading and began to laugh out loud. She had always enjoyed reading but school had taken so much of her time, it had been a while since she could just read for pure pleasure.

"What's so funny?" Zack asked.

"This book by Janet Evanovich. It's a series and enjoyable," Jace said, then noticed Zack looking at the rest of her books.

"King, Koontz, Cussler, Brown, and Patterson . . . you seem to have a variety here," Zack said.

"I needed a break to clear my mind for a few days. You seem to be busy outside. Want to fill me in, or will you have to kill me?" Jace said and smiled.

Zack sat down. "Practicing with the weapons we have here. Borrowed the sheriff's Glock, same model that the company uses. Sorry about disappearing for a few days. Checking some hunting blinds and needed to reacquaint myself with nature."

"You're different," Jace said.

"I'm being trained to focus my inner sight. For once in my life I'm attempting to control the flood of information that comes at will, to open and close the door."

"When are you going back?" Jace asked.

Zack showed Jace an envelope. "Special delivery today: airline ticket."

"Where?"

"Las Vegas. Looks like desert training, but I didn't tell you that," Zack said. "I don't want to worry mamma. She believed the interpreter story. Papa didn't, but he promised not to ask. Jace, when are you leaving?"

"I'll stay a day or so after you're gone so your parents won't feel ..."

"Thanks, I appreciate that," Zack said.

"Besides, my contract doesn't start until the eighth, and I might stop back in Waynesboro and stay a night or two," Jace said. She looked up to see Zack staring off.

"Ask Denise who stayed there during Christmas," Zack said.

"Why?"

"One of the men that stayed there is looking for you."

"Are you sure?" Jace asked.

"Just ask."

"I will, and speaking of Waynesboro ... all the pictures you took came out crystal clear: dates, names, everything," Jace said.

"Thanks for the gift. I had forgotten that Daniel took that picture of us on the front porch," Zack said.

"I thought it turned out nice. I had one printed for me, too."

Gloria came to the den and told them in Spanish that lunch was ready. Jace thanked and asked in Spanish what was being served today.

"Leftovers," Gloria said in English and walked back to the kitchen.

Zack looked at Jace. "You're improving."

"Your mother is a good teacher and has been very patient with me. French, I'm sorry to say, will be another story," Jace said and laughed.

"Jace, once my training starts again, I may not be able to write or call as often."

"Hey, let's focus on New Year's Eve in New Orleans and we'll worry about the rest of 2001 later."

"It's all set; Uncle Ernest has a daughter who is married to one of the assistant managers of the inn on Bourbon Street. We have a top-floor room with a balcony that faces the street!" Zack said.

"No one will believe I spent New Year's Eve on Bourbon Street," Jace said.

"Oh, we'll have plenty of film to prove it."

"Girls, come," Gloria said.

"Yes, mamma," both answered.

White Daily Journal Office
Manhattan
2:00 p.m.

Louisa, Sherman's secretary, signed for the package that arrived for Sherman. She noticed there wasn't a return address and sighed, thinking he was involved with Aaron Cayden again. She remembered the last time Sherman had ARC Investigations do work for him, people died. She stood and headed into the office.

"This just came for you," Louisa said as she handed Sherman the package.

"Thank you." Sherman took the box. He waited until she had returned to her desk before he opened it. The phone he expected sat in the bottom along with the following message, "01-01-01, 0101." The door opened and Ron Edwards walked in, followed by Louisa.

"I'm sorry, Mr. Shaw, but I couldn't stop him."

"It's fine, Louisa. Come in Agent Edwards," Sherman said.

"I was in the neighborhood and thought I would stop by to see if you've heard from Caydon," Ron said and sat down across from Sherman.

Sherman took the box and placed it in his bottom drawer. "Since your visit at Thanksgiving? No, I've had no contact."

"Well, just wanted to stop by and wish you a Happy New Year. I'll be in touch," Ron said. With that, he stood and exited the office.

Sherman wiped the sweat off his forehead, took the phone and note, put both of them in his briefcase, and called Louisa over the intercom.

"Louisa, I'll be gone for the rest of the day, the rest of the year," Sherman said.

"What about your appointments?"

"Cancel them!" Sherman shouted.

Chapter Seventeen ❧

Aaron stood facing the loch, waiting a few more minutes before he called Sherman. This was his refuge, the only place he felt at ease, where the demons never bothered him. Time stood still here, peace, rest. At that moment his watch alarm buzzed. Aaron took a deep breath and dialed the number. All he could hear on the other end of the phone was babble.

"Shaw, shut the fuck up and listen to me. I can't come back right now, but I have people working on your case. Someone will come by your house with a delivery. When I come back I'll be in touch." Aaron then hung up the phone and threw it in the loch. He looked up and watched Kyleigh MacNiel walk toward him in jeans, a cream-colored Shetland sweater, and a plaid shawl from her clan. Every clan had its own unique color and pattern. The plaid pattern with green, lavender, black, and white combination was perfect for her.

"'Tis early to be out on the loch, good sir," she said and handed him a hot cup of tea.

"Aye, lass," Aaron said. "Come let me hold you for a moment on this New Year's morn."

He pulled the tall redhead into his side and held her as the sun rose higher in the sky. Aaron's feelings for Kyleigh were different from the other women he had been with over the years. There had been no attachment to those other women, only sexual release, but not with her. This poised a problem. His feelings to protect her were the same as those for his sister. Here with Kyleigh is where he wanted to be now and always.

"How long this time, Aaron?" Kyleigh asked.

"Spring," Aaron answered.

"And then?"

"Back to the States."

"Then we'll winter away until the flowers bloom," Kyleigh said and kissed him.

Sherman Shaw's Brownstone
Upper West Side, off 77th
New York
12:10 a.m.

"Bastard!" Sherman said. None of this would be happening if Taylor had just taken the easy way out. He would have paid Taylor nicely for Larry's part of the newspaper. Larry Shaw couldn't have had enough property or money to be worth all this irritation. A holy quest and the reward would provide what? Satisfaction for honoring the ravings of a dead man? Sherman had tried numerous times to identify Larry's assets, but to no avail. He was surprised his uncle had not died penniless. Sherman walked over and looked out the library window. All he needed now was for Ron Edwards to show up. He started out of the library and then stopped, walked back to his desk, and picked up the phone to call Honolulu.

"Taylor Shaw residence, can I help you?" Harry said.

"Who the hell is this?" Sherman asked.

"Who the hell are you?" Harry responded.

"Sherman Shaw. Where is Taylor?" Sherman said.

"Oh, Mr. Shaw, sorry but it's very early here. How are things in New York? Taylor said the weather there is frightful in the winter;

supposed to be a beautiful day here in Honolulu. Happy New Year to you. Say did you have a big party at your house? Taylor said you would probably have a lot of folks there. Pretty quiet here, not a lot going on. How many times have you seen the ball fall in Times Square? I bet that would be a sight to see, yes siree," Harry continued to ramble on.

"Can you—I need to speak—yes, it is cold here. Damn it!" Sherman screamed and hung up the phone.

❦

LONG BOWE B&B
GEORGIA
NOON

Taylor and Eric sat at the breakfast nook waiting for lunch at Denise's insistence. Both men had become relaxed since their arrival, despite not being totally honest with the Longs about why they were really there.

"Mrs. Long, you really didn't have to fix lunch for us," Taylor said.

"Nonsense, it's New Year's Day and everyone has to have their black-eyed peas for good luck. You boys have been so busy with your Civil War research and visits to the cemeteries that we haven't really had much time to visit."

"Your family cemetery was immaculate. I took some nice shots of the headstones," Eric said.

"I've never seen a cemetery so manicured; who takes care of it?" Taylor asked.

"I can answer that question," Daniel said. "Susan Bowen was my aunt. The story goes, the day she left for the war my aunt made a trip to the family cemetery. Aunt Susan walked into a cemetery that had been ignored, overgrown with weeds, headstones needing repair, and said her good-byes to family." She told my grandfather to have the boys, Jacob and Joshua, take better care of our family." Daniel cleared his throat. "After Aunt Susan's body was brought back, my uncles began to clear and clean the cemetery. The signs on the gates were put there by their sons."

"Who are the caretakers now?" Eric asked.

"Their boys take care of it now and the responsibility will continue to be passed down until there are no longer Bowens or Longs alive to understand the importance of the signs that hang on the gate," Daniel said.

"We were hoping to talk with Dr. Benjamin and his wife before we leave," Eric said

"Daniel, when are Bill and Donna supposed to be back?" Denise asked.

"I believe sometime today," Daniel answered.

"We have a couple of days left. Mrs. Long, would you call to see if we could meet them, say, Wednesday, if that's convenient?" Taylor asked.

"I'd be happy to call Donna this evening. I don't think it will be a problem," Denise said. "I have more information about our family history and pictures to show you that aren't on the wall. I no longer have any pictures of the original Bowen family.

"We appreciate all your assistance with our research; you've given us information we could've never found in any history book," Taylor said.

"You should gather all this information and put it in written form for generations to come," Eric said.

"Do you boys know anyone that could help us with that?" Denise asked.

"We might know someone that can help you," Taylor said and smiled at Eric.

Denise placed hot cornbread, ham, and black-eyed peas on the table family style.

"Sweet tea?" Eric asked.

"Right here," Daniel said.

Denise and Daniel sat down at the table; Daniel reached out and all joined hands for grace.

Chapter Eighteen ❧

The drive to the airport had been quiet, only the sound of the radio. Zack's father took her bag and carried it to the counter, where she got her boarding pass. They all walked to the gate and stood until it was time for Zack to board. Jace watched Zack say good-bye in French and Spanish to her parents. There were tears in Gloria's eyes. Jace knew she had continued to assure her mother that her job was safe and simple. She smiled as Zack walked over and hugged her.

"I'll get in touch when I can," Zack said.

"I'll be busy with my new assignment, it's fine. Got your raven?" Jace asked.

Zack patted her left jean front pocket. "I'll keep it close for luck; Jace, don't forget to ask Denise about her guests over the holidays."

"I won't forget," Jace said.

Jace watched Zack turn and head toward the door, but stopped once more to hug and kiss her mamma. Jace walked over and put her arm around Gloria.

"Jace, when are you leaving?" Gloria asked.

"Not until Saturday."

"Gracias."

❧

Bill and Donna Benjamin's Home
Waynesboro, Georgia
Noon

Taylor was apprehensive about the meeting with the Benjamins. They had been able to fool the Longs, but if they had any photographs of his uncle he would have to be forthright about their visit.

"Eric, I think we should have left a bread crumb trail when we left the B&B," Taylor said.

"According to this map Daniel drew, it should be just around this bend," Eric said.

Taylor stopped the jeep. "What a beautiful home."

"It provides what they obviously desire most, privacy," Eric said.

"I see now why Daniel insisted we take the jeep and not the rental. Let's see if they have something to add to the Longs' information," Taylor said and knocked on the door.

The door opened and Bill Benjamin was startled by the sight of the taller man.

"My God, Larry."

Bill Benjamin felt like a fool. He knew Larry Shaw was dead, but the man before him had startled him into the belief the dead man had returned. The family resemblance was shocking.

"Please come in and forgive my outburst, but you have no idea how much you look like your uncle," Bill said.

"No apology necessary," Taylor said.

"Bill, is that our guests?" Donna said and gasped as Taylor walked into the dining room.

"I know, I have already embarrassed myself. This is Taylor and Eric Shaw, Larry's great-nephews," Bill said.

"My goodness, such a strong family resemblance. Denise didn't tell us you were related to Larry," Donna said.

"You're not the first to tell me this but thank you, it is a very nice compliment," Taylor said.

"We didn't tell the Longs about our relationship with Larry," Eric said.

"Oh, why the secret?" Bill asked and motioned for everyone to sit down at the table.

"We're here to fill in some blanks on a book my great-uncle started and was unable to finish," Taylor said. "By your reaction, I assume you met my uncle, but we were told he never came to Waynesboro."

"He didn't," Bill said. "Once we've had lunch we'll talk and Donna can get the scrapbook."

An hour later Donna removed the dishes from the table and left to obtain the family scrapbook.

"Bill, Donna, thank you for that wonderful lunch," Taylor said.

"Bill's the gourmet chef here. I just watch and clean up," Donna said as she returned to the kitchen.

"Bill, you said that our uncle never came to Waynesboro," Eric said.

"No, he didn't, but Donna and I made a trip to Honolulu. I had a conference there and he was a guest speaker. Later, I introduced myself to him and we spent the rest of the evening talking. Young man, you have many of your uncle's physical attributes, including his unusual eyes," Bill said.

"Did Uncle Larry ever tell you why he didn't come to Waynesboro?" Taylor asked.

"No, not sure if it was because my father and Susan were involved at one time, maybe out of respect for him and mother," Bill said.

"It sounds like we'll never know," Eric said.

Donna reached over and handed Eric the scrapbook. "There are many photographs of Bill's mother and Susan in there."

"Eric, have you got the envelope Denise gave us before we left?" Taylor asked.

"It's in the jeep. I'll be back in a minute," Eric said and left the house.

"Do you know what Denise sent?" Donna asked.

"No, I'm sorry, she didn't say," Taylor said and looked up as Eric returned and handed Donna the envelope.

"It's a recipe for her special orange cranberry nut muffins," Donna said and smiled. "She's such a wonderful cook."

"Do you have any photographs of Uncle Larry and Susan Bowen?" Taylor asked.

"I did but gave it to a family member last fall. You might contact—" Donna was interrupted by Taylor.

"It's fine, I don't want to trouble anyone." Taylor took out a notepad. "If you don't mind, could you tell me about your father before he married your mother?"

Donna looked at her husband. "I'll make some coffee."

Chapter Nineteen ❧

Taylor looked at his watch. It was nine p.m. there but his watch said three a.m. Georgia time. He yawned and looked at his brother as they headed to pick up their bags. The trip to Waynesboro had been beneficial; a lot of information they didn't have could now be added to his own notes. The only thing he could think of right now was his bed.

"Taylor, I bet Harry's waiting for us in baggage," Eric said.

"I hope he's waiting, I'm beat," Taylor said.

Both men were not surprised when Harry met them with a porter to get their luggage.

"You two look like something the cat drug in," he said.

"Good to see you too, Harry," Eric said.

"Did you find what you were looking for?" Harry asked.

"Uncle Larry would be proud of us," Eric said.

"His manuscript is one step closer to the publisher. But what I found is the beginning of our history with the Bowen family, some of it anyway," Taylor said.

"Good to hear, good to hear. Let's get you two home," Harry said.

"Yeah, but you still have a lot of footwork to do," Eric said as they headed out the door to the waiting taxi.

Taylor was happy to open the doors to the penthouse. "It's good to be home."

Eric walked over to the kitchen table and looked at the messages stacked in separate piles. "Whoa, that's a lot of messages."

"Most of them are for you, Don Juan," Harry said and opened the blinds to the balcony, then headed into the kitchen.

"Harry, what are you doing?" Taylor asked.

"Helping myself to one of your beers, payment for watching the penthouse," Harry said and grinned.

Eric walked over to join him in the kitchen, then got deli meats and cheeses for a sandwich. "Taylor, Harry, snack?"

"Sure, but no mayo on mine, please," Harry said.

Taylor took a beer and picked up his messages and walked out on the balcony. Harry followed him outside and sat down.

"Beautiful night," Harry said and then picked up the remote. "Star Dust" began to play.

Taylor sat down. Eric brought out sandwiches and chips. "Here we go." All three dug into their snack and clinked their beer bottles together.

"Good to have you guys back," Harry said.

"Thanks, good to be back," Eric said.

"Harry, Uncle Larry used to have an extensive record collection, but I haven't been able to find it. Do you have any idea where it might be?" Taylor asked.

"Where do you think I got that song that's playing?" Harry said and smiled. "In your bedroom, check the bookshelf; pull the book on Glenn Miller and it will open the library."

"Harry, any secret chambers in my bedroom?" Eric asked.

"Nope, just in the master bedroom," Harry said and got up to go get more beer.

Taylor took another beer and waited for Harry to sit down. "Anything happen of importance while we were gone, Harry?"

Harry smiled. "Nothing I couldn't handle."

Chapter Twenty ❧

Bevan had just returned from his morning meeting at the White House. His desk had been clear when he left this morning; now there was a stack of files and at least fifteen messages he would need to respond to, not counting emails. He sat down and leaned back in his chair. There were some days he wished he was back in Atlanta walking a beat.

"Boss, how was the meeting?" E. asked.

"It would've been better if I had been able to tell them we were closing in on Aaron Caydon," Bevan said.

"Off the grid, no movement anywhere across the world. He's hiding in the trash bin, so to speak. Sorry, I've used everything I have available, even used the new program. Who trained him?" E. asked.

Bevan turned around in his chair and looked at E. "I did."

"Well that explains why we can't find him," E. said. "I'll keep the network humming; if he moves, I'll find him."

"Thanks, you're the best," Bevan said.

"That's what you pay me for," E. said and then left the office.

Bevan turned back and picked up his phone and hit the speed dial. "Ron, tell me you have some news."

"Sorry Bevan, the only activity I have is an early morning New Year's call that was untraceable. Shaw has been receiving occasional deliveries to his house."

"What kind of deliveries?"

"Florist, parcel service, a cable service truck. Why?"

"How often are these deliveries coming?"

"Every couple of weeks."

"That's how Aaron is getting his information to Shaw," Bevan said.

"Last one was yesterday. We'll stop the next one."

Bevan looked at the calendar—it had been almost three months. "No, don't waste your time. You can't stop everyone and he's mixing phony with real needs."

"What makes you so sure?" Ron asked.

"His training. If he's been out of the country, which I suspect, he'll be coming back soon, and he'll go to a safe house," Bevan said.

"You sound like you know his patterns."

"He learned most of them from us, which means he'll be moving on soon. Ron, thanks for your help."

"Well, I'll keep an eye on Shaw from time to time, rattle his cage, and see if anything falls out. I just don't believe he's as squeaky clean as he claims," Ron said.

"Just don't let it interfere with your other work. It sounds like there's not much of a case, but let me know if you do come up with any information that can help me find Aaron."

"Will do. Oh and congratulations on your engagement."

"Damn, is nothing sacred?" Bevan said and hung up the phone.

Bevan put the lack of information about Aaron in the back of his mind for now. He dug through the stack of reports on his desk and found the standings on the physical training in the desert. A shiver ran down his back as he thought of the cold nights, little or no water, and snakes; he hated snakes. He smiled as Zack still had a commanding lead over Blain. Bevan knew Blain would not be happy being in second place, but that would be where he would end up. He would never tell Blain that Zack had a somewhat unfair edge over everyone. That was a secret that needed to be kept or it could get her killed in the field. Bevan felt her inner sight would only grow stronger, but she had to get control over it. The agent that had been working with Zack said her ability was above his own and would only improve over time.

Bevan reached over and pressed his intercom. "Darlene, can you come in here?"

He looked up as Darlene walked into his office. "Yes, sir."

"I need you to contact these embassies and set up video conferences for me with the lead field agents," Bevan said. "I want to talk to them individually, so set up one a week for the next five weeks."

"Right away, and when do you want to start these meetings?" Darlene asked.

Bevan looked through his calendar. "Starting next week, and if I need to meet them on the weekend then do it. I have some hard decisions to make and I want to be sure I send my people to the places they will be the most effective."

"I'll get started right away," Darlene said.

Bevan looked at his list: Algiers, Baghdad, Casablanca, Riyadh, and Tunis. It would be a long five weeks and his triple latté was now cold. Bevan got up and headed to the microwave.

"Where are you going?" Darlene asked.

"To nuke my coffee."

NSA DESERT TRAINING
NEVADA DESERT
5:00 A.M.

Zack had been awake for about an hour since a lizard ran across her nose. She thought she had made her nest secure but those smaller lizards got in regardless. Footsteps outside belonged to Blain. She smiled; he was so determined to get ahead but kept making the same mistakes. Blain was a creature of habit, easy to read, which allowed her to benefit. Zack had slept peacefully last night with the knowledge his camp was the last one on her list. She waited until he passed, then slid out and made her way to the small mound he had poorly made two days ago. Zack found the last item on the list, smiled, and slipped away before daybreak. The directions to a satellite phone with a code only she could use to contact and schedule her pickup was about two hours away. She had memorized her code days before they were left in the desert and burned it so no one else could use it. Zack could not wait to wash six weeks of dirt and grime off her body and eat a real meal. She really couldn't complain, as she ate the last piece of rattlesnake meat and then took a small amount of pulp she cut from a barrel cactus and sucked the juice out of it. Zack stopped for a moment and smiled.

"Damn you, Zack!" Blain's voice carried across the desert.

Zack not only had obtained all the items on her list, but she also had all fifteen satellite codes. She hadn't planned to take them, but this would make all of them realize the seriousness of the situation. Zack stuck her hand in the front pocket of her jeans and made sure the raven fetish was still there. "With me always," she said out loud and thought about the hot bath and pitcher of sweet tea as her personal reward.

Chapter Twenty~One ❧

Bevan was sitting in front of his fireplace warming his feet and wished Laura was waiting in his bed, but it was only him and his chocolate lab, General Lee. When the phone rang, General Lee looked up and whined.

"I know, boy, maybe it's a wrong number," Bevan said.

"Bevan, sorry to call you so late but I couldn't wait another minute," the male voice said.

Bevan recognized the voice of Roger Steel, agent in charge of the desert training. Bevan was worried. When he got called like this it usually meant someone was hurt. "Roger, I hope you don't have bad news."

Roger started laughing. "Well, let me tell you the good news first. That spitfire of a woman you sent out here, she called early yesterday morning and we picked her up. She's two weeks early."

"Not possible. No one has ever finished two weeks early," Bevan said.

"Well, after her hour-long cleanup, prime rib, and a pitcher of sweet tea, we debriefed her. You're gonna love this. Not only did she obtain all the items from her list, but she had all fifteen satellite codes."

"She did what? Why?"

"She said that no one out there was taking this exercise seriously and now they would have to think about the possible consequences."

"How are we going to find all of them?"

"Well, they still have two weeks left out there," Roger said.

"Roger, for the most part the exercise is over. Zack has won, and to leave the rest of them out there is really cruel. Since none of them were smart enough to memorize their codes, the locations of the phones are useless."

"Look, Bevan, I agree, but policy is policy, and the earliest we can pick them up is next week. They need to pull together and learn to survive. Zack drew a map of their last locations. She said the only health issue was sunburn."

"What about her?" Bevan asked.

"Her skin is darker, said she used some aloe for her sunburn, ate a lot of rattlesnake, and from what the doctor said she is not dehydrated. She actually seems rested, no major weight loss, almost none. Where did you find this woman?" Roger asked.

"Louisiana. Did she say anything else about the others?"

"Yes, said she individually tagged all of them with locater dots in case they really got lost," Roger said.

"Body tagged?" Bevan asked, stunned at what he was hearing.

"She told me most of these candidates are city folk and not used to the hardship of the elements. Zack said she wouldn't have anyone's death on her conscious. She borrowed enough tags so that no one would be left behind."

"Did she say how she got the tags on them?"

"No, said it was her secret," Roger said. "We didn't push her; figured it will make interesting reading when she writes her report. Listen, Bevan, everyone here at the command center all agreed to leave the rest of them out there another week. We believe Zack wouldn't have left anyone behind that was struggling or in real danger."

"Where is she now, on her way back to D.C.?" Bevan asked.

"We were all impressed with her performance so I asked her what she wanted to do with a free week. Know what she said?"

"Home."

"We flew her home around nine this evening. Bevan, this woman is a goldmine; she translated every clue correctly in three different languages and four of our own codes. We'd like to have her, any chance?"

Bevan began to laugh into the phone.

"Well, guess that answers my question. Sorry again to call so late," Roger said.

"No, this was a call I'm happy to take," Bevan said, then hung up the phone. He then looked at General Lee. "How about a quick walk, General?" Bevan watched General Lee go get his leash.

❧

NEVADA DESERT
8:30 P.M.

It took Blain the better part of the day to gather the rest of the candidates together. The Nevada evening was cold even with the fire they all sat around as they contemplated their next move.

"Okay, does anyone have their code for the satellite?" Blain asked.

"No! For the last time, stop asking us that. That Louisiana bitch took them all with her!" Grant Adams screamed.

"Blain, do you have any idea why she took the codes?" Aiden Stewart asked.

"She left me a note where I had hid my code that said we were not taking things seriously and maybe some alone time would help us focus," Blain said.

"When can we expect to be picked up?" Diane Melbourne asked.

"Not for another week at least," Blain said.

"This is just great—no food, no water, and it's fucking cold!" Grant screamed.

"Well, I suggest we pull what resources we have together and make the best of the next seven days," Blain said.

"I can only imagine what we're going to have as punishment for this one," Diane said.

"I'll gladly take it over being out here in the sun and bitter cold. Does anyone know what this plant is?" Jennifer Austin said and held up a spire.

"It's aloe," Diane said.

"What?" Jennifer said.

"It's for your sunburn. Take the gel from the plant and put it on your skin. Where did you get that?" Diane asked.

"Found it in my stuff," Jennifer said.

"Zack left it," Blain said. "I bet if all of you check your belongings she has left something for all of us to get by until we're picked up."

"Why?" Grant asked.

"Because that is the type of person she really is," Blain said.

"I say we make this fire a little bigger now that we don't have to sneak around anymore," Aiden said.

"I'll take first watch, four-hour shifts," Blain said.

"Why? The exercise is over?" Jennifer said.

"If you haven't noticed we're still in the desert—snakes, scorpions, coyotes—and when is the last time any of us had four hours of sleep?" Blain said.

"Tomorrow we need to make a shelter, so we can stay out of the sun and look for water," Grant said.

"It seems Zack has made her point," Jennifer said.

"Yeah, loud and clear," Blain said and wrapped a blanket around him for first watch. He hoped once everyone became rested they could go to six-hour shifts at night. There were enough of them that no one person would be screwed on watch. If everyone could get some rest there would be less arguments and inner fighting. Diane was correct: they would all be given extra work in one form or another for failing this exercise. Blain thought about the note Zack left about no one taking this seriously, and he had to agree. Even he had not given this exercise much thought, something he would regret for months to come, he was sure of that fact. He sat for the next two hours thinking about what they could do for food and water.

"Blain, go rest, its two a.m.," Grant said.

"I've been thinking about the next week. Food, water, and shelter," Blain told him.

"Diane said she had been drinking fluid from barrel cactus. I would imagine Zack was, too," Grant said.

"I'm not sure, but I think that Zack was eating rattlesnake. I found some heads. I hear it tastes like chicken," Blain said.

"Guess we'll find out," Grant said. "Go sleep, you need it."

Chapter Twenty~Two &

Jace had finished loading her truck. This assignment had only been thirteen weeks, just long enough to cover maternity leave for one of the nurses. As a traveler, this was only one reason for assignments. Travelers were needed for vacations, maternity leave, staff shortages while new nurses were being trained, et cetera: all needs that must be filled, and Jace enjoyed her work no matter what the need of the hospital. She had a little over a week before her assignment started at Bethesda.

Jace felt bad she hadn't been back to Waynesboro during her assignment, but the volunteer work at the women's shelter had been rewarding. Denise was sweet and understood when Jace called to apologize. She had told Jace not to worry, that a room was waiting for her. Jace needed to walk back through the cemetery once more and make sure she had the family tree correct up to Susan's death. She had made copies of the Keens family trees from the bibles and photographs from the albums that she felt might be important for her research. Jace was disappointed that the publisher of the original book on Northern and Southern nurses had nothing to tell her—all records had been lost or destroyed. They were surprised she had been able to find a connection at all. She had sent a letter to the newspaper in Honolulu where Larry White had worked hoping she would receive an answer about the man and his family. She received a package yesterday from the twins—there was no news from Honolulu but there was a letter from Zack. She would read it once she got to Waynesboro. Jace had another idea: she wanted to look up Larry White online to see what she could find. She would borrow Denise and Daniel's computer. Jace needed to purchase a laptop but libraries, friends, and family had free computers to use for now. Jace was almost ready to leave; just one last thing to do before she turned the key.

"Denise, I'm on my way. See you in about an hour," Jace said and placed her cell phone back in her purse.

PORT OF OBAN
OBAN, SCOTLAND
6:00 P.M.

Aaron stood with his arms around Kyleigh. He could smell the scent of roses in her hair and the warmth of her body stirred his. He kissed her and then watched as she walked back to her car and left. She was accustomed to his comings and goings over the years, so there were no tears or begging him to stay with her. Kyleigh was special to Aaron. The job for Sherman would be his last. Aaron would come back to Scotland and never leave again. He turned and looked at the barge and walked up to the man waiting at the gangway.

"Mr. McDonald?" the attendant asked.

"Aye, Ryan McDonald 'tis," he said in a proper accent.

"We're ready, sir, please come aboard."

Aaron walked up the gangplank and hoped for smooth waters to Austria.

Sherman looked up as his secretary brought in a package. He could tell by the expression on her face she was not pleased. Sherman was aware of her feelings toward Aaron Caydon after the last situation he had hired him for ended badly.

"This just arrived," Louisa said.

"Thank you," Sherman said and took the small box. He already knew what was inside the box: another cell phone, date, and time. Sherman looked at Louisa. "Do you have something to say?"

"You're in bed with Caydon again, aren't you?" Louisa asked.

"That will be all."

"I hope you don't regret this," she said and left the office.

He pulled out the files in his bottom drawer that had been delivered to him since Caydon disappeared. There were pictures of the building with now condos (that once were the apartments Larry lived in), some information from the newspaper (which he already knew about), copies of Eric and Taylor's plane tickets to Georgia over the holidays, and the most interesting thing was a picture of Eric on a vintage Harley. There was no information that Aaron or his people had been to Waynesboro. The door to his office opened.

"Sherman, how's business?" Ron Edwards said, then walked over and sat down.

Sherman closed the file and then reached over and called his secretary. "Louisa, could you bring some coffee for Agent Edwards, black with three sugars."

"Right away."

"What can I do for you, Agent Edwards?" Sherman asked.

"I was in the neighborhood and thought I would stop by. I saw the picture of you and the mayor last week in the society section. You look a little tired," Ron said.

"The newspaper business is competitive, always someone else out there trying to get the edge away from you," Sherman said. He could feel his shirt starting to stick to his back.

Ron looked up as Louisa brought his coffee. "Thank you. Any contact from Caydon?"

"No, and I told you I would let you know. The last thing I need is the newspaper being investigated by the FBI or any government agency." Sherman's voice was increasing in tone as he watched Ron drink his coffee.

"We appreciate your willingness to assist the FBI to locate Caydon. If you're not already aware, this man is dangerous and will not hesitate to dispose of anyone he feels is a threat."

"Thank you for your concern," Sherman said.

"Have a great day. We'll be in touch," Ron said and left the office.

Sherman waited until he had left the office and then went to the bar and poured a drink. He downed the Scotch and then took a cocktail napkin and wiped the sweat from his forehead.

"Mr. Shaw," Louisa called from the door.

"What!" Sherman shouted.

"The mayor is on line two. He is asking if you will be joining him for dinner."

"Please tell him I'll be there and, Louisa, my apology for yelling. Things have been a little stressful for me lately."

"I'll tell the mayor; and your tuxedo is in the wardrobe," Louisa said.

"Thank you."

LONG BOWE B&B
GEORGIA
6:00 P.M.

Jace had settled in after her short trip from Augusta. She was happy to be back and was hoping to be able to do more work on finding Sarah's journal.

"Denise, what a wonderful dinner. I can't thank you enough for letting me stay," Jace said.

"Nonsense, we have plenty of room and it's lovely to see you again. Most of our business is on the weekend, so during the week this big house is usually empty," Denise said.

"If you ladies will excuse me, I have some work in the office to do, tax time. Denise, I have taken a few reservations," Daniel said.

"He's done our taxes ever since we opened the B&B. I'll look over the reservations tomorrow," Denise said. "How's Zack?"

"I just got a letter from her but haven't had a chance to read it yet. Denise, do you think Daniel would mind if I borrowed the computer while I am here? I have some things I need to do for work and I'd like to check my emails," Jace said.

"Anytime, Jace. Daniel is going over to help Bill and Donna tomorrow so the computer will be open," Denise said.

"I hope I get to see them again," Jace said.

"Donna and I are going to a spring bazaar on Saturday. Why don't you go with us?"

"That sounds like fun. I'd love to go. Let me help with the dishes."

"No, you are our guest. Go read your letter and the next time you talk to Zack tell her we send our love."

"I will." Jace went upstairs to the Rose room; a queen-sized bed covered with a yellow rose quilt sat under the window that faced the back of the B&B. Jace could hear birds singing from the wooded area. Later she would soak in the claw-foot tub, but right now she wanted to read Zack's letter, and relax. Jace picked up the remote and turned the TV on to disturbing news in the Middle East. She listened for a bit, then turned the TV off; she worried that Zack would be sent overseas. A worry Jace knew she had no control over. After all, Zack is a resourceful, intelligent, and careful woman. She opened the letter and began to laugh at Zack's story of a Louisiana woman that outsmarted fifteen city folk to win a prize. The letter was generalized and said it would probably be longer before she was able to send another, but not to worry, she would get word to her. Jace looked at the envelope; it was from Louisiana.

"I guess it was a big prize," Jace said, and then headed to the bathroom for a soak.

SHERMAN'S BROWNSTONE
UPPER W. 77TH
NEW YORK
11:30 P.M.

Sherman sat in his library and drank his Scotch. The small package had been opened; it contained a phone and note that read, "5-29 at 5:29 a.m." He was not sure how much longer he would be able to stand this cloak and dagger or the unwelcomed visits from Ron Edwards. Caydon had put everything he loved and desired in danger. Sherman must make some decisions about Taylor and the newspaper very soon.

"Sherman, are you coming to bed?"

Sherman looked up at the woman he had known for years standing in his favorite black teddy.

"In a moment, Louisa."

"Hurry or I'll start without you," Louisa said.

Sherman smiled and followed her out of the library.

PENTHOUSE
HONOLULU
6:30 P.M.

Taylor sat on the balcony and listened to one of the Artie Shaw albums from the music library. Harry was right about it being a library; however, what he failed to say was how large a library. Enormous would be the word to describe it. Taylor could listen for the next ten years and probably never play all of them. He picked up

136

one of the local magazines and saw the photographs in the article Eric had contracted to write. Eric had become bored since they returned from Georgia. The original job Eric had was a short assignment, only a few days. Taylor suggested he contact the local magazines and get his foot in the door. He smiled because now Eric was being called daily for jobs. Taylor was not the only one impressed with Eric's quality of work. He knew that Eric had been considering a contract in the Middle East. He was proud of Eric but a little jealous; there was a lot of activity overseas. The kind of activity he wanted and needed to report. He would make some calls and send out a few emails to see if he could get an assignment before Eric made any decision. If he was able to find an assignment, maybe Eric would go and be his photographer. Taylor heard the door open.

"That you, Eric?" Taylor asked.

"Yes, bro," Eric responded.

Taylor could hear him getting a beer from the fridge. "Hard day?"

"Damn picky, bitchy models. Divas, all of them! If it weren't for the money, I would tell them to bite me," Eric said. "Taylor, why are you laughing at me?"

"Just funny to hear you talking about beautiful women like that, since you spent most of your time at the beach when we first got here trying to pick them up," Taylor said.

"Totally different situation, trust me. Anything new on the search?"

"I've put everything together that we obtained in Waynesboro— all your photographs at the cemetery, names, dates, and information from the Benjamins. . . . The manuscript is finished but I will need to hold it until I can finish the will. What I'm doing now is for another book."

"What about the phrases on Sarah and Susan's headstones?" Eric asked.

"Remember the necklace?"

"Yes, with the pink stone."

"Well, there was a note with it."

"Let me guess. 'I promise'?"

"'I promise . . . Sarah,'" Taylor said.

"And the 'Wait for me' on Susan's stone?"

Taylor walked over and handed Eric the letter written to Larry from Susan.

"I found it in Sarah's journal."

"Damn, this gives me a chill," Eric said. "Where do you go from here?"

"Now I'm at a standstill. I need to do a search on Frank and Deelyn Bowen, go to San Antonio, and find their children," Taylor said.

"Any word from Sherman?"

"No, and I hope it stays that way. Eric, have you made any decisions about the Middle East offer?" Taylor asked.

"I was going to talk to you after dinner. It's been great hanging with you, bro, but I have bills to pay and bumming off you isn't fair—fun but not fair. There's work here but it's not what I really want to do. If I intend to make a name for myself, I need to go where there's something to photograph that will put my name out there as a serious professional," Eric said.

Taylor smiled. "When do you think you'll be leaving?"

"I told them I needed to discuss this with you first, but probably June first. Plus, I have some work I need to finish for *National Geographic*," Eric said. "What are you going to do?"

"I need to take a break and go back to work. When I come back I can take a fresh look and see if I'm still on the right road to finish Uncle Larry's request," Taylor said. "What we're doing here doesn't have a time restraint."

"Good, because I told them that unless they hired you to report I wouldn't go," Eric said.

Taylor smiled and his heart started to race. "It's going to be hot—no beer, no bikinis, probably a lot of dirt and dust."

"Good thing we have Honolulu to come back to then," Eric said.

"Guess Harry can take care of things while we're gone. He seems to feel comfortable up here," Taylor said.

"I wish we knew more about Harry. He definitely was more than just a mail clerk at one time."

"I thought that when he said to call him Bulldog. I hope one day he'll tell us since I'm not sure about trying to interview him," Taylor said.

"He's kind of become family, and it doesn't feel right asking too many personal questions."

"Some people prefer to leave the skeletons in the closet."

"You probably need to contact Milton, too."

"We have some time to get things in order," Taylor said.

"What's for dinner?"

"Whatever you want, I'm buying. We need to celebrate."

"What are you going to do about Sherman?"

Taylor shrugged his shoulders.

"Just thought I'd ask."

Chapter Twenty~Three 🔊

Donna drove up to the Long Bowe anxious to spend the day with Denise and Jace. The spring bazaar always had fun items for the house and fresh vegetables, fruits, granola, and flowers. As she got out of the car she looked at the front porch and saw all the hanging baskets of flowers and plants. This only added to the warmth of the B&B. Donna opened the front door and walked inside to the smell of something wonderful.

"Denise, where are you?"

"Be down in a minute! There's coffee, and muffins in the kitchen—help yourself."

Donna poured a cup of coffee and she could never resist Denise's blueberry muffins. She walked into the dining room and sat down. There were several pieces of paper spread out over the table. The information was about Larry White—the books he'd written, his work at the paper, and information on his family in New York. She could hear Donna coming down the stairs.

"More coffee?" Denise asked her friend.

"Denise, did you make all these copies on Larry White?" Donna asked.

"No, Jace did; she is trying to find his family and see if she can get Sarah's journal back."

"Those two young men that were here during the holidays were his great-nephews," Donna said.

"No, why didn't they tell us?" Denise asked.

"We asked them the same question. Taylor said they obtained important information from you already and didn't want to pry. I don't think they realized how much more you could have told them if they had simply asked," Donna answered.

"I could have told them about Jace and her family," Denise said.

"Do you still have their information?"

"Yes, but this puts me in a predicament. I can't just give her his name and phone number. But I could call him to see if he would be interested in talking with Jace," Denise said.

"This is wonderful! I hope Sarah's diary is still in their possession."

"I can't wait to tell Jace."

"Tell me what?" Jace asked as she entered the dining room.

Jace couldn't believe the relatives of Larry White had been at the B&B. Maybe this was the man Zack was talking about. "This is wonderful news. Maybe he'll know who has the diary."

"Will it be okay if I contact them in the next couple of weeks, Jace? Since you arrived, Daniel made several reservations and I need to do some prepping," Denise said.

"What will a couple more weeks matter after all this time? Do you need my room?" Jace asked.

"No, no, but you can help me if you have time."

"I'd love to help."

"Ladies, we need to go—the bazaar is waiting," Donna said.

"When we get back, I found something in Elise and Sarah's herb book I want to show you," Jace said.

"Something special?" Denise asked.

"I think so; there is an entire section on herbs that could have only been found in the Orient."

❦

Bevan and General Lee were on the final lap of their run. Bevan tried to run daily but lately it just hadn't happened, so today had been enjoyable.

"We're almost done, General; then it's home, a shower, and . . . Damn it!" Bevan said, and answered his cell phone. "Hello."

"Mr. Benjamin? It's Darlene," she said.

"Do I need to come in?" Bevan asked.

"No, I had some things that need to be completed before Monday and found paperwork on your desk that you should be aware of now," she said.

"What is it?" Bevan asked.

"Two more of the recruits resigned," Darlene answered.

"Which ones?" Bevan inquired.

"Jennifer Austin and Bryan DeGoss both turned their letters and credentials in after we left the office on Friday."

"They make six since the field training exercise. I'll look over their letters; just leave everything on my desk. Did you ever get a hold of the agent in Algiers?" Bevan asked.

"Yes, but the call will have to be made late on Monday."

"How late?"

"He said between nine and ten that night."

Bevan sighed. Another late night. "I'm going to need you Monday night so don't come in until three. We'll be there a few hours after the conference."

"See you Monday, and enjoy your weekend," Darlene said.

"Thank you." Bevan looked up as Laura caught up with him and the General. "Thought I'd lost you."

"I took another lap around the track before heading back," Laura said. "Do we still have reservations tonight?"

"Yes, and I invited a couple of the recruits if that's acceptable with you?" Bevan asked. "Cool-down walk home?"

"They must be pretty special for you to invite them out and pay for dinner," Laura said and agreed to the walk.

"They are more than special, and in a month they'll both be given their assignments," Bevan said.

"This will be an interesting night. You've always had a celebratory cookout in the past. What's changed?" Laura asked.

"The world climate has changed, which makes where they're going even more difficult; but if I tell you anymore, I'll have to kill you," Bevan said and wrapped his arms around her.

"I meant to ask you something when I came in—about your work," she said.

"You can ask but I can't promise to answer," Bevan said.

"Do you have some sort of protection detail following you?" Laura asked.

"No, why?" Bevan asked.

"Well, I stopped to tie my shoe before the last lap and noticed a dark van pulling out after you and General Lee passed. I just figured you'd been threatened again and my hard-earned tax dollars were at work," Laura said. "What are you doing?"

Bevan had his phone and was making a call to his office. "Darlene, is E. in his office? Good, transfer me. E., hang on. Laura, I need as much information as you can give me," Bevan said.

"I guess that's a no on the security detail," Laura said.

"No, it's something else," Bevan said and then reported all the information Laura could remember about the van to E.

"I'll see what I can find, boss," E. said.

"E., this involves our friend," Bevan said and closed his cell phone.

"Is that a no on dinner out?" Laura asked.

"We'll go; I just need to be more observant than I have been lately. I want you to consider staying with me for a while," Bevan said.

"Bevan, I can't. That's too much, and I have a big case next week."

"Laura, if this is what I think it is you could be a target, too. Humor me for a few weeks."

"Do you really think this could affect me?"

"Please, at least until I can get some answers or an agent to watch you."

"We'll discuss it later after dinner. I don't need a babysitter, Bevan." Laura's tone was stern.

"Then stay with me, and do me another favor? Don't say anything tonight."

"An evening with stimulating conversation other than work, not sure I can handle it," Laura said and smiled at Bevan.

Bevan shook his head. "Smart-mouthed attorney."

"Company man," she said.

Bevan opened the door to his home. "Shower and a nap?"

"Do you really intend to sleep?" Laura smiled.

"No, probably not."

Long Bowe B&B
Georgia
4:00 P.M.

The morning had passed too quickly for Jace, Denise, and Donna at the market and bazaar. Jace was happy and pleased to be able to find natural-made items and spend time with Denise and Donna. They now sat around the table laughing, drinking tea, and sharing what they had each bought.

"Fresh honey, handmade soaps, fresh granola, and herbs—this was great," Jace said.

"There'll be a wonderful famers market later," Denise added.

"That's why this B&B is so popular. Denise's local and natural food menu," Donna said.

"Jace, let me see the herb book from your ancestors. I want to see what you're talking about."

"Donna has a degree in plant stuff," Denise said.

"Herbology, and it's more of a hobby," Donna clarified.

"I knew there was a reason I liked you," Jace said.

"I have a root cellar and large warming cupboard that once belonged to your family. I don't use it anymore except to store things," Donna said.

"Donna . . . " Jace hoped to see the cupboard.

"Of course, any time, Jace; you're always welcome. I probably have some extra creams and carrier oils you can have for your own use. I've practiced natural healing for years; there are still a few of us around," Donna said.

Jace ran upstairs, got the book, and returned to the dining room table. "Let me show you what I was talking about."

Donna looked through the book and said, "This is interesting, and I think you may be right about some of these herbs and their origin in the Orient."

"I haven't finished going through the book yet. Elise and Sarah made notes and I've just taken my time on it," Jace said.

"I'm going to write some of these names down and check my books. I'll have an answer before you leave," Donna said.

"Take it with you and I'll pick it up when I come to see the cupboard," Jace said. "If you ladies will excuse me, I need to call Galveston and check on my B&B."

Donna continued to look through the handwritten book as Jace left the room. She began to realize this was more than just a book on herbs.

"Denise, do you know anything about these women?" Donna asked.

"Nothing more than Sarah was a nurse during the Civil War," Denise said.

"I think she was more than just a nurse. The information I've read so far indicates she and her mother were probably the local healers."

"Wouldn't that be something?" Denise said.

"Yes, it would be something, indeed," Donna said.

❦

MANGIONI'S
RESTIN, VIRGINIA
7:30 P.M.

Zack looked at the address she had written down when Bevan called and asked her to dinner. She was excited about meeting Laura and having a nice evening out. It had been some time since she had worn a dress and put makeup on.

"Thank you," Zack said to the doorman as he opened the cab door. She walked into the restaurant and was immediately bombarded with information from the crowded room. So much coming at her from every direction! She stood for a moment, took a deep breath, and focused her thoughts. A moment later she was able to stem the flood of information. *Control, control, control... damn it!* she thought.

"This is a surprise. I didn't think you owned a dress," Blain said.

Zack turned and smiled. "For your information, I have several dresses, heels, and jewelry. And I wear makeup on occasion."

"Well aren't you the diva."

"Oh and for your information—yes, I'm wearing underwear," Zack said, then turned and walked directly to a table where Bevan and Laura sat.

Bevan stood as Zack walked up to the table. "Thank you for coming. This is . . ."

"Laura, it's nice to meet you. Congratulations on your upcoming win in court," Zack said and held out her hand.

Laura looked at Bevan.

"Laura, I forgot to tell you about Zaveen's special talent," Bevan said.

"Please call me Zack, and I promise to keep my talent under control tonight," Zack said as she sat down.

"Blain, good to see you," Bevan said and shook hands.

"Nice to see you, Uncle Bevan, Laura," Blain responded. "I didn't realize I would be eating dinner with the star of the class."

"Tonight I would appreciate it if you two would stop competing long enough to just have dinner," Bevan said. "Waiter! Champagne."

Zack looked at Bevan and knew this was his way of congratulating them. The next thought was his concern for Laura and the possibility of someone following both of them. Zack quickly scanned the restaurant and found a thought: *Keep Bevan's movements recorded.* She stood up and turned toward the bar.

"Zack, what's wrong?" Bevan asked.

Zack turned back to the table. "You two have been followed: the small man in the blue jacket, American flag tie, and blue jeans. He's standing at the end of the bar."

"Bevan," Laura said.

"Is he armed?" Bevan asked.

"Yes."

"What the hell is going on?" Blain said.

Zack quickly told Blain in Arabic to go to the front door and wait for her. She watched Blain as he stood and headed toward the door. Before Blain was able to get to the door the man pushed a waiter with a full tray of food into him and ran out the door. Zack turned back to the table and closed her eyes.

"I'm sorry; I should've been more subtle."

"I guess this means pizza and beer back at the house," Laura said.

Bevan's residence an hour later . . .

Bevan paid the delivery man for the pizzas and turned to the argument that had been brewing on the way home from the restaurant.

"You cheated!" Blain said to Zack as he exited the bathroom.

"It's not cheating when you are expected to use whatever an agent has at their disposal to accomplish their assignment," Zack said.

"Blain, what happened tonight can never be spoken of again, to anyone," Bevan said and handed him a pair of sweats. "It could get Zack killed and it puts my decision to make you partners in question."

"What? Partners!" Blain said.

"You're not my choice either but your arrogance is only surpassed by your ability to watch my back and do a good job," Zack said.

"I think you have excelled in the arrogance section!" Blain continued.

"Zack, what happened tonight? I thought you had better control," Bevan said.

"My training has been in controlled situations. The schedule I have for the next two weeks includes all public trainings, in more crowded areas. I thought I had a better handle on it," Zack said.

"You have to do better, better control, smoother transitions to the objective," Bevan scorned.

Blain looked at Bevan. "Why did you invite both of us to dinner tonight?"

"In four weeks you two will be assigned to senior field agents. You still have a lot to learn before you'll be qualified to take any type of lead position. You're the best of the class. I have agencies across the world begging for one or both of you. I have to make the decision where your talents will be best served for the security of this nation. Do not make me regret my decision," Bevan said.

"Bevan, I'm going to bed. I think I have heard more than I need, and it seems there is more to be discussed tonight," Laura said. "Zack, it's nice to meet you and your talent. Blain, don't be a stranger."

"Uncle, what can you tell me about tonight?" Blain asked.

"And who is Aaron Reece Caydon?" Zack asked.

"I'm so screwed," Bevan said.

Chapter Twenty~Four 🐾

HOME OF BILL AND DONNA BENJAMIN
GEORGIA
WEDNESDAY, APRIL 11, 2001
6:00 P.M.

Jace parked her truck in front of the Benjamin house. The B&B had received an urgent call for a room. Denise had told her she could stay, but she knew they needed her room. Paying guests should come first, so Donna and Bill had offered a room. As Jace got out of the truck she looked up to see Donna standing in the door.

"Hello," Jace said.

"Can I help you with your suitcase?" Donna asked.

Jace handed Donna a pie instead. "Denise sent this for dinner and apologizes that they can't come tonight."

"Praline apple pie, one of Bill's favorites."

"I want to thank you for allowing me to stay the night. The Long Bowe is a very popular place right now and they needed the room, even though Denise said they didn't," Jace said.

"Are you sure you won't stay here until Saturday?" Donna asked.

"That's very sweet of you but I need to get to my apartment in Maryland, unpack, buy groceries, and see if it will be easier to take the metro or drive to the hospital. It's not a long drive from here—nine hours, if I don't get lost," Jace said.

"Jace, good to see you again," Bill said and handed her a glass of red wine. "Let me know what you think of it; found it in town today. A light but flavorful Shiraz, I'm told by the owner of the store."

"Thank you, I will. I have two bottles of wine from Brushy Creek for you. They are two of my favorites: a Merlot, full bodied, and a white Rkatsiteli, fresh pear and floral tones. What's for dinner? It smells wonderful," Jace said.

"Prime rib, my special garlic mashed potatoes, and steamed asparagus," Bill announced proudly.

"Oh my, I didn't bring formal attire," Jace said.

"Jeans will be just fine," Donna said. "While he finishes, let's go look at the warming cupboard."

Jace followed Donna to the back of the house and outside to a building next to her root cellar.

"Nice," she said. There was a huge cupboard and then another one standing next to it.

"Bill had the second one built for me. I had the carpenters use the original one from your family as a guide. We found it in the clinic and I had it brought here so that it could be saved. It's my understanding Susan Bowen and Angie Long taught classes on natural healing back in the 1940s. Angie's father and brothers built it to Susan's specifications. There would be no other reason for such a large warming cupboard," Donna said.

"This is amazing," Jace said and opened the doors.

Donna handed Jace the book on herbs. "I want to thank you for allowing me to have time to look at the contents of something that is very special. Jace, this is more than just a book of herbs. I believe your ancestors were the healers in this area during the 1800s. Please sit down; there are a few things I need to show you."

"You're obviously seeing something I've missed," Jace said.

"I want you to remember that hospitals, doctors, and pharmacies haven't always been available like they are today. Women often died in childbirth, and infection was responsible for thousands of deaths during the Civil War. A simple cold or cough could kill an entire family. The things in this book go far beyond simple herbs for teas and minor injuries. This is a book that a healer would keep. The notes that were made indicate the correct herb used, mixtures, what difficulties were encountered, and the many successes both women had with their treatments," Donna said.

Jace was shocked and mad at herself for not realizing the treasure she'd been given. "I should've paid more attention when I first looked at it," Jace said. "What about the section I thought might include herbs from Asia?"

"Elise made reference to a name that goes back to the Ming dynasty," Donna began.

"Ladies, dinner is ready," Bill said.

"We're right behind you," Donna said. "Jace, at some point in Elise's life she was taught a form of healing by this family in China."

Jace picked up her glass of wine, drank what was left in one swallow, and then took the book and followed Donna back into the house, attempting to understand what she had been told. "Donna, I need to ask you more questions after dinner."

"I should hope so," Donna said.

"Jace, I hope you like your prime rib medium rare," Bill said.

"Perfect," Jace answered and held her glass out for more wine.

Dinner conversation consisted of questions about Jace's new assignment at Bethesda, the B&B in Galveston, and what plans she had for her future. Donna cleared the dishes off the table and made coffee to go with Denise's pie.

"The perfect ending to another great meal," Donna said and kissed Bill.

"Thank you, thank you. Just leave your tips on the table," Bill said. "If you two will excuse me, I'm going to walk 'the ladies' and read upstairs. Jace, I'll see you in the morning."

"Good night, Bill," Jace said. "The ladies, I assume, are the retrievers out back."

"Betty and Marilyn; Bill walks them every night. Jace, let me see the book. I want to show you something else."

"Donna, you seem to know more about my family than I do."

"Jace, we've been here a long time, and when you become a part of a community you learn about the area by listening and talking to your neighbors. I like history, so I checked the library and courthouse for records in the area. I read a lot, and Yue was a name I have come across more than once in herbology. There are some references in the back of the book to acupuncture."

"I have to find Sarah's journal. The more I discover about her, the deeper the drive to know who Sarah was as a person. I want to know her feelings and thoughts about family, those she cared for and who she loved. I'm praying Taylor has or knows where the journal is located. Denise said she would contact Taylor and give him my name and number," Jace said.

"You need to take some time to really read all the notations made by Elise and Sarah. The more information you have, the easier the answers to your questions. Our lives are like puzzles—each piece fitting with another to present the total picture. The pieces you need are there, you just have to find them," Donna said.

"You have certainly given me the edge pieces, so to speak. I can't thank you enough. I hope you'll let me come back," Jace said.

"Our door will always be open—come back any time. I have Bevan's room opened for you. I hope you'll be comfortable." With that, Donna took Jace upstairs.

"You don't happen to have any chamomile tea, do you?" Jace asked.

Donna smiled. "What kind of hostess would I be if I didn't? You get comfortable and I'll make some for you. Honey?"

"Please."

🍃

FRIDAY, APRIL 13, 2001
8:00 A.M.

Jace waved as she drove away from Bill and Donna's home. She was excited about the information Donna was able to obtain from the book. Donna was right: she needed to find the rest of the puzzle so that the picture was complete. Hopefully the diary was safe and would soon be back where it belonged, with family.

Chapter Twenty~Five ✌

Gloria was dressed for mass and waited for the rest of her family. The house was lonely since Zaveen had left for Washington. As Gloria walked into the dining room to get her purse and bible she looked at the gift her daughter had sent for Mother's Day. She picked up the silver frame with Zaveen's photograph at the Lincoln Memorial. She pressed the button on the corner and Zack's voice said, "Mamma, Happy Mother's Day. I love you and please don't worry about me." The message was in Spanish.

Gloria looked up as Doyle walked into the room and tears ran down her face. "I miss my daughter."

"Me too, mamma, but you know she is smart and the best damn tracker/hunter in the parish," Doyle said and put his arms around his wife.

"*Si,* but a mother still worries."

Bevan had been awake since six a.m. and should've taken General Lee for a run, but Laura was lying nice and warm on his shoulder.

He had thought about waking her for early lovemaking and possibly a long shower together, at least that's what his body had in mind.

"You need to call your mother," she said.

Bevan sighed and reached for his cell phone. He knew what she was going to say, but his mother needed to know what she meant to him.

"Happy Mother's Day," Bevan said. "Did the flowers get there?"

"Yes and they are lovely. You shouldn't have, but thank you," Donna said. "When are you and Laura coming home?"

"Maybe in the fall, just depends on our schedules," Bevan said. "How is everyone?"

"Your father is well and had to make an early morning call to the Longs. Denise slipped and fell down the steps."

"Anything serious?" Bevan asked.

"Your father said she broke her leg. It looks like Daniel will be running the B&B for a while. I volunteered to help and your father will do the cooking and baking."

"They're lucky to have friends like you," Bevan said.

"We're a close community, you know that. Bevan, your brother and sister are here, I need to run."

"Love you, Mom." Bevan said, hung up the phone, and then looked at Laura.

"I've seen that look before and it will cost you."

"Name your price," he said and took her in his arms.

JACE BOWEN'S APARTMENT
BETHESDA, MARYLAND
11:00 A.M.

Jace had been on the phone for almost an hour talking to her mother. It was never easy to have a short conversation at anytime with Mom, and especially today.

"I'm fine, and working at Bethesda is very interesting. I'm learning something new every day. I found a free clinic and have been volunteering when I can. Tell Dad I love him. I need to run. Love you."

"I thought it was hard to get off the phone with my mom," Linda said.

"I haven't been home in a while. Do you mind if I make another call before we head out?" Jace asked her new friend and traveler.

"No, we have plenty of time; the metro runs right to the mall where the movie is showing," Linda said. "I found this awesome restaurant in downtown Alexandria; metro then a short walk."

"Thanks. You have no idea how I love not having to drive in the traffic here," Jace said and dialed Denise and Daniel's number. "Daniel, hi, it's Jace. Is Denise there? Oh no, when? Is she okay? Is there anything I can do? Tell her to get well soon."

"What was that all about?" Linda said.

"Denise is part of my family; she fell this morning, broke her leg," Jace said.

"Is she okay?"

"Yes, but will be out of commission for a while; guess I'll have to wait a little longer to get some family information I need," Jace said.

"What kind of information?"

"A name and number; maybe while she is recovering she can get it for me," Jace said.

"We need to go grab that umbrella just in case," Linda said.

Baghdad
Monday, May 14, 2001
2:00 p.m.

Zack walked with other women dressed in an abayah and hijab. She had blended well into the community over the past two weeks since her arrival as her partner's "niece." Zack had obtained information that was passed to her partner and sent for evaluation back home. She thought about her home and hoped the gift to her mother had arrived safely, that her parents were well. The most difficult thing she had ever done was to get on the military transport in the middle of the night and leave everything and everyone she loved. What she had to remember was this was her choice and that she would make a difference. The women stopped when they arrived at her house and said their good-byes. Once inside, Zack shed the coverings and relaxed in a cooler cotton shirt and slacks.

"How was the market?" Mark asked.

"Good, and I have more information for you to look at," Zack said and looked at her senior partner. Mark had been in Baghdad for eight years. He was an established trader and seller of goods. Zack had been given an information packet on him a week before she left the states. As his niece, she must be familiar with his history there and her part in his life.

"You know what's funny?" Mark asked.

"What?"

"In the two weeks since you arrived I've had twenty offers of marriage." He laughed.

"I assume the price isn't high enough yet?" Zack said.

"Not yet, but five are still in the running."

"Thanks, that makes me feel secure," Zack said and began to look at information he handed to her.

"We have work tonight," Mark said. "It's time to see if you can pass as a man."

"Then I'm going to take a nap," Zack said and headed to her room. She wondered if Blain was still in Washington. His assignment had been delayed. The senior field agent he had been assigned to had been killed. Blain was told it could be another month before he was sent out. Zack hoped he had taken that last week of the field exercise seriously, because the next time he was alone in the desert she wouldn't be there to save him. She lay down on her bed, looked at the raven, and then picked up the boning knife she had brought with her. Deelyn had sent it to her shortly before she passed away. It was one of the sharpest knives she had ever owned; it had been useful many times out hunting, on the desert exercise, and was now possibly the only weapon she could carry and easily hide. Hours later, Zack felt a hand on her shoulder. She moved like the wind, placing the knife on Mark's neck.

"Stop! It's Mark."

"Sorry," she said.

"Time to go."

Chapter Twenty~Six 🐚

Sherman had been in his library since four a.m. drinking Scotch. He intended to tell Caydon to forget it, keep the money; that he would just wait it out. Sherman hoped it would only take another one, maybe two months, and this would all be finished and he would write Taylor a check. He couldn't take the chance for problems. Sherman's hands were shaking as he reached for the ringing phone.

"Shaw here."

"My office, July Fourth, noon," Aaron said and hung up the phone.

Sherman stood up, walked to the fireplace, and threw the phone in it.

Ron sat in his minivan watching Sherman. His wife didn't even ask when he told her he had to run to the corner market for beer. He was lucky to have such a wonderful woman.

"Why would you have a fire on a night when it wasn't needed?" Ron said from the backseat; then he reached for his cell phone. "Bevan, get a hold of that boy genius of yours and see if he can find any calls to Sherman Shaw in the past five minutes."

"Ron, do you know what time it is? I'm still in bed," Bevan said.

"Well rise and shine, buddy. Shaw has a fire burning in his library and it just ain't that cold here," Ron said.

"It'll be at least two to three hours before I can get everything running," Bevan said.

"I tagged the time. I need to get the minivan back home, but I'll come back and see what falls out of the cage today."

Bevan cursed under his breath as he hung up his cell phone. He turned back and wrapped his arms around Laura. *God she felt so good*, he thought.

"Laura, I have to go," Bevan said and kissed her shoulder. "I'll have an agent pick you up."

"Bevan, it has been what, two months. I think the manpower can be better spent somewhere else. I have a conference in L.A. this weekend. Please call off the detail," she told him.

"I'll see what this is about and consider it," Bevan said.

"It's a short week with the holiday and conference so I took the next few days off," Laura said.

"Good. See you tonight, and take General Lee if you go for a run," Bevan said and got out of bed.

"He's better company anyway," Laura said.

"Love you, too," Bevan said as he got in the shower.

AMERICAN AIRLINES
NEW YORK DEPARTURE GATE
HONOLULU AIRPORT
8:00 A.M.

Taylor and Eric stood at the gate waiting with Harry. The flight crew had just arrived, so it wouldn't be long before passengers would be allowed to board.

"Harry, take care of everything and we'll send word when we're on our way home," Taylor said.

"Wish you guys wouldn't go. I got a bad feeling in my left foot."

"What did you say?" Eric asked.

"Nothing, you two be careful and come back safe," Harry said. "Oh, say hello to your brother for me."

Taylor and Eric looked at each other, then began to laugh. The attendant called for first class and business class to board.

"That's us!" Eric said.

"Take care of yourselves," Harry said.

Both men shook hands with Harry and headed down the gateway.

"What do you think that was about?" Eric asked.

"Not sure," Taylor said.

"Did you call Sherman and let him know we were coming?"

"No."

"This is not going to be good."

"I felt telling him in person was better than from Baghdad," Taylor said. "Got your passport, right?"

"Close to my heart," Eric said.

Taylor stopped and felt for the necklace—safe and secure next to his.

NSA
MARYLAND
NOON

Bevan looked over E.'s shoulder at information he had accessed from numerous information sites, phone lines, security cameras, and satellite images at the time Ron had given him.

"Is this the program you sent months ago for approval?" Bevan asked.

"Yes, and thanks for getting it through so quickly," E. answered.

"I think you need to thank Darlene. What have you found?"

"First, let me update you on what I have so far. The man in the restaurant was probably one of Caydon's ex-military associates.

There were five in his squad that left when he did. Their records have been compromised in all databases. I had paper files brought up and even these have been gone through, photographs destroyed. I sent information out to local agencies, names and what descriptions I had, but they've all gone underground. Nothing on the men that made the deliveries to the Shaw residence or newspaper; the license tag on the van that followed you home was reported as stolen. Everything we have found has been sterilized."

Bevan rubbed his forehead and eyes. "Is there any good news here?"

"The time tagged by your friend in the FBI was a disposable phone. The conversation was less than ten seconds, sorry," E. said.

"Do me a favor and go back through surveillance videos from the major airports one more time and see if you can find anything," Bevan said.

"Will do. I have this program set up to compare even the slightest similarity to Caydon's description," E. said.

"You didn't have anything major planned today, did you?"

"Some updates for the building, but I can put it off a day or so, maybe do them late tonight," E. said and reached for his energy drink.

"DeAnna out of town?" Bevan asked.

"Yep, just me and the new flat screen," E. answered.

Bevan walked back and sat down at his desk. He still had Jennifer and Bryan's files on his desk; all that was needed was his signature. Jennifer Austin had been a stretch from the beginning, but her computer skills would have been put to good use in England. Bryan DeGoss's resignation was a surprise. His job offer had been there at the NSA. Bevan had not signed off because, in the past, agents had left—went home, thought about their decisions, and came back, usually in two to three weeks. He felt they were not coming back, so he signed their files and put them in his outbox for Darlene. He looked at his phone and punched Ron's speed-dial number.

"Bevan, I know there is a lot of red tape there in D.C. but this is a bit much," Ron said.

"Well, you're not going to like the rest of what I don't have to tell you either."

"What the hell, Bevan? This guy is fucking with us, you know that?" Ron said.

"Yeah, I know. I wish I had something to give you. E. is going back over airport surveillance with a new program. If he comes up with anything, I'll let you know," Bevan said.

"This whole day is a bust. I think I'll go home, drink some beer, and watch my kids play. You should try that sometime," Ron said.

"I drink beer," Bevan said.

"You're an ass. I don't know why my sister puts up with you," Ron said.

"She likes my dog."

White Daily Journal Office
Manhattan
5:00 p.m.

Taylor dreaded the confrontation that was inevitable with Sherman, but he would just have to deal with their decision. He would not let Sherman dictate what he did with his life as he had Eric's.

"Eric, is there anything you need to do before we leave the country?"

"Bro, I made what arrangements I needed on the computer, let the credit card company know I would be out of the country for several months . . . The only thing left is to get some cash and exchange it at the airport here before we leave," Eric said.

"Guess I wasn't as prepared as I thought. After listening to you, I'll be busy for the next two days," Taylor responded.

"Let me know if I can help," Eric said and stopped at the front door of the newspaper. "Ready?"

"I guess. What can he do, eat us?" Taylor said.

"With Sherman, you never know," Eric said.

Louisa looked up as the door opened and was shocked when Taylor and Eric walked inside the office. *This was not what Sherman needed right now.* She wasn't sure what was bothering him, but his performance in the bedroom had been a disappointment as of late. She demanded more and would look elsewhere if he didn't give her the satisfaction she deserved. Her computer skills were not the only talent she possessed.

"Is he in?" Taylor asked.

"Mr. Shaw didn't come in today. If you had called and informed him I'm sure he would have been here waiting for you both," Louisa said.

"Must have someone entertaining him at home then; Sherman doesn't miss work for any reason other than sex," Eric said.

"No, he had several appointments today, including one with the mayor," Louisa lied.

"Then let's go, Eric," Taylor said.

Louisa watched both men leave; as soon as the doors closed she picked up the phone. "Sherman, your brothers are on their way to the house."

Taylor hailed a cab from the corner. "Eric, how many times have you known Sherman not to come to work?"

"Hmmm, good question. Before he took over running the paper he had a bed in his office, used the shower on the main floor, and always had a change of clothes, including a tux. I remember him staying all night. He never leaves before seven or eight," Eric answered.

A cab pulled to the corner and both men got in. Then Taylor gave the driver the address. "Doesn't sound like Sherman. Maybe something has happened since we've been gone. I might need to contact the accountants and make sure the newspaper isn't in any trouble before we leave," Taylor said.

"Let's see what Sherman has to say about missing work; I'm sure it involves a woman," Eric said and laughed. "She's probably married."

❧

This is so like Taylor to just show up without calling, Sherman thought. He looked in the mirror at his reflection. He'd sat in the library and drank all day, hadn't showered or shaved. He looked at the sweat suit that hung on him. He had let his daily swim at the club slip, stopped eating properly, and it was beginning to show. Sherman had come to the family penthouse to take care of personal business but had not accomplished anything. He reached over and pressed the call button.

"Yes, sir," a male voice answered.

"Rutherford, my brothers will be arriving soon. Open their rooms and have Bethany fix dinner for us, please. I'll be in the shower," Sherman said.

"Right away, Mr. Shaw. Can I assist you?" Rutherford asked.

"No, I'll be fine," Sherman said.

Taylor and Eric exited the cab, got their backpacks out of the trunk, and headed to the front door.

"Do you have your key?" Taylor asked.

"Of course," Eric answered.

The door opened before Eric could get his key.

"Mr. Taylor, Mr. Eric, it's good to see you both. Your rooms have been opened," Rutherford said.

Both men looked at each other.

"Louisa," they said.

"Dinner will be ready at seven thirty. I'll take your packs; Mr. Sherman is in the library waiting for you," Rutherford said.

Taylor looked at Eric. "Let's get this over with. I'm hungry, tired, and don't want to make a scene in front of the staff. There's no telling what they've had to endure since we left."

"Lead the way," Eric said.

Taylor opened the door to the library. "I see Louisa called to let you know we were on the way."

"I'd say it's good to see you, but I have a lot of business to attend so I hope you two do not expect me to entertain you while you're home," Sherman said. "Drink?"

"Always the bright star in the sky," Eric said. "Thanks, don't mind if I do. Taylor, what are you having?"

"I don't suppose you have completed that ridiculous request?" Sherman asked.

"Nothing for me at the moment, Eric; and, no, I haven't completed it," Taylor said.

"I suppose you've run out of money, Eric, or you would still be in Hawaii. You are well aware of grandfather's stipulation on your inheritance money," Sherman said.

"Fuck you, Sherman—and the money!" Eric said and walked out of the library with his drink.

"Sherman, why do you insist on making everything difficult?" Taylor asked.

"Because he's throwing his life away on a fantasy that he will become a famous photographer without the education to go with his work," Sherman said.

"Eric has the right to be whatever he chooses—with or without a college degree. And for your information, he is a wonderful photographer," Taylor said. "When is the last time he has asked you for any money? He's been so busy that he turned away work in Honolulu. He just finished a shoot for *National Geographic*. You need to take some time and interest in your family."

"Why are you two here?" Sherman asked.

"We're leaving the country," Eric said as he walked back into the library.

"When?" Sherman asked.

"Friday. That's why we're here," Taylor said. "I'm at a standstill with my search on the will for now. I was given an opportunity to go with Eric and report while he photographs."

"Where the hell are you going?" Sherman asked.

"The Middle East," Eric said.

"You're going to get yourselves killed," Sherman said.

"Guess that would solve everything for you then, wouldn't it?" Eric asked.

"Gentlemen, dinner is ready," Rutherford said.

"We need to talk about this after dinner," Sherman said.

"Sherman, there isn't anything to discuss. I'll finish the terms of the will once Eric and I return," Taylor said.

"When do you think that will be?"

"Depending on the assignments, four to six months," Eric said.

"Unacceptable! You both need to realize the only thing that is important here is the newspaper."

"No! Sherman, what's important is your need to control everything. We're leaving Friday and for once in your life you'll wait for me. I have the controlling interest and at this point I'm allowing you to run the paper. Deal with it! Or should I call the paper's attorneys and let them explain it to you, again? Now, if you don't mind, I don't want to disappoint Bethany; I'm sure she has made a wonderful hot meal at the last minute when a sandwich would have sufficed."

Taylor and Eric headed toward the library door.

"Are you coming?" Taylor asked.

"In a moment. I want to refresh my drink," Sherman said.

Sherman walked to the bar and filled his glass. *Fools.* This simply won't do. It would be another month before he would be able to talk with Aaron. Something had to be done; he simply couldn't wait months before he obtained what was his, not to mention the continued irritation of Agent Edwards appearing whenever he wanted. Sherman thought about where his brothers were headed and Eric was right, in a manner of speaking. If they never returned, his problems would be solved. Sherman downed the drink, filled the glass once more, and left the library to have dinner with his family.

🍂

TAYLOR'S ROOM
11:00 P.M.

Taylor was relieved that dinner had proceeded without further conversation or argument. Taylor did notice that Sherman had lost weight and seemed to enjoy his Scotch.

"What's up?" Eric asked.

"I'm looking for the account information on the newspaper," Taylor said.

"A little online banking after Sherman's performance?"

"I'm concerned—his drinking, he looks terrible."

"His arrogance hasn't changed. Sorry, but I was about to deck him in the library earlier," Eric said.

"Understandable. More reason to make sure there are no irregularities in the paper's assets before we leave. Help me out here, will you?"

"Okay, let's set up your ID, then password, and voila."

Taylor began to look over all the accounts for the paper. "Eric, I don't see anything out of the ordinary here. Day-to-day expenses, payroll . . . nothing out of place, as far as I can see."

"Okay, get out of the bank and let's pull up the information from the finance department at the paper."

"Can you do that?"

"Move aside; let me show you what I did learn in college."

Taylor watched his brother hack into the newspaper's finances. He looked over numerous pages for the past six months. "I don't see anything out of place. What about you?"

"Again, the day-to-day finances and business of the paper. Aunt Beatrice, it seems, didn't trust any one individual and had several checks and balances on the newspaper's money. It appears she had two separate accountants basically watching each other's work," Eric said. "Whoa, no wonder Sherman is so determined to own the newspaper. Taylor, look at the profit for the past two years."

"Money and power go hand in hand, Eric. I'm beginning to think that our brother has political aspirations, and it wouldn't look good for his younger brother to be holding all the money," Taylor said.

"Well, I can't find anything that would indicate he misused company money," Eric said.

"That makes me feel somewhat better about leaving now. I just have one other question."

"I can read your mind, and I've already pulled his personal account up," Eric said.

"I'm looking for some type of investigative service," Taylor said.

"There is one check only to ARC Investigations—the night you came in for Aunt Beatrice's funeral," Eric said.

"There has to be more than one check."

"Nothing here."

"He wouldn't have been that stupid," Taylor said and then looked at Eric.

"Louisa," they said in unison.

Taylor watched Eric pull up Louisa's checking and savings accounts.

"It seems Sherman has a taste for his secretary. Numerous transfers to her private account in the Caymans and several checks to Aaron Caydon signed by Louisa," Eric said. "That has to be who was screwing with Harry in Honolulu."

"Now we have a name and know that Sherman passed on the same information to ARC Investigations that we have," Taylor said.

"This is all about the money. Sherman would die if he knew about the penthouse and what was in the garage."

"I don't understand why Sherman called in a private investigator. Nothing can be done until I finish the terms of the will," Taylor said.

"He can't stand for you to own the controlling part of the paper, it's killing him," Eric said.

"Yeah, but Sherman wouldn't spend that kind of money unless he had a plan," Taylor said.

"Like what, force the Bowen family into some deal? It would never hold up in court," Eric said.

"That or something worse."

"Do you really think Sherman's capable of something other than writing a check?" Eric asked.

"I think where the newspaper and his ambitions are concerned, Sherman is capable of anything while keeping his hands free and clean. Eric, you've seen how much money is involved with the paper. Once he buys me out, our family name has been established for hundreds of years; he'll be one of the most powerful men in New York. What would that be worth to you?" Taylor asked.

"What are you going to do?" Eric asked.

"This is a delicate situation, but before we leave I'm going to call Mr. Milton and tell him what I suspect. I can't tell him we hacked Sherman or Louisa's account but I can explain my concerns," Taylor said.

"Sherman changed after Aunt Beatrice told him about your controlling interest in the paper. He was convinced that you would just sell out, but that was before the actual reading of the will," Eric said. "I'll never forget the expression on his face that night."

"I'll just feel better if someone else knows what we found," Taylor said.

"I can't think of anyone I trust more than Milton."

"Me either, except maybe Harry."

"Oh crap, we forgot to call him," Eric said and picked up the phone.

"Wait, he won't be home."

"Bingo, I'll just leave a message."

Chapter Twenty~Seven 🍂

NSA
MARYLAND
FRIDAY, JUNE 1, 2001
MIDNIGHT

E. was on his last can of energy drinks. It had been a long day and he still had updates to make before morning. The new program had been searching for the past two hours. He was about to give up when the sound of "Stars and Stripes" started to play.

"Got you!" E. said to his computer, then punched the direct number to Bevan. "Boss, boss! I found him."

"What time is it?" Bevan asked.

"Midnight," E. said.

"Is he stateside?"

"No," E. answered.

"Go home, be back at nine, and . . . " Bevan started.

"Can't do, working on company updates. Once started, I can't leave until they're finished," E. said.

"Blanket and pillow in my office."

"Got it an hour ago. Boss, wake me when you get here; and can you bring me a couple of my energy drinks?" E asked.

"Consider it done. See you in a few," Bevan said.

E. smiled, put his earphones in, plugged into his private section of music, and began to finish the updates. If he was lucky it would only take another hour and he would be snoozing away by one thirty.

🍂

5:30 A.M.

Bevan had prepared for his a.m. briefing on ARC Investigations with his superiors. The comparisons on the new program E. had written were amazing and would be beneficial to the company in the future. Bevan looked at the copies that had been printed; the detail was impressive and indicated the similarities were a 98 percent match.

"Hey, boss," E. said.

"Outstanding work," Bevan said.

"Let me show you why we had so much difficulty finding him," E. began.

"You mean besides the disguises," Bevan interrupted.

"It's not just the disguises; he has found a way to change the shape of his eyes. I really need to find out how so that I can add that to this program."

"So tell me how you found him?"

"Even though he was able to change the shape of his eyes, I set this program to look for skin anomalies," E. smiled.

"Like what, scars?"

"Yes, but I focused on something that has become more common in the recent years."

"Okay, I give up. Tell me."

"Tattoos. My program will pick up on the slightest change on the skin's surface and the one thing Aaron couldn't hide was his Special Forces tattoo," E. said.

"You're telling me that your program can pick this up through clothing?"

"Shirts, makeup, it becomes less effective with heavy jackets. Let me show you," E. said.

Bevan watched as E. began to use the program he had written to look for the irregularities on the body.

"Aaron may have been able to change his appearance, but the outline of the tattoo on his lower arm was unmistakable," E. said proudly.

"Is there any possibility that we can set this up at entry points?"

"At this point no, there may be an issue of privacy. For the moment this whole program is set up for only one person. I will be able to change parameters down the road. I'll check daily, but if he gets through before I'm notified he could have several hours jump on us. It's the best we can do right now. I could use some help," E. said.

"I'll get you whatever you need. I don't want you living here more than you already do."

"Thanks, I have someone in mind."

"Send the name to Darlene and she can get the paperwork started," Bevan said and stood to go to his six-thirty meeting. "Tell me again where this last photograph came from?"

"Scotland, where he boarded a barge to Austria, and that was where I lost him. Unfortunately, boss, there were at least seven places he could have disembarked. We simply lucked out with this one."

"Did you get the name he was using?"

"Ryan McDonald. All papers were forged and extremely well done. I had a difficult time finding irregularities."

"Damn it, he can be anyone he wants with those types of forgeries. Just stay on top of the entry points best you can and let me know if he comes back home," Bevan said and headed out of his office.

"Will do. Boss?"

Bevan turned around. "Something else?"

"Any chance you can get me some extra days off July Fourth?"

"With what you have been able to accomplish with this program, consider it done."

"Appreciate it. DeAnna and I are going home."

"Stop by and see my parents; they'd love to see you," Bevan said.

"Will do, thanks."

Bevan stopped at Darlene's desk. "Did Blain get out this morning?"

"Yes sir, his flight should be leaving in about twenty minutes, a short stop in New York and then on to his destination," Darlene answered.

"Finally there is some positive news in this office. I should be back in a couple of hours," Bevan said and left the building.

❦

LaGuardia Airport
7:30 a.m.

Taylor and Eric entered the 747 and were shown to the first-class section. The last two days had been trying with Sherman. This morning when they left the penthouse the only people to say good-bye were the staff.

"For once, Eric, I'm actually glad to be in this section. It's going to be a long day," Taylor said.

"I did opt for business class with this contract but the boss said something about liking my work," Eric said.

"You begged."

"Something like that," Eric said and smiled.

"Who is supposed to be there to pick us up?"

"No one. We're to take a taxi to the hotel and then meet in a restaurant. Our contact will be there."

"Sounds good. I'm ready to get to work."

"What did Milton say when you called him?"

"He said that all this was quite interesting since Sherman has no claim to any of Larry's inheritance, but he will watch things a little closer there in Honolulu," Taylor said. "Did you hear from Harry?"

Eric laughed. "Yeah, said he hit the blackout yesterday for seven hundred dollars and not to worry about anything, as Bulldog was on the job."

Taylor laughed and looked up at the man that walked on board and took a seat two rows behind them. "Eric, that man looks familiar," he whispered.

"He should. You've seen several of his photographs," Eric said.

"What?" Taylor said.

"Waynesboro—the home of Bill and Donna Benjamin. If I'm not mistaken his name is Blain, their grandson," Eric said.

"You seem to be a little more observant than I was. Wonder where he is headed?" Taylor asked.

"We'll know if he gets off when we do," Eric answered.

Taylor looked up at the stewardess who began the preflight instructions and then another stewardess offered both men Irish coffees.

❧

BETHESDA, MARYLAND
11:00 A.M.

Jace waited for her friends, Linda, Kyani, Jayton, and Zoe, at their favorite place downtown for her birthday brunch. She was fortunate to have met such great women. They had made her feel comfortable at work even though none of them understood holistic nursing. They had explored so many places on their days off together and enjoyed what the nightlife here had to offer. Jace had enjoyed this assignment and promised her manager she would consider extending her contract. She must give her an answer by July Fourth. Jace already knew she wanted to stay a few more weeks; she would consider another ten weeks, maybe less. She had heard Gettysburg was lovely in October, so maybe on her way home she would stay there a few days, walk the grounds and see if she could find a connection and some answers she had about Sarah. Jace's thoughts then turned to Zack and wondered what the Louisiana sprite was involved in.

"Happy Birthday to you, Happy Birthday to you . . . " Jace's friends sang and delivered a cake and gifts to the table.

"Eat, drink, and let's all be merry," Linda said and hugged Jace.

"Thanks," Jace said.

"What are you going to do today?" Kyani asked.

Jace smiled. "Spend it with my new friends."

Zoe handed a hibiscus cocktail to everyone. "Cheers, drink up everyone—time to celebrate!"

"We need to start making plans for the Fourth of July. They have a lot of activities on the Mall and we need to be there," Jayton said.

"Will dates be allowed?" Kyani asked.

"I hope so, since I have already asked someone to join all of us," Linda said.

"Jace, I guess we need to find a date then," Jayton said.

"Sorry, Jayton, but I already asked someone," Jace said.

"Let me guess. A captain who works in the anesthesia department, at Bethesda, tall and extremely handsome," Linda said.

"I would say that is a good guess," Jace said.

Long Bowe B&B
Georgia
2:00 p.m.

Denise sat on the couch and watched Donna pick up and straighten things in the house. She hated not being able to help but her fracture was taking its sweet time healing.

"Donna, if it hadn't been for you and Bill these last few weeks helping us out, I don't know how we could've kept things running."

"We're happy to help, and you know how Bill loves to cook and bake. I'm glad you're doing better."

"Better, but it will be a while before I'm back to managing the B&B without help. I hired a couple of girls home from college to help through the summer. One of them is a culinary student and she has asked to do the cooking."

"Very nice. I may send Bill over to get some new recipes," Donna said. "I meant to ask if you were able to contact Taylor."

"No, with all that happened I haven't had a chance; but no time like the present, right? Let's see what this young man has to say when I tell him about Jace." Denise found Taylor's number and picked up the phone to call Honolulu.

Harry was sitting on the balcony in the penthouse drinking coffee when the phone rang. *Damn it! Should have brought that contraption out here*, he thought and walked inside to get the phone.

"Hello, Taylor Shaw residence. This is Harry, can I help you?"

"My name is Denise Long. Taylor and Eric were at my B&B over the holidays and I would like to speak with Taylor, please," Donna said.

Harry remembered the brothers' stories about the wonderful people in Waynesboro. He felt comfortable but a little cautious with giving information over the phone.

"I'm sorry, Taylor and his brother are out of town. May I ask what this concerns?"

"Oh my, do you know how long they will be gone?" Donna asked.

"I don't have an exact return date but it may be several months, and I don't have a number to contact him at this time," Harry said.

"I would like to leave my name and number. Just tell him Denise Long called and to please call when he returns. It concerns his great-uncle," Denise said.

"I'll be happy to give this to him when he returns," Harry said and took the information and then hung up the phone. He walked back to the balcony with the information and sat down for a morning nap. While Harry slept a simple breeze from the ocean took the paper and sent it over the railing into the landscape below where the groundskeeper speared it and placed it in the bag he carried with the rest of the trash.

Denise looked at Donna. "He's not there. The man that answered the phone said Taylor and Eric were gone and it would be months before they returned," Denise said.

"Did he say where they had gone?"

"No, just that he would give Taylor the information when he returns."

"Too bad, I think his information would help Jace with her questions and the location of the journal."

"It seems she'll just have to wait."

Chapter Twenty~Eight ஒ

Jace sat at the kitchen table with her coffee and looked over the book of herbs and began to read the notes made by her ancestors. Donna was correct; this book was much more than just herbal remedies. Once Sarah's journal was found, Jace hoped to connect the cures with injuries she was sure Sarah would have logged for future reference. Jace looked up and smiled at Dawson Raines as he walked out of the bathroom wearing a pair of green scrub pants and toweling his hair. Dawson's company had been enjoyable over the past month and she hoped they would continue to see each other until the end of her contract. Dawson was one of the best anesthesiologists on her unit.

"Good morning, what's on the menu for today?" Dawson said, then leaned down and kissed Jace.

"You smell good," Jace said.

"I think it's your shampoo," he said and smiled.

"I would like to go to Chinatown today."

"Anything special or just sightseeing?"

"Research on the book I showed you. I want to see what I can find out about the name Yue."

"I know a place where you might be able to find the information you need, or he can point you in the right direction."

"A colleague?"

"A friend and an acupuncturist I have used in the past."

"Wonderful, maybe I can get some answers about the herbs that are listed in this book."

"Now that this is settled, breakfast in or out?"

"Out, our favorite place."

"Be ready in ten," Dawson said. Then he headed into Jace's bedroom.

Jace stood and followed Dawson into her bedroom.

Dawson turned around and looked at Jace. "Did you have something else besides breakfast in mind?"

"Let's do lunch instead."

FRANKFURT, GERMANY
2:00 P.M.

Aaron looked at the face of Günter Stanek on his German passport. He sat in the back of a bus that was en route to the airport at Frankfurt. Aaron looked at his watch, adjusted the heavy black-rimmed glasses, and pressed the moustache he had applied quickly and hoped it would stay put until his next stop. He disliked this disguise and alias; his German was not up to par so he would avoid conversation on this flight as much as possible.

The day would be long and boring so he was glad he had made copies of the information on the Long and Bowen families during his stay at the hotel. He had made friends with the night clerk and was able to get this information using the clerk's computer ID. He would head to Waynesboro after his meeting with Sherman on the fourth. He couldn't stay in one place for any length of time. His mechanic had found and destroyed the tag on his plane. A new paint job and numbers on the tail would make him harder to track. His plane had been moved to a hangar in Gettysburg, where he would meet his pilot and fly to Georgia.

He thought about the meeting scheduled with Sherman. Aaron's contacts in New York had advised of the frequent visits from the FBI. He tired of Sherman's whining and felt he was becoming a liability that would have to be dealt with at some point, but not before he obtained another payment.

Aaron thought about the visit in Honolulu and felt there was something more to Larry Shaw's inheritance. The last report he had received confirmed that the penthouse was where Taylor and Eric had been living since their arrival. Aaron was sure there was money—possibly a fortune—that only a couple of people might know about, and he intended to find it. Aaron had discovered more about Larry Shaw's financial history than Sherman. He had contacted the publisher for his books and was able to get the total sales of both books and that there was a contract for a third book that had yet to surface; he also knew of Larry's total years at the paper in Hawaii and estimated salary; with his contacts in the government, he had obtained the amount of money Larry had been paid for his service during World War II. Larry Shaw had never been involved with the newspaper in New York, had never received money that was rightfully his. This was because he didn't need the money—he was rich.

The bus stopped and Aaron took his carry-on bag with another disguise, plane ticket, and the new passport he would need at the next stop. He would arrive in Miami late with all the detours he had arranged, a necessary irritant for the moment.

JACE'S APARTMENT
MARYLAND
8:00 P.M.

Jace waited as Dawson opened the door. She had enjoyed the trip to Chinatown. She bought herbs and was pleased with the treatment that stopped the migraine that had begun shortly before they arrived at the shop. They had had tea with Mr. Chin; he answered her questions and confirmed the herbs in the book were from China. Mr. Chin was interested in the book, the reference to the name Yue, as well as how Elise had obtained the herbs and at one time had been instructed in the art of acupuncture. Questions Jace was unable to answer.

"Dawson, I rented a movie for tonight," Jace said. Then his cell phone rang.

"Damn it," he said.

Jace watched as Dawson frowned, then hung up his phone.

"Sorry," Dawson said, then walked over and hugged Jace. "The way it sounds I probably won't be back tonight."

"I picked up an extra shift tomorrow night, so I guess I'll see you on the fourth?" Jace said.

"Maybe sooner," Dawson said and kissed Jace before he headed out the door.

Jace picked up her cell phone. "Jayton, I've been stood up for the evening. Interested in a movie and popcorn?"

Chapter Twenty~Nine ❧

NSA FIELD HOUSE
BAGHDAD
WEDNESDAY, JULY 4, 2001
2:00 P.M.

Zack looked over the new intel that had been sent on movements and possible bombing sites over the next few days. She pushed these thoughts away and began to think about her family and the celebration that would be going on today at her home.

"What are you thinking about?" Mark asked.

"Home and what will be served at my parents' house. Shrimp, crawfish, corn on the cob, enchiladas—" Zack was interrupted.

"Enchiladas, I thought you were from Louisiana?" Mark said.

"Mom is Hispanic so there is always a blend between Cajun and Mexican food at our house," Zack said. She smiled thinking about all the work her mother would do for family and friends.

"Beer?" Mark asked.

"The coldest beer in the parish will be served at my home today."

"Think I need to come and meet your folks," Mark said.

"Anytime."

"Anything new?" Mark asked and pointed to the papers in Zack's hand.

"Nothing that we weren't already aware of. It seems our sources are better than what is coming from home," Zack said.

"I should hope so or we wouldn't need to be here. I do have information about an American journalist moving back and forth between here and Israel."

"Mark, there are a lot of American journalists over here, what's so special?" Zack asked.

"Nothing special, just information being passed on. Americans are targets here. I try to keep up with who comes and goes in the area."

"You're not planning on babysitting, are you?" Zack asked.

"No, but I want to know the players in the area. They're all on their own," Mark said.

❦

Taylor and Eric sat in the back of a truck with Israeli soldiers and several journalists from around the world.

"So, Eric, is it all you thought it would be?" Taylor asked and smiled as he watched Eric wipe the sweat off his brow, leaving a dust smear across his forehead.

Eric looked at his hand, and then made the international sign of friendship toward his brother.

Taylor laughed and passed Eric some water. "Here, maybe this will improve your attitude."

"Any idea where we're headed?" Eric asked.

"The West Bank."

"Any chance we can cross over so I can get photos from the other side?"

"Not sure, we can try. Things the past few days have been tense. I would say we just wait and see what the temperament on both sides is when we arrive," Taylor said.

"Well we didn't come over here to sit on the sideline. I say we try," Eric said.

Taylor smiled and nodded his head.

Blain sat in the cab of the truck with two soldiers and looked in the rearview mirror at the two men he recognized from the flight to Israel. Blain had changed his appearance since his arrival for obvious reasons; today he was an observer. His skin was darker; he had dyed his blond hair brown, and wore brown contacts. His need to blend had become even more necessary with the increase in bombings. Blain had new orders and would be transferred in the next forty-five days to Baghdad. He would be teamed up with his rival. Blain had kept up with the work Zack had done and his cover was being prepared as another family member. His Arabic was rusty, so bantering with Zack would be welcomed and necessary.

Washington, D.C.
Mall
8:00 a.m.

Jace sat in the car with Dawson, inching their way to the Mall, where many activities for the fourth would take place throughout the day.

"God, I can't believe I'm doing this," Jace said.

"You're in the nation's capital on the Fourth of July! It's a little foggy, but that will clear. We're off work, I packed a wonderful lunch, our friends are waiting—parades, bands, venders—and you are in for the best fireworks display anywhere. There are people that pay to come to see this. I can't believe you are complaining," Dawson said and parked his car.

Jace stuck her tongue out at him. "I'm just not a morning person."

"That I know. Grab your water and camera. Let's go!" Dawson said.

Dawson and Jace gathered their cooler and blankets and then headed to the center of the national Mall to meet at the agreed place near the Natural History building. Jace knew this would be another adventure she would remember for years to come. There were hundreds of people already milling around looking for a place to claim for the day. There were flags flying, red white and blue being displayed in every way imaginable, and music coming from several areas—all of which made Jace smile. She saw her friends and looked up at Dawson.

"I love being a tourist."

❦

TWIN TOWERS, NORTH TOWER
NEW YORK
10:00 A.M.

Hannes Brunner signed into a dummy corporate office at the front desk with the security officer.

"Welcome back, Mr. Brunner, it's been a while," the officer said.

"Yes, it has, hasn't it?"

Aaron walked to the first elevator and entered, careful not to look at the camera he knew recorded his movements. He had arrived two days ago in Atlanta and was happy to be back in New York, even if it would only be for a few hours. The elevator stopped at his floor; he walked to the dummy office that connected directly into his private office. Aaron entered and immediately took off the blond wig and the rest of his disguise, and then entered the supply closet and punched in the sequence of numbers that opened the door to ARC Investigations. He headed for a greatly needed shower and shave before his client arrived. If he timed it just right, he would have time for a cappuccino.

Sherman sat in the back of a cab, the third he had used since he'd left his home an hour ago. He kept checking to see if he had been followed. Sherman hoped that the FBI was on holiday like everyone else, but he had to be cautious.

"Where ya want out?" the cab driver asked.

"Here!" Sherman said and jumped out of the cab, throwing a hundred dollar bill at the driver as he ran down the side street.

Aaron sat finishing his coffee when the door opened to his office. He turned and began to smile at what now stood in front of his desk.

"Nice to see you, Sherman; I see you've been dieting. Cappuccino?"

"No, but if you have any Scotch I'll take one; make it tall," Sherman said.

Aaron walked to the bar, poured a large Scotch for Sherman, and turned back to see his client looking out the window.

"Sherman, sit down," Aaron said and handed him the Scotch. "You look like shit."

"While you've been vacationing I've had to put up with frequent visits from the FBI. I'm tired, I can't sleep, my brothers are in the Middle East trying to get killed, and the newspaper is nowhere close to being mine. I've seen no return on my investment with you. I want to forget about all of this and get my life back. I'll just wait and see if Taylor can fulfill Larry's will or get himself killed. I'm done, Caydon. I want you out of my life!" Sherman said and downed the Scotch.

Aaron smiled. "Well, you have a pair after all, but you've decided to grow them a little too late."

Sherman stood up. "Fuck you! You bastard! I don't have to put up with you or your shit! You're not innocent and the FBI wants you, not me. Maybe I should give you to them and get back to living."

Aaron watched Sherman go to the bar and fill his glass again. "Sherman, stop making threats you can't deliver. Ron Edwards won't be bothering you much longer, and I haven't been vacationing. I have some updated information on your uncle's finances and I think you'll want me to continue my investigation." Aaron took out his file and showed Sherman the information he had obtained on Larry's possible worth and pictures of the penthouse.

"The man was wealthy beyond his need for profits from the newspaper. I always wondered why he never asked for a check."

"Have you found out his total worth?" Sherman asked.

"Not yet, but I believe it's greater than anyone in your family could imagine," Aaron said and watched Sherman begin to understand what was at stake.

"I assume you need another check."

"That would help me continue the investigation. If your brothers don't come back from the Middle East, you will be the only heir to the Shaw wealth left by your uncle," Aaron said.

"The lawyer in Hawaii, Milton?"

"Easily handled," Aaron said.

"I don't want to know anything else but I want that bastard Edwards out of my life!" Sherman said.

"Being arranged as we speak," Aaron said and watched Sherman take out his checkbook. "If you don't mind, this time I need cash."

"Tomorrow I'll send my secretary to the bank," Sherman said.

"Have her leave the money with the woman in the exchange department in the basement," Aaron said.

"I assume this is going to cost me more this time," Sherman said.

Aaron smiled. "Inflation, I'm afraid, has caught up with me."

"I doubt that."

"Double the usual should cover my future cost," Aaron said.

"Done. Anything else?" Sherman asked.

"One last meeting here in New York."

"When?"

"September eleventh around seven a.m. I'm closing this office for obvious reasons," Aaron said.

"Where will we meet after that?" Sherman asked.

"I hope to have our business concluded by this date," Aaron answered.

"That fast?"

"Money opens a lot of doors," Aaron said and poured Sherman one more drink. "Can I call you a cab?"

"No," Sherman said and opened his cell phone and called his driver.

"Sherman?"

"I'm not a fool," Sherman said and gave his driver an address blocks away from the twin towers.

"You need to do something else," Aaron said.

"What?" Sherman asked and downed the Scotch.

"Clean yourself up and lay off the Scotch. I'm not asking."

Aaron sent Sherman down a freight elevator and gave him

the code to get out the door without setting off the alarm. Once Sherman left the office, Aaron locked the door and went back to his desk and sat down. He took out a new disposable cell phone and dialed the number he had memorized before Sherman had arrived.

"Long Bowe Bed and Breakfast, can I help you?" the female voice said.

"Howdy, ma'am, I need me a room. I have some business there in your fair city. Y'all got one available for me, darling?" Aaron asked.

"We're booked up through the weekend but I do have a room opening up Sunday. How long were you planning to stay with us?"

"At least a week, maybe a few days more if you kin squeeze me in there at y'all's place."

"We can more than accommodate you," the female said.

"Then book me, little lady," Aaron said.

"Wonderful. Now all I need is a name and credit card number, please."

"Bud Johnson from Muleshoe, Texas, and it will be a Visa," Aaron said and gave a number to a card with the same name. It was good to have friends with skills and beautiful women that worked in banks.

"We'll see you then."

"Thank you, ma'am, y'all have a happy fourth," Aaron said and hung up the phone. He now would have to find another place to stay until Sunday. He opened the cell phone again and punched in more numbers.

"Caren, I need a place to stay for a couple of days, my room still open?" Aaron asked.

"Of course, the kids will be thrilled to see their uncle. Everything okay?"

"The story of my life, messed up reservations on a holiday, nothing serious. See you this evening. Tell Stephen I'll bring the beer," Aaron said.

"The traffic is bad, so be careful," Caren said.

"Not a problem; see you soon." Aaron hung up. He then made one last call. "I need a complete clean on two offices. As soon as possible and discretely; there are new tenants waiting." Aaron hung up and then gathered anything that could be traced to him. He left the building the same way Sherman had and waved a cab down.

"Where ya headed?" the cab driver asked.

"Boston. Need to catch a train."

"Hope you got a reservation with the holiday and all."

"Always."

Chapter Thirty 🐌

NSA
MARYLAND
SUNDAY, JULY 15, 2001
9:00 A.M.

E. had settled back to the routine of his work after being at home in Waynesboro over the fourth relaxing and being constantly fed. His mother had agreed not to use his room as a rental with the B&B; he had told her that strangers sleeping in his bed would creep him out. E. had brought a book back for Bevan from his father: one of Clive Cussler's newest. E.'s favorite books were programming manuals, new equations, numbers, code—all exciting and challenging. He looked for the information on Aaron and discovered his new assistant had found him entering the States in Atlanta on the second; the rest was sketchy at best and not reliable. He grabbed the book and headed toward Bevan's office to update him. E. could hear a loud conversation coming from Bevan's office.

"Ron, I don't know anything, but if you're going to be transferred I can think of worse places to be sent. I'll tell Laura and we'll come by before you leave. I need to go." Bevan looked up at E.

"What was that all about?"

"A transfer of Laura's brother and family to Hawaii," Bevan said.

"And he's complaining."

"Ron said he hadn't put in for a transfer; that he was called in and told he was being sent, no questions, and he was not to refuse if he wanted his career to proceed. He said his wife and kids were thrilled, but he's not convinced something else isn't at play here," Bevan said.

"Well, there are a lot of cold and desolate places he could've been sent, so if I were him I would grab the suntan lotion and buy some new shades."

"This seems a little strange to me too, but without a paper trail he may never know where this came from. Is that for me?" Bevan asked.

"A gift from your dad," E. said and handed Bevan the book.

"Thanks. Did you and DeAnna have a chance to spend some time with them?"

"We had dinner and DeAnna showed your mom her new line of clothing and gave her a pair of shoes she designed. Your dad has become quite the gourmet chef."

Bevan smiled. "Laura and I have to go home; mom keeps asking."

"Well, you won't leave there hungry, that's for sure."

"What else do you have for me?"

"You are aware Aaron was in Atlanta on the second?" E. asked, hoping that his assistant didn't screw up.

"Yes, but I did receive information that he arrived in Miami on the twenty-ninth of June. Have you got anything new?"

"I think he may be back in New York. I found some calls made on a prepaid cell, when I checked this morning, coming out of his office on the fourth."

"Damn it!" Bevan said and picked up his phone. "Wait just a minute, E. . . . Ron, can you send some people to the ARC Investigations office at the twin towers? See if anyone has been there, check all the logs at the security desk, and call me back later."

"Boss, he's not going to be there."

"No, but maybe someone screwed up and left something that might tell us where he has gone now," Bevan said.

Darlene called into the office. "Mr. Benjamin, there is a call for Ethaniel, his mother."

"You want to take it here?" Bevan asked.

"No, I need to make this short, company time and all," E. said and left. Bevan's secretary transferred the call.

"Mom, is something wrong?" E. asked.

"Oh no, I just wanted to let you know DeAnna left some of her things here and I wanted to tell you about the wonderful man that has been staying with us," Denise said.

"Mom, I'm working and these lines are recorded, you know that."

"I know, but when Bud Johnson left this morning to go back to Muleshoe, Texas, he said for me to pass on a big howdy from him," Denise said. "Hello, Ethaniel? Are you there?"

E. dropped the phone and ran down the hallway to Bevan's office. Bud Johnson was an alias Aaron used and they had confirmation on it. "Aaron's been in Waynesboro, left this morning."

Bevan stood, grabbed his coat, and both men headed toward the door. "Darlene, call Billy and have him get the plane ready—fast."

Once both men were out of the building, they opened their cell phones and called the women they loved.

"Laura, I'll be back in a couple of days, stay close to home," Bevan said, then dialed another number for protective services for both women.

"Damn it DeAnna, stop arguing with me, I don't want you to go to New York until I get back. Yes, it's serious," E. said and then hung up. He looked at Bevan. "What the hell was he doing there?"

"I don't know. Let me call my parents," Bevan said. He hit the speed dial. "Dad, yes it's good to talk to you, too. Listen, there was a man at the B&B this past week. Did he come to the house? Okay, nice man, stayed for dinner. I'll see you in a few hours," Bevan hung up and looked at E. "We've got a problem."

JACE'S APARTMENT
MARYLAND
NOON

Jace sat at the kitchen bar and looked over her extension contract for the next ten weeks. She had called the twins to see if the extra time would be okay, even though she knew the answer. Casie was very curious about the good-looking doctor Jace had been seeing while there and wanted to know if he would be coming home with her. Jace heard the disappointment when she said no. This contract would run until Monday, September twenty-fourth. She wanted to take a couple of weeks to do some sightseeing before heading home. Jace knew the one place to go for a few days would be Gettysburg. Dawson had offered to take her for a long weekend, but she felt she needed to do this alone. There were some places she wanted to walk, and she wanted to spend time where so many had died. She felt there were answers there for her, and maybe she would find a ghost or two. Dawson was a wonderful man, but the time would come when she had to leave. His life was the military—a little too structured for her. Jace enjoyed the ability to go when and where she pleased; the choice was hers to make and the loss of that ability was not acceptable. She would enjoy their time and when she left she would wish him a safe journey. With that thought, she picked up her cell phone.

"Denise, it's Jace. I'm calling about Taylor."

"Oh honey, he's out of pocket right now, but a good friend of his said he would have him call me when he got back," Denise said.

"I hate to hear that. I haven't had a lot of luck either. I sent the letters to the newspaper in Hawaii about information on Larry Shaw, but I received a standard reply letter informing me to check the internet. I'm ashamed to say, I haven't really done much research in New York in regards to family that may be still running the *Journal*. I hope Taylor calls when he gets back. How's the B&B?"

"We've been so busy I had to get extra help. I'm healing well and we had the nicest man here for about ten days. He was curious about our family and the Benjamins. I told him all about you and the Jolly Roger. He bought a gift certificate for a friend," Denise said.

"Well, we'll be happy to have him. What was his name?"

"Bud Johnson from Muleshoe, Texas. He said his friend would be down Galveston way in a month," Denise said.

"Okay, I'll tell the twins you've sent us some good business," Jace said.

"Honey, come see us when you leave there."

"If I have the time," Jace said. With that conclusive thought they said their farewells and hung up.

Jace wasn't that far from New York; maybe she could take the train, find the newspaper, and get some information on her own. Jace decided she would go to the pool, relax this afternoon, and think about the trip to New York.

"Jace?" Linda called from her front door. "Any chance you can work extra? I just got a frantic call and two nurses have called in sick. The charge nurse sent me to ask, said you probably wouldn't answer the phone if you saw it was the hospital."

"Call-back pay?" Jace asked.

"They promised," Linda said.

"Okay, I can use a little overtime. You know we work in the only profession where we abuse ourselves to care for others," Jace said.

"I know what you mean; a twelve-hour shift and no restroom time makes my bladder unhappy." Linda laughed.

"I need a nap. Then I'll come by and we can ride together," Jace said.

"See you around six then."

"We need to stop for coffee and pick up something to eat," Jace said.

"If we get to eat, you mean," Linda said and left the apartment.

Jace looked at her new laptop and decided she would make a decision on New York another day.

BURKE COUNTY AIRPORT
GEORGIA
3:00 P.M.

Bevan and E. exited the plane and headed toward the waiting sheriff's vehicle. Bevan looked at the man leaning on the car. His old friend, Dale Billings, had aged and added a few extra pounds since the last time they had seen one another. His hair was thinner on top but he still had the same smile he had always had since high school.

"Bevan, it's good to see you; Ethaniel, it's been a while—you staying out of trouble?" Dale said.

"Sheriff, you know me—as long as I have a computer, I'm good," E. answered.

"Yeah, that's what worries me," the sheriff said and laughed.

"Dale, thanks for meeting us here. We have a problem named Aaron Reece Caydon, aka Bud Johnson from Muleshoe, Texas," Bevan said and began to give a report to the sheriff.

"Sounds like you may have your hands full," Dale said as they all got into the cruiser. "Bevan, your house or the B&B?"

"B&B for now. I'll have Dad pick me up later," Bevan replied.

"My concern is why he was here and that our families may now be in danger," E. said.

"Well, if the man you're talking about was the one here, he's after something besides threats to your families," Dale said.

"What makes you say that?" Bevan said.

"This Bud Johnson came to my office asking questions about the Bowen family. Told him what I knew and sent him to the Bowen family cemetery. He did some research in the county courthouse— old records back to the Civil War on all the land the Bowens used to own."

Bevan handed a photograph of Aaron to Dale. "This is Aaron Caydon."

"The height is right but facial features are off. The man that was here: heavier around the middle, bulbous nose, and heavy eyebrows."

"He has numerous disguises," E. said.

"And he learned from the best," Bevan said.

"I assume you are talking about the military. Then I say you're right about him being a problem," Dale said and stopped in front of the Long Bowe B&B.

Chapter Thirty~One 🙟

Aaron stood outside his sister's house and waited for the fire in the pit to get just a little bigger before he began to burn the documents for the aliases he had used over the past year. *Time to find some new ones,* he thought. Aaron decided even Bud Johnson was now a liability. He heard the screen door open.

"Aaron, is the fire ready?"

"Just about, sis," Aaron said, then watched as passports, credit cards, and many forms of identification disintegrated. He then walked into the house. "Caren."

"What?" Caren answered.

"I have a gift for you and Stephen. A late anniversary gift," Aaron said and pulled out an envelope.

"What's this?"

"It's a trip for your family to Scotland, Ireland, and Wales for two weeks," Aaron said. "I made them for Labor Day so Stephen can arrange his schedule early. Please, I want you two to go and take the kids. I have friends over there and your accommodations have all been arranged and paid for—all you have to do is go and enjoy." Aaron was worried she might refuse.

Caren walked over and hugged her big brother and called to her husband. "Stephen, you know that trip we wanted to take this year?"

Aaron watched as she ran to the family room to show him the tickets and itinerary. He took a deep breath and was thankful they would be gone. He took the business card from the Long Bowe B&B and turned it over, opened a new prepaid cell phone, and dialed the number.

"Jolly Roger, this is Casie."

"Good afternoon, I need to make a reservation, please."

"What date?" Casie asked.

"September twenty-fourth. I'll be driving in late."

"Not a problem, someone will be here," Casie said. "Can I get your name and a credit card number?"

"Dennis MacKinnon, and I have a gift certificate from the Long Bowe B&B. I was told it would be good for any B&B," Aaron said.

"Absolutely, I just need the number on the certificate and how many nights you want to stay."

Aaron read off the certificate number. "I'll be there at least a week, maybe longer."

"We're looking forward to meeting you; if you should need to cancel, we need a twenty-four-hour notice," Casie said and read off a confirmation number.

"If possible, I would like a room facing the canal," Aaron said.

"I see you have been looking at our website, and since you've called so early it won't be a problem."

"Thank you," Aaron said and hung up the phone. He had pulled up the website for the Jolly Roger a week ago and had looked at the layout of the B&B and the photograph of the three owners, Candi, Casie, and Jace Bowen.

"Aaron, let's burn some steaks and celebrate," Stephen said and put his arm around Aaron.

"Sounds good."

Bevan wasn't happy about Aaron's visit to Waynesboro. This man was getting too close to those he loved. He turned the corner and headed for home.

"I hope Laura was able to talk DeAnna into coming to the house," Bevan said.

"I see DeAnna's Lexus, so I would say she was successful," E. replied. "I'm starved."

Bevan laughed. "Really? For the past four days we've eaten like kings, and I saw your mom give you a brown bag when we left."

"It was just a snack."

"If I know Laura there's something wonderful in the oven, and I have two bottles of Shiraz waiting to be enjoyed," Bevan said.

Bevan and E. entered the house. The agents that had been sent to watch the two women were dismissed after a full report was given to Bevan.

"Where's DeAnna?" E. asked.

"Outside with the General," Laura said and kissed Bevan. "Find what you were looking for?"

"What do you think?" Bevan returned the question.

"That's what we figured," Laura responded.

"I figured it was an excuse to go back and eat at home," DeAnna said as she and the General entered. She walked over and hugged E.

"Mom sent your things back," E. said.

"Something smells good," Bevan said and began to open the wine. Bevan handed glasses to the women and E.

"Prime rib—we've been cooking all day. I used your father's new marinade recipe," Laura said.

"Then it should be outstanding," E. said.

"I hate to ask, but did this little trip give you any direction?" DeAnna asked.

"Sorry, I already asked. It seems you were right, they just spent four days visiting and eating home cooking," Laura said and laughed.

"It seems Aaron Caydon has become interested in the Bowen family," Bevan said.

"Anyone special or the whole family?" Laura asked.

"He asked a lot of questions about Susan and Jace," E. said.

"Susan was killed in World War II and Jace bought into a bed and breakfast in Galveston. What's the interest?" DeAnna asked.

"I haven't talked to Jace in years. She had a bad divorce and after that bought into the B&B," E. said.

"Monday morning I need you to try to find her," Bevan said.

"Do you believe she's in some kind of danger?" Laura asked.

"Honestly, I don't really know what to think at this point. Aaron is involved in many enterprises. I'm not sure how Jace fits into this or why, but she needs to know for her own safety," Bevan said.

"I'm glad you two are back; the protection detail was killing my style," DeAnna said.

"How much longer before dinner is ready?" Bevan asked.

"We just need to set the table," Laura said.

"I'll be back in a minute," Bevan said.

"Bevan, don't start something now, I want time with you and our guests." Laura's voice was harsh.

"Promise! Just need to wash up," Bevan said, then walked to the bedroom and took out the file on Aaron. He could not understand where Aaron was headed. The report from Ron said the office looked as if no one had been there for months. All of this was something he would have to try and wrap his mind around, but not tonight if he intended to stay in Laura's good graces.

"Bevan!" Laura called.

"Coming."

Chapter Thirty~Two ❧

NSA
MARYLAND
MONDAY, AUGUST 20, 2001
7:00 A.M.

Bevan looked over the information out of Baghdad. He was ready for his usual Monday morning report to the president, but he wasn't going to have the answers to questions that would be asked in references to Iraq. Blain and Zack were accumulating reports on increased activities in Iraq and Iran. Their contacts had indicated something of great importance was about to take place. His only concern was the information was limited and at this point could not be substantiated. He reached for the folder on Aaron. Bevan had left contacting Jace up to E.

"Boss," E. said.

Bevan looked up and nodded his head for him to come inside.

"I have good news and bad news."

"Of course you do."

"I talked with Jace. She's here working at Bethesda."

"Did she join the military?"

"No. She's a travel nurse on assignment. Jace said she had never heard of anyone named Aaron Caydon but that Bud Johnson had stayed at the Long Bowe. He bought a gift certificate and said a friend of his might be coming to the Jolly Roger. She had no name or date. It has been months since she was home in Galveston. She did tell me that she had been sent a package a year ago containing personal items that belonged to one of our ancestors, Sarah Bowen, who was a Civil War nurse. Jace said she's looking for a journal belonging to Sarah that may have been given to a journalist during World War II, by Susan."

"This is interesting; does she know the name of the journalist?" Bevan asked.

"Larry White," E. said and handed a large file to Bevan.

Bevan looked at his computer guru. "This says Shaw."

E. smiled. "He used his mother's maiden name."

"Larry Shaw related to New York Shaws?" Bevan asked.

"One in the same. I pulled his file out of the archives," E. said. "It makes interesting reading on his activities for our government as a civilian during the war."

"I don't suppose he's still alive?"

"No, he died in 1995. I did some checking on his financial status after the war and he was extremely wealthy," E. said.

"Well, the White family goes back to before the Civil War. They are established and considered old money. The Shaws were steel providers during the war. Major government contracts were given to them," Bevan said.

"When did you become such a history enthusiast?" E. asked.

"I've always loved history. What about his finances?"

"Larry never used or received money from the family business in New York. He didn't need it."

"Did he ever marry?"

"No, but this is where it gets weird. His wealth has never been touched. It's in a trust, according to attorney Bentwood Milton, in Hawaii."

"Why is that weird?" Bevan asked.

"Mr. Milton was able to tell me that Larry was romantically involved with a nurse during the war. That nurse was Susan Bowen," E. said and handed Bevan another folder. "Larry Shaw has three nephews that are heir to his fortune: Eric, Taylor, and . . . "

"Sherman Shaw," Bevan said. "This is beginning to make a little more sense, why Aaron is involved."

"Boss, there is an enormous amount of money involved here, money worth killing for to get control over. Are you going to call Ron?"

"Yes, Laura and I are going to see him and his wife over Labor Day. Their flight is Friday morning, the seventh, to Honolulu. I think maybe a visit from the FBI and NSA might impress upon Mr. Shaw the seriousness of withholding information of national security."

"Anything I can do to help?" E. said.

"Financial reports on Sherman Shaw and the location of his brothers," Bevan said.

"Running the financials as we speak. Taylor and Eric are in Baghdad."

"I need recent pictures of them," Bevan said.

"In your email," E. said and headed out the door.

"I guess you're expecting another raise," Bevan said.

"No, but if Ron has an extra room for guests in Hawaii that would be nice," E. said.

"I'll run that by him in a couple of weeks," Bevan said and watched E. head back to his dungeon. He then looked at all the information that sat on his desk. Homework that he needed to read before he and Laura arrived in New York. He needed to be prepared when he talked to Sherman Shaw and his attorneys. Bevan now felt the connection between Aaron and Sherman was Jace and the wealth of Larry Shaw. Bevan opened the email and looked at the faces of Taylor and Eric Shaw. He recognized them. Bevan had read many of Taylor's articles when he was in Africa. The younger brother he also recognized. He picked up the *National Geographic* on his desk and turned to the article Eric had done on Hawaii.

Bevan picked up the phone. "E., I need financials on the younger brothers." Bevan's computer notified him of another email from E. "Never mind." Bevan sat for a moment and then picked up his phone again.

"Ron, I need you to make a formal appointment with Sherman Shaw and tell him to bring his legal counsel."

"When?" Ron asked.

"Labor Day. Let's shake the tree and see if he falls out of it," Bevan said.

"I can't wait to see how he responds to this; he looked like hell that last time I saw him," Ron said.

"I need some answers. Aaron is involved in what could be construed as terroristic activities and has involved my family in a personal investigation for his own gain. If Mr. Shaw hasn't realized it by now, someone is going to prison. I would prefer to see Aaron there, but I'll be happy to accommodate Sherman in one of our facilities," Bevan said.

"I'll be happy to pass that on when I make our appointment. See you and Laura soon," Ron said.

Bevan looked at his watch; it was time to head to the White House.

Chapter Thirty~Three ✌

Laura had sat in silence since they left Bevan's house. She decided it was time to say something about this trip to supposedly help her brother prepare for their move to Hawaii. She had been a part of too many supposed family gatherings that turned into work. Not this time.

"Bevan, I can't believe you've turned another family visit into a work project. Elizabeth is not going to take this well," Laura said.

"It appears she's not the only one who will be upset. It's just one day. I promise, we'll spend the largest part of this holiday with them as a family," Bevan said.

"I know how your promises usually turn out, but damn it! You're going to do what's right! It could be a while before I get to see my brother and his family after they move," Laura said.

He looked at her and smiled.

"Bevan, I mean it this time. I don't want to be sitting at their house while you and my brother disappear for hours or days!"

"One day, Monday. I'll give all my attention to Elizabeth and the kids. If I don't keep my promise this time I'll spend a week in Hawaii without my cell phone," Bevan said and smiled at her again.

"And hell will freeze over, too!"

❧

HOME OF AARON CAYDON'S SISTER
BOSTON
10:00 A.M.

Aaron walked through his sister's house picking up toys and putting them away. He reached down and patted the Border collie, then picked up his sister's Yorkie, rubbing the back of the dog's neck. Aaron kept a watchful eye out the window of the main room. *Force of habit,* he thought.

"Caren, I made reservations at the Marriott; was Stephen able to get off?" he asked.

"Yes, since you called early he was able to get the extra days. How were you able to change our tickets? I know that costs extra," Caren said.

"Not when you have friends in high places with the airlines," Aaron said and smiled at his sister.

"Well thank you, and we'll enjoy the extra days sightseeing," Caren said and hugged her brother.

"I'll take everyone to the motel tonight and kennel the dogs before I leave," Aaron said and put the small dog down. He knew whatever was about to happen on the eleventh would affect his travel plans. He would be safe; not even the government knew he had found his sister. A secret he intended to keep.

"Aaron, can you help me upstairs with the kids?" Caren asked as she headed toward the stairs.

"Just a minute, I need to make a quick call," Aaron said. He walked outside and dialed the number of a trusted friend.

"When and where?" the male voice said.

"Boston, 9-11, five a.m., keep it plain; something that disappears on the road," Aaron said.

"Address?"

Aaron gave an address that was two blocks from his sister's. "Yellow house with a 'for sale' sign out front."

"Done."

"Envelope will be under the mat at the front door," Aaron said and the connection was ended. He would relax and let things unfold in New York. Then he would slip away in the midst of whatever chaos was about to happen. He hoped it would take the heat off him.

"Aaron!" Caren called.

"On my way."

❦

JACE'S APARTMENT
MARYLAND
1:00 P.M.

Jace had been pacing her apartment for the past week. She needed to leave; there was something pulling at her.

"Jayton, I can't stay longer. I really need to go home and help the twins, plus I want to spend a few days in Gettysburg," Jace told her friend.

"What about Dawson?" Jayton asked.

"You know, career military, duty to country, et cetera, et cetera. That's just not the life for me. But I will miss him," Jace said and grinned.

"I bet you will," Jayton said.

"What about you and the rest of our merry band of travelers?" Jace asked.

"Kyani has taken a permanent position in one of the local hospitals. I think she's about to get a proposal. The rest of us are extending again. We'll miss you; please think about it," Jayton pleaded.

"I've been here long enough. I need to make a trip to New York and try to find information on the White family, but honestly, I'm ready to go home," Jace said and then thought about Zack. It had been a while since she had any word. She was worried but concerned more for Zack's parents. Jace would make a trip to Morgan City or maybe she could talk them into coming to Galveston.

"Are you working the holiday?" Jayton asked.

"No, Dawson and I are taking a trip."

"Where?" Jayton asked.

"Camden, to a place called Whitehall Inn," Jace said and smiled.

"Maine, how romantic. Maybe he will talk you into staying."

"No, it's his way of saying good-bye."

Chapter Thirty~Four 🕊

Sherman sat in the library with his attorneys. Sweat was already running down the back of his neck. This meeting was just what Ron Edwards would do to continue to screw with him. He looked at his hands; they were still for the moment, but he knew that would not last unless he got a drink and soon.

"Why now? I have cooperated with them so far, bastards!"

"Sherman, calm down. While they're here I want you to listen to us and stay away from the liquor," Christian said.

Sherman looked at Christian Black, who had been the lead attorney at the *Journal* for almost twenty-five years. He knew Christian had seen a change in him over the past six months and was aware his drinking had increased along with his temperament.

"At least I was able to get the meeting here and not at the newspaper," Christian said.

"That would have been disastrous. Christ, I need a drink," Sherman replied and stood up.

"Sherman, what have you been involved in that would cause this meeting? The FBI and CIA don't demand meetings on a holiday without a reason," Bradford Stewart asked.

Bradford was Sherman's best friend from college, a fraternity brother, and closer to Sherman than his own brothers. This friendship assisted in a prestigious and well-paying job at the *Journal* for Bradford once he passed the bar.

"Nothing, I haven't been involved in anything illegal. They're investigating Aaron Caydon," Sherman said. He walked toward the bar but stopped for a moment, then poured a cup of coffee.

"Who?" Bradford asked.

"ARC Investigations?" Christian asked.

"Yes," Sherman answered.

"Fuck, have you lost your mind! I told you three years ago to stay away from him," Christian said and looked at Bradford. "You don't know, do you?"

"Know what?" Bradford asked.

Sherman replied, "I was in some difficulty a few years back and Aaron helped me out."

"Help? Is that what you call it?" Christian said.

"I don't want to know any more," Bradford said.

"This is over Larry's will, isn't it? Don't you have enough money and power, Sherman?" Christian asked.

"No! As long as Taylor has controlling interest, I'll never have what I want," Sherman said, his voice growing louder.

"We told you to just wait, let this all play out—but it's obvious you didn't take our advice. Your interference with Taylor has brought the FBI to your front door," Christian said.

Bradford walked over to his friend. "When they get here, keep your mouth shut and let us do the talking. Don't answer anything unless we tell you to, understood?"

Sherman shook his head in agreement.

Christian walked over to the window and looked out. "Sherman, what time are they supposed to be here?"

"Nine," Sherman answered.

"They're early," Christian answered.

"Sons of bitches!" Sherman replied and his hands began to shake.

Ron drove up to the Shaw residence and stopped. Both men looked toward the brownstone. Lights were on in several rooms.

"Nice job getting us here early," Bevan said.

"Thanks. I always like to push things just a bit," Ron said.

"How many lawyers do you think he has in there?"

"Two. I had an agent here all night. He called when they showed up around six this morning. They're preparing their client for the government bad guys," Ron said.

"Nothing to prepare, he either tells us what we want to know or he goes to jail today," Bevan said.

Ron smiled. "Then let's do it."

Bevan and Ron were shown to the library. Introductions were made and both men helped themselves to coffee and pastries. The expectation of immediate business had been replaced with a relaxed attitude on Ron and Bevan's part for the moment. This was a tactic Bevan enjoyed and excelled at. When both men finished their coffee, Bevan cleared his throat and looked at Sherman.

"Gentlemen, I assume Mr. Shaw has advised you to the reason for our meeting today," Bevan began.

"Mr. Benjamin, this meeting, time, and entire situation is inappropriate and—" Christian stated.

"What's inappropriate is the relationship your client has with someone who is now considered a national threat," Ron interrupted him.

"We're here for answers. What is your relationship with Aaron Reece Caydon?" Bevan asked.

Sherman started to answer when he was stopped by Bradford. "At this time, I'm advising my client not to say anything."

Ron stood and reached for his cuffs. "Then Sherman Shaw, you are under arrest for subversive activities against the United States."

"Fuck this shit!" Sherman said and stood up.

"Sherman!" Christian said.

"Shut up!" Sherman walked around behind his chair and attempted to steady the shaking in his hands and legs. "You're not the one about to be arrested. These assholes are about to put me in a cell or ship me off to some Godforsaken place. I'm not going to jail for anyone!" Sherman was screaming.

Ron looked at Bevan, smiled, and sat back down.

Sherman took a deep breath. "What do you want to know?"

Ron and Bevan walked out of the Shaw residence around noon. The information Sherman gave them helped to place a direct focus on just what Aaron was after. Bevan had been correct from the beginning, money.

"Well that was productive. What do you think?" Ron asked.

"I believe Sherman knows the consequences of any further lies to us," Bevan said.

"I'll pass all this information on to my replacement. There will be a team waiting for Caydon on the eleventh. They can wire Sherman before the meeting," Ron said.

"You don't intend to stay and finish this?" Bevan asked.

"No, I promised Liz that today was it. We leave Friday morning, as planned," Ron said. "What about you?"

"I'll let your people make the arrest. They can call me when they're finished with him. I do have a few questions that don't involve the Shaw family," Bevan said. He sat for a moment and rubbed his forehead. "I'll feel better about Sherman's brothers once Aaron is in custody."

"Me too; hard to think of your own flesh and blood trying to do you in over money," Ron said.

"Not just money but power. Sherman Shaw will not be satisfied with the newspaper. I imagine he will run for office when all this is settled," Bevan said.

"He doesn't need a scandal to interfere with his political plans," Ron said.

"We have not heard the last of Sherman Shaw," Bevan said.

"I have. And now all I want to think about is what kind of suntan lotion to buy," Ron said.

"So you've come to terms with the transfer?" Bevan asked.

"Liz reminded me there are far worse places we could have been sent. She and the kids are happy, so why should I complain about paradise?" Ron said.

Bevan smiled. "Laura and I will come once you're settled."

"We'd love to have you, and tell that computer guru he can come and bring his girl anytime."

"Speaking of E., I need to borrow your computer and forward this information," Bevan said.

"Don't let Laura catch you," Ron said.

"Maybe we better run by your office before we go home," Bevan suggested.

"Good idea, it's on the way," Ron said and laughed.

NSA Field House
Baghdad
Tuesday, September 4, 2001
2:00 p.m.

Zack had returned home with the women of the town. There had been a pervasive silence over the past week. There seemed to be a gloom settled over the city and its people. As she entered she could hear Blain talking.

"I don't know what's going on. He wasn't there?" Blain said to Mark.

"This is not good," Mark said.

"What's not good?" Zack asked.

"Our contacts in Iran have not checked in."

"That happens, why the concern?"

"The concern is there are forces gathering around a leader named Bin Laden," Blain said.

"This man is dangerous and has a hatred for America that knows no boundary," Mark added.

"I haven't been able to pick up anything; everyone is silent, even in their thoughts," Zack told them.

"Then we're blind," Blain said.

Chapter Thirty~Five 🐌

"Sherman, stop fidgeting," Tynesha Coleman said as she finished placing a camera and microphone on him. At twenty-nine she was the lead agent in charge and was uneasy about the job ahead of them today. She had been promoted along with her partner when Agent Edwards was transferred. She liked Ron and would miss his banter. Since she had been given this assignment, Tynesha was not confident in Sherman's ability to carry through without putting the team in danger. She had read the file on Aaron and knew he was not a person to underestimate or attempt to second-guess. Tynesha's team of ten men and women would be located in strategic places in and out of the twin towers.

"I need a drink," Sherman said and wiped the sweat off his face.

"The only drink you're getting is water. It's time to go," she said.

Tynesha, Sherman, and her team left the office, then entered company vehicles and headed toward the north tower.

🐦

BETHESDA NAVAL HOSPITAL
SHIFT CHANGE, 7:15 A.M.

Dawson was in the elevator heading up to find Jace. His orders this morning were to report with other physicians to the Pentagon. This could only mean one thing. The doors opened and he could see her coming out of the report room.

"Jace, wait up," Dawson called out.

"Dawson, I need to go. My friends are meeting at my apartment for a congratulatory breakfast for Kyani's engagement," Jace said.

"I'm being transferred."

"Where?"

"The Middle East," Dawson said.

"When?" Jace asked.

"If I was to guess, immediately," Dawson said.

ARC INVESTIGATIONS OFFICE
TWIN TOWER, NORTH
8:30 A.M.

Things had not gone as planned this morning, and Sherman knew he was going to be blamed and probably sent to prison.

"Agent Coleman, I'm not lying," Sherman said. "I was told to be here at seven a.m. for a final meeting."

"Well, it's obvious this office has been sanitized, which means he wasn't planning to come back," Tynesha said. She was concerned. The report from Ron had suggested the offices were empty of personnel, but nothing out of place. Furniture, filing cabinets, computers—all still in place. What they had found this morning were empty offices, void of all life or any indication an office had ever existed.

"I've been set up; the son of a bitch set me up," Sherman said and watched Tynesha turn and head to the next room to make a call.

Sherman walked to the window and looked at the street below. Why would he set up a meeting and not show? That's not like Caydon. Sherman was lost in thought when Tynesha and the rest of her team walked into the room.

"God in heaven! Run!" she screamed.

Sherman looked up as the jet hit the tower several stories below him.

"Caydon, you bastard!"

❦

JACE'S APARTMENT
MARYLAND
10:00 A.M.

Jace and her friends were congratulating Kyani and arguing over the color of their bridesmaids' dresses when Jace realized Zoe wasn't there.

"Where's Zoe?" Jace asked.

"She had to stop and pick up something special from the corner bakery," Linda said.

"Well she better hurry or there won't be any hibiscus cocktail left for her," Kyani said and held her glass out for Jayton to refill.

"Good thing none of us have to go back to work tonight," Jayton said and laughed.

Ten minutes later the door flew open and Zoe ran to Jace's TV and turned it on.

"What's going on . . . " Jayton started.

"Look!" Zoe said and sat down on the floor.

The rest stood in silence as they watched the north tower burning.

"What's happened?" Linda asked.

"They're not sure but . . . Oh my God, no." Zoe said as the second plane crashed into the second tower and exploded.

"Linda, call the hospital and everyone stop drinking," Jace said.

"I can't get a signal—it's dead," Linda said.

The rest grabbed their phones and it was the same.

"Landline, we need to find a landline," Kyani said.

"The manager," Jayton said and headed downstairs.

Jace sat down and stared at the TV. There was a break and an announcement that a plane had also crashed into the Pentagon. *Dawson*, she thought.

"This has to be terrorists," Linda said.

"Dawson," Jace said.

"What about Dawson?" Linda asked.

"He was headed there this morning after work. A meeting, he's being transferred," Jace said.

"Transferred where?" Zoe asked.

"The Middle East."

Jayton returned. "The charge nurse said to stay put and come in for our regular shifts; she'll call if we're needed before that."

Jace looked at the faces of her friends. What was supposed to be a celebration had turned into a wake.

"Jace, can I stay here?" Zoe said.

"Me too," Linda said.

"Why don't all of you go get your pillows and some blankets? I think we all need to be together right now," Jace said.

Over the next few hours one by one they dozed off, leaving the TV on to replay the nightmare that was sure to change everything.

NICK'S DINER
SOUTH OF ROCHESTER, NEW YORK
NOON

Aaron sat in a local diner in Henrietta, New York, drinking coffee and eating lunch. He had listened to the news since nine. A year ago when foreign clients first asked for information he had known there might be the possibility for heavy damage somewhere in the city, possibly even close to his office, but never did he think the towers would be the target. Aaron's original plan was to have Sherman killed by one of his associates when he arrived for their meeting and then whatever happened would delay anyone from finding Sherman's body for days. But when his people had informed him of the FBI raid, he then felt that Sherman would spend the next thirty years in a cold jail cell when they found the empty office. The attack conveniently took care of Sherman, and now he could concentrate on finding Jace Bowen and pressure Taylor into a financial deal that will allow him to retire. All facets of the government including the FBI would be up to their necks in investigations, and mountains of paperwork for the next year. He hoped Bevan would put finding him on the back burner and out of the spotlight.

"More coffee?" the red-eyed waitress asked.

"Yes, thanks, are you okay?" Aaron asked, attempting to show concern.

"Those poor souls, terrible just terrible," she said and walked away wiping her nose with a tissue.

Once she left, Aaron opened the map he had brought inside the cafe. He purposely made the trip to Rochester to avoid the issues now in New York City. He would stop early in Columbus, Ohio, and spend the night. That would still leave him twenty hours of driving to Galveston. His reservation at the B&B wasn't until the twenty-fourth, so he would detour into Louisiana and stop in New Orleans for a few days. He opened his cell, and then stopped. The waitress walked up and offered more coffee. Aaron covered his cup.

"Will that be it for you?" she asked.

"Yes, and is there a pay phone close?" Aaron asked.

"Outside; it's been used a lot this morning," she said.

Aaron nodded his head. He left a twenty with his bill and went outside. He walked to the pay phone and searched for change. *Damn, forgot about how inconvenient these are.* Aaron punched in the number and waited. He looked at the white minivan that had been left with two child car seats and a "baby on board" sign in the back window.

"Rosie, it's Dean. I'm coming through New Orleans. Any chance I can come by for a few days?" Aaron asked. "Thanks, see you Friday. I'll be there early. Yes, I know; tragic, just tragic. Souls gone to heaven."

❦

WHITE DAILY JOURNAL OFFICE
MANHATTAN
4:00 P.M.

Alfred Prichard was on the printing floor of the paper checking on the story of the century. He knew regardless of the tragedy that had befallen New York the news must be printed and papers sent out. One story had already gone out over the *Journal's* website. He was lost in thought on the day's tragedy when he chanced to look up to see Louisa waving her arms.

"There's a call for you from the FBI," she said.

"The FBI? Are you sure?" Alfred asked.

"Yes, they're asking for the next person in charge after Sherman. I told them that would be you," Louisa said.

Alfred followed Louisa back to Sherman's office and shut the door. He left her outside and away from his conversation. He picked up the phone and hit the blinking light.

"This is Alfred Prichard," he said.

Alfred sat down and listened to an official voice tell him that Sherman had been in the north tower on an FBI sting this morning. He and the entire team were missing and presumed dead.

"I see. No, his brothers are out of the country, but I'll see if I can contact them," Alfred said and hung up the phone.

Alfred sat down in Sherman's chair. He knew Sherman had not been the same since Taylor returned, but he had no idea he was involved with the FBI. Alfred was fifty and had been with the newspaper for thirty years. He was the only person besides Sherman that knew the ins and outs of the daily workings of the *Journal.* He would now have to take charge until Taylor and Eric returned. He reached for the bottom drawer of the desk and pulled out a bottle of bourbon. Sherman had always kept one there just for him. He poured a drink and sat for a moment holding the glass. He looked in the bottom at the amber liquid and thought about the next decisions he needed to make for the betterment of the paper. He smiled and emptied the glass. Alfred made two more calls, stood up, and walked out of the office. He watched Louisa filing her nails.

"Louisa, I need you to bring your keys and come into the office."

Louisa stood up, took the keys from her desk, and followed Alfred. "Is something wrong?"

"I'm afraid Mr. Shaw was in the north tower this morning. He is missing and presumed dead."

"No!" Louisa said. She sat down in front of Sherman's desk.

"I'll be taking over until his brothers return, so I would appreciate it if you would show me all of Sherman's files. I'll need the keys to his secret filing cabinet, computer passwords, all of his backup systems, and the combination to the safe. I want all checkbooks, account numbers—and I mean every account he had here and abroad." Alfred now waited for the answer he knew was coming from her. He was one of the only employees that knew about Sherman and Louisa's relationship. She was paid highly for services that had nothing to do with her secretarial abilities.

"You don't have the authority to do this!" Louisa's voice was shrill.

Alfred took a moment and smiled at her as he sat down behind Sherman's desk. "I do, and you will give me what I have asked for. Sherman was not willing to give up control, but he was not a fool either. He had prepared for any possibilities should he not be here to run the paper. I have a power of attorney to manage and control the office in his absence, or the absence of his brothers." Alfred looked toward the open office door and motioned for Christian, the *Journal's* head accountant, and two security officers to enter the office.

Alfred stood, walked around the desk, and sat down on the edge facing Louisa. "When you have completed this task, you will clear your desk and these officers will assist you out of the building. Your services at the *Journal* are no longer needed."

❦

BEVAN'S OFFICE
NSA
MARYLAND
6:00 P.M.

Bevan and his staff had been cloistered since the attacks. Darlene had brought so many reports to him it would be weeks before he could read them all. His private line rang.

"Ron, we're all fine and thanks for calling," Bevan said.

"I guess you heard about Sherman and the team?" Ron asked.

"Yes, my sympathies are with the team and their families. Sherman is where he was headed years ago. I'm convinced Aaron knew some type of attack was coming," Bevan said.

"Any word on him?" Ron asked.

"For the moment, a ghost; and all of our attention is on the attacks. His dealings are for the most part cash, untraceable phony credit cards, and disposable cell phones, so not much of a paper trail to follow. He has so many aliases; even E. is having a difficult time keeping up with all of them," Bevan said and rubbed his forehead.

"How does he manage to keep them all straight? He's bound to make a mistake; no one is that good," Ron said.

"Unfortunately, he is that good, and this ability was one of his many attributes that brought him to the company. He had many aliases while he was on assignments with the company. Aaron never once failed to play the right part with the right name and situation," Bevan said.

"What happen?" Ron asked. "The company doesn't usually let those types of individuals go."

"I'm not at liberty to say but he left, opened his own business, and the money began to flow. He still has friends here and in many areas of the government. I can't even imagine the contacts he has outside the States," Bevan said.

"If he was involved with today's tragedy he doesn't have much of a conscious either," Ron said.

"That was the other quality we discovered. It was an asset we built on and polished while he was here. Now he is a monster that we trained and can't find to stop," Bevan said. "Ron, I have another favor to ask of you once you're settled in your office."

"Found the condo address. I'll go in a few weeks after I get my feet under me here in paradise," Ron said.

"Be sure to take a picture of Caydon, maybe someone has seen him there," Bevan said.

"I was told there is an old man that manages it. Hopefully he's not too senile," Ron said.

"Let me know what you come up with."

"Will do. I'm just glad you and Laura are safe; my love to her. Keep me informed and I'll do the same," Ron said.

"Will do," Bevan said and hung up the phone.

"Boss," E. said.

Bevan looked up and could see the concern in this young man's face. "Did you find her?"

"Not yet."

"Where was she supposed to be this morning?" Bevan asked.

"I thought the garment district, but she didn't leave an address. She had an appointment in Boston but I can't remember if it was today or yesterday. I don't listen when I should, now I can't find her."

"Keep looking and don't worry."

"I didn't want her to go. We had an argument," E. said.

"We both have strong women in our lives. They do what they want, but that's why we love them, right?" Bevan asked.

"Mr. Benjamin," Darlene called over the intercom.

"Yes, what is it."

"FBI field office, Boston. They said there is a young woman that showed up and demanded them to call you. She is refusing to leave the office and told them to arrest her," Darlene said and laughed.

"Put the call through."

"Bevan, this is DeAnna. Will you tell these people here I'm not crazy, and can I talk to E.?"

Bevan laughed and handed the phone to E.

Chapter Thirty~Six ❧

NSA FIELD HOUSE
BAGHDAD
WEDNESDAY, SEPTEMBER 12, 2001
11:30 P.M.

Zack had just returned from her nightly explorations for news. "Mark, Blain, where are you? I have information and it's not good." She found both men sitting and staring at a piece of paper.

"Zaveen, terrorists hijacked four planes. Two were flown into the twin towers in New York, one into the Pentagon, and a fourth was headed to the White House. Passengers fought back and the plane went down in a field outside Pennsylvania," Mark said.

Zack sat down. "Jihad, that's all I heard outside tonight, jihad."

"Things are going to get worse; it won't be long before troops will be coming," Blain said.

"We will be in more danger once they arrive, because—" Mark started.

"Because we look like everyone else," Zack finished.

❧

MARKET SQUARE HOTEL
BAGHDAD
FRIDAY, SEPTEMBER 14, 2001
9:00 A.M.

Taylor sat outside the hotel where he and Eric had established a friendship with the owner. This man had the ability to send and receive information for them from home, for a small fee. He looked at the message from Alfred Prichard. The news about New York had spread like wildfire across the world. Taylor had sent a message once they had returned from the field; he had to know about Sherman and the *Journal*.

Eric walked up and looked down at Taylor. He could see where tears had run down his cheeks, leaving a trail in the dust caked to his face. "Is the Journal okay?"

"Yes, it appears fate was kind. You might want to sit down." Taylor looked up at his brother.

"What's wrong?" Eric asked and sat down.

"It seems our brother was involved in something he shouldn't have been," Taylor said and handed the message to Eric.

Eric read the message and looked up at his brother. "Taylor, what do you want me to say? Sherman and I were never close; you know that; the arguments never stopped, even after you left. His constant badgering before I went to college; then while I was there my grades were never good enough; and when I quit, his barrage of insults never ceased. According to him, I was an embarrassment to the family name, on and on—it was never-ending. What I feel at this moment is pity for his soul and joy for the employees of the *Journal*. Alfred is a great guy and the newspaper is in good hands."

"I can't decide if we should go home or stay here," Taylor said and wiped his eyes.

"If you feel you must go, then go. I'll understand: duty, respect, responsibility . . . all of it. But I won't shed one tear for him and neither should you. Whatever he was involved in got him killed, and I can assure you it had to do with money and power," Eric said.

"Those are the only two things he ever cared about in his life, above his friends and above his family."

"Death comes in three," Taylor said.

"What?" Eric asked.

"Nothing, old wives' tale."

"Taylor, it won't be long before America retaliates. We're already here, our contacts are reliable, and we're established. I say we stay. Then when we get back you can finish Uncle Larry's will at your leisure, with no one looking over your shoulder pushing or demanding you hurry," Eric said.

"What about the *Journal*?" Taylor asked and looked at Eric.

"Don't look at me. You know how I feel about a day job, the New York weather, and who would want Louisa as a secretary?" Eric said.

Taylor thought for a moment before he answered. Sherman was gone, the paper would continue with or without him in New York. "Then we'll stay a little longer and see what happens. Maybe you can get that picture to catapult you into the fame you desire."

"As long as it doesn't get us both killed," Eric said and stood, then held his hand out to Taylor. Taylor grabbed it and pulled himself up.

"Where to now?" Taylor asked.

"There's a merchant up the street that I've been told has information from time to time."

"The one with the niece that refuses to be married off?"

"Yep, that's the one."

"Are you looking for information or a date?"

"Don't know just yet. Are you going to send Alfred a message?"

"What do I say to him?"

"Tell him congratulations and we'll see him when we see him," Eric said and turned around to head up the street. "Are you coming?"

"Right behind you," Taylor said, then thought about Sherman again. How had his family come to this point? Brothers who were strangers. His heart was saddened but Eric was right, power and money is why Sherman died. The *Journal* would be in good hands until he could return and take care of the legal issues that would be waiting. Alfred Prichard had been at the paper longer than anyone besides the Shaw family and he was someone that could be trusted. Taylor thought about the name in the book—the one Samuel had started but was finished by someone else. Wasn't it Prichard, too? He would look when they returned to Hawaii. There was so much to do, to finish, people to find, but now war had come again to America and he would do what his ancestors had done before, report it.

"Taylor!" Eric asked.

"On my way."

Chapter Thirty~Seven ❧

JOLLY ROGER B&B
TEXAS
MONDAY, SEPTEMBER 24, 2001
NOON

Aaron rang the large bell outside the door of the Jolly Roger. He had obtained another vehicle in New Orleans and was happy to be in the new silver Cadillac. Getting a car had not been easy but, again, money talks. He started to reach for the bell again when the door opened and he was let inside.

"Dennis MacKinnon, I have reservations," Aaron said.

"Come in and welcome. Your room is ready," Candi said.

Aaron looked around at the huge house. The large windows at the back showed the canal. "This is lovely, and were you able to save the room facing the canal for me, ladies?"

"Absolutely; now if I can get that voucher from you, we'll be set," Candi said.

"How about a drink. Its past noon, isn't it?" Casie said and handed Aaron a glass of white sangria.

"Thank you." Aaron looked at the twins, identical. He handed Candi the voucher.

"We usually ask for a credit card for incidentals," Candi stated.

Aaron reached in his wallet and took out four one hundred dollar bills. "I lost my credit card last week, so I stopped by the bank for cash. Will this do?"

"Of course, and would you fill our guest book out?" Candi asked.

Aaron quickly entered his alias; the address he gave them was the Wal-Mart in Baton Rouge, and home phone was the Catholic church in New Orleans. Aaron finished the glass of sangria and smiled. "That was very refreshing."

"Well, if you liked that we have wine and cheese every evening out by the canal, please join us," Casie said.

"I'd love to once I have unpacked and rested. I understand there are three of you that own and run this B&B. Where is your partner?" Aaron asked and smiled at Casie.

"Jace, oh that girl is in the D.C. area. She won't be home for at least three maybe four weeks. She's going to Gettysburg and then home; after that she'll be here for a while before taking another assignment," Casie rambled on and on.

"Is your visit business or pleasure?" Candi asked.

"For the moment, pleasure. I'm in need of a long overdue vacation so I will be here at least two weeks, if you have room," Aaron said.

"Not a problem, we have had some cancellations due to 9-11, so stay as long as your bank account will let you," Casie said and smiled.

"I might just take you up on that," Aaron said. "Now ladies, if someone could show me to my room, I'm ready for a nap."

Chapter Thirty~Eight 🐝

As Ron got out of his car, he looked up at the condos. He felt like this was a wasted trip as far as Aaron Caydon was concerned, but maybe he could get some information on the two Shaw brothers. He walked up to the front doors and looked at the cameras.

"Well this is hopeful," Ron said out loud.

Before he could ring the buzzer a voice came over the intercom.

"Who are you and what do you want?" the man's voice said.

Must be the old-man manager. "My name is Agent Ron Edwards; I'm with the FBI, and I have some questions," he said and held his badge to the camera.

"Who are you looking for?"

Ron took the photograph of Aaron and held it to the camera. Before he could answer the question put to him, the door opened.

"It's about time you G-men showed up. Come in. I'm Harry Hawthorne, the manager, but you can call me Bulldog."

🐝

Linda's Apartment
Bethesda, Maryland
3:00 P.M.

Jace took her backpack and put it in the front seat of the pickup. She had stayed for two weeks after her contract had ended and had volunteered at the Red Cross. The attacks in New York had made her trip there impossible, and she now felt that Sarah's journal would never be found or returned to her family. This thought saddened her to know so much history could be lost forever or in the hands of someone who couldn't understand its importance. Jace finally received word from Dawson. He had been on the opposite side of the Pentagon that morning and ended up helping with the wounded that survived the attack. He asked to see her one more time, but Jace decided their weekend in Maine was where she wanted her memories to stay.

Linda had donated her couch to Jace for as long as she wanted to stay. Jace thought back on all that had taken place. This was the first time since Pearl Harbor that America had been attacked on native soil. The strangest part of all this was the empty sky, the only things allowed to fly: birds. All commercial air carriers were grounded for three days, people were stranded everywhere across the states and Canada. The rush to get home filled buses and trains, and it was impossible to find a rental car anywhere. She did hear helicopters one night and knew they could only be military. It had taken the better part of two weeks to get the planes back in the air, and now there was talk of added security at all airports, which meant extra time to check in and longer lines.

"You all packed?" Linda asked.

"Yes," Jace said and looked at the four women who had become an important part of her life. The bond between all of them had grown and now strengthened due to 9-11.

"Don't you dare cry, damn it," Jayton said and hugged her.

"You'll be back for the wedding and I promise you won't have to wear an ugly bridesmaid dress," Kyani said.

The hugs and tears came. Addresses were rechecked along with phone numbers.

Zoe handed her a bag of donuts from the bakery. "They're your favorite."

"I'll see you down the road, and if you're ever in Galveston you have a place to stay—my treat," Jace said.

She got in the truck and rolled down the window. "Safe journey, my friends, wherever the road leads." She started the truck and turned on the radio; her Willie Nelson tape was playing "On the Road Again." She smiled and drove out of the apartment complex and headed for 270 North toward Gettysburg. It would be a short drive and she should get there before the sunset.

NSA
MARYLAND
5:00 P.M.

Bevan looked up at the clock and decided to wait a little longer before leaving. Ron had left a message that he was going to the condo this morning.

"Mr. Benjamin, Ron Edwards line one," Darlene said.

"Ron, anything or a bust?" Bevan asked.

"Oh, you won't believe the information I got from Bulldog."

"Who?"

"The old senile manager I thought ran this place; well, he wasn't so senile and was full of surprises. I'm faxing you some photographs taken here a few months ago. You need to see them before we go on with this conversation," Ron told him.

Darlene entered his office and handed him several sheets.

"It's him," Bevan said.

"Yeah, and from what Bulldog said, Aaron had been snooping around for a while before trying to 'pull one over on him,' as he put it. He said Aaron pretended to be a potential buyer but kept asking about the penthouse."

"Who is this man, Bulldog?" Bevan asked.

"Real name is Harry Hawthorne, a World War II veteran, kind of tight-lipped about that part of his life but spry and smart. He took me up to the penthouse and showed me where Taylor and Eric had been living. Multimillion-dollar condo all paid by their uncle Larry White-Shaw. Darlene should be bringing his file to you."

"Got it," Bevan said and pulled Larry's file from his bottom drawer.

"This family has been involved in wars since the 1860s in one form or another, mostly as correspondents. Taylor is the heir to a fortune that has more zeros at the end of it than you can count. That doesn't include the newspaper in New York, which he had never taken a dime from. The controlling interest in the paper was left to him by his great-uncle."

"I knew some of this information," Bevan said. "What else?"

"Bulldog sent me to see Bentwood Milton, the attorney in charge of Larry Shaw's estate. When he realized the seriousness of my visit he was more than happy to share what information he thought would be helpful. Taylor has no idea what is at stake here. This is the kind of money people kill for. Oh, and there is another little twist to all of this," Ron said.

"What's that?" Bevan asked, wondering how this could get any stranger.

"Do you know the name of the family that owned all that land where your parents live?" Ron asked.

"Yes, the Bowens, why?"

"Well there is a large amount of money that will go to the heir of Sarah Jane Bowen at some point. I didn't really pay much attention but the attorney shared that part, too," Ron said.

"Jace Bowen and E. are related to this Sarah Bowen. This case is evolving around my family and friends. What about Sherman, did he know about any of this?" Bevan asked.

"According to Bulldog, no. He said Sherman was a fool, and was easily played. It appears Harry has appointed himself as Taylor and Eric's protector."

"What about Aaron?"

Ron laughed. "Bulldog said he ran him a merry chase, too, and left him with more questions than answers."

"Aaron is no fool and if there was any way he could obtain financial information he might have knowledge of what Taylor might inherit, but not the extent of what you have discovered. If he found anything of importance he may have shared it with Sherman. Something we will never know unless we catch him," Bevan said. "Taylor's worth now as the owner of the *Journal* makes him one of the wealthiest men in New York. Aaron will use that to his advantage in one way or another."

"It's beginning to sound like Aaron is looking for a way to retire and disappear permanently. Any leads on him?" Ron asked.

"No, but I have received some information that there were men in his office a year ago, foreign, with a lot of money," Bevan said.

"Terrorist?"

"Can't confirm that at this point," Bevan said. "Any word on where the Shaw brothers are?"

"Last Bulldog heard they were headed to Baghdad."

"Shit!"

"My thought, too, but nothing much I can do about that right now," Ron said.

"Well not from your end but I have other options here," Bevan said.

"Bulldog took my card, told me to stop by anytime for a beer in the penthouse. He said that if Caydon showed up again he'd let me know," Ron said and laughed.

"What's so funny?" Bevan asked.

"You know, sometimes you get the best surprises when you least expect it and this old man was a diamond. I will think twice before ever doubting the wisdom of the elderly," Ron said.

"I may have E. call Jace again and see who has checked in at the B&B since the attacks," Bevan said.

"I'll keep in touch with Harry; and when the brothers come back, I'll go see them. I promised the attorney not to say anything to them but they are both in danger until Aaron is arrested."

"Agreed; I need to go, your sister is waiting. My love to Liz and the kids," Bevan said and hung up the phone.

Darlene entered the office with the files on Zack and Blain. "Good night, Mr. Benjamin."

"Always reading my mind. Good night, Darlene," Bevan said and took the files and opened them. He would have to make some decisions about these two. He could have them look for the Shaw brothers. Taylor and Eric could be anywhere, and with military plans progressing, they were in as much danger in Baghdad as here with Aaron looking for them in the States. Bevan knew at some point Zack and Blain would be brought home. There were new concerns here that would need to be addressed, and their time in the Middle East would be advantageous to the company. He would also use them to help search for Aaron. Zack's special ability would be an asset. The reports he was receiving indicated an ever increasing control and something he hadn't expected. She had begun to manipulate thought. He smiled at the report from Mark that said, *I observed Blain making Zack's bed and folding her clothes while she sat reading. When asked why? His comment was, "I don't know I just thought it needed to be done." Mark said he looked at Zack and she pointed to her forehead and tapped it.* This is extraordinary. The report had been for his eyes only, and until he was sure she had a firm control on this he did not intend to share it. There were always decisions to make, but he could make them tomorrow or next week; now Laura would be waiting at the restaurant and he needed to go. Bevan walked down to the "cave," as he called it, to check on E.

"Heading out, what about you?" Bevan asked.

E. turned, smiled, and opened a blue box with a huge diamond ring in it. "It's what she wants."

Bevan smiled. "Well congratulations, when are you going to propose?"

"This weekend."

"See you tomorrow."

"Running some updates again so I'll be here a while," E. said.

"Blanket and pillow in the usual place, and there's a six-pack of those energy drinks you like in my fridge."

"Thanks boss, see you tomorrow."

Bevan turned and walked away. He would put E. in for another raise when his review came up. The company had better hope he never left.

❧

Battlegrounds
Gettysburg, Pennsylvania
5:30 p.m.

Jace stood at Cemetery Hill and looked out over the battlefield. She had made good time, missed the traffic out of D.C., and had driven into Gettysburg shortly before five. She checked into a local hotel, grabbed a bottle of water and map, and then headed out for an evening walk before the sunset. She decided to take the bus tour tomorrow and get a true feel for the battles that took place here. Jace was glad she had chosen to come now in the fall. The summer heat would hopefully have subsided, and she loved the changing colors of the Northeast. She closed her eyes and took a deep breath of crisp air and felt the beginning of an October chill. Jace thought about the history, the great amount of death, and how nurses had worked with little or nothing to try to save the men and boys that were injured on the ground she now walked. A shiver ran over her arms as she smelled gunpowder and heard horses galloping toward her.

There were the stories about Sarah, her ancestor that was a nurse here at Gettysburg. Jace remembered the book written about Northern and Southern nurses that had traveled during the Civil War. She regretted not bringing it with her for reference but felt it was safe in Galveston with her friends. This ancestor had actually traveled from Georgia with other nurses to heal. *Must be in our blood,* she thought and smiled.

Jace walked over and looked at the monuments that marked the leaders that were injured or killed along with troops from across the nation that had fought and died. As the sun began to set she walked back toward town to find a place to eat. She smiled at the locals that walked the streets in costume, part of the charm in Gettysburg.

As she walked up the street toward her hotel, Jace could see a man in costume sitting on a bench. He was wearing a cream-colored pullover shirt with what looked like suspenders, but they weren't stretchy. The brown pants he was wearing appeared to have been homespun. His boots were worn and scuffed as though he had walked a great distance in them. She started to pass him but changed her mind; she walked up to him and smiled.

"Mind if I sit down?" Jace asked.

"Please," the stranger said and pointed to a place next to him.

"Nice evening," Jace said and looked into the greenest eyes she had ever seen. They were almost haunting.

"Yes, so much nicer than the summers here," he said. "Are you staying long?"

"Couple of days, tourist," Jace answered and turned to the sound of music that had started up the street.

"Be sure to go out to the Monfort farm," he said.

"Oh really, why?" Jace asked and turned back to an empty seat where the stranger had been sitting. She looked up and watched as he walked away. The man stopped and turned around to look at her.

"There is a special story there; one you will want to hear." He then disappeared into the dark.

Chapter Thirty-Nine 🕭

NSA
MARYLAND
MONDAY, OCTOBER 8, 2001
6:00 A.M.

E. was asleep on the couch in Bevan's office when the door opened. Bevan smiled when E. peeked out from under the blanket, his hair sticking straight up and matted to one side.

"I see it took all night," Bevan said.

E. opened his eyes. "Yes, but only because there was a glitch that took me some extra time. It's all fixed, good as new and working faster all over the building."

"Did you get hold of Jace?"

"Yep, late last night. She's in Gettysburg sightseeing for a few days. Said she would call and see who was at the B&B. She'll leave a message on my personal phone," E. said and closed his eyes.

"Why don't you go home?"

"DeAnna's not there and you buy better energy drinks than I do."

JOLLY ROGER B&B
TEXAS
7:00 A.M.

The twins had been busy since daybreak cooking and preparing for the guests that would be arriving later. The table was set and buffet ready. Their star guest seemed to always be the first one up and the first one downstairs for breakfast.

"Have another slice of quiche and a muffin, Dennis," Casie said. "It's my own special recipe."

"Well, maybe just one more, you ladies are spoiling me," Aaron said and laughed.

"Are you going to stay longer?" Candi asked.

"Yes, at least another week, if it's possible. I have decided to look at property here and I have an appointment with a realtor to go look at homes," Aaron lied to them.

"Wonderful, I'll write up a bill for you," Candi asked.

"I won't get my credit card until I return home. I hope cash will be sufficient," Aaron said and smiled at Casie.

"Cash is always okay," Casie said. "Oh, I heard from Jace last night and she will be home sometime this weekend or Monday."

"I hope it's while I'm here. I really want to meet her," Aaron said.

"You'll just love her," Casie said. "Can we count on you to join us for dinner?"

"With your gourmet meals, how can I say no?"

THE GETTYSBURG HOTEL
GETTYSBURG, PENNSYLVANIA
9:00 A.M.

Jace sat in the restaurant at the hotel and made the decision to rent a bicycle and do the tour on her own. They were audio tours, so she could stop and replay if she felt something important had been missed. She walked back to her room and looked at the names of people staying at the B&B. She wondered why Ethaniel or his boss was so interested in their guests. Jace would call before she left to head home and leave the names. She put a few things in her backpack: water, granola bars, and her new digital camera. She loved the fact she could see the pictures immediately, and if one was bad she could just delete it and take a new one. Jace hoped to find some herbs and plants to add to her collection. She walked to the rental and got a bike and audio set. She then headed out to really listen and learn about what took place at Gettysburg those three days in July.

As Jace rode down the streets she passed more locals, again many dressed in costume. She smiled as soldiers tipped their caps, women curtseyed, and children played with toys that didn't require batteries. She looked for the man she had talked with the night before, but didn't see him. Jace had hoped he would go with her since he seemed to have such interesting information about this town and its history. She stopped for a moment, looked at her map, and headed toward the first site.

As the day progressed, Jace kept thinking about the Monfort farm. *Why was it so important she go there?* She finally gave in and looked for its location on the map. If she went to the Monfort farm now she could stay a couple more days and finish the tour of the battlefields later.

As Jace rode up to the Monfort farm she could see a few cars and people walking around. She walked up, pulled out her camera, took a photo, and then looked at the image. *That's funny, he wasn't there a minute ago*, she thought. The man she talked with last night was in her photo and now beckoned.

"You found it!" he said.

Jace walked up to the man. He was dressed in the same clothing from the night before. "You said there is a story that I need to hear?"

"There are many important stories on all the battlefields here, but this one, I feel, will touch you in a special way," he said. "Please sit down with me."

They both sat down. Jace looked at this very handsome man with haunting green eyes and listened to a story he seemed to think would be of interest to her.

"There was a young nurse here that fell in love with a man who fought the war with a pen, not a weapon," he began.

"A reporter," Jace said.

"Yes, these two were destined to be together, for they had known one another since childhood but had never met until the war. They found love in the midst of pain and suffering all around them. They

243

became separated at one point. He searched for her until he was led to this farm, a hospital, where she was working to save lives. He professed his love and intent to be with her forever. But fate can be cruel, and an unfortunate accident stopped their happiness. He was injured and died in her arms here at this place." The stranger stopped his story. He then reached out for Jace's face.

"Oh my God, what a sad story," she said and felt the tear running down her face gently disappear. She looked at the man sitting in front of her. *This man knows the story of my ancestor, but how is that possible?*

The stranger smiled. "But there will always be hope where there is true love. The nurse, his love, promised to search for him for eternity until they were reunited. She had given him something very special . . . her heart."

Jace listened to this story and her own heart ached for these two lost souls. A cool breeze blew across her face and made her realize the day was rapidly ending and she needed to return to town before dark.

"Thank you, thank you for sharing this story. And you were right—it is a special story. I have so many questions but I need to go. If it's possible, I'd like to talk to you again about all you've told me. I need to apologize for not introducing myself last night; it was very rude of me," Jace said and stuck out her hand. "I'm Jace, Jace Bowen."

The stranger smiled again. "I'm Samuel, Samuel White."

With what seemed to be the lightest touch he took her hands and helped her to stand.

"Did you say White?" Jace asked.

"Yes."

"Do you have relatives in New York?"

"Probably, but I can't say for sure," Samuel said and walked Jace to her bike. "Remember, there can be no rest when a part of the heart is missing . . . lost. It must be found."

Jace turned to get on her bike. She wanted to ask him what he meant about the heart and she needed to know how he could possibly know the story of Sarah.

"Samuel, who . . ." Jace started to ask, but when she turned back he was no longer there. All that was left was the scent of lilacs where none were growing.

Chapter Forty &

Jace had packed her truck the night before. She was disappointed she couldn't find Samuel and perplexed no one in town knew him even when she showed them his photograph. *How could anyone forget this man once you saw his eyes?* She had made a few purchases and needed to get on the road. It would be late Sunday before she got home. She had left the names of all the guests on Ethaniel's phone in a message. She picked up her backpack and started to leave when the smell of bacon and eggs stopped her at the front door of the hotel.

Jace looked at the attendant at the front desk who smiled and pointed toward the dining room.

"Well maybe I should go ahead and eat first."

JOLLY ROGER B&B
TEXAS
8:00 A.M.

Aaron returned to his room after a morning swim in the canal. He was enjoying this all too much, but he was going to have to leave if

Jace didn't show up over the weekend. Casie wasn't a problem but her twin Candi was beginning to ask too many questions.

"Dennis, breakfast," Casie called.

"On my way," Aaron said. As he passed by the message center set up for the guests, he noticed a note to the twins. *Candi or Casie, Call Ethaniel Long Immediately.* There were two numbers listed and one Aaron knew well. He took the note and put it in his pocket. This was a problem. He was now going to have to leave before he could talk to Jace. He would check out in the morning, drive down the sea wall, and check into the Galvez. He would need another car; air travel at this point would be a risk, even with a new identity and disguise. Aaron's mind was already processing a new plan. Taylor Shaw's wealth, now that Sherman was gone, would be immense. He thought about Scotland and New Year's morning with Kyliegh. Aaron walked into the breakfast area.

"Ah, ladies, each meal here just gets better."

NSA Field House
Baghdad
Friday, October 12, 2001
2:00 p.m.

Mark had been standing outside talking with other traders, making deals, ordering and fending off another marriage proposal for Zack. He looked down the street and could see Eric Shaw walking toward his shop. *Damn it, she's at it again!* He quickly ended the conversation and headed upstairs where Zack was standing at the window.

"Zack, you have to stop," Mark said.

"Nice looking man, don't you think?" Zack said and smiled as Eric stood outside their door again.

"You're going to raise suspicions."

"But you must admit, I'm improving? Eric was two blocks away when I sent the thought to come here," Zack smiled.

"Yes, and last week you had a herd of goats that showed up at our door," he said. "Be careful, my niece. I can't allow you to see this man."

Zack looked down at the tall man from her window.

"Then maybe it's time I go back home."

Chapter Forty~One ❧

The twins had seen the last guest off and were preparing rooms and menus for the upcoming week. They noticed Jace's truck outside as they headed to the beach for their early morning run. Both knew she was not a morning person and would be down in her own time.

"Jace!" Casie said.

Jace stumbled into the kitchen with her camera, still dressed in her scrub bottoms and tank top. She had put on her sunglasses to block out the brightness of the room. "Coffee, please."

"Honey, when did you get in?" Candi said, then handed her a cup of coffee and huge blueberry muffin with butter melting on it.

"Mmmm—around three a.m. I took a wrong turn out of Birmingham and ended up lost. Found an awesome little town with all kinds of shops so I stopped, spent the night, and explored. What the heck. I feel if you don't turn around at least once it wasn't worth the trip," Jace said and drank her coffee. "Oh yuck! Where's the creamer?"

"Well, glad to have you home," Casie said and handed her two containers with different flavors.

"How's business been since 9-11?" Jace asked.

"We had some cancellations, which were to be expected, but then there was a man here for three weeks," Candi said.

"Nice looking; he was interested in meeting you but he left Saturday morning suddenly. Said he had received a call from his business partner and needed to leave. Left us a huge tip in his room," Casie told Jace.

"Oh, did you guys get a call from Ethaniel Long?" Jace asked.

"No, is he a friend?" Candi asked.

"He's family and works in D.C. He called asking about our guests and I told him to leave a message if he couldn't get hold of you."

"Never talked to him or saw a message," Casie said.

"Ditto," Candi said.

"Candi, hand me the phone and let me call him," Jace said and called the work number he had given her.

"Ethaniel, it's Jace." She talked for almost an hour. She hung up the phone and looked at the twins. "Ethaniel's boss will be here tonight."

"Why?" Candi asked.

"He said there is a possibility the man that stayed here is wanted by the FBI and CIA," Jace said.

"Dennis? No way, he was a sweetie," Casie said.

"Mr. Benjamin is bringing pictures and wants us to leave his room alone. He asked that we do nothing to it," Jace said.

"Too late, you know how we are when someone leaves. Clean and set up for the next guest," Candi said. "He's welcome to stay in it when he gets here. I'm sure he'll be here at least one or two nights."

"Well maybe he can find something, but I think he really wants to talk to you two since you saw him every day," Jace told them.

"Jace, who is this?" Casie asked and held out the camera.

Jace pulled down her sunglasses. "Said his name was Samuel White."

"Like the name in the book?" Candi asked.

Jace shrugged her shoulders. "I asked him if he had relatives in New York. He said he wasn't sure."

"Did he give you his phone number?" Casie asked.

"No, he just disappeared, and no one in Gettysburg knew him. How could you forget a man with eyes like that?" Jace asked.

❦

GULFSTREAM II JET
GALVESTON-BOUND
4:00 P.M.

Bevan had been in the air about an hour and was looking over all the photographs he had of Aaron. How many times was he going to miss this man by just a few days or hours? Three weeks was a long time for him to stay in one place. He must have felt safe. He hoped the room he had stayed in was not disturbed, but he didn't plan on it. He would talk with all of them and see what they could tell him; maybe someone there took a photograph. He needed to see what disguise he had used for three weeks. He looked at his watch; it would be late when he got to Galveston. E. had pulled up information on the owners at the B&B. He found the twins to be honest and financially secure. Bevan opened the file on Jace and almost dropped it. The resemblance to Susan Bowen was frightening. The eyes and hair, facial structure—all similar; there were some differences, but no question to family ancestry. He was surprised when he read that Zaveen Keens was her relative. *Had he just missed that part of her application and background?* This whole case just continued to get stranger and stranger. Bowen, White-Shaw, Long, Keens, and Benjamin; families that have been connected in one way or another from the 1860s, through the1940s to present. *Why now? What is the connection that is pulling all of them together?*

"Bevan, buckle up, we're running into a little turbulence," Billy told him.

Bevan put his files away, buckled up, and decided to take a nap. He would worry about the families later; right now he had to find Aaron before someone else died.

❦

SCHOLES AIRPORT
GALVESTON
10:00 P.M.

Jace waited outside the fence as the plane landed and watched the two men exit the plane. She waved at them and both walked over to her.

"I'm Jace Bowen," she said and shook hands with the tall man in the suit.

"Bevan Benjamin. Do you have room at the B&B for my pilot?" Bevan asked.

Jace smiled. "We'd be pleased if you both stayed."

The pilot made arrangements for fuel and security for the night. Bevan followed Jace to a jeep that had Jolly Roger B&B painted on it. The pilot walked up behind Bevan.

"For real, Bevan? Skull and crossbones?" Billy asked.

"I guess so," Bevan answered.

Jace laughed. "Welcome to Galveston. I hope you both are hungry! And if you're not, good luck telling the twins."

After introductions, room assignments, and a meal that was impressive by any standard this time of night, it was time for questions.

"Bevan, I'm going to bed. Ladies, thank you and I'll see everyone at breakfast," Billy said.

"We'll plan an eight a.m. breakfast for you but there is always coffee and muffins at six a.m. for any early risers," Casie said.

"Sounds good," Billy said and headed to his room.

Bevan looked at all three women. "Jace, I know you just got home so I want to talk with you tomorrow morning."

"Okay, but can I sit here and listen?" Jace asked.

"Yes, I think you should," Bevan said. Over the next two hours he explained why it was necessary for him to come and interview them personally. He then stressed this was a case of national security involving terrorism. "Did either of you get a picture of this man?"

"Damn it, I knew something wasn't right," Candi said.

"Why?" Bevan asked.

"He always moved or made some excuse for not having his picture taken," Casie answered.

"I was afraid of that," Bevan said.

"But I just received some photos online from guests who were here when Dennis, I mean this Aaron, was also here. He obviously didn't know he was being photographed. There are several of him in the file," Candi said and went to the computer to make copies for Bevan.

"Wonderful, at least I can see what type of disguise he was using," Bevan said.

"Do you have pictures?" Casie asked.

Bevan pulled the file out and Casie looked at the pictures. Candi returned with copies and laid them down next to the file photo from the company.

"It looks to me like he didn't wear a disguise, Bevan," Casie said.

Bevan gathered the pictures from the B&B and thanked the twins for their time. He would gather more information tomorrow after he talked with Jace. He was pleased the room Aaron had stayed in was open and figured it had been cleaned. He would look through everything anyway, but if Aaron was true to form this room had been sanitized. Bevan walked out on the deck and sat for a moment looking at the sky. Peaceful, pleasant, and he hadn't seen stars like that since he was a child in Georgia. He wished Laura was with him; this was a lovely B&B. He would bring her one day.

His thoughts changed back to Aaron. He had taken a huge chance staying here with no disguise. It was like he was on vacation, swimming, going to the local bar, mingling with other people, sightseeing . . . none of this made any sense. This was not like him, he had always been so careful, had been taught to be cautious. Bevan was tired and his mind couldn't process all this now. Maybe it was this place that made him drop his guard. He undressed, lay down, and thought no more of Aaron.

Chapter Forty~Two 🙠

Bevan had been awake since six and thought he had heard someone downstairs at five. He had slept so peacefully he couldn't stand the thought of getting up early. He could smell coffee and something wonderful baking downstairs. Happy Hour had even been singing a nice wake-up call. Bevan wandered down thinking he would catch Jace early.

"Jace around?" Bevan asked and sat down at the bar.

"I guess Jace should have told you that as a night nurse morning for her will be around ten," Casie said and handed Bevan his plate and directed him to the buffet.

"Where's Billy?" Bevan asked and picked up the digital camera and turned it on.

"Had his breakfast at six thirty and is out in the canal kayaking," Candi answered.

"You ladies have quit a nice set-up here, beautiful views, peaceful, relaxing. I would love to come back and bring Laura," Bevan said.

"Your wife?" Casie asked.

"Fiancé," Bevan answered.

"Anytime, you'll always be welcome here," Candi said.

"Ahhh, there she is, good morning sunshine," Casie said.

"Ugh, sorry, Bevan, I work nights so don't expect much until I've had my coffee," Jace said.

Bevan smiled. "Jace, I hope you don't mind but I turned on your camera and looked through your pictures."

Jace poured a little coffee in her creamer. "No, I don't mind."

"I do have a question, though," Bevan said.

"Sure, what?" Jace responded.

"How long have you known Taylor Shaw?"

"Who?" Jace asked. "Wait, I'm trying to find him. His family may have a journal that belonged to my ancestor. He and his brother stayed at the Long Bowe B&B last year. I've been trying to contact him ever since he was there. But I've never met him. Why are you asking?"

"Because, the man in this picture is Taylor Shaw," Bevan said and showed her the picture she had taken of Samuel White.

"No, that man said his name was White, Samuel White," Jace said.

"No, this is Taylor Shaw," Bevan said. "You need to look at something." He went upstairs and returned with a magazine that had a picture of Taylor Shaw.

The three women looked at the magazine. Jace couldn't believe what she was seeing. "What's going on here? None of this is making any sense. That picture was taken in Gettysburg last week."

"Let me make a phone call," Bevan said and walked out on the deck. A few moments later he returned.

"You look confused," Candi said.

"Who did you call?" Jace asked.

"A colleague in Hawaii. He said that Taylor Shaw and his brother are still out of the country."

"So that can't be him," Jace said.

"No, but whoever this is could be his twin," Bevan said. This conversation had answered most of what Bevan had intended to discuss with Jace. She had had no contact with Taylor and was not aware of the fortune at stake.

"What did you want to talk to me about this morning?" Jace asked him.

"You've already answered that question. Part of this case revolves around the Shaw family, but since you haven't met Taylor there isn't anything for me to ask," Bevan told her. "Just one question about the man in Gettysburg. Did he have relatives in New York?"

"He said possibly but he wasn't for sure. Now I have a question. What does this Aaron want?" Jace asked.

"I can answer that, money," Candi said.

"And no good ever comes from the lust of wealth," Casie said.

Bevan thought about Sherman and where his lust for power and money had led him. "You both are correct; no good comes from that type of greed."

"I have a request," Jace said.

"What?" Bevan asked.

"My cousin, Zaveen Keens, has a job somewhere in D.C. and I guess her phones aren't working, but if you happen to speak with her, please tell her hello and I miss her," Jace said and made a crooked smile.

Bevan didn't even ask, he just nodded his head. Bevan spent a couple of hours talking with the twins again. It appeared that Aaron used this three weeks as a rest stop, so to speak. The total use of cash instead of phony untraceable credit cards was new. He called E. at the office.

"Anything?" Bevan asked.

"The guy is screwing with us again," E. said.

"I have where a Bevan Benjamin checked into the Galvez Saturday afternoon and left Monday morning. The picture they sent shows him looking directly into the camera smiling. Do you want me to call the local FBI and send them?"

"He's gone, waste of time. He's showing off, always a step ahead. Anything on car rentals?" Bevan asked.

"No, he has to have someone getting them for him, no trail to follow," E. said. "How's my cousin treating you?"

"This place is nice; you and DeAnna need to come," Bevan said and hung up.

Billy walked through the door and looked at Bevan. "What time you want to go? I need to call and make the flight plan."

"Tomorrow morning will be fine, around nine a.m. I'm going to the Galvez to see where he stayed. Jace, can I borrow the jeep?" Bevan asked.

🐦

BORDER BETWEEN IRAQ AND IRAN
WEDNESDAY, OCTOBER 17, 2001
6:00 P.M.

Taylor sat with his brother, writing out another note to Alfred Prichard. When they returned, decisions would need to be made and papers signed. They both felt the paper would be run as if they were there to do it themselves, as long as Alfred was there. Taylor watched his brother in action, taking photo after photo and ducking in between gunfire.

"I have to get these back to the States," Eric said.

"Then let's head back in tomorrow. I can send this back to Alfred," Taylor said.

The sound of gunfire let Eric know larger rounds were coming. He grabbed his brother and they both flattened out on the ground. They were pelted with dirt and rocks when the shell exploded.

"Damn! That one was close."

"No, close is when it falls in your lap," Taylor said. "We need to get to Baghdad."

"You don't have to tell me twice," Eric said and they crawled away.

Chapter Forty~Three ❧

Bevan and Billy had finished breakfast, said their good-byes, and attempted to pay for their rooms. Bevan had insisted, but the twins told both of them to come back and they would take their money next time. Both men now stood at the jeep waiting for Jace.

"Do you think she's awake?" Billy asked Bevan.

Bevan had seen her coming around the back of the jeep with her I'm-not-a-morning-person coffee cup.

"Of course I'm awake! Not functioning properly, but awake," she said.

Bevan had warned the twins again how dangerous Aaron was and to contact him if he returned or called. He doubted either would happen. Bevan put his bag in the back of the jeep and all three got in for the very short drive to the airport.

"Jace, be careful and I'll have the agent in Hawaii give your number to Taylor when he returns," Bevan said.

"I appreciate that more than you realize. If he has the journal, I would like to have it. It's my family history and it belongs with family," Jace said. "Did you find anything at the Galvez?"

"Another beautiful place I need for Laura to see and a note from Aaron."

"What'd it say, or can you tell me?" Jace asked.

"Stop now before someone else gets hurt." Bevan looked at Jace.

"Sounds like a threat," Jace responded.

"Watch your backs," Bevan said.

"You better watch yours, too," Jace said and drove into the airport.

The plane was out and ready for Billy's preflight check. Jace walked out to the plane with Bevan.

"Billy, nice meeting you and have a safe journey," Jace said and shook his hand. She then turned and hugged Bevan. "Be careful and come back. Maybe the next time I'm in Waynesboro we can all get together, family reunion-style."

"That would be nice." Bevan said.

Jace watched until the plane took off; she had an uneasy feeling about all of this, but there wasn't much she or anyone else could do right now. She drove back to the B&B and told the twins she had gifts from Gettysburg for them upstairs.

"Jace, you didn't have to do that," Casie said as they went upstairs with Jace.

"I know, it isn't much but it suits you two," Jace said and put a gray hat on one and a blue hat on the other. "Now you two can battle it out." They all laughed. She then reached in another sack and gave them the real gifts, handmade jewelry of the 1800s from a jeweler in Gettysburg and cast-iron molds for the kitchen.

"These are beautiful," Candi said as she looked at the jewelry.

"Love it, love it," Casie said and took the dress out of the sack on Jace's bed.

"Where did you get that?" Candi asked.

"I found a small dress shop just outside of Gettysburg. It's strange, when I went inside the house-shop I didn't intend to buy anything. The lady that owned the shop told me she was the seamstress and made all the dresses. She insisted I try it on. It fit like it was made for me. I bought it because I felt like it was mine."

Casie took the blue checkered dress with pink flowers inside the squares and held it up to Jace. "The color suits you, brings out your eyes. Now all you need to do is pull your hair back in a bun, find a necklace, and you'll look like a lady from the 1860s!"

🍂

NSA FIELD HOUSE
BAGHDAD
THURSDAY, OCTOBER 18, 2001
3:00 P.M.

Zack was sitting in the window reading. She found she could pick up more from the men on the streets by just being still and concentrating. Zack had thought about the comment to Mark about going home. She realized it was not her decision, but she missed her family.

"Picking up anything important out there this afternoon?" Mark asked.

"No, where's Blain?"

"On the border for a couple of days. He said his contact had information," Mark answered.

"I wish he wouldn't do that, too much going on to be alone. I ..." Zack stopped talking and stood up.

Mark had been around Zack long enough to know this was not good. "Zack? What?"

"Bomb, at the hotel where Eric and his brother are staying. We have to go now!" she said and grabbed her veil and covering.

"Zack! Wait!" Mark called out.

"Hurry, a lot of people are about to die and Eric's brother is already in the hotel."

Eric was a few buildings away from the hotel waiting for Taylor to send the message home. He looked down the street, people out trying to stay normal, if that was possible.

"Where's your brother?" the voice of a woman asked.

Eric turned and looked down at a small figure covered in appropriate dress. He was confused, since there should have been a male relative with her and talking to him could get her killed.

"What? Who are you and why are you . . . " Eric didn't finish.

"Where the hell is your brother? A bomb is about to explode!" she said.

"Eric!" Taylor called as he headed toward his brother. "Who . . ."

"Run!" The woman screamed.

Before Taylor could finish his statement the building he had just left exploded.

Gunfire, screams, dust, and fire now was the main scene at the hotel. Eric and Zack had been thrown against the building and were both face down in the street. Zack shook her head, pulled off the veil, and checked Eric for a pulse. *Alive.* She stood up and was headed to help Taylor when the sight of the woman kneeling beside him stopped her. The woman was wearing a long, blue checkered dress and she had blonde hair; when she stood and turned around, Zack fell to her knees.

"Jace!" Zack said.

The woman smiled and put her hand over her heart. Zack began to shake when she heard the woman's thought. "Mack, it's good to see you again." Zack closed her eyes and when she opened them the woman was gone.

Taylor lay on his back, ears ringing, pain in his left arm and hand, confused about his surroundings. He opened his eyes to the sight of a beautiful woman kneeling next to him. She was Caucasian and her blue checkered dress was stained with blood. Was it his blood? Her hair was blonde and she had the bluest eyes he had ever seen. Lilacs, he smelled lilacs. She smiled at him and put her hand on his chest where the heart necklace was located.

"It's time, you must find me, find me again," she said.

Taylor watched as she stood, turned, and disappeared into thin air.

Mark ran into a scene of chaos and death. He had to find Zack before anyone realized she was alone. He refused to believe she was dead.

"Zack, Zack!" Mark called. Why was she just standing there? Why had she taken off her veil?

Zack turned to face Mark, who had her veil. "Did you see her?"

"We have to go. If anyone has seen you without this we're in trouble," he told her.

As she started to leave, a hand grabbed her arm.

"Who are you?" Eric asked.

"A friend."

Chapter Forty~Four 🍂

NSA
MARYLAND
FRIDAY, OCTOBER 19, 2001
6:00 P.M.

Bevan was completing his report on Aaron and the visit to Galveston when E. walked into his office. "You and that lovely lady of yours have plans for the weekend?" Bevan said and then looked at the expression on Ethaniel's' face. He could tell whatever was in the folder was not good news. "What is it?"

"I think you better read this," E. said and handed Bevan a report out of Baghdad.

Bevan read over the report from Mark about the explosion. He was relieved the Shaw brothers had not been killed. Taylor had been taken to a US military hospital and would be coming back to the States once he was stable. The report that Zack's face had been seen on the streets was an issue. Bevan leaned back in his chair and looked up at E.

"Bring them home."

🍂

US Military Hospital
Baghdad
Saturday, October 20, 2001
8:00 a.m.

Dr. Dawson Raines had finished a twelve-hour night shift and decided to go see Taylor Shaw before heading "home" for some much-needed rest. Dawson had been sent to triage to help with the wounded after the bomb blast at the Market Square Hotel. So many civilians were killed, and when he first saw Taylor Shaw he didn't expect him to live, but most of what looked like major injuries were only minor cuts on his face and head. Taylor was lucky to have only had a broken arm and lost a thumb; it could have been his life.

"Good morning, doc," Taylor said.

"You're in a good mood to have been almost killed."

"Painkillers are wonderful, aren't they?"

Dawson smiled, "We're going to keep you for a few more days, then hopefully you can head back home. Honolulu, right?"

"Yes, Dr. Raines, thank you for what you did to save me," Taylor said.

"All in a day's work."

"Doc, I have a question about that day."

"Okay."

"Did anyone see a woman dressed in a long blue checkered dress, blonde hair and blue eyes out there that day?"

"No, why?"

"Nothing, maybe just my mind playing tricks on me. After all I did get hit pretty hard on the head."

"Well, if you see her again let me know, she sounds like someone I know," Dawson said and left.

Chapter Forty~Five 🐚

Harry stood on the balcony of the penthouse and wiped the tears away from his face. He had received the email from Eric about the bombing, injury, and the news that they were coming home. He was happy they were both back.

"Harry, I hope those tears are because the sun is so bright this afternoon," Taylor said and wrapped his arm around Harry's shoulder.

"It's nice to have you two back. How's your arm?" Harry asked.

Taylor looked at his left arm in the sling. "I was lucky. Broken arm, a few cuts and scrapes." Taylor saw him looking at this hand. "Who needs a thumb anyway?"

"What, no tears for me, old man?" Eric teased.

"Glad you're okay, too," Harry said and patted him on the back.

"Stop babying Taylor. Those cuts on his face give him character. Something for him to brag about with the women," Eric said.

"Anything happen while we were gone?" Taylor asked.

"Had a G-man here asking about that fella, and old Bulldog was right. He's a bad dude. That G-man turned out to be alright, wants to talk to you two but not until you're all healed up," Harry said.

"Harry, really I'm fine, but I want to settle back and catch up on some things before delving into what was probably Sherman's doings."

"Well, when I got the message about you two coming home I stocked the fridge," Harry told them and headed for the door. "Gotta run. Bingo starts at four."

"I don't know about you but it's good to be home," Taylor said.

"Home, glad to hear you say that!" Eric said.

"Eric, I need to ask you about the day this all happened," Taylor said.

"Bro, the only thing I remember is that woman telling me there was a bomb in the hotel, then waking up and seeing her face, just before her uncle drug her away. Her English was perfect. I'm beginning to believe there was something else going on at that shop," Eric said.

"The government has been in foreign countries for years with set-ups like that to obtain information. That was probably one of them," Taylor said.

"When I went back a few days later the shop was closed and they were gone. Some story about her shaming the family, blah, blah, blah," Eric said.

"You'll probably never see her again," Taylor said. He sat down and thought about Larry's will, Sherman, the newspaper, things that must be tended to . . . and soon. "Eric, I need you to call Alfred and have him, Christian Black, and the head accountant fly out here next week. I want to take care of that first before I go back to working on the will. Call Bentwood if Harry hasn't already, let him know we're back and have him leave an opening when the rest arrive. I want him to be involved in all of this, too."

"Not a problem, big brother," Eric said. "Do you really think I'll never see her again?"

Taylor started laughing and hit the button on the remote. "Fools Rush In" by Glenn Miller started to play.

MARRIOTT HOTEL
OLD TOWN
ALEXANDRIA, VIRGINIA
9:00 P.M.

Bevan looked around the party room that he had reserved and decided it was time for announcements to be made. He walked to the center of the room and began.

"Attention everyone!" Bevan said. "I have a toast as the future best man."

Everyone in the room stood and raised their champagne glasses.

"To the future Mr. and Mrs. Ethaniel Long. May your lives be forever blessed," Bevan said. Everyone in the room agreed, glasses were clinked, and E. kissed the love of his life. The music started and everyone moved into the next room.

E. walked up to Bevan. "Thank you for agreeing to be my best man, boss."

Bevan smiled. "The honor is mine. Where's your family?"

"Tonight is for DeAnna's family and our friends here. Mom is planning something when we go home at Thanksgiving. I hope you and Laura will be there."

"Yes, we're coming home this year," Bevan said.

"Good," he said. Then DeAnna walked up and took his hand; they left to spend the rest of the evening celebrating.

"Bevan, I'm tired and need to get home," Laura said.

"Are you okay? Usually I'm the one insisting we go home?"

"Fine, huge case tomorrow in court," Laura responded.

"I figured something was up with your absence at the house. Let me have them bring the car," Bevan said and watched Laura say good-night to Ethaniel and DeAnna.

After Bevan and Laura were home, he turned his computer on before taking General Lee for a quick walk. Bevan had a meeting scheduled on Monday with Zack and Blain. They had been brought back, debriefed, and were given time to go home and see their families. Mark's shop had been closed. The story given to his friends and neighbors was his need to protect his family in another city and find a husband for his niece who had brought shame in the market. Bevan was headed back to the house when General Lee stopped and began to growl. The hair on the back of his neck rose and he reached for the gun he carried on late-night walks since the incident in the restaurant with Zack and Blain.

"What is it, General?" Bevan asked. A moment later General Lee began to wag his tale. Bevan relaxed and they turned the corner. When Bevan got to the house there was a note taped to his front door.

"She's pretty, Bevan. Your taste is improving. Stop searching for me, ARC."

Bevan turned and looked around: nothing out of place.

"Damn it!"

PENTHOUSE
HONOLULU
8:00 P.M.

Taylor sat on the balcony thinking about how lucky they had been in Baghdad. Eric walked up and handed him a beer.

"What's in the big envelope on the table?" Taylor asked.

"When we were about to head back, I left a message for my boss to find something simple until we got on our feet. They're hoping you might write the story when you feel up to it," Eric said.

"What's it about?"

"Travel nurses," Eric said.

"Hmmm, let me think about that for a week or so," Taylor said.

"Not a problem. If you can't or don't want to do it, they have someone else that can write the stories," Eric said. "What are you doing?"

"Writing a thank you to Dawson Raines," Taylor said.

"Who?"

"You remember the doctor that put me to sleep so they could fix my arm and hand."

"I remember him, tall, military captain, told me he had been in D.C. before being transferred here," Eric said.

"Nice guy, hadn't been over there very long," Taylor said.

"I've been meaning to ask you something. One of the nurses told me you kept talking about a blonde-headed woman at the bombing. What's up with that?" Eric asked.

"You're going to think I'm as crazy as Uncle Larry," Taylor said and told Eric about the woman that appeared at his side when he was injured, what she had said to him, and then how she had just disappeared.

"Crazy shit. Are you sure you weren't dreaming?" Eric asked. "They pumped a lot of drugs in you at the hospital."

"Maybe, at this point who knows?" Taylor said.

Eric stood up. "Bro, I'm beat. You're all unpacked and if you need some help later let me know. I'm done for the day; need to shower and head to bed."

"I'm fine; if you get up before I do start making those calls for me. I want to get started again on Uncle Larry's will," Taylor said.

"Got it," Eric said.

Taylor sat and thought about the woman in Baghdad.

No, it wasn't a dream.

Chapter Forty~Six

Zack was late getting to the office. The late flight back from home and then an alarm that didn't get set was not the way she had intended to start a week she had been dreading. The incident in Baghdad was her fault, and she knew Blain blamed her for him being pulled back, too. She walked into the conference room where Blain sat drinking coffee.

"How was your trip home?" Zack asked Blain.

"Good, and yours?" he asked.

"It was hard to leave but at least we got to go home. My cousin Jace spent a couple of days there, too. Always good to catch up. She said Bevan had been to the B&B but didn't go into details," Zack said.

"Have you found a place yet?" Blain asked.

"An apartment in Alexandria; small but I love it. What about you?" she asked.

"Nothing yet, but I have a buddy that's letting me sleep on his couch for now," Blain said.

Zack braced herself for the next statement Blain was about to make.

"Zack, I'm not sure why both of us were brought back; you, I understand, but there was no reason for me. I hadn't screwed up."

"You were coming home whether this incident had happened or not, both of you," Bevan said as he walked through the door. "Things have changed with 9-11 and I have another problem, which is connected. I haven't been able to catch this man." Bevan gave them folders. "I need something new and you two are it. He is the best of the best. Trained by the government and has contacts everywhere. I believe he is attempting to obtain money from this man and disappear permanently." Bevan then handed them a file on Taylor Shaw.

Zack quickly read through some reports and looked at the copy of the note that had been left on Bevan's door. "This is not going to be easy."

"No it's not," Blain agreed.

"Zack, I can't go into a lot of details but your cousin Jace is involved in this and it could be dangerous at some point for her," Bevan said.

The door opened and five boxes of files were brought into the room by Darlene.

"You both have a lot of work ahead of you and I will expect you to know this man intimately when you're finished. Everything in here is for your eyes only; nothing is to be removed. Educate yourselves with these files because if you don't, he'll kill you," Bevan told them.

"You trained him, didn't you?" Zack asked.

"Yes."

JOLLY ROGER B&B
TEXAS
10:00 A.M.

Jace sat on the deck outside her room, drinking coffee and reading the invitation to Ethaniel and DeAnna's engagement party the Saturday after Thanksgiving in Waynesboro. She smiled. *Why not?* The B&B had made money, so she had extra money; and she didn't plan on going back to work until after the first of the year. Jace would drive to Waynesboro and spend the holiday with her family, then go to D.C. for Kyani's wedding on the fifteenth of December. The thought of the wedding reminded Jace she needed to go into town and pick up the red dress that had been altered. Kyani had kept the promise she made to all of them and chose dresses that were lovely, flattering, and could be worn again. Jace thought about the holidays and hoped her parents would come to Waynesboro. She put the invitation down and looked over at the magazine Bevan had left. Jace compared Taylor Shaw's photo to the one she had downloaded and printed of Samuel White. They were the same, just like Candi and Casie. She felt her arms get cold. She hoped Taylor would have the journal belonging to Sarah. The hardest part now was to wait. Jace thought about what Samuel had said to her before he disappeared that day. Something about the heart, missing . . . lost? She went in and pulled out a box that she still hadn't unpacked since moving into the B&B. She found the brown envelope, opened it, and took out the photograph of Sarah.

"Jace, are you up?" Candi asked and entered, after knocking on the door. "What are you looking at?"

Jace turned the photograph around to show it to Candi.

"I can never get used to that, you look so much like her," Candi said.

Jace pointed to the necklace that hung around Sarah's neck.

"I think I know what Samuel White was talking about now."

Casie entered Jace's room with a new batch of muffins. "You two need to try these. I mixed blueberries, cranberries, and mandarin oranges."

"I'm not going to fit into my bridesmaid dress if you keep this up," Jace said and took one.

"Jace seems to think Samuel wants her to find Sarah's necklace," Candi said.

"Why?" Casie said and looked at the picture.

"I hadn't paid much attention to the picture except the strong resemblance, but the things he said about true love, souls, promises, and the heart . . . I remembered that Sarah was wearing a necklace, it has to be what he was talking about," Jace said.

"Two souls lost," Casie said.

Jace opened the book written by Samuel White. "Look at the dedication in this book."

"Do you really think that this man is the Samuel White that loved your aunt?" Candi asked.

"I have always tried to keep an open mind about the paranormal. I believe there is more than heaven and earth. I feel it is possible to leave this earth too early, leaving unfinished business," Jace said.

"You think there is unfinished business between them?" Casie said.

"No, I believe they're searching for each other," Jace said.

"Where's her heart?" Candi asked and pointed to the necklace in the photo.

"I don't know," Jace said.

Chapter Forty~Seven 👂

Taylor stood on the balcony and watched Eric help the driver load the luggage in the limo he had rented to take Alfred and Christian back to the airport. He felt it was the least he could do for all their hard work. The last week had been mentally exhausting. Files, accounts, the house and staff, so much paperwork it took more days than he had planned; but, for now, things would be settled in New York. Alfred had continuing power of attorney to run the office, as he had done since Sherman's death. There had been an increase in sales and the website had been improved. Eric was right, Alfred could be trusted and the employees seemed to be happier. Louisa had not caused any trouble since her dismissal, and her monthly check no longer flowed out of Sherman's personal account. All accounts had been double-checked for potential issues or problems. Any accounts in question had been closed and corrective measures taken. Taylor refused to take any money from the *Journal*. His money would be given back to the employees of the newspaper. He would let Alfred and the accountant decide the best way the money should be distributed. Eric would be given a reasonable monthly allowance from his inheritance. Taylor loved his brother, but he did not want to lose him to the greed that caused Sherman's death. Taylor's arm was healing nicely and the original cast had been replaced with something lighter and more flexible. The orthopedic specialists advised just a few more weeks and it would come off, and then he could start physical therapy. He looked at his left hand. *Hope I can learn to type with four fingers.* Taylor walked toward the kitchen to find something for lunch when he stopped to look at the pictures on the table. There were men and women of every color, size, and race. He picked up a stack and started to look through it. The fourth photo in the stack stopped him from going further. He didn't hear the door open.

"What's for lunch?" Eric asked.

Taylor looked at his brother and turned the photo of a woman around to show him. "Who is this?"

"I don't know. I just opened the envelope this morning. I haven't had time to match names and faces yet, why?" Eric asked. "Taylor, your hands are shaking."

"This is the woman I saw in Baghdad, the one that said I needed to find her," Taylor said.

"Give me a minute to find the list of names," Eric said.

Taylor watched Eric dig through the paperwork on the table.

"Here, it says her name is Jace Kindle, San Antonio, Texas," Eric told him.

Taylor sat down and stared at the picture.

"I have to find her."

Chapter Forty~Eight 🙠

OFFICE OF DR. ROSE MARIE CACCIATORI, ONCOLOGIST
HONOLULU
TUESDAY, NOVEMBER 13, 2001
4:00 P.M.

Harry sat in his physician's office instead of an exam room. He had been preparing himself for this day. Taylor and Eric were back home safe; he had taken care of the business Larry had left for him to do, and Bentwood would see to his last wishes. He could hear the sweet voice of Dr. Cacciatori as she was coming down that hallway, giving instructions to the nurses. She was a striking woman, tall, dark hair, olive skin, and light blue eyes. She had told him once her eyes were not from her father's Italian heritage but from her mother's Scandinavian side of the family. She was always dressed professionally, but today she took off the white coat so that the colors of the island greeted him. She walked over and sat down next to him like a friend.

"How are you feeling, Harry?" Rose Marie asked and put her hands on top of his.

"Oh, you know, doc, right as rain," Harry said and smiled at her.

"I received a report on your lab work and we talked about this before we drew blood," she began.

Harry smiled and squeezed her hands. "You know, doc, I think it's time I went home, back to England. I have a few loose ends that need to be tied up before I take that final jump."

She smiled. "You never cease to amaze me."

"I've had a good life, no complaints, no regrets; and there are friends waiting for me," Harry said and stood up. "It's been nice knowing you, doc. You're a straight shooter and I've always appreciated that."

Rose Marie stood and hugged Harry. "I'll write you a prescription for pain and . . . "

"Nope, that's okay, got all I need at home," Harry said.

"Is there anything I can do for you?" she asked.

"Find a cure," Harry said.

Penthouse
Honolulu
7:00 p.m.

Taylor had spent the day reading through the information on Jace Kindle. Most of what was with the photographs was work history, the reason she had been chosen for a possible interview, her specialty, et cetera, everything except what he needed, like where she was working now. He had sent Eric to trace down family, friends, anyone that might know her and where he could find her. Taylor looked up as the front door opened.

"Hello Harry, did you win at bingo?" Taylor asked.

"No, not today. Say, you and that brother of yours going to be around Thanksgiving?" Harry asked.

"Hadn't made any plans, why?"

"I'm going to be gone for a while and wanted to make sure you two would be okay without me," Harry said and helped himself to a beer from the fridge.

"Sure, something wrong?" Taylor asked.

"I've been needing to go see some friends and thought now would be the best time. You two back here safe and all," Harry said and gave Taylor a beer.

"We'll be fine. How long will you be gone?"

"Few weeks, maybe a month. You know how family and friends are when you haven't been there in a while," Harry said.

"We'll take you to the airport, how's that?"

"Don't want to put you to any trouble now," Harry said.

"No trouble, you're family," Taylor said and they clinked bottles.

"I thought you might want to call that G-man and visit now that you're feeling better," Harry said and gave Taylor the card Ron had left. "He's a good guy."

"I'll give him a call," Taylor said.

"Well, gonna head home and watch TV for a while," Harry said and started toward the door.

"Harry, got a question," Taylor said.

Harry stopped and turned around. "Shoot."

"Why are you called Bulldog?"

Harry smiled and left the penthouse.

Harry walked into his apartment and looked around. He had had a good life, good friends, and memories, but all things end. There was business to take care of at home. He made a phone call to the airlines and booked a first-class, one-way ticket home to London. Harry had a niece that had kept in contact with him through the years. She had said there would always be a room for him there, and now he would take her invitation. He always knew he would go home to die. That's where the rest of his buddies were and that's where he wanted to be. He went to the closet and pulled out a suitcase and placed it in the corner of his bedroom. Harry decided to watch TV and visit his buddies. He went to the kitchen, got a beer, took out the scrapbook, and thought again about that frigid night in France so many years ago. Before falling asleep in the oversized chair he loved so much, he took the photograph of a bride and groom from the back of the album. He needed to get this to Taylor. It belonged with the rest of the Bowen history.

❦

NSA, Conference Room
Maryland
11:00 p.m.

Zack was reading over Aaron's reports from his assignments overseas. She heard footsteps in the hallway and knew they were Bevan's. She began to speak as he walked into the room.

"I know I'll go home soon," Zack said.

"Zack, your abilities continue to improve. Where's Blain?" Bevan asked.

"Sent him home around seven. His mind hasn't been focused the past few days," Zack said.

"Oh?"

"Her name is Lyssa. He needs to get that situation tended to before we have any interaction with Aaron. He can't be thinking of anything or anyone else when we find him," Zack said.

"You think you can find him?" Bevan said.

"Of course, that's why you brought me back, isn't it?" Zack said and smiled. "The major concern for me is that this man has no conscience, and that is going to cause issues for me."

"Explain," Bevan said and sat down.

"The people that I connect with have emotions, pain, fear, love, anger. My gift allows me to understand and hold those emotions. It gives me an edge, so to speak. This man has nothing. No family, no love, he uses and moves on without thought to what he has done," Zack said.

"Yes, I am aware of all of that," Bevan said.

"I'm not sure I'll be able to connect directly to him. I'll have to use the people around him, and any thought control will probably not work," Zack told him.

"I knew this could be an issue," Bevan said.

"But, from what you have said about his friends and connections here, I'm hoping to obtain information from those individuals. I will need freedom to roam the building. Can you get that for me?" Zack asked.

"I'll make some calls but I don't see a problem. You should be able to start by the end of the week. As for Blain, I'll talk to him if things don't settle in the next week," Bevan said.

"If he doesn't put his personal life aside it could get him or me killed. Where did you find this man?" Zack asked and tapped Aaron's photograph.

"That information I can't give you right now, but I will when the time is appropriate," Bevan said and stood up.

"I know. I'll follow you out," Zack told Bevan and closed the file on Aaron.

"Will we see you in Waynesboro next week?" Bevan asked.

"Yes, my entire family is coming. It's funny but there is the wonderful feeling of joy surrounding this holiday. Not just because of Ethaniel and DeAnna but it seems things are coming full circle," Zack said.

"Funny, I was just about to say the same thing."

Chapter Forty~Nine ❧

Eric took Harry's luggage out of the taxi. Harry tried to lighten the conversation, talking about his family and friends. He couldn't bring himself to tell them he wouldn't be coming back. Harry had grown attached to them like family and it wasn't good to lie to family.

"Harry, are you sure there isn't anything we need to do while you're gone?" Taylor asked.

"No, no, I've made arrangements with the owners to have a temporary manager come to the office and take care of everything," Harry said.

"Old man, I'll be expecting a gift when you come back," Eric said and patted Harry on the shoulder.

"I left you two gifts," Harry said and smiled.

"Well you're just full of surprises," Eric said.

"I left it with the album collection," Harry responded.

"What is it?" Taylor asked.

"Wouldn't be a surprise if I told you!" Harry laughed.

"Guess you better go get in line. It looks like this might take a while," Taylor said.

"I got time and enough to read," Harry said and held up the magazines with Taylor's articles and Eric's photographs from Baghdad. "Oh, can I get you to sign this before I go? My niece asked. She's somewhat of a fan."

"Taylor, we're famous," Eric said and signed the magazine, then handed it to Taylor.

"Thanks." Harry walked over and hugged both men. "I'll see you down the road," Harry said, then turned and headed toward the long line.

"What was that all about?" Eric asked Taylor.

"I don't know," Taylor said and tried to shake the feeling he would never see Harry again.

Both men headed out to get a taxi. "Eric, did you find anything for me on Jace?" Taylor asked.

"I have information coming to the office, but it's going to be after the holiday," Eric said.

"Why so long?"

"When this story about travel nurses was first initiated, emails were sent to thousands of travel companies across the US. The files on theses nurses have been cut down six or seven times before they were selected for interviews. It's my understanding they are some of the best in their specialties. My boss said they have to hunt down the companies and request the information from their recruiters. It's going to take some time," Eric said.

"I guess I can wait."

"How about breakfast while we're out?"

"We need to get back. I called Agent Edwards and he'll be at our place in about an hour. Besides, I prefer your cooking."

"Yeah, you're right. I am a good cook, outstanding at times."

"And humble," Taylor interrupted him.

"I want to see what Harry left us," Eric said.

"Harry's a cool old man. Did I tell you I asked him how he got the name Bulldog?" Taylor asked.

"What'd he say?"

"Nothing, just smiled and walked away."

Eric went straight to the kitchen once they arrived home and began to prepare something "wonderful," as he put it to Taylor. Taylor took the remote and hit play. He was heading to the bedroom to find Harry's gift when the intercom buzzed.

"You're being paged, Taylor," Eric called out.

Taylor walked over and pressed the button. "Agent Edwards?"

"Yes."

"Come up to the penthouse. I'll let you off the elevator once you arrive," Taylor said.

"On my way."

"Eric, make enough for three. I have a feeling this is going to take a little time."

"Not a problem. I hope he likes *migas*."

Taylor walked to the elevator and waited. Once the elevator stopped, he opened the door with his key. Ron Edwards walked off and showed Taylor his credentials. Taylor shook his hand.

"Nice to meet you," Taylor said as they entered the penthouse.

As Ron entered the penthouse he heard 1940s music being played. "Artie Shaw?"

"Yes, our uncle was quite a fan. Artie Shaw, Glen Miller, the list goes on, his collection is massive."

Eric walked over and shook hands. "Hungry?"

"It smells pretty good to me."

"We'll eat out on the balcony," Eric said.

Ron walked by the dining room table and looked at all the pictures. "What's all this?"

"My next assignment," Eric said.

Ron stopped and picked up a photograph. "What is Jace Bowen's photograph doing in all this?"

"Who?" Taylor asked.

Ron handed the photograph to him. "Jace Bowen. Why do you have her picture?"

"It says Kindle."

"Kindle was her married name; she's divorced and took back her maiden name. This is Jace Bowen, related to the Bowens in Waynesboro."

Taylor looked at Eric. "Ron, I hope you don't have any other business today. I think this is going to take a while to explain."

"The day is yours, but Jace Bowen is not the reason I'm here. My visit involves your brother and a man named Aaron Reece Caydon."

Morning turned to afternoon, then into evening at the penthouse. Ron called his wife and told her he would be late and asked her not to wait up. Eric fixed two more meals after breakfast. The beauty of the day helped with the unpleasant information about their brother and his connection with ARC Investigations.

"Ron, we both knew that Sherman's death had to do with money. We were also aware of checks written to ARC Investigations," Taylor said.

"Sherman's ambitions knew no boundaries apparently," Eric said.

"If he had just waited, I would have sold him the paper."

"Patience was never a quality he admired."

"I believe he may have wanted a political future of some kind," Ron said. "What I would like now is for you two to look at these photographs of Aaron and tell me if you recognize him or have seen him here."

Taylor and Eric looked at the photographs of Aaron. Eric looked at Taylor. "We have something to show you," Taylor said.

Eric grabbed a file from his briefcase. "These are pictures of Danfield Williams, probably Aaron Caydon."

"I have the same copies from Harry," Ron said.

"Neither of us have had direct contact with him and I hope I never do," Eric said.

"We believe he has gained information about your uncle's estate here in Honolulu."

"Well, I have no access to whatever has been left to me until I complete the provisions of the will."

"So, you need to find Jace in order to complete your uncle's will, is that correct?" Ron asked.

"Yes, I have some things that need to be returned to her family. Uncle Larry's last novel is basically complete and I have begun to gather information on the Bowen and White family history," Taylor said.

Eric went to the fridge and pulled out three beers. "Ron, I think it's time you were off the clock."

"Agreed," Ron said and took a beer. "Where's Bulldog? He's quite the character."

"We put him on a plane to England this morning," Eric said.

"England, you say? Do either of you know anything about him?" Ron asked.

"No, but give me a minute—he left something for us. I haven't had time to get it," Taylor said, then headed toward his bedroom.

Ron waited until Taylor returned with a package.

"Did Harry ever say anything about being in the war?" Ron asked.

"No, he never talked about much other than how Uncle Larry got him the job here at the condos," Taylor said and began to open the package.

"Well, after I was here the first time I did a little research on Harry Hawthorne. He was born in London and came to America after the war. He has dual citizenship. It appears he was a member of a group called the Jedburghs during WWII. Most of what I found was classified. I was able to get information about a jump he and the team made behind German-occupied lands. He was injured after landing, shot actually. It's my understanding he was patched up and finished his mission. Apparently that's where he earned his nickname," Ron said.

"Damn, tough old bird," Eric said.

Taylor was listening to the conversation but was more interested in the contents of the package.

"Taylor, what did Harry leave us?"

"The story of his life," Taylor said and then laid the book on the table for them to see. Harry had documented his life from the time he entered the military through the end of the war, his citizenship ceremony in Honolulu, and finally Harry's association with Eric and Taylor.

"Who's the woman with the curly hair?" Ron asked. He then looked at the picture closer. "She's wearing allied clothing and insignias."

Eric took the photo out of the corners that held it in place and turned it over. "I don't believe this."

"What?" Ron asked.

"All the names are back here, including Frank Bowen and a Deelyn Keens," Eric said and looked at Taylor.

"More Bowens?" Taylor said.

"Yes."

"In Uncle Larry's manuscript he talks about two people who were secretly married in France during the war. He never gave their names," Taylor said and smiled.

"I can tell you that Frank Bowen was a captain whose B-17 was shot down over German territory. He and his men were involved for some time helping the Maquis. Frank Bowen is from Waynesboro. After the war he and his wife, Deelyn, moved to San Antonio," Ron told them.

"You seem to have a lot of information," Taylor said.

"The Bowens have a lot of history. Most of it very interesting, even back to the Civil War," Ron told them.

"What's that?" Eric asked Taylor.

"There's a letter," Taylor said, then opened and read the letter.

Eric waited a few minutes. "What's it say?"

"What I suspected. Harry won't be coming back," Taylor said and handed Eric the letter.

"Sick?" Ron asked.

"Yes, it appears he has gone home to die," Taylor said.

"Why didn't he tell us?" Eric asked and sniffed.

"Probably didn't want you two to worry," Ron said.

"He said he fulfilled his promise to Uncle Larry," Taylor said.

"Gonna miss him, damn it," Eric said and wiped the corner of his eye.

"I hope his family will notify us," Taylor said.

"If you don't hear from him by Christmas, I'll see what I can do," Ron said.

"Thank you, he's become family," Taylor said.

Eric was looking through the book when a photograph wrapped in tissue slid out. Eric gently opened it.

"It's her! Taylor look at this." Eric's voice was trembling.

"Who?" Taylor said and took the picture.

"The woman in that picture is the woman that warned me of the bombing in Baghdad," Eric said.

"Can't be, this is dated 1860 something . . . can't make it out," Taylor said and handed the picture to Ron.

Ron turned the photograph over. "It says Bowen wedding, James and Martha."

"Taylor, what the hell is going on?" Eric asked.

"I don't know, Eric. Ron, do you know where Jace is working or living?" Taylor asked.

"I have a number I'm supposed to give you. I believe you will be able to contact her there," Ron said and gave him the number from Bevan.

"Excuse me," Taylor said and walked into the house and opened his cell phone.

Ron leaned back and looked at the ocean. "You guys have a gorgeous place."

"Not me, this all belongs to Taylor. I'm just along for the ride," Eric said and smiled.

Taylor walked back out on the balcony.

"Well, did you talk to her?" Eric asked.

"No, it was a number to the Jolly Roger B&B. Apparently she is one of the owners?"

"Did you leave a message?"

"No, I want to check something first."

"Well gentlemen, I need to go; wife and children, you know," Ron said.

"Come back anytime and bring your family," Taylor said.

"I may do that. You two need to be careful. We believe Aaron is trying to further his financial empire. You have just inherited a multimillion-dollar business, and the opportunity to obtain more Shaw money will be very tempting. I'm going to leave this picture of him."

Eric and Taylor walked Ron to the elevator. "Keep my number handy and call if you have any problems or information. Even if it appears small or unimportant to you, it could lead us to him."

The three shook hands again and Taylor locked the elevator door once it closed. He returned to the penthouse and turned on the computer.

"What are you doing?" Eric asked.

"I need to see if this Jolly Roger has a website," Taylor said.

Eric walked up and looked over his shoulder. "Well, this is interesting."

Both men watched as the website showed the location, rooms, and a lovely view of the sunset off the canal. Taylor was more interested in the owners and held his breath as the picture of Jace and a set of twins appeared. Taylor started typing.

"What are you doing?" Eric asked.

"Making a reservation."

"Guess I'd better pack, never been to Galveston," Eric said and headed to his room.

Taylor quickly checked for open dates and booked them. He then booked their flight and car rental. Eric returned to the main room.

"When do we leave?"

"Sunday night. It appears the only seats open are first class; everything is booked due to Thanksgiving," Taylor said and rubbed his forehead.

"Sweet!" Eric said. "What's wrong, bro?"

"Every time I get close, something blocks my path."

"You didn't honestly think it would be easy, did you?" Eric asked.

"Well, so far it has been interesting," Taylor said.

"Maybe she will know who the woman is in the old photograph."

"We need to take everything with us," Taylor said, then stood and walked out on the balcony and sat down. He felt the weight of the necklace next to his heart. He looked at the cast on his arm. He hoped his appointment in the morning would be his reprieve, but the chances were slim. At least he didn't have to wear the sling anymore. Taylor had never been one to take pain medications and had stopped after returning to Hawaii. He had adapted to typing with only four fingers. The mind was an amazing thing. It was like he had never had a thumb.

Eric followed Taylor outside and handed him a beer. "I've been overloaded with way too much information today, what about you?"

"Agreed."

"What's bothering you, Taylor?" Eric asked.

"I can't wrap my thoughts around everything right now—Sherman, Caydon, Jace, your mystery woman, Uncle Larry's will, and all this," Taylor said and waved his hand at the penthouse.

"Well, hopefully Jace will be in Galveston and we can get some answers."

"I hope she has them."

Chapter Fifty ❧

Aaron drove into the RV park pulling a small Airstream trailer with an ATV in the bed of the truck. He was far enough away from Waynesboro, and with it being late season there would be few campers. He didn't need anyone trying to be friendly. His contacts at the NSA had told him Bevan was going home for the holidays this year. Now seemed a perfect time to have a conversation with his mentor and encourage him strongly to stop pursuing him. He looked in the rearview mirror and checked his disguise. This one seemed comfortable; it was new and no one knew this alias. He had a long graying wig with one braid down the center of his back, American flag bandana tied around his head, scruffy beard, and moustache. He wore an army jacket; he had added a fat suit, which he covered with fatigues and his own combat boots. Aaron had made sure the NRA sticker was displayed for all to see along with his rifle in the rack behind his seat. Aaron looked up as an older man exited the office. He stepped out to greet him.

"Howdy, I'm Dudley Sikes, owner and manager," he said and held out his hand.

"Gordon Morres, retired from the world," Aaron said in a gruff voice and shook hands.

"We don't get many travelers this time of year but you're welcome. You can pick whichever spot you'd like—everything is open.

I have a few coming in tomorrow; most are on their way to family for the holidays. But first come first served, I always say," Dudley said and laughed.

"I'd like something in the back, close to the trees. I'm a solitary individual and like my privacy, if you get my meaning?" Aaron said and winked.

"Not a problem. Got a spot in mind. Come in and we'll get you signed in and settled," Dudley said.

"Right behind you," Aaron said and watched Dudley go back inside. He looked around, getting his bearings and as always watching. "This'll do."

Aaron signed in with his new alias and gave Dudley a handful of cash, which he quickly put in his pocket. He gave Aaron a map, marked the spot, and gave him instructions on the hook-up.

"No one will bother you back there, and unless you need something you're good for two weeks. I'm heading into Augusta in a bit, you need anything?" Dudley asked.

"No, and if I need something I'll come to you," Aaron said. He left the office and drove to the spot he had rented. Once everything had been hooked up and the ATV taken off the truck, he locked himself in the Airstream and shed the disguise. He had sketched a map of the land surrounding the B&B and the Benjamins' home when he had been there as Bud Johnson. People were such fools, and that made obtaining information much simpler for him. Bevan's father had given him a tour of their land and the Long Bowe B&B. He would take a trip tonight and recon. He intended to confront Bevan but timing would be everything. Family and friends all around would keep Bevan from attempting something foolish. Aaron grinned. *Always to my advantage, even on enemy soil.* Now he would rest, and once the sun set he would go play in the darkness.

ả

AUGUSTA GEORGIA AIRPORT
NOON

Jace sat in the concourse waiting for the plane that carried Zack, Bevan, and his fiancée, Laura. She was excited about the next few days, especially the chance to connect with family again. The twins were understanding and encouraged her to come even though the Jolly Roger was booked through Monday. Jace watched families coming and going, smiles, hugs, and tears. Many travelers were having some difficulty with the new restrictions but most understood the necessity and extra security. Jace heard the announcement of the plane she was waiting on. She stood and began to look for Zack, just like the rest of the people waiting for loved ones to appear.

"Jace!" Zack ran up and hugged her.

"Where's Bevan?"

"They're right behind me," Zack said.

Laura and Bevan appeared in the main terminal. "Jace, it's good to see you again. Laura, this is Jace Bowen," Bevan said.

The two women greeted each other and all proceeded to get luggage and head home. Jace had borrowed the Long Bowe van instead of the jeep. Conversation was general about family while on the road to Waynesboro.

Jace handed Zack the directions back to Waynesboro as they drove out of the airport. She drove up to the stoplight. "Your parents are here."

"I know, mother called me three times yesterday and . . . " Zack said, then stopped mid-sentence.

"Zack, what?" Bevan asked.

"Not sure . . . it was too fast. I need to think a minute," Zack said. *Money, ATV,* her only thoughts. She then looked out the window at the older man in the truck next to them. He drove off before she could read the sign on the door.

"Jace, anyone new in the area, any strangers been to the house?" Bevan asked.

"No, all family. I've been watching," Jace said.

"Maybe it's just someone's thought with the holidays, Bevan," Laura said.

"We're all a little jumpy," Bevan said.

Jace drove on to Waynesboro listening to the directions Zack was giving her. She missed the turn to the Benjamin house.

"Jace, I think you need to turn around; that was the road," Bevan said.

"Damn it! I was hoping I wouldn't miss it," Jace said.

"Jace, don't let Bevan kid you. He still misses the turn, too," Laura said.

Bill and Donna were waiting outside when they drove up. "Zack, Jace, it's so good to see you two again," Donna said and hugged both of them. She then kissed Bevan and Laura. Bill took their luggage and went inside with Laura.

"Donna, we need to run," Jace said.

"Denise called and gave me the times for tomorrow and Saturday. We're all looking forward to this. I hope you two will come and spend at least one evening with us," Donna said.

"We'll try," Jace said.

"Mother, I'll be a moment," Bevan said.

"See you tomorrow, ladies," Donna said and went inside.

Bevan walked Jace and Zack back to the van.

"Be watchful, both of you. Zack, you need to stay close to Jace this weekend; and see if you can put that thought together—it could be important," Bevan said.

"I will," Zack said.

"I'll get what you need when we get back. The holidays stopped me from getting you the clearance. I don't believe it will be a problem. Do you have a weapon?" Bevan asked.

Jace laughed. "Are you kidding? Every vehicle at the Long Bowe has at least one gun in the back window."

Zack smiled. "I'm good."

Bill stood in the door and watched the exchange between his son and the two young women. He grabbed two glasses and a bottle of wine, then walked outside to his oldest son.

"Here, try this," Bill said and handed Bevan a glass of wine. "Thanks."

"Things a little stressful, I understand," Bill said.

"That's putting it mildly," Bevan said and took a drink. "This is good, and I'm surprised—you don't usually drink white."

"Something I just added to my collection, it's from Texas; I believe Jace called it Rkatsiteli," Bill said.

"Dad, do me a favor, don't walk the dogs after dark and don't go alone while we're all home," Bevan said.

Bill looked at his son. "Normally I would say you're overreacting, but since I know who you work for and the climate since 9-11, if I go, you or Blain can go with me. You know where the gun locker is and the code to get in it."

"Thanks, that makes me feel better," Bevan said and looked up as Laura came outside. She had changed into a pair of yoga pants and red turtleneck sweater.

"Son, you better marry that woman before someone takes her away from you," Bill said.

"It's not me, it's her. I'd marry her tomorrow but . . . " Bevan said.

"What's going on?" Laura asked.

"Just telling Bevan how lucky he is," Bill said and kissed Laura on her cheek. Then he headed back inside.

"Bevan, go change. I want to go for a walk," Laura told him.

"Yes, ma'am," Bevan said and both walked back to the house. "I'll be back in a minute. Don't leave without me."

Laura sat on the steps of the house and waited for Bevan. It was so peaceful here. She loved coming home with him. The air was clean; the only noise was children playing or dogs barking at each other or the laughter of family. The door opened and she looked up. She loved to see him in his jeans and a sweatshirt.

"I'm ready. Where do you want to go?" Bevan asked.

"Nowhere particular. I need to talk to you about something," she said.

"Sounds serious," Bevan smiled and they started out toward the pond.

She smiled back at him. "I wouldn't call it serious, but a decision that involves both of us. I'm considering resigning from the firm. I want something a little slower paced, less tense. We seem to have enough of that in our lives right now."

"Well, this is a surprise," Bevan said.

"I found a small office close to your house. There are only three attorneys there and they need one more. I wouldn't be working late every night and only an occasional weekend. I can sell my place and move in with you. Save some money," Laura told him.

"Who are you trying to convince?" Bevan said and stopped. "You can do anything you want as long as you stay in my life."

"Then I'll write my letter effective January 1. I still have two cases to finish," Laura said.

Bevan hugged and kissed her. "I'll tell General Lee when we get home. He'll be as happy as I am."

LONG BOWE B&B
1:30 P.M.

Zack's parents were outside visiting with family when they drove up. Jace stood by as Zack greeted her family and conversed between Spanish and French. She was amazing. Jace looked at all the family that had gathered and was a little sad her parents couldn't come.

"Zack, I have your family staying in the guest house down the road," Denise said. "I thought you might want to stay here with Jace."

Zack said something in Spanish to her mother and she nodded. "That's perfect."

"Everyone, come inside—there's food on the tables," Denise said.

Jace watched Daniel wave and music started. Family moved outside in, where a feast was waiting. Laughter could be heard throughout the house. There were local wines, hot food, meats, desserts—anything you could dream of was here. Jace could not imagine what tomorrow or Saturday would be like. She watched Ethaniel and DeAnna. It was nice to see two people in love. She thought about her life and wondered if she would ever find someone to love again. Jace sat in a corner of the main room and wondered what life had been like here for Sarah.

"This very gathering probably took place and, yes, you will find someone to love," Zack said to Jace.

"Mind reader."

"Guilty," Zack said and laughed.

"Zack, I have something to show you later when this all settles down," Jace said. She smiled as the children ran by them.

"You think all this will settle down before midnight?" Zack laughed.

"Probably not, but it's nothing that can't wait. Did you ever make sense of the thought you heard?" Jace asked.

"No. This gift has a mind of its own sometimes," Zack said and looked up.

"What?" Jace asked.

Zack smiled. "Mother needs me. She can't think of the right words."

"Go. I'll see you later," Jace said and headed back to the table for seconds.

❦

RV Park
8:00 p.m.

Aaron stood in the Airstream assessing his needs for the night. There would be little moonlight this evening, which was to his advantage. The military gave him all the things he needed to survive, and tonight was his favorite type of mission: search, prepare, and wait. If you were a patient person, what you needed, wanted, would always present itself, and Aaron was very patient. He looked out the window and then exited the Airstream. Aaron pushed the ATV to the back where he had found a trail before nightfall. He mapped these trails and found a place to hide the ATV about three miles from the Benjamin home.

❦

BENJAMIN HOME
9:00 P.M.

Bevan walked outside and sat down on the large porch. He had been uneasy since the trip in from the airport. His talk with Blain before dinner had not gone as he had hoped, but he felt Blain now understood what was at stake. Dinner had been nice this evening and he was actually looking forward to the next few days connecting with extended family. He looked at his watch and thought about calling Ron to see how his visit went with the Shaw brothers, but thought about his walk and conversation with Laura. For once he would put work away and put his family and the woman he loved first. He looked up as Laura walked out the door with a bottle of wine.

"I always eat too much when we come home. Bill sent me out with the Rkatsiteli, said you seemed to enjoy it earlier this afternoon," she said.

Bevan smiled. "I'll take another glass, please."

Laura filled his glass and then sat down in his lap. "Did you call Ron?"

"No, and whatever is happening will have to wait until Tuesday," Bevan said and kissed her.

"The new Bevan Benjamin?"

"For the next few days anyway," he said.

The door opened and Betty and Marilyn came outside followed by Bill. "I hate to break this up but I could use some company."

Laura stood up, taking her glass and the bottle with her. "We'll be upstairs when you're done."

"Give me a minute, Dad."

Bevan went in, opened the lock box, took out a Glock, put in a clip, and chambered a round. He put the gun in his waistband and walked back out. "Ready."

"Smart man, Bevan," Aaron said. He had been watching the conversation between Bevan and his lady. Aaron knew Bevan had gone inside to arm himself. Aaron would wait until everyone had gone to bed, then reacquaint himself with the Benjamin home and property. The dogs would not be a problem; he had a special touch with animals—always had, since childhood. He took off the night vision goggles and leaned against the tree. He had time for a quick nap.

LONG BOWE
11:30 P.M.

Jace had helped to clear the tables and loaded one of the two large dishwashers in the kitchen. She had enjoyed talking with everyone and watched as Denise and Daniel prepared the turkeys.

"I don't know how you two do it, but I'm glad you do," Jace said.

"Jace, thanks for all your help tonight with dishes and the children. You've been a blessing today," Denise said.

"Not a problem," Jace said.

"Jace, did Taylor ever call you?" Daniel asked.

"No, but Bevan has a friend in Hawaii that is supposed to give him my name and number," Jace said.

Zack walked in at that moment. "What can I do to help?"

"You two go to bed. The next few days are going to be busy," Denise said and hugged them. "Daniel and I will be up early getting these birds in the ovens. Now go, get to bed."

Zack and Jace headed up to their room. "I didn't think I was tired until we started up these stairs," Jace said.

"What did you want to show me?" Zack asked.

"It'll wait until breakfast," Jace answered.

WOODS NEAR BENJAMIN HOME
MIDNIGHT

The sound of leaves moving woke Aaron. He sat motionless for a moment until he realized it was only a deer that had come to drink near the pond. As he prepared to leave his hiding spot he checked again with his night goggles for any movement inside the Benjamin home. Satisfied, he began his way to the house, entered without difficulty, and began his search. He placed a number of listening devices in family areas so he could time his meeting alone with Bevan. He had no interest in the majority of the family in the house. He was, however, interested in Bevan's nephew who had just returned from Baghdad. Aaron stood and looked at him while he slept. He would send for records on this Benjamin when he returned to the Airstream. Aaron took a memento from this young man's room. He would see how well he had been trained. Aaron then entered Bevan's room. He stood and looked at his mentor and the beautiful woman sleeping in his arms. He smiled and then removed the watch lying on the nightstand next to her. Aaron entered the kitchen, helped himself to leftover chicken and pie, then made his way to the wine cellar and removed two bottles that Bill had shared with Bud. Bevan's father had good taste. He left the house as he had entered, gave the dogs their treats, and disappeared into the trees. It was a quick three-mile hike to his ATV.

Chapter Fifty~One

The morning came all too soon. The smell of fresh sheets and lilacs had put her to sleep, but now Jace was beginning to stir under the covers and could smell fresh coffee and muffins. She pulled the covers off her head and looked at Zack smiling and pointing to the table.

"You really aren't a morning person, are you?"

"Pardon my French but screw you and morning," Jace said.

"Where's the pictures you were going to show me last night and didn't?" Zack asked.

"You really have to stop, it's way too creepy," Jace said and smiled. "Where's the creamer?" She sat up and reached for the small pitcher Zack was handing her. Jace fixed her coffee and took a long drink. "What time is it?"

"Seven thirty," Zack said.

"I'm going to kill you."

"Careful, remember who I work for," Zack said and both women laughed. "Denise had muffins made so I brought our breakfast up here."

"Thanks, I guess I won't kill you after all," Jace said and got up to find the pictures and magazine Bevan had given her. "I want you to look at all of this."

Zack took the pictures and spread them on her bed.

"I haven't had a chance to tell you what happened to me in Gettysburg," Jace said and proceeded to tell Zack about the man and the story about her aunt Sarah. "The man in the picture at Gettysburg looks like the man in the magazine."

Zack had seen the photograph of Taylor but could not discuss it with Jace. "What else happened to you in Gettysburg?"

"I heard things like horses in full charge, I smelled smoke from guns . . . and then I bought this." Jace took out the blue checkered dress that matched the one Sarah had worn. "Zack, what's happening to me?" Jace asked.

"Jace, whether we realize it or want to accept it, we are tied to the past, especially where family is concerned. You have a gift," Zack said.

"No, I don't think so," Jace laughed.

"Yes, you have ignored it and tried to pretend it isn't there. Listen to what is around you. Don't deny what you know to be true; accept and embrace it. Where's her necklace?" Zack asked.

"It's missing," Jace said. She then told Zack the last thing Samuel told her about the heart.

"They're lost."

"Yes," Jace said.

"We have to find the heart," Zack said.

"I don't think anyone in the family has it. And if they do, how do I ask for it?" Jace asked.

"I can use my gift to eavesdrop on family," Zack said and smiled.

"Just see if anyone here today might know anything about it. I'll bring it up in general conversation," Jace said.

Zack smiled. "I need to practice."

BILL AND DONNA BENJAMIN RESIDENCE
8:00 A.M.

Donna had been up since six preparing food to take to Denise's and a simple breakfast for her family. When she started coffee this morning she found a plate and fork left on the bar. She thought nothing about it and placed it in the dishwasher and started the load left from last night.

"Good morning, my love," Bill said and kissed his wife. "Coffee ready?"

"Almost. Did you get up last night and have a snack?"

"No," Bill said.

"Guess it was one of the boys then," Donna said.

"That or one of the grandchildren. Come on, ladies, let's go for a walk," Bill said and took the dogs out.

One by one the Benjamin household came to life. Everyone began to prepare for the day at the Long Bowe and to celebrate.

"Laura, Mom made breakfast," Bevan said and walked into his bedroom. "What are you looking for?"

"My watch. I could have sworn I put it on the nightstand last night when we went to bed," she said.

"It's here, we'll find it later," Bevan said.

"Now this is a thought, no watch and you not worried about work. Who are you and what have you done with the real Bevan Benjamin?" Laura said and laughed.

"Sometimes change is good," Bevan said. He kissed her and they left to join the rest of the family for breakfast.

RV Park
8:00 a.m.

Aaron lay in his bed and listened to the morning conversations taking place at the Benjamin house. He was interested in Blain Benjamin's file from NSA. Aaron was impressed with Blain's scores but obviously they had not been good enough to graduate first in his class. Bevan would bring in someone fresh to find him, someone like his nephew. Aaron was interested in who surpassed

Blain. That individual would be someone he would have to be concerned about, someone he might have to kill. He looked at the items he took from the Benjamins. The watch had already been missed but assumed misplaced. The signed baseball in the case should be a no-brainer. He would return them but not the wine. He enjoyed a nice Bordeaux. Bill Benjamin's choices were outstanding. Later today he would grill a steak and enjoy the wine; it would be a nice Thanksgiving after all.

Long Bowe B&B
1:00 p.m.

Due to the large gathering, the barn had been turned into the dining hall for today's dinner. No one on either side of the family could remember a time when so many people had come home. Daniel had been waiting for the few stragglers to come in and whistled for everyone's attention.

"I want to thank everyone that has flown, driven, or walked to our home today. We have all tried to remember a time when the family had been together en masse as we are today. And the only time we can think of is when Frank Bowen brought his bride Deelyn Keens home. It's been far too long since family has gathered together. We hope today will be the beginning of something good and a tradition," Daniel said. The crowd clapped and yells went out.

"Now, if you will join hands with the person next to you, we'll say grace." One by one family members big and small held hands, forming one continuous line, back to Daniel where the circle was completed with Denise.

"We thank you, God, for your blessing of home and family, for the bounty you have given us. We ask that your love and peace be here today for all family past, present, and future. Amen."

Multiple amens were heard throughout the barn.

"Let's eat, folks!" And at that moment the music started and the feasting began.

Jace filled her plate and sat with Zack and her family. She had talked to so many family members she lost count.

"Anything?" Zack asked her.

"No one remembers her ever having a necklace. Denise didn't even remember it in the photograph she gave me. The main thing all the family remembers is the journal," Jace said. "What about you?"

"Nothing about the necklace, but there is some interesting information about moonshine and back taxes," Zack said and both women laughed.

"I don't think anyone here has it. There's a possibility it was buried with her," Jace said.

"No, I don't think so," Zack said. "Hello Blain."

"I wish you would stop that," Blain said as he walked around a stack of hay.

"This is Jace," she said.

Jace stood and shook hands. "Zack has told me a lot about you, Blain."

"I'm sure she has; most of it isn't true," he said and smiled.

"Ladies, good to see you," Bill said.

"I was looking for one of your good wines on the beverage table today," Jace said.

"Well, I had two reds to bring—a Bordeaux and a nice Merlot I just discovered—but apparently I've given them away. They weren't there this morning when I checked the cellar for them," Bill said.

"Pity, you have great taste," Jace said.

"Flattery will get you invited to the house for wine and cheese. Tomorrow night, sevenish," Bill said.

"We'll be there," Zack said.

"No poker, unless Zack sits out," Blain said.

"Now that's not nice," Bevan said. "Dad, did I hear you say you were missing wine?"

"Not a big deal, probably gave it to someone at the clinic," Bill answered.

"Is Laura having a good time?" Jace asked.

"Yes, and we're looking forward to the celebration for E. and DeAnna Saturday," Bevan said. "This has been wonderful for our family."

"Ours, too," Zack said. "Papa has found family he hasn't seen in years."

"How is your mother doing?" Bevan asked.

"She found some family that speaks Spanish. She has made new friends for life," Zack said.

"Full circle," Bevan said.

"Almost," Jace responded.

Chapter Fifty~Two ❧

The day had started early, cleaning inside and out in order to get the barn ready for Ethaniel and DeAnna's engagement party Saturday. Jace and Zack didn't make the eight a.m. call but showed up about nine thirty and began to clean and make preparations, as family should, to help.

"I hope the weather holds and we have a good turnout tomorrow night," Zack said.

"Is your family going to stay?" Jace asked.

"Yes, they want to take me to the airport Monday and then they'll head home. Bevan got me and Blain an extra day."

"Wonderful."

"What about you?"

"I have a wedding in D.C. on the fifteenth so I'm going to stay here for a week or so, then head north."

"Ladies, you're needed inside; Denise said something about polishing silver," Daniel said.

Jace and Zack looked at each other. "Silver polishing? I haven't done that since I was nine years old," Jace said. "I thought this was going to be casual."

"Well, at my house I polished silver once a week until I went to college. We need to hurry. The Benjamins are expecting us at seven," Zack said.

"I'll put on, you wipe off," Jace said.

"Right, give me the hardest part."

BILL AND DONNA BENJAMIN RESIDENCE
6:30 P.M.

Bevan stood on the porch and watched Laura play with his sister's children. *She would make a good mother*, he thought, then turned around when Blain walked outside.

"Have you seen my baseball?" he asked.

"Your Mickey Mantle?" Bevan asked.

"Yes."

"It should be where it's always been."

"It's gone."

Bevan went in and checked. He and Blain went through every corner of the room. "Don't say anything to your grandfather just yet."

RV PARK

Aaron sat drinking a glass of the Merlot he had taken, listening to Bevan and his nephew looking for the baseball. He smiled.

"It took you long enough to discover it was gone. Not the brightest star in the sky," he said and left the Airstream for supplies.

Jace pulled her truck up to the Benjamins. Zack got out and stopped. She looked across to the line of trees. Jace noticed.

"What's wrong?"

"Someone's been here that doesn't belong," Zack said and turned around as Bevan and Blain walked outside. Zack held up her hand and then put a finger to her lips. Both men walked to Jace's truck.

"Bevan, any chance you can get your family to leave for about an hour?" Zack asked.

"Tell me," Bevan said.

"Someone was here last night and not family. I need to check your house," Zack said.

"Bevan, let me call Denise," Jace said and opened her cell phone.

"Blain, what are you missing?" Zack asked.

"Collector baseball signed by Mickey Mantle," Blain answered.

"What else is missing from the house?" she asked.

"Laura's watch and two bottles of wine," Bevan said.

Jace finished her call and looked at Bevan. "Denise said she could use some help if they could come now."

"Give us a minute," Bevan said.

Blain and Bevan went inside and fifteen minutes later everyone but Laura, Bevan, and Blain was headed to the Long Bowe.

"I want to go in alone," Zack said. She entered the house and moved straight to the kitchen. She looked at the dogs. They wagged their tails as she walked up and gave them a treat from the jar in the pantry. She then moved from room to room, downstairs to the cellar, the main floor, and then to the bedrooms. She returned to the kitchen, opened the refrigerator, and then sat at the bar. She stood and went back outside where the four stood and opened her hand to show the six transmitters she had found. Bevan pointed to them and then to his ear.

"Dead, disabled now," Zack said.

The five went inside and Zack proceeded to tell them what she felt had happened Wednesday night. "He entered through your mother's herb room, gave the dogs a treat, started to place the devices in main rooms, then upstairs—first to your room, Blain, where he took your baseball and planted a device, then to yours and Laura's room. He stood for a long period of time in your room before he took Laura's watch. He went back to the wine cellar, took two bottles after reading many of the labels, came back to the kitchen to eat something, and, finally, gave the dogs another treat. He purposely left his plate and fork on the bar. He then walked to the tree line by the pond and disappeared. I lose him after that," Zack finished.

Everyone at the table was speechless.

"Bevan, is it him?" Laura's voice was shaking.

Bevan put his arm around her. "He's here for information or he would have killed all of us. We're not his target; he's showing off to prove he's uncatchable."

"He knows about you, Blain, but not me," Zack said.

"How were you able to get so much information? I thought you said he had no emotion?" Bevan asked.

"He has one emotion, arrogance," Zack said.

"What do you want to do?" Jace asked.

"Nothing, Aaron has made his point. I'm not going to let this ruin our holiday. But I will be more vigilant," Bevan said and looked at Blain and Zack. "I want you two armed from now on, and especially tomorrow at the party."

They all looked up as Bevan's family returned from the Long Bowe.

"Let's keep this to ourselves. I don't want to upset the rest of the family," Bevan said.

"Well, I don't know about anyone else but I could use a drink," Jace said.

RV PARK

Aaron returned from the market and was surprised by all the conversation about the engagement party from the locals. He put the food away and opened a beer, not his favorite but the clerk said it was from a local brewery.

"Time to see what's happening at the Benjamins," he said out loud. As he sat down, the first thing he noticed was the lights on his monitor were dark. *Not possible,* he thought. Aaron checked his equipment. "What the hell is going on in that house?" he said. Now he was blind. He could not believe anyone in the house could have found them, but it appears they had. Aaron didn't believe Blain was smart enough to find them, but Bevan may have run into one and then checked the house. He had to make a decision whether to chance another trip to the Benjamin home or insert himself into the party tomorrow night. The engagement party had an open invitation to the community. This would be a good test of his new disguise and alias. Aaron smiled, thinking about having a face-to-face conversation with Bevan. It would be nice to see his mentor again.

Chapter Fifty~Three ❧

The party had turned into another wonderful night of food, music, and celebration. Bevan had just finished his second toast of the night to Ethaniel and DeAnna. The night had been uneventful and no new faces had appeared. Blain and Zack were armed, and though they appeared to be relaxed they were not. Bevan couldn't remember a happier time than tonight with his family and friends. He and Laura had danced and laughed all evening.

"Son, I need to run back to the cellar and get a few more bottles of wine," Bill said.

"No, I'll go, you stay and enjoy yourself," Bevan said and kissed Laura on the cheek. "Be back in a few."

"Bevan, take Blain or Zack with you," Laura said.

"No, they need to stay here. I won't be gone long," Bevan said and headed for his father's truck.

As Bevan drove to the house he made a decision. He would ask Laura to marry him. He felt he knew her answer, but this weekend had made him realize how precious family was to him. When he approached the house all the lights were still on. He had left a few on this evening as a precaution and he hated entering a dark house. Bevan opened the door and both dogs ran to greet him. Bevan reached down and patted both. He looked in the main room and kitchen. *Nothing's out of place.* He headed to the cellar and found the four bottles his father had asked him to bring back. He started up the stairs and both dogs ran ahead of him wagging their tails. He turned and shut the door with his foot. He walked into the kitchen and put the bottles on the center island. "Marilyn, Betty! Come, girls." Bevan called for the dogs; they didn't come. He walked into the main family room and looked at Aaron sitting in his father's chair petting them.

"Damn dogs," Bevan said.

"Come in, Bevan, it's good to see you. I took the liberty of clearing the house of weapons. I wanted this to be a civil conversation," Aaron said.

Bevan walked in and sat down. "There are others coming soon."

"Bevan, you're a horrible liar. You have about twenty minutes until someone will start to wonder why you aren't back," Aaron said.

Bevan looked at Aaron and carefully chose his next question. "Aaron, what happened to you?"

"You happened to me, remember? Or have you and the company forgotten," Aaron said.

"You've stepped over the line, too deep now to get out. Selling information to the wrong people and involving my family and those close to me in Sherman Shaw's greed. The FBI, the company, we're all looking to take you one way or another," Bevan said.

"I'm a business man. There are expenses that must be covered and money is money, regardless of where it comes from."

Bevan shook his head. "What do you want?"

"You need to call off the dogs. If you stop now no one else needs to get hurt or die."

"I can't do that."

"Then their blood is on your hands," Aaron said and looked at his watch. "Time to go. I would appreciate it if you would stay put for the next five minutes. The guns are in the attic and I returned the items, except the wine. Your father has excellent taste."

"This isn't going to end well, you know that," Bevan said.

"Of course it will, Bevan. If you haven't noticed by now, I never lose. The company taught me that," Aaron said and walked toward the kitchen. "Five minutes." The dogs followed him.

Bevan sat and watched Aaron leave through the kitchen. It wouldn't do any good to call, and he had left his gun here at Laura's request. He stood and walked to the kitchen. Aaron had taken two of the four bottles of wine he had placed on the island.

"Bastard!"

Chapter Fifty~Four 🍃

LONG BOWE B&B
MONDAY, NOVEMBER 26, 2001
8:00 A.M.

Jace stood on the front porch of the Long Bowe and hugged Zack. The weekend had come and gone so rapidly. It always seemed they were saying good-bye.

"Jace, come stay with me next month when you're in D.C. for the wedding. I can't go home for Christmas and we can celebrate together. My apartment isn't big but we'll have fun," Zack said.

"Deal. And I want you to consider going to Gettysburg with me next July. I want to see the reenactment, and I might as well use the dress I bought for something. I've made reservations at the hotel I stayed in this year. Please think about it," Jace said.

"Hoping to meet Samuel again?" Zack asked.

Jace smiled. "His eyes were so beautiful, haunting, and he was very handsome for a ghost. But what I want is Sarah's necklace. We have to help them find each other and peace."

"I'll see what I can do to get some time off," Zack said. She hugged Jace one more time, then smiled. "Coming, mamma!" Zack looked at Jace since no words had been spoken. "She's worried I'll miss my flight."

Jace watched as the Keens left to take Zack to the airport. Zack and Blain were leaving this morning. She had been asked to take Bevan and Laura to the airport for their flight later in the afternoon. Jace had been invited for lunch at the Benjamin house and wondered where she could possibly put any more food. She felt like a squirrel with both cheeks full. Ethaniel and DeAnna would be staying a few days longer. They would be helping Daniel and Denise put things at the B&B back together and get ready to open up for business again. Jace thought about Taylor. She was anxious to talk to the man who may hold all the answers.

1:00 P.M.

It's always hard when the party is over and people leave. Jace's trip back to the B&B, after dropping Bevan and Laura off at the airport, was a little sad, but knowing she would be seeing Zack again in a week or so brightened her smile. She was anxious to see her friends from Bethesda and catch up on all the gossip since she had left Maryland. Jace was happy there had been no trouble from Aaron to ruin the weekend. As she drove up to the house she could see Daniel talking and laughing with someone. As she got out of the jeep the man got in his truck and left. She walked up to Daniel.

"Who was that?"

"Old war veteran named Morres said he was lost and needed directions," Daniel said.

O'HARE INTERNATIONAL AIRPORT
CHICAGO, ILLINOIS
2:00 P.M.

Taylor and Eric stood in the line waiting to go through security. Taylor had not slept well. The overnight flight and late check-in at the hotel had left him tired and his arm aching. The call this morning about the added delay didn't help either, but with the holidays you are always at the mercy of the airlines. He looked at the cast on his arm and cursed under his breath. The physician said, "Next visit in three weeks." He had dreams of death and war; promises made and respects yet to be paid were all tumbling in his mind. There were so many questions he had for Jace. He hoped she would be able to answer them. He placed his carry-on items in the container to be scanned and was called through. He stopped when the buzzer went off. He backed up, reached for his breast pocket, and took out the heart necklace and placed it in the basket.

"Thought you'd packed that," Eric said.

"No, not a chance," Taylor said and picked it back up once through the scanner and placed it back where it belonged.

Both men found their seats and settled in for the flight to Houston. They were served coffee before the plane took off and gave their orders for breakfast. Taylor took Jace's photograph out and looked at it. He could not believe how much she looked like the woman in Baghdad. He took the necklace and laid it on her picture. The scent of lilacs filled the plane. Passengers commented as they entered and the attendants searched for the source. Taylor smiled.

Eric looked at his brother. "Guess that's a go on the trip to Galveston."

Taylor leaned back; he put the necklace in his pocket and the photograph in the envelope. The flight to Houston would get them there at four thirty, they'd wait to get their luggage, a rental car, and then it would be at least an hour to two depending on traffic to get to the B&B . . . so they were looking at an arrival time of seven thirty or eight. It was going to be another long day. He hoped the weather would be agreeable and Jace would be waiting.

JOLLY ROGER B&B
TEXAS
7:00 P.M.

The twins had been busy all morning, cleaning, prepping, and baking. Several guests had checked out late today so now there was a hurry to get rooms cleaned. The past week had been busy and they needed to get the B&B ready for guests that would be arriving today and over the weekend. Happy Hour was singing and dancing on his perch in the main room when Casie walked into the kitchen to check on muffins and breads she had baking.

"Candi, what time will these guys get here?" Casie said.

"I was expecting them now, but I heard that there had been delays on several airlines from some of our guest, hence the later checkouts. Better to sit here and look at the water than the airport," Candi answered.

"What's their names?" Casie asked.

"We've been so busy, I can't remember," Candi said and the bell rang out front.

"It doesn't matter, let me check on the muffins and breads in the oven and I'll help you finish whatever is left to do," Casie said.

"And answer the door," Candi said.

Taylor rang the huge bell outside the Jolly Roger and could feel his heart starting to race. He looked at his hands and they were shaking. He turned to look at Eric.

"Taylor, what's wrong with you?" Eric asked.

"I don't know. I guess it's because I finally found where X marks the spot, so to speak," Taylor said and turned when the door opened. The woman that met them became pale and backed away from the door screaming.

Eric looked at Taylor. "Well, that's not good."

Taylor opened the door and they walked inside.

Candi had heard the door open and Casie screaming. She ran downstairs, not sure what had happened to her sister or whether someone had been injured. As she ran into the main room she saw Casie shaking and pointing to the two men standing there.

"For Christ's sake, Casie, what's wrong?" Candi said.

Casie's voice was trembling. "It's him, it's Samuel White!"

Candi began to shake when she looked at the man with the

green eyes. This man was either a twin or the ghost of Samuel White standing in their home.

Both men stood for a moment trying to understand what had just happened.

"I'm sorry, what did you call me?" Taylor said.

"I think she called you Samuel White," Eric said.

"Ladies, my name is Taylor Shaw, and this is my brother Eric. We have reservations."

"Mr. Shaw, I'm so sorry, please come in and forgive our shock and my sister's outburst," Candi said. She tried to stop her hands from shaking.

"Taylor Shaw from New York?" Casie said.

"Hawaii actually," Eric said.

"I'm looking for Jace Kin . . . Bowen, is she here?" Taylor asked.

"No, I'm sorry she's in Waynesboro," Candi said.

"Damn it! I keep missing her," Taylor said.

"Why did you call Taylor 'Samuel White'?" Eric asked. "And what is that wonderful smell coming from your kitchen?"

Casie laughed and relaxed. "That's dinner and breakfast. We knew there had been some delays at the airport and hoped you might be hungry."

"If you'll come with me I'll show you to your room. We can worry about the formalities of checking in later. If you haven't figured it out, we need to sit down and have a talk," Candi said.

"Talk, talk, talk," Happy Hour repeated.

Candi took them upstairs to a large room with two queen beds and a view of the canal. "I hope you will be comfortable here. I apologize for the welcome you received but I think after you see what we have to show you, you'll understand." She then left the men to unpack.

"Well, this has got to be the strangest day ever, bro," Eric said.

"Why can't I catch this woman? She's always out of reach one step ahead or behind me!" Taylor said.

"I guess this means another flight or road trip back to Waynesboro," Eric said and smiled.

"Yes, but not for a day or two. I want to see what the hell is going on here and get some answers once the twins stop shaking," Taylor said.

8:30 P.M.

Casie and Candi were putting the final touches on the dinner for their guests. Candi had chilled a bottle of Chardonnay and the grill was on, waiting for the steaks and shrimp.

"I hope they have recovered from your welcome," Candi said.

"I'm sorry, sis, but damn, I just knew the ghost of Samuel White had come to find Jace," Casie said.

"Well, you should have realized ghosts usually don't have travel buddies with them," Candi said.

"I wasn't really looking at Eric. Taylor's eyes are haunting, just like the photograph," Casie said.

"Well, I'm giving them a free night. How the hell would that look on our website? Had a wonderful time except for the screaming banshee that greeted us at the door. Not one of your better moments," Candi said.

"What's grilling?" Eric asked as he entered the kitchen.

"In about two minutes, steak and shrimp, with my special marinade," Casie said.

Eric walked over and took a spoon and tasted the marinade. "Hmm, that's pretty good, but let's add some red wine and . . . "

"Please excuse him ladies, humility is not his better quality. But he is a hell of a cook," Taylor said.

Casie looked at Eric. "Lead on, I'm always interested in new and interesting challenges." They took the steaks and shrimp out to the landing where the grill stood.

"I hope your room is satisfactory and, again, our apologies," Candi said.

"Forget it. So much strangeness has happened to us lately this will just be another chapter in a book yet to be written," Taylor said.

"Please leave out the crazy woman you met when you arrived," Candi said.

Taylor smiled. "You have a beautiful place here. Peaceful."

"Thank you; it's our Hawaiian island, Texas-style," Candi said and they both laughed. "Wine?"

Taylor held out a glass and took a drink. "Local?"

"A winery outside of Bowie called Brushy Creek. We carry a number of their wines and others located in the state, Lubbock and Fredericksburg just to name a couple more," Candi said.

"Very nice; it's light and not too dry. After dinner I think we need to talk," Taylor said.

"Well, that is an understatement," Candi said.

Casie returned to the kitchen and set places at the bar. "I hope it's okay if we sit here tonight; there's a nice view as the sun sets."

"You'll get no argument from me," Taylor said.

Eric entered the kitchen with the steaks and shrimp. "I simply amaze myself at times."

Taylor looked at Eric and shook his head and the twins laughed. As dinner was served, the kitchen was filled with talk of Hawaii and laughter from Eric's bad jokes.

After dinner, Taylor and Eric walked out on the landing and sat while their meal settled and both enjoyed another glass of Texas wine.

"They're pretty cool ladies after all," Eric said.

"Once you get past the screaming," Taylor said and they laughed.

Casie walked out on the landing and sat down next to Taylor. "I have something special for dessert."

"Can't wait," Eric said.

Candi joined everyone outside. "I never tire of the evenings here."

"I understand. I have a view in Hawaii I feel the same way about," Taylor said.

"You two should come one day," Eric told them.

"We might take you up on that offer," Casie said.

"I'm going to get a few things for you two to look at so take your time out here," Candi said and went inside.

"I saw a couple of kayaks, any chance?" Eric said.

"Anytime. You might want a wetsuit, the water may be a bit chilly," Casie said and looked up to see Candi waving at them. "I think she's ready for us."

Everyone gathered back at the bar. Candi had opened another bottle of Chardonnay and refilled everyone's glass.

"Taylor, we have known Jace for some time and trust her as if she were family. She was sent a package from her mother with items belonging to her ancestor Sarah Bowen," Candi said, then showed both men the pouch.

"I don't believe she'll mind you looking at these things," Casie said and opened the pouch and took out the books, including the bell.

Taylor picked up the book and looked at the first edition that matched the one he had on nurses in the Civil War. "This book is one my ancestor wrote. It is worth a substantial amount of money being a first edition." He then looked at the other books, including the handwritten book on herbs.

"She had an aunt who was killed in World War II. This aunt took a journal with her that belonged to Sarah. Jace was told the journal was lost during the war," Candi said.

Eric looked at Taylor. "Well, we have good news. Susan Bowen sent the journal to my uncle who was in love with her. It's safe and intact," Eric said.

"That is the best news ever," Casie said.

"She'll be thrilled," Candi added.

"My uncle left me with a daunting quest to find a present heir that's a nurse and return items that belong to the Bowen family. I was to find her personally and build a bridge so that his final book could be finished and published. There will be royalties from the book to go to the heir. That will be Jace," Taylor said.

Eric was looking through photographs Candi had brought to show them when he recognized the one of Aaron. "Why do you have this picture?"

"The CIA and FBI are looking for him. National security threat, maybe terrorism, is what we were told by Bevan Benjamin," Casie said.

"And the fact he stayed here for three weeks basically waiting for Jace. Why? We haven't figured out just yet," Candi told them.

"He's looking for me and a way to get money," Taylor said. He then explained to them about Sherman, particularly his need for money and power at any cost.

"Sorry to hear about your brother," both twins said.

"Who's this woman with Jace?" Eric asked.

"That's a cousin, I believe," Candi said.

"Her name! I need her name!" Eric was almost screaming.

"Whoa, brother, you sound like Casie," Taylor told him.

"Zaveen or Zack, that's what we call her," Candi said.

"Her last name, please," Eric was begging.

"It's Keens," Candi said.

"Can you make me a copy of this picture?" Eric asked.

"Of course," Candi said and took the picture to the copier.

"When did Jace have this picture made?" Taylor asked.

The twins started laughing.

"That's not Jace," Candi said and handed Eric Zack's picture.

"That's Sarah Bowen," Casie said.

Taylor now knew who the woman was he had seen in Baghdad.

"Bro, you have to look at this," Eric said and handed Taylor the photograph of Samuel White that Jace had taken in Gettysburg. "It's you."

Taylor looked at a photograph that truly could have been of him in period costume. He stared at the picture. He couldn't ever remember seeing a photograph of Samuel White. "I don't understand any of this."

"Jace believes that Sarah and Samuel are lost, searching for each other," Candi said.

"If this conversation had taken place two years ago, I would be calling the authorities to have you two committed. But after what I have seen and been through, nothing is strange anymore—to either of us," Taylor said and looked at the necklace around Sarah's neck in the photo.

"Jace is trying to find that necklace. She believes it holds the key to them finding each other and being at peace," Casie said.

Taylor reached in his breast pocket and took out the necklace. "I have that key." He then laid it on the photograph of Sarah and the kitchen filled with the scent of lilacs.

"You should call Jace," Candi said.

"According to the will, I must contact her in person. Since I know where she is right now, we'll just fly to Augusta and drive to Waynesboro next week. I need to put all the information you've given me together," Taylor said.

"There was a last-minute cancellation and we won't have anyone else here until Friday late, so take the cart and drive to the beach, go into town and walk the Strand, get to know our city before you leave," Casie said.

"Sounds good. Where's the dessert?" Eric said.

Balcony
Taylor and Eric's Room
11:30 p.m.

Taylor stood on the balcony of their room and looked at the sky. There was a cool breeze that almost had a slight chill to it. He looked at the photo of Samuel and then of Sarah. The note with the necklace said *I promise . . . Sarah.* He now knew what that meant. Promise to search for him, to find him, to be with him. He then picked up the picture of Aaron and a shiver ran down his back. What did this man plan to do to get more money from him? Jace had no fortune, his own inheritance was tied up, paperwork had yet to be completed in Hawaii . . . Taylor couldn't figure Aaron's next move at this point. Whites, Bowens, Keens, evil-doers, CIA, FBI, beautiful women, spies . . . all real life; damn, what a book this would make. He had been so close this time. He had to find Jace before Aaron did. He walked back into the room and looked at his brother asleep with Zack's picture on his chest. He shook his head, undressed, and lay down in a bed that enveloped him. That was the last thing he remembered.

Chapter Fifty~Five 🙢

Aaron sat in the Airstream waiting for information on Taylor. The last report he had received was that the brothers were in Galveston. He didn't understand why the man didn't just call and tell Jace to wait for him. Playing leapfrog all over the country wasn't necessary—and on that point, he now agreed with Sherman. He felt Taylor would be coming to Waynesboro to find Jace. Aaron would stay another week, as his plan to increase his bank account was developing nicely. He needed to work quickly and disappear before Bevan set the hounds loose again. Aaron had become very comfortable with his present disguise but would have to change again. He stood and refilled his coffee cup from the French press and then walked outside and looked at the sky. Winter was coming and he would adapt, though he would prefer to be in sand and sun. If he could put the right plan in place he and Kyleigh would spend the rest of their lives together someplace where it never got cold or snowed.

LONG BOWE B&B
GEORGIA
9:00 A.M.

Jace looked at the bedroom she had been in for the past week and a half. She had packed everything except her clothes for tomorrow. Ethaniel and DeAnna had left yesterday, which left the B&B empty and lonely. Donna had invited her to lunch and then they would come for dinner tonight at the Long Bowe. She would call the twins after she arrived in Alexandria and check on them and the B&B. Jace could smell coffee and knew Denise had made blueberry muffins. She hoped for a to-go bag in the morning.

JOLLY ROGER B&B
TEXAS
10:00 A.M.

Taylor was sitting at the computer printing boarding passes for himself and Eric. It didn't seem like they had been there for almost a week. He had taken their suggestions and spent time learning about Galveston and its history. They had walked the Strand, took a tour of homes, and walked the cemetery on Broadway. They had eaten dinner at the Galvez and Eric continued to kayak every morning.

"Are we set?" Eric asked

"Yes, noon flight out to Augusta," Taylor said.

"Breakfast, you two?" Casie said.

"I'm going to miss the food here," Taylor said.

"Casie has been kind enough to make me a small recipe book," Eric said.

"Taylor, have you been able to get the information you needed?" Candi asked.

"For now, Jace will have to fill in the rest. The connection between our families is amazing," Taylor said.

"Did you say you have a book from your uncle that wasn't finished?" Casie asked.

"Yes, I have been able to complete it, except for a dedication."

"We'll be expecting copies," Candi told him.

"Absolutely, and signed."

"Ladies, I was wondering if you give to-go bags when your customers leave," Eric said.

"It can be arranged," Casie said.

"Do you two have plans for dinner tonight?" Candi asked.

"Dinner at the Jolly Roger," Taylor said.

"Wonderful, since I put prime rib on this morning," Casie responded.

"I may have to move in here permanently," Eric said.

NATIONAL SECURITY AGENCY
MARYLAND
1:00 P.M.

Bevan was headed to the conference room to brief Blain and Zack on the incident at the house. He obtained total freedom for Zack to roam the building, but only for thirty days. Bevan didn't need someone asking questions he wasn't ready to answer at this point. He hoped she would have some information for him today; how was Aaron obtaining files and information he shouldn't have? The man seemed to be three steps ahead of him. The fact he knew about Blain was going to be an issue. He would now be forced to use Blain as bait. Zack and Blain needed time in the gym, and on the range he was going to push them over the next few weeks. As Bevan got on the elevator he thought about Laura and their conversation over Thanksgiving. She had returned, written her letter, and was making arrangements to put her house on the market. Her partners had offered an increase in shares if she would stay but she turned them down. She would leave with a substantial amount of money, and the last two cases would be taken over by other attorneys at the firm, if she wanted. Bevan hoped she would take the offer. He intended to ask Laura over Thanksgiving to marry him. The timing never seemed right for some reason, but he would do it this weekend, get down on one knee and propose. Zack had said Jace would be in town tomorrow so he would ask them and Blain to come to dinner. As Bevan got off the elevator he could hear Zack and Blain arguing outside the conference room door.

"What makes you think you can find him!?" Blain asked.

"He stood in your room, memorized your face, and stole property you didn't even know about for over thirty-six hours!" Zack responded.

"Excuse me, but can we take this conversation inside? You two are drawing a crowd," Bevan said and opened the door.

Zack and Blain entered and went to opposing sides of the table and sat down facing each other.

"It appears my new schedule for both of you has come at a good time. I have scheduled gym and range time starting Monday morning at five a.m. If you want to argue, do it in the gym. I didn't bring you two back from Baghdad to be at odds with each other. You're partners; work together and watch each other's back. Do I make myself clear?" Bevan said.

"Yes sir," both said.

"Because if you can't, Blain, I will find someone who can," Bevan said.

Zack stood up. "I'm not his favorite!"

Blain now stood and faced Bevan. "Damn it! How am I supposed to work with her when she knows everything I'm thinking?"

"Deal with it, or I'll fill the empty position in Fairbanks," Bevan said. "Now sit down, both of you. I need to go over the incident at the house during the reception." Bevan spent the next hour discussing the incident and his plans for the two of them.

"So, you're planning to use me as bait?" Blain asked.

"Do you have a problem with that?" Zack asked.

Blain thought about the weather in Fairbanks right now. "No, I don't have a problem with that."

"Good. Blain, I want you to head to the gym for the rest of the day. Zack, I'll need your report in just a minute. Both of you are invited to dinner Sunday, seven p.m.; bring Jace," Bevan said and stood. "Zack, my office."

The three left the conference room. Blain headed to his appointment in the gym and Zack followed her boss, paying attention to everyone and every room she passed. Zack entered Bevan's office and sat down. Bevan shut his door and picked up the phone.

"Darlene, I don't want to be disturbed; you know the exceptions," Bevan said and hung up the phone. He took out the file on Aaron. "What have you found?"

"He has friends everywhere in the building and they are loyal for one reason or another, not necessarily for money," Zack said.

"How many are we talking about?" Bevan asked.

Zack took a deep breath. "On this floor five, the next floor up and basement another three to six."

Bevan leaned back in his chair. "That's why he is so arrogant. He can get whatever he wants and by the time I stop one source he will have five more take their place."

"Aaron has built a network of individuals that owe him for favors done for them or family. He's been doing this type of thing for years; the network probably goes way beyond this building. What are you going to do?" Zack asked.

"Is there any one individual he uses above the others?"

"No, he keeps it spread out over many. Most of them don't realize they are helping him. There is a system where information is obtained by one person then passed to another and another," Zack said. "Unfortunately, I haven't been able to narrow the field to just one or two."

"Christ!" Bevan said.

"Anything you can tell me about him besides what I have memorized in the files?" Zack asked, knowing there was more.

"No, it's all classified," Bevan said. "How many more floors do you have to check?"

"Two more and the perimeter of the building."

"Go home, I need to think about what to do with all this information that I can't use. I never expected such a web," Bevan said.

"Because there are so many I can't obtain the information you need until it's already in his hands. Since there is no direct contact, my abilities aren't really useable. I'll keep roaming and maybe we'll get lucky," Zack said.

"Luck is what it'll take; you only have thirty days. Go, see you Sunday," Bevan said.

Chapter Fifty ~ Six 🕭

AUGUSTA REGIONAL AIRPORT
GEORGIA
SUNDAY, DECEMBER 2, 2001
4:30 P.M.

Taylor waited as Eric picked up the rental car. The twins had said their good-byes with a to-go bag for Eric. Taylor left a large tip in their room since they had only been charged for half their stay. They had given him copies of the photographs and as much information as they had available. He had Candi call the Long Bowe B&B and hold a room. Taylor wanted to apologize to the Longs for not telling them the first time who they were, and hopefully that would help on his next request. He would need a more detailed family history.

"Ready?" Eric said and loaded their luggage into the car.

Taylor looked at Eric and took a deep breath. "I think so."

"You're not going to start shaking again?" Eric teased.

"I hope not."

"She's just a person."

"No, she's not. Jace is connected in the same way I am to the past. That also connects us to one another."

"Well, guess we better go, destiny waits," Eric said, then drove out of the airport and headed to Waynesboro.

"I need to find a florist tomorrow and honor another one of Uncle Larry's requests. I need to finish something he was not able to do for one reason or another. I believe Uncle Larry could never bring himself to come and say his good-bye to Susan," Taylor said.

"Not a problem. I'm sure there are several here."

"I want to contact the Benjamins again and see if Donna will let me make some copies of the scrapbook. The information they have and what the Longs know will help me," Taylor said.

"More research for family history, I presume."

"Yes," Taylor said. "There is a story that needs to be written about the Whites and Bowens. A family history . . . I think that's what he really intended for me to do all along."

"You'll need a top-notch photographer, of course; one with charm and style," Eric said.

"Of course! Let me know who you have in mind. He'll have to work cheap," Taylor said.

"I work for food and keep—oh! And beer, too!" Eric said and laughed.

I'll locate as many family members as possible and obtain their photographs to go along with their stories. I'm hoping they have old family photographs as that will just add to the book," Taylor said. "Jace will definitely be the one to help me."

"She can help me meet her cousin," Eric said.

"Didn't you send her an email from the Jolly Roger?" Taylor asked.

"Yes, still waiting for an answer."

"If she's smart, she'll put your email in the trash bin," Taylor said.

"Such support! She would be lucky to know me and my gallant ways," Eric said and waved his hand. He then turned down the road to the B&B.

Taylor's stomach was hurting and his left arm ached. "I need to get this damn cast off."

"Call your doc and see if it'd be okay for Dr. Benjamin to take it off," Eric said.

"Works for me."

❦

LONG BOWE
5:30 P.M.

There had been a lot of scurrying at the Long Bowe preparing for the Shaw brothers. As usual there was food, drink, and dessert, and Denise kept running to the front door checking for them. She began to turn back toward the kitchen when she heard a car.

"Daniel, they're here!" Denise said. "I'm anxious to talk with them and see why they didn't tell us who they were the last time."

"Now mother, people have their reasons, not our place to pry," Daniel said.

"Not this time, something is going on and I want answers. My curiosity is killing me," Denise said and walked out to greet the Shaw brothers. "Welcome back!" Daniel and Denise assisted the men inside and settled them in their room upstairs.

"It's nice to be back," Taylor said.

"What's cooking downstairs?" Eric asked.

"Ham, sweet potatoes, cornbread, and blueberry pie," Daniel said.

"I now know I've died and gone to heaven," Eric said and swayed.

"You two are our only guests. Bill and Donna are on their way to join us," Denise said.

"Where's Jace? I need to talk to her," Taylor asked as they all walked downstairs.

"Hello, are we late?" Bill said and walked in and over to the Shaw brothers and shook hands. Donna followed her husband and hugged both the young men.

"Taylor was just asking for Jace," Denise said.

Everyone stopped and silence consumed the group.

"I missed her, didn't I?" Taylor asked.

"She left this morning," Daniel said.

"Where?" Taylor asked.

"Alexandria for a wedding. She'll be staying with Zack," Daniel said.

"How long this time, Taylor?" Eric asked.

"At least a week. I have a lot to do," Taylor said.

"Well nothing is ever decided on an empty stomach," Denise said.

"I have a new wine from a local winery; it's made with peaches, but not too sweet, I was promised," Bill said.

"And I brought the scrapbook. I thought you might want to look through it again," Donna said.

"Eric, do you have film?" Taylor asked.

Eric smiled. "What kind of photographer would I be if I didn't?"

Outside, just inside the tree line, a lone figure watched all that was taking place inside the Long Bowe. Another opportunity had presented itself. Aaron thought about all the money Taylor and Eric had inherited. The money from the newspaper and from the Shaw estate in Hawaii was worth killing for to obtain even a fraction. He didn't intend to kill anyone at this point.

"If you're patient, all things will come to you," Aaron said.

Dinner at the Long Bowe was always comforting. Laughter, warmth, and a feeling of friendship surrounded the table. Eric helped Denise clear the dishes, then she served coffee and pie. Taylor now felt the time was right to discuss his uncle's book, the will, and what was at stake for everyone, especially Jace. He talked about his decision to write a full history of the White, Bowen, Benjamin, and Keens families. He decided not to say anything about seeing the ghost of Sarah Bowen. He looked at the faces that sat around the table after a couple hours of explanations. To his surprise most everyone had a smile.

"Taylor, that's quite the story," Daniel said.

"Yes, sir, it is but it's the truth," Taylor answered.

"If everything you have said has a purpose, Jace could be in danger," Bill said.

"We feel that Aaron's main focus is Taylor and his inheritance," Eric said.

"Our inheritance. You're now worth more than you were a year ago, brother," Taylor said.

"Jace is with Zack or I would be worried," Denise said.

"What I want to do over the next few days is to have everyone come together so that I can explain what I'll need from them. I want to give everyone plenty of time to go through pictures and old bibles. When I come back with Jace, I'll gather everything and begin to write the book. The proceeds of the book will be distributed among the families involved, except ours," Taylor said.

"And I'll want to take pictures of everyone," Eric said.

Daniel looked at his wife. "Well, mother, it appears we are going to be famous."

Everyone at the table laughed.

"I'll start making calls tomorrow and see if we can gather those closest and get started," Denise said. "And the family far away can email you the information with pictures."

"We'll do our part for you, too. Taylor, be sure to go to the county clerk's office and pull all the files with the Bowen name so you can see just how much land they once owned," Donna said.

"I'll do that, and I appreciate anything you can do to help make this a completed story."

"Donna, it's time to head home. The girls will need to be walked," Bill said. "Taylor, could you walk us out?"

"Certainly."

Taylor left Eric to answer questions and list what would be needed from family outside of Waynesboro.

Bill walked up to Taylor. "You're aware our family is connected in Washington, are you not?"

"Yes, sir."

"This man, Aaron, is not to be taken lightly—be cautious," Bill said.

"It sounds as if he has little or no conscience, and I have seen what lust of wealth and power can do to a person first-hand," Taylor said.

"Then take care," Bill said.

Taylor stood outside and listened to the night. He thought he heard movement out toward the trees. Taylor started walking away from the house.

Eric opened the door and yelled. "Taylor, can you come back? Denise has questions I can't answer."

Taylor looked at the trees again. "Yeah, be right in."

"Good idea," Aaron said and headed to the ATV. Once back to the Airstream he started preparing for the trip north. He hated the cold weather but D.C. held his Ace of Hearts, and that is where he needed to be.

Chapter Fifty~Seven ❧

Jace sat with the rest of the bridesmaids and the bride-to-be at the hotel bar. The past week and a half had gone so fast she barely had enough time for herself since arriving at Zack's apartment. She had spent as much time as possible with Zack since this weekend would be catching up with friends and wedding plans, including tomorrow night's bachelorette party for Kyani. Jace would be staying at the hotel with everyone else the next few days. Zack had been invited to come and stay, but she declined the invitation. She did promise to be at the wedding Saturday night. Jace appreciated Zack's kindness to give her time with friends. Zack had been preoccupied with work and the email from Eric Shaw. Jace found Zack's attitude toward Eric somewhat amusing. She was trying to pretend she wasn't interested, but Jace knew that was definitely an act. Zack told Jace that Taylor and Eric would be arriving sometime over the weekend and would contact her. Jace couldn't think of a more fitting time to finally meet Taylor. She only hoped he didn't think she was a nutcase when she told him all she had discovered.

"Jace, what are you thinking about?" Kyani asked.

"What else, your wedding and tomorrow night's festivities!"

"Well, I've rented a party bus for us," Linda told them.

"When will Zoe be in?" Jayton asked.

"In about two hours, we need to pick her up at Reagan," Kyani said.

"It's nice to all be together again," Jace told them.

"Are you bringing a date, Jace?" Jayton asked.

"No, just me," she answered.

"Well there will be plenty of single men there, so don't you worry about a dance partner," Kyani said and winked at her.

There were a couple more rounds of drinks when Linda looked at her watch. "Time to go. Grab your coats and gloves," she said.

"Good idea to have your wedding and reception all in one place," Jayton said.

"With the weather here we felt it would be best for everyone, even for those staying in other hotels downtown," Kyani said.

"I'm so glad we can take the Metro to the airport. I still hate the traffic here," Jace said and made a face.

As they headed toward the front door the man in front of them held the door for all to exit.

"Thank you," Jace told him.

"My pleasure," he said.

The group huddled together and continued to talk about the wedding. When they entered the Metro no one noticed the same man get on their train two cars away.

Chapter Fifty~Eight &

HILTON INN, RECEPTION HALL
ALEXANDRIA, VIRGINIA
SATURDAY, DECEMBER 15, 2001
4:00 P.M.

Aaron was stacking glasses and bottles of liquor along with other bartenders. He had inserted himself into the night festivities; after all, mixing drinks was like making bombs; easy. If all worked well he would lure Jace away from the party, sedate her, and slip out the back to a van that would be waiting for him. Simple and no one would get hurt.

"Gordon, how you doing there, buddy?" the other bartender asked.

"Good, but I have an errand I need to run; cleared it with the boss. I'll be back in time for the festivities," Aaron said.

"Well just don't leave me high and dry."

"No chance of that."

BRIDAL SUITE

Jace and the rest of the bridal party were celebrating early with several bottles of champagne. The party bus the night before almost did them all in, but thanks to Zoe's old family concoction for hangovers they were ready for tonight. She looked at the red dresses they were all going to wear. Jace was actually glad to put this one on. It fit nice and complemented all of them.

"Jace, phone!" Jayton yelled across the room.

"Who is it?"

"Zack," Jayton answered.

"What's up?" Jace said.

"Well it sounds like the party never stopped," Zack teased.

"Are you on your way?"

"I'm still at work, running late, but I'll be at the reception," Zack told her.

"I was hoping you'd be at the wedding, but I'll make sure your place is saved at our table. Any word from the Shaws?" Jace asked.

"No, but I emailed my cell number to Eric and told him to call when they got to their hotel. I don't expect them for at least another day," Zack said.

"Sounds good; see you tonight."

Marriott Hotel
Old Town
Alexandria, Virginia
5:00 p.m.

Taylor was tired but excited; finally he was in the same town as Jace. All the leapfrogging had come to an end. He looked at his hands—they were shaking. He passed it off to muscle weakness in his left arm now that the cast was gone. He thought about leaving Waynesboro again, not paying his uncle's final respects to Susan. He would; the time just didn't feel right.

"Thank you, Mr. Shaw, all we had left was a suite on the top floor," the desk clerk told him.

"That'll be fine. I need to get some information about a wedding at the Hilton on King Street," Taylor said.

"That's on the next block from here. Do you have a name?"

"No, just a time, wedding at seven with reception to follow," Taylor said.

"I'll see what I can find and call you shortly," the clerk said.

"Taylor, let's go! I have a phone call to make," Eric said.

5:30 P.M.

Zack walked into her apartment and was happy the week was over. Bevan had been true to his word, and her time in the gym and gun range had been tiring. She had not been able to obtain any further information on her daily trips through the building or outside. Aaron had not made any contacts as of the past two weeks. She needed to work fast; after the first of the year, Aaron would have the advantage. All she would be able to collect as information would be in common areas. Blain had been better since Thanksgiving and his break-up with Lyssa. That decision was best for everyone. She looked at the clock and knew she had time for a long bath and glass of wine before heading to the reception. Zack looked at the black pants and sequined top she intended to wear and headed to the bathroom when her cell phone rang. She smiled and answered.

"Zaveen?" the male voice asked.

"Eric," Zack said.

Taylor stood and watched his younger brother act like a teenager asking a date to the prom. He smiled and wondered if he, too, would stutter and stammer when he met Jace. It had seemed an impossible task, but now everything had come together. The knock on the door would be the name for the wedding.

"What's that?" Eric asked.

"Information on the wedding," Taylor answered.

"I could've saved you the trouble. Zaveen just invited us to the reception," Eric said and smiled.

"I hope shirt and tie will be acceptable," Taylor said.

"Guess we better find something for the bride and groom," Eric said.

"When in doubt, cash always works," Taylor said and headed to the bathroom.

"I saw an ATM in the lobby," Eric said and headed toward the door.

Taylor turned and looked at his brother. "Is this really going to happen?"

Eric smiled, "It's sure looking that way."

Aaron needed to check into the suite, get out of this disguise, set his room up for tonight, and get back to the Hilton to bartend. He had little tolerance for inept individuals, and the bellman that came up with him had no idea how close he was to meeting his early demise.

"Let me help you with that, sir," the young man said.

"Thank you, it's so nice to see young people that still respect their elders," the old man said and watched Eric Shaw open the door.

"My pleasure, have a good night."

Aaron watched as Eric walked away. "Well isn't this a pleasant surprise."

"What did you say?" the bellman asked.

"Nothing. You can leave, and don't ask for a tip."

RECEPTION HALL
HILTON INN
8:30 P.M.

Jace had taken a moment to get a glass of wine and take a breath. She was thankful the ceremony had been short and very sweet. They had taken many of the photographs before the ceremony so that groupings afterward could be done quickly. One thing about Kyani, she meant for everyone to have a good time partying, and that didn't include wasted hours on pictures. Jace had been surprised at the choice of music, a lot of Big Band, 1940s. Hence Kyani's choice of dresses that definitely had a forties flair to them. Jace had pulled her hair to one side with a set of rhinestone clips to finish off the total look. She finished her glass of wine and looked around the room and down the hallway, hoping Zack would show up soon. All of her friends had brought dates, even Zoe. The bartender filled her glass again.

"Thank you," Jace said and looked at the older man tending the bar.

"Not a problem. Nice wedding, and you ladies are all lovely," the man said.

"Well, thank you," Linda said as she walked up to get Jace. "Jace, where's your friend?"

"She'll be here, she promised," Jace said.

"I hope she didn't get tied up at work," Linda said.

"You ladies have a good time and come back to see me," the bartender said.

Both women smiled and headed toward their table to waiting friends.

Taylor, Eric, and Zack walked into the foyer of the Hilton and found a sign pointing to the wedding reception. Taylor had not been able to get a word in since Zack had shown up at their room. Eric babbled like a school boy but Zack didn't seem to mind. She actually seemed amused. Taylor put his hand over his breast pocket and took a deep breath as they entered the room. The band announced the next song and Taylor scanned the room and found Jace. He was stunned at her beauty; she had similarities to Susan but she was the exact image of Sarah. He walked to the table.

"May I have this dance?" Taylor asked.

Jace looked up into the same haunting green eyes and handsome face she had seen in Gettysburg. It was the same man, but it couldn't be. *Did he just ask me to dance?*

Taylor didn't wait for her to answer; he took her hand and walked out to the dance floor. He turned, pulled her close, and took a breath of a fragrance that had become all too familiar, lilacs. The band started playing "At Last."

As the music played, Taylor listened to the words. This song was on an album in Larry's collection. The song had been circled and marked "Ours."

"I can't believe I finally found you. There's so much I need to tell you," Taylor said. He could feel Jace's heartbeat on his chest.

Jace could feel her heart racing. She took a deep breath and let her body fold into his embrace. Jace looked up into Taylor's face. "Does it feel to you like we've done this before?"

Taylor took in the beauty of her face and blue eyes, the same blue eyes that had stared down at him in Baghdad.

"Maybe . . . but in another time and place."

Everyone at the table sat speechless as they had watched a total stranger take their friend to the dance floor.

Linda looked at her friends. "Does anyone know who that is?"

"It appears they know each other," Jayton said.

"I don't remember her telling us about him," Zoe said.

"Good evening, everyone. I would like to introduce Eric Shaw, and his brother, Taylor, is the one dancing with Jace," Zack said and was bombarded with a flood of questions only she could hear. Then everyone started talking at the same time. "Ladies, there are just some things that simply can't be explained."

Aaron watched the scene unfold and was now concerned he would have difficulty getting Jace away from Taylor. He had to get her alone! Her disappearance was the key to all he had planned. He scanned the exits closest to her table and quickly recalled where restrooms were located. Maybe just once there wouldn't be a group effort.

"Hey, Gordon, can you run and get more champagne? They're about to start the same old boring toasts," the other bartender stated.

"On my way, buddy," Aaron said and left. He looked back to the dance floor as the song ended. He could see Jace kiss Taylor and point toward the exit. Aaron grinned.

"Easy."

Taylor returned to the table where all eyes were on him. He stood while Zack introduced him to Jace's friends and their dates.

"Where's Jace?" Zack asked.

"Said she had to make a stop before coming back to the table," Taylor said.

"Damn, she has a lot of explaining to do," Linda said.

"Let me see if I can answer those questions. I don't think she can tell you what you want to know about me and why I'm here," Taylor said and sat down.

For the next twenty minutes he felt like he was being interviewed but gave as direct answers as he could as to why he was there, minus the story about the ghost of Jace's ancestor appearing to him in Baghdad. These answers seem to have satisfied everyone at the table.

Zack had been preoccupied with Eric but was beginning to wonder why it was taking Jace so long. She stood and looked around the room. At the bar Zack could see one of the bartenders pointing and arguing with the man in charge of the reception. Things didn't seem right, so she walked over to the bar.

"I don't know where he went. I told him to go get champagne and he never came back," the man told the manager.

Eric walked up as Zack put her hand on the top of the bar.

"Oh shit!" Zack said and handed Eric her cell phone, gave a fast request, and left.

Taylor looked up and saw Zack run out the door. He stood and went to the bar.

"Eric, what's going on?" Taylor asked.

"Problem, hang on. Bevan, this is Eric Shaw, we have a problem. Zack said to come." Eric gave him the hotel name.

"Where was Zack going?"

"To get Jace. She said Aaron has her," Eric said.

"What! How does she know that?"

Eric shrugged his shoulders. "I think it's the same thing that happened in Baghdad. The woman has a gift for trouble. She said to stay here. Taylor, where are you going? She said to stay . . . shit!" Eric then followed his brother, not knowing where they were going.

Bevan was uncomfortable with the call from Eric. This was bold for Aaron. He made another call to Blain to meet him. Bevan holstered his weapon and walked toward the front door. Laura had called and said she and her friends were going to have a late dinner and show. He left a note on the kitchen table for her not to wait up for him. Bevan looked down and patted General Lee.

"Watch the place and Laura when she gets home."

Marriott Old Town
Alexandria, Virginia
10:30 p.m.

Aaron entered the suite next door to Taylor's. When he came through the front door of the hotel carrying Jace no one seemed to be too concerned. The only person that even looked was the desk clerk, and she smiled.

"I tried to warn her about those Long Island iced teas. She just wouldn't listen," Aaron told the clerk.

Once he got to the room and put Jace on the bed he looked at his watch, knowing he had about a thirty-minute head start. More than enough time to finish here and head out. Flex cuffs around legs and wrists, he placed her head on a pillow. She really is beautiful, he thought, and then he thought of Kyleigh. Jace made a moaning noise and Aaron stuck her in the neck one more time.

"Sorry, but I just can't have you waking up before I get out of here." He put a piece of duck tape over her mouth and left a white rose on her chest. He left something special in the suite just for Bevan. As Aaron got to the door, he turned and smiled.

"Perfect."

Zack stood outside the Hilton trying to focus, blocking out everything but what she needed to find Jace. How could she have been so stupid and careless? Arrogance, remember, arrogance is his emotion. She turned and saw Eric and Taylor coming toward her.

"What are you doing?" Taylor asked.

"I'm trying to find where he took her," Zack said.

"What are you, psychic?" Eric asked.

Zack knew she didn't have the time to explain. "Yes, in a manner of speaking, I am—so stop talking, back off, and let me focus."

Both men slowly backed away.

Eric looked at Taylor. "And I thought things just couldn't get any stranger when we were in Galveston."

Bevan and Blain arrived at the same time. Bevan could see Zack standing in front of the hotel attempting to find Jace and Aaron. He walked up and waited for Zack to break. Eric and Taylor walked up next to Bevan.

"How long?" Bevan asked.

"Almost an hour," Zack said.

"He must have been one of the waiters or bartenders to get so close," Blain said.

"Bartender," Zack said.

"Zack, I don't understand any of this but if he's kidnapped her for money I'll give him whatever he wants," Taylor said.

"It's partly money but it's the game, control. I can't explain it for reasons of national security, but I can't allow you to give him money," Bevan said.

"Jace! She's in the room next door to Taylor and Eric's room. She's in trouble. Blain, call for EMS, she's drugged, he's given her too much!" Zack said.

Taylor and Eric stared for a moment. Neither could believe what they had just heard.

"Let's go," Bevan said.

"We're coming," Taylor said.

I don't think . . . " Bevan started.

"It's not an option," Taylor said and headed toward the Suburban.

MARRIOTT

Bevan obtained the key to the suite while the rest took the elevator to the top floor. Zack looked at Eric and then to Taylor, whose hands were shaking.

"Are you alright?"

"They only shake when I think of her. It can't end this way, it just can't, all this time searching and she dies because of money," Taylor said.

When everyone was at the door, Eric and Taylor were ordered back until the room was cleared. Bevan, Blain, and Zack entered as all had been trained. "Clear, clear, clear!" could be heard out in the hallway. Zack was the first to get to Jace. She removed the tape and cuffs. Her breathing was shallow, her color gray. Eric, Bevan, and Blain waited outside the bedroom. Zack wouldn't leave.

Taylor sat down on the bed. "Jace, Jace, come back." He reached in his pocket, took out the necklace, and placed it around her neck. "Jace, stay with me." He leaned down and kissed her. Jace opened her eyes, the bridesmaid dress turned to blue checkered gingham, and at that moment Taylor knew this was Sarah. She placed her hand over his heart.

"You found me, now take me to Gettysburg." She then looked at Zack and smiled. "Hello, my friend, it's been too long." The gingham faded; Jace took a breath and coughed.

Taylor picked her up, held her to his heart, and then looked at Zack. "You saw her, didn't you?"

"Yes."

Bevan had searched the room and found something he had not realized was missing. He turned to Blain, gave quick instructions, and pushed him out the door. What he held in his hand was a warning. He walked to the bedroom door.

"Zack, I need you out here," Bevan said.

"Yes, sir."

"Is everything in there okay?" Bevan asked.

"I believe it will be," Zack said. "Where's Blain?"

"En route to my house," Bevan said and handed her a black case.

Zack opened it and looked at Bevan's badge now retired from Atlanta. "Where?"

"My house," Bevan said. "I didn't even know it was missing. The bastard comes and goes at will."

"Laura?"

"Not home, cell phone going to voice mail," Bevan said and started to the door.

Zack followed and then stopped, looked up at Eric, motioned for him to bend down, and kissed him. "Don't go anywhere."

Eric wasn't sure what was going on but knew she could take care of herself. He walked into the bedroom and could see Jace was beginning to come around. Taylor looked up at him.

"Everyone left," Eric said.

"Why?" Taylor asked.

"It appears Jace wasn't the real target. He apparently has a grudge against Bevan," Eric said. "They're on the way to make sure Bevan's fiancé is alright."

"My God, who is this man?" Taylor said.

"Not sure, but I never want to meet him," Eric said and backed away as paramedics brought a stretcher into the room.

Chapter Fifty~Nine ❧

BEVAN'S RESIDENCE
RESTIN, VIRGINIA
SUNDAY, DECEMBER 16, 2001
1:00 A.M.

Laura was tired, but had enjoyed her evening out with the girls. She didn't tell Bevan, but this was her "going away" and "congratulations, you're pregnant" party from her friends at work. Laura intended to tell Bevan this weekend and would give him the small silver picture frame that said "Daddy." The pregnancy was a surprise but a most welcomed one. She could see the light on in the kitchen as she opened the door.

"Bevan, General Lee? Anyone home?" she said and locked the door behind her.

"Bevan's out and General Lee is taking a nap," Aaron said.

Laura turned with nowhere to run. "Aaron Caydon, I presume."

"At your service," he said and took the bags. "I'm afraid I have made somewhat of a mess in the kitchen. Blain thought he was up to the job of saving you."

"Oh God, you didn't kill him," Laura's voice was shaking.

"My, I'm not the ruthless killer Bevan is telling everyone. No, just a broken arm and some bruises. He's resting in the guest bedroom, afraid he will be out for a while. But the breakfast table and chairs are not repairable," Aaron said and pulled out a syringe. "I hope you're not allergic to anything."

Laura held up her hands. "Stop! I'm pregnant! I'll go with you! I won't fight you! Just don't give me anything."

"Well, counselor, this is an interesting turn of events. Please sit down. Bevan will be home soon," Aaron said and proceeded to tie her feet and arms to a chair and taped her mouth. He placed her in the center of the living room, built a fire, and opened a Guinness.

"I would offer you some, but pregnant women really shouldn't drink," he said, laughed, and turned off the lights.

Bevan stopped three blocks from his house and waited for Zack to get off the phone. His mind was not where it needed to be. This was all too close to home for everyone involved. Bevan hated this man and he had to be stopped, put away, or killed.

"Jace doing better?" Bevan asked.

Zack laughed. "Yes, Taylor said when she finally woke up in the ER she started arguing with the doctors. The doctor wants her to stay the night."

". . . and?" Bevan asked.

"Well, Taylor will be sleeping next to her on one of the God-forsaken sleep chairs. They promised to let her go if she would stay until morning. Nurses are the worst patients. What do you want to do here?"

"He knows I'm coming but not you; he may suspect there is someone else, but let's see if I can keep him occupied," Bevan said. "Anything on Blain?"

"Hurt, tied up, and drugged," Zack said.

"You get that from him?"

"No, Laura. She's tied up in the living room. Not hurt, no drugs," Zack stopped.

"What?" Bevan became concerned.

"Bevan, she's pregnant. Sorry, she wanted to tell you." Zack stopped.

Bevan sat unable to speak for a moment; a world of emotions now surrounded him, shock, happiness, worry, and a building anger.

"Sir, you have to stop and put the anger away. It'll get us all killed. You have to put it away!" Zack was almost screaming; she reached out and shook his arm.

Bevan knew she was right and focused on what they needed to do. "I would assume he has drugged the dog, too. Zack, I need you outside. Position yourself to the greatest advantage. I don't want to know where. He has the control here and reads people almost as well as you, only he doesn't have your gift. I'll do what I can but don't intend to use any weapons. I'll leave that to you. Give me ten, then you're on your own." Bevan gave Zack his weapon and exited the car. Ten minutes later he was out of sight.

Zack smiled, checked her weapons, and pulled the boning knife out of her vest. She ran a finger across the blade.

Aaron had checked all windows, doors, and anywhere someone might try to enter. He knew Bevan better than most, and any conflict that might arise would be minimized for the sake of those in the house. He checked on Blain and General Lee, and then sat back down. Aaron knew Bevan had taken his service weapon with him, and the back-up in the house was empty of bullets and sitting in the bottom of the dishwasher that was cleaning the empty racks. Aaron heard the front door open.

Bevan had prepared the best he could in the ten-minute walk. His best weapon would be what it had always been with Aaron—his ability to talk him down. He opened the front door to the sight of Laura tied to a chair. He then scanned to where Aaron was sitting. No weapon pulled . . . that wasn't his way. Aaron's training followed through even now, to show the threat to someone else in order to keep others at bay.

"Come in, Bevan, and let's talk, have a beer, and see if we can come to an agreement," Aaron said.

"Laura, are you okay?" Bevan asked.

Laura nodded to the affirmative.

"Bevan, you know I would never hurt a woman unless provoked. She is my Ace of Hearts, so to speak; oh, and congratulations, Daddy."

Bevan sat down across from him. "Aaron, why all the theatrics and this?"

"Making a point that none of you are safe. I can get to anyone, anywhere, anytime—and make anyone disappear. Tonight is the last time I will leave without taking. No more checks; back your people off. You now have more to lose," Aaron said and pointed to Laura.

Bevan looked at Laura and back to Aaron. "I want you to go; I'll do what I can to leave you alone for now."

Aaron smiled. "I guess that's the best you can give me but it is my last warning." He stood and headed toward the back door and turned around. "She's pretty, Bevan, let's keep her that way."

Bevan watched as he left out the back door. He knelt in front of Laura and cut her free. He gently took the tape off her mouth. "Are you okay?" But before she could answer gunfire erupted and he pulled her to the floor. "Stay down." He opened his cell and punched in one number, then ran to the back and out the door.

Zack had positioned herself in a tree that hung over the roof. She lowered herself to the edge and waited. Time had never been an issue for Zack; she used her mind to calm and prepare just like waiting in the woods back home. She heard footsteps and crouched to spring.

Aaron stepped outside and began to holster his weapon when he was knocked to the ground and the gun fired, injuring the side of his left foot. The next thing he felt was a sharp and burning sensation down the left side of his face and shoulder. Someone was cutting him! He turned to see something small backing away, preparing to strike again.

"I don't think so!" he said.

Zack said nothing; if this did not go well she didn't want to give him any advantage. She felt they would meet again. She had read his files, memorized them, and was aware of his combat experience in hand-to-hand. She could not let him get the upper hand or he would kill her. She ran, jumped, but he caught her and threw her into some bushes. Zack recovered as Bevan came through the back door. Aaron turned, pulled his weapon—but Zack was quicker and fired, which disarmed him. She ran toward him but mistimed her jump; he caught her arm and she hit the ground.

Aaron had had enough of this tick! He was bleeding and his foot was making it hard to keep balanced.

"Not this time," he said. He threw this man to the ground and then realized his attacker was light and . . . was that perfume he smelled? No, not possible. A woman could not have inflicted all this injury to him. He leaned down and back-handed her to unconsciousness and pulled out his back-up weapon just as Bevan reached him.

"Not this time, Bevan! Back away or she dies," Aaron said. "On the ground! Hands beneath you!" Aaron could hear sirens and knew he had to go. He looked at her hand and saw the boning knife. He reached out, took it, and put it in his belt. He stood and looked at Bevan. "Impressive, but I'll be walking away; tell her I'll keep the knife as a souvenir. And Bevan, be careful you don't do to her what you've done to me." Aaron turned and left out the gate into the alley.

Bevan got to Zack to make sure she was alive. Police, EMTs, and agents were arriving in force, but it would be too late. It was always the same story with Aaron, too late!

Chapter Sixty ❧

NSA
MONDAY, DECEMBER 17, 2001
9:00 A.M.

Bevan looked at the clock on his desk. He had been in his office since five a.m. completing his report and preparing for the debriefing that would take place in the next fifteen minutes. Everyone involved in the weekend events had been requested to be present. Blain was still in the hospital and would be out of commission for several months. This incident at the house had destroyed all of Bevan's plans. Jace had recovered from the sedative without any lasting effect and Zack was sporting a few bruises and a black eye. Bevan was not sure where his course would lie now that Aaron had made his point. He and Laura hadn't talked much after the incident at the house; he had just held her throughout the night thinking of their future together and as parents. He was somewhat confused about Aaron's actions. No kidnapping? This had not played out as he had anticipated. Maybe money had never been the issue. His job now was to keep all this information contained from those involved. Bevan thought about the turn of events that had brought all their families together. Hopefully the ghosts of the past could now be settled and the living could progress.

"Sir, it's time," Darlene said.

"Yes I know, thank you."

Bevan made a call for the added personnel he would need for statements, gathered his files, and headed to the conference room.

He was still concerned about the toll it had taken on everyone involved. He was trying to decide whether or not counselors would be needed to help Jace, Taylor, Eric, and Laura. As he rounded the corner, Bevan could hear laughter coming from the conference room. He stopped outside and smiled.

"Sir, sir, is there something wrong?" the agent asked.

"No, everything is just fine."

Chapter Sixty~One ❧

The past few weeks had seemed a blur to Jace. She was still trying to adjust to all that had happened and to the constant feeling of contentment since she danced with Taylor at Kyani's wedding. Everyone including Zack had returned to the B&B for the holidays and a wedding. Bevan and Laura were married Christmas Eve at the Benjamins in a simple ceremony. They would be leaving for Hawaii for two weeks on New Year's Day and Bevan had promised "no cell phones."

Jace looked out the window and saw Eric and Zack walking toward the barn. She believed there was something taking root between those two and she smiled. Jace looked at all the items Taylor had brought with him: photographs, Harry's scrapbook with grandmother Deelyn's picture with the Jedburghs . . . things now made more sense. The medals in the case were Deelyn's and Frank's. She would have Eric correctly and carefully copy the photograph of Mack and James on their wedding day. Jace watched the color drain from Zack's face when she looked at it. It seemed their families had very strong genes. The most special gift was the heart necklace and Sarah's diary. There was so much history in the diary, and now it was where it belonged, with her. Taylor and Jace had looked at the pictures of Sarah and the man who called himself

Samuel White. They were both carbon copies of these people. It took a few days, but both had finally discussed their own experiences with visions, smells, and feelings that had led them to this point. Jace was relieved, but she felt Taylor was holding back on his visions of Sarah. Taylor had explained the terms of Larry's will and that the money from the book would go to her to do as she wished. The family history he intended to write and any money would be split among family. This was all so overwhelming she wasn't sure how to fit it into her life. The one thing Jace knew for sure was she wanted Taylor to be there each step.

"Jace, are you ready to go?" Taylor asked as he knocked on her door.

"Yes."

Jace, Taylor, Eric, and Zack drove to the family cemetery. Taylor was now ready to honor Larry's request. As the four got out of the jeep, Taylor took four dozen peach-colored roses out of the back and they all walked to Susan's grave. Taylor knelt down and placed them in front of the marker.

"From Larry, who could not bear to say good-bye and loved you until the day he took his last breath on this earth," Taylor said. He stood and put his arm around Jace.

"We have something else we have to do for our family," Jace said.

"What's that?" Taylor asked.

"We have to go to Gettysburg," she answered.

Taylor was silent and looked at Zack.

"I already have reservations for the reenactment in July. It's time to go back and settle the past so that we can all move forward," Jace said.

"I'll make arrangements when I get back to D.C.," Zack said.

Jace took Sarah's diary out of her bag and looked at Zack. "I have something I need to show you."

Everyone followed Jace to Martha's marker.

"Martha Ann Catherine Keens, Martha, and also known as Mack," Jace said.

"I don't understand," Eric said to her.

Jace opened the diary to the back cover and peeled it back. She took a piece of paper out and tenderly opened it, then began to read.

"I promised to not speak of this but never promised not to write about it. I destroyed all information that Samuel White had written on the Night Walker in order to protect the best friend I have ever had, Mack. May she always be remembered for the love she gave to James and her friendship to me and Samuel."

"That will have to be put somewhere in the family history," Zack said and wiped a tear from her face.

Taylor turned and wrapped his arms around Jace. "I have a gift for you."

"You've given me so much already. I can't imagine; what is it?" Jace asked.

"New Year's in New York," Taylor said.

Chapter Sixty~Two ❧

Taylor had called in some favors at the last minute to see this night would be everything it should have been for his uncle and Susan Bowen. He would honor their memory with something special for Jace. They had arrived Friday morning in New York and Taylor had the limo driver take a drive through Central Park before arriving at the Crowne Plaza. He smiled watching Jace take in every sight they passed. Taylor had purchased tickets for *Phantom of the Opera* for Saturday night. They had walked the streets on Time Square; visited the newspaper, where he introduced her to Alfred Prichard; rode the subway; went to SoHo; and, because no visit is complete without it, rode to the top of the Empire State Building.

Taylor had been a gentleman and reserved a double room suite for them. He didn't want Jace to have the wrong idea, but when he looked at her his body couldn't deny what he was feeling. Jace was a beautiful woman and there was a connection between them.

"Taylor, can you help me?" Jace asked and pointed to the zipper in the back of her dress.

"My pleasure," he said and zipped the dress, then leaned in closer to her. He could smell the light scent of lilacs. "You're beautiful, that dress matches the blue in your eyes."

"You look pretty spectacular in that tux. Where're we headed?"

"Downstairs to the bar for a drink, then to 21 Club for dinner."

Jace walked over and kissed Taylor. "Thank you for everything."

The evening progressed with all the flare of New York. Dinner, champagne, roses bought from a vendor on the street as they left the restaurant . . . They stood for a moment and watched the increasing number of partygoers smiling and singing in the street.

"It's so nice to see everyone celebrating after all that has happened here," Jace said.

"We are a resilient group."

"Are we going to Times Square with the rest of the world?"

"No, I want to go back and watch the ball drop from our suite, if that's okay with you."

"Sounds good. I love to dress up, but these heels weren't made for walking all night."

"Then, my lady, your carriage is waiting," Taylor said and waved to the limo.

CROWNE PLAZA, TOP-FLOOR SUITE
11:45 P.M.

Taylor had taken his jacket off, turned on music to a 1940s station, and was opening champagne while waiting for Jace to return to the main room so they could watch the New Year come in together. He looked at his hands trying to open the bottle; they were shaking.

"I'm glad to get those shoes off," Jace said, coming out of her room. She saw Taylor's hands. "What's wrong? Is your arm and hand hurting?" Jace walked over and put her hand on his arm.

"No, they only do this when I think or worry about you," he said as the cork popped.

Jace took the bottle and poured two glasses for them. "You don't need to worry; I have the best protector in the world."

"Zack?" he asked

"No, you."

They touched glasses, then drank. They could hear the people in Times Square singing.

"To 2002, may it bring happiness and healing to everyone," Jace said, then moved into Taylor and kissed him.

Taylor held her and hoped this moment would never end. When they parted, she smiled at him and nodded toward his bedroom. Taylor's body shook from his need to have her. He picked her up and carried her to his bedroom. As he unzipped her dress he kissed her neck, shoulders, and all the way down to the small curve in her back, stopping when she shivered. Taylor took his hands and slid them through the back of her opened dress, pulling her gently to him.

"Tell me, tell me, Jace, what do you want? I will give you anything you want," he said.

"All I want now and always is you."

Taylor gently lowered her down on his bed, turned out the light, and gave her all he had, body and soul.

Tuesday, January 1, 2002
6:00 a.m.

Taylor watched as the sun rose on the New Year. He looked at the woman lying on his shoulder and now knew what it meant to love and need someone beyond death. Jace would forever be tied to him and he would not be parted from her in this world or the next. Taylor now understood what they must do to help their ancestors to find peace.

Chapter Sixty~Three ॐ

Zack sat at her desk reading over an email from Jace.

Zack, I hope you're not working too hard trying to find Aaron Caydon these days but enjoying the all too frequent trips Eric is making to Washington. I fear his time there may be shorter, as Taylor has been stockpiling extra work for him here. We have been busy here in Waynesboro working on the story of our families. Eric will be heading to Louisiana in a week to photograph a number of the Keens families. He is hoping to be able to stay with your family in Morgan City. Zack I want you to read all the stories Sarah wrote about the brave women that traveled to heal in her journal. These women were strong, brave, and loving individuals, and Taylor has decided to add those stories to the history and hopefully Eric will be able to find relatives we can talk with and photograph.

We are excited about the trip to Gettysburg in July, and I'm anxious to see you. Please give our love to Bevan and Laura, take care of yourself, and call me when you have time.

Love,

Jace

Zack smiled; since January, Jace and Taylor had become insepa-
rable. She felt it was more than just the work on the book that Jace
kept insisting on, but Zack knew that was for appearances with
family. They were in love, and the trip to Gettysburg would be more
than just to bring peace to ghosts; it would be a new beginning.

"Jace and Taylor send their love to you and Laura," Zack said
before Bevan entered her office.

"What are they up to these days?"

"According to Jace, the book on our family's history."

"Dad told me last week they had been over there taking pictures,
copying the scrapbook, gathering a lot information. I need to check
about releasing information on Deelyn and Frank's dealings with
the Jedburghs for Taylor."

"How's Laura?" Zack said and smiled at him.

"Pregnant and bitchy right now. She is on bed rest for the next
three weeks due to some bleeding issues. It's driving her crazy."

"Things will get better."

"God, I hope so, even General Lee is hiding from her," Bevan
said.

" Does E. have anything on Aaron?" Zack asked.

"Nothing, disappeared off the face of the earth for now. He'll
resurface, but with all of his connections it could be anywhere on
the planet."

"I don't think he's finished with Taylor. I can't get a clear thought
on it, but he's going to cause problems again for him," Zack said.

"Sorry about Deelyn's boning knife. I know it meant a lot."

"Not a problem, I intend to get it back," Zack said.

Long Bowe B&B
Georgia
8:00 p.m.

Taylor sat on the porch swing and read over papers that had been
faxed from Bentwood's office this evening. There was a note from

Harry Hawthorne's niece advising that he had passed away peacefully January fifth, 2002, surrounded by family. The next pages were the accumulated wealth of Larry Shaw. Taylor had to stop and look at the numbers several times before he began to realize what had been at stake from day one and that it was possible Aaron Caydon had also obtained this information. He looked up as Jace came out the front door with two glasses.

"Sweet tea?"

"Sounds good," Taylor said and moved over for her to sit down.

"Are those the papers from Hawaii?"

"Yes, Harry died in January and Bentwood is reminding me I have papers to sign when I get back there," Taylor answered.

Jace sat in silence for a moment. "When do you have to go back?"

"Well, I thought we'd go back after the trip to Gettysburg."

"We?"

"Unless you'd rather go somewhere else," Taylor said.

Jace smiled and kissed Taylor. "No, there's nowhere else I'd rather be, but I need to make some arrangements with Candi and Casie. I've been gone too long."

"I'd like to visit with them when you call. I have a proposition for them that will be beneficial to everyone."

"Like what?"

"I want to buy your share of the B&B and be their silent partner."

"That's nice, but where does that leave me?" Jace asked.

Taylor reached up and touched the heart necklace that Jace continually wore since the night he almost lost her. "With me."

Chapter Sixty~Four ?❧

Taylor waited for Jace to return from Zack and Eric's room. She had bought something for Laura and Bevan's daughter born on Jace's birthday, June first. Sarah Catherine Benjamin arrived healthy and beautiful, according to Bevan. Taylor thought about the name Laura and Bevan chose for their daughter. Names are important in families, they give us character and strength, and they tell stories about who we were, are, and will be in life. Taylor thought about the initials on the back of the necklace. Jace now wore SJB, Sarah Jane Bowen, Susan Jane Bowen, and Sarah Jace Bowen, coincidence? If he believed that, then Eric Samuel White Jr., Lawrence Samuel White-Shaw, and Taylor Samuel White-Shaw were right up there, too. He walked over to the table and looked at the tintype photograph he and Jace had made the day before. A chill ran down his back. Jace wore the dress she had bought here the year before and he had picked out clothing similar to that of the man in Jace's photo. Taylor and Jace were mirror images of Samuel and Sarah. Today they would walk the grounds where Sarah had held Samuel in her arms and made a promise to search for him for eternity until they were reunited and her heart returned. Jace had asked to go toward evening, just before sunset, to Monfort farm.

The door opened. "You ready to go, Taylor?"

Taylor looked at Jace and smiled. She wore a pair of white linen pants, and her blue short-sleeved cotton sweater matched her eyes and Sarah's necklace. "Always ready. Where's Eric and Zack?"

"Zack said that what needed to be done should be done by the two of us, alone. They would see us later."

"Well, I would never question Zack," Taylor said. He smiled and reached in his front jean pocket; he had one more thing to give Jace.

Monfort Farm
Gettysburg
8:30 p.m.

Jace smiled as they drove up to the Monfort farm. She felt silly thinking she would see Samuel and Sarah waiting. Zack had told her she would find love again. She looked at Taylor and knew he was who she had been looking for, waiting for, and now had found. Jace hoped this evening she would be able to bring peace to her ancestors. She prayed that Sarah and Samuel, Susan and Larry would come together and the promise would be fulfilled. Jace held the heart in her hand as they arrived at the farm, and the scent of lilacs filled the car. Jace and Taylor looked at each other. Taylor opened the car door and put his arm around Jace as they walked into the field.

Jace turned and looked at Taylor. "I was told that there could be no peace when a part of the heart was missing, lost, waiting to be found." She held the necklace. "It has been returned. I ask that those who are lost or searching now, come together, be whole and at peace."

Taylor stood watching the sun as it was beginning its descent to what appeared to be a beautiful evening ahead. He could feel the weight of the centuries and the hands of his ancestors upon his shoulders. They were there, next to him, Samuel and Larry. The scent of lilacs again rode on the wind. The time had come to finish what they had intended so many years ago. He turned to the woman he loved, knelt, and took her hands.

"When this journey began I promised to return all that belonged to the Bowens," Taylor said. He reached in his pocket and took out the ring that Samuel had made for Sarah. "Jace, will you take what was made for Sarah, made out of love, made for eternity, and marry me?"

Jace could feel them, her family, Sarah and Susan. They were here at this very moment to support her, thank her, and to let her know this was meant to be, love and happiness.

She knelt, reached for his face, and kissed him. "Yes, I will."

Chapter Sixty~Five ❧

Jace stood looking out the balcony of the bridal suite. In an hour all the planning she had quickly done was complete. Friends and family were all gathering downstairs waiting for the ceremony to begin. She wanted to keep their wedding simple but special. When they first came to Hawaii and Taylor showed her the penthouse, he attempted to explain the wealth of Larry Shaw and the worth of the Shaw family. She was pleased as they discussed a life of giving to others and living a simple life together as much as possible. They agreed their lust would be for life. What they had would help others, as Jace had always tried to give back wherever she worked and helped where there was need, and she never wanted that to change. Jace could hear Zack talking to her parents. She looked at them and smiled. Their love and strength was an inspiration to her, especially today.

Jace's father walked over and kissed her forehead. "Time to go."

"I'm ready."

❧

Beach
7:00 p.m.

Jace stood with her father waiting for their cue. The wedding coordinator had done a wonderful job, managing to have a gazebo placed just at the water's edge, as she had asked, and flowers around the top and down both sides. Zack had picked an emerald green sundress and opted for bare feet instead of sandals. Eric and Taylor complemented each other with linen pants and cream-colored pullover shirts and sandals. There were leis draped around the members of the wedding party.

"I've never worn flowers before," Eric said.

"It's quite becoming, maybe you should wear them all the time," Zack teased.

"I don't understand why you two didn't just make this a double wedding?" Jace said to them.

"Oh, we haven't decided just yet if we like each other," Eric said and thumped Zack on the head.

"I have work to do and he just keeps getting in my way," Zack said and stuck her tongue out at him.

"Adult, very adult," Eric said and kissed her.

"We're up," Zack said and turned, hugged Jace, and straightened the heart necklace. "See you in a min."

Jace could see Taylor as he stood and waited as his brother and Zack walked toward him. Eric smiled at Zack, then took his place as best man and she as maid of honor. Jace waited for the next song to start, "At Last," and then she walked in her cream-colored 1940s-style dress to meet Taylor. The feel of the sand on her feet made this day real, no dream. She had once again pulled her hair to the side and placed a rhinestone clip in it along the natural wave. They had forgone suites and ties for sandals, bare feet, shorts, sundresses, or whatever was comfortable for their guests. Jace looked around at the family and friends that had been flown into Honolulu for this day, Taylor's wedding gift. The twins smiled as she walked by and then she laughed when Sarah reached out for her from Laura's arms.

Jace stopped and kissed the child, then progressed on. Jace reached the man she loved; her father gave Taylor her hand, kissed her once more, then took his place next to Jace's mother.

"You may all be seated," the pastor said.

Jace and Taylor turned to each other and repeated traditional vows. When the ceremony ended they kissed and turned to meet their friends as husband and wife. Taylor squeezed Jace's hand. She looked at him.

"We have some special guests," Taylor said and nodded his head to the back of the crowd.

Jace turned and could see the shape of two couples, one in Civil War dress and the other in World War II uniforms.

"Well, after all, they are family," Jace said.

Taylor kissed his bride again and headed for the reception area.

The evening progressed with food, dancing, laughter, and many toasts to the bride and groom. Eric found Zack talking to Candi and Casie. He reached out and took her by the hand.

"Let's take a break and go for a quick walk," he said and headed out the open doors toward the beach.

"Fun day," Zack said.

"Absolutely. I'm going to be gone through the first of the year. I've taken a job that is paying way more than it should and I just couldn't resist," Eric said.

"Wow, why so long?"

"It's in Jackson Hole, Wyoming. Some author writing a book on nature," Eric said.

"Well, guess Christmas will have to wait then," Zack said.

"Maybe not," Eric said and reached in his pocket and pulled out a ring. "Kind of anticlimactic after today, but wanted you to have–"

Zack grabbed and kissed him.

"Guess that's a yes?" Eric said.

Zack just looked at him and smiled.

"Let's keep this quiet right now. I don't want to ruin Taylor and Jace's day," Eric said.

"When do you have to leave?" Zack asked.

"In the morning. Taylor already knows; he and Jace will be headed to Italy for a month so decided it was the best time to go," Eric said.

"Jace and Taylor are coming, should we tell them?" Zack said and put the ring in her pocket.

"Hey, you two," Taylor said.

"Why are you out here? The party is up the beach," Jace said.

"Oh, just telling Zack about my job," Eric said.

"You have a ring!" Jace said.

"Damn it! I hate this psychic thing you two have," Eric said.

Taylor smiled at his brother and shook his hand. "It's about time."

"I didn't want to ruin your day, so don't say anything right now. After I get back from Wyoming, we can make a proper announcement," Eric said.

"Let's go; we have silent celebrating to do," Jace said.

Both couples headed back, to family and friends, secrets kept but hope and love for the future.

Chapter Sixty~Six ❧

Taylor was going over instructions and arrangements he had made and what would still need to be completed for all of their guests with his friends, Bevan and Ron. Both men had arranged for Zack and the two of them to see Jace, Taylor, and Eric to their gates safely.

"If you need anything," Taylor started.

"Go. We got it handled," Bevan said.

"Have a great time; see you two when you get back," Ron said.

"I have to meet with Bentwood, finish paperwork on the will, and then we'll see how many people we can help," Taylor said.

"So you've told Jace just how much money you're worth?" Bevan asked.

"I've given her an estimate but actual numbers, no, it's overwhelming even for me right now," Taylor said.

"Go!" Bevan told him.

"Bye, bro, see you in a few months," Eric said and hugged Taylor.

"You leaving, too?" Bevan asked.

"Yep, on my way to Jackson Hole, Wyoming; work to do, money to make," Eric said.

"Keep in touch and be careful," Bevan said.

"Oh, I will—I have a girlfriend now," Eric said and looked at Zack.

Zack hugged and kissed Jace and Taylor. "Have fun and be careful, gotta run—Eric's plane is here."

"Do you think they'll wait until we get back to get married?" Taylor asked.

"I think so," Jace said.

"Well, Mrs. Shaw, time to leave," Taylor said and kissed Jace. "You smell lovely, not lilacs, something new?"

"Yes, Zack gave it to me," Jace said as they headed to the waiting attendant.

Ron and Bevan watched as Zack walked Eric to his gate and kissed him good-bye. She then returned to where Bevan and Ron stood.

"Heard you ask Taylor about Larry's money," Ron asked.

Bevan looked around the gate at the people, not sure if he would recognize Aaron if he was there. "That's a discussion for another time and place," Bevan said.

"You look like something is wrong, boss," Zack said.

"Still worried about Aaron, aren't you?" Ron asked.

"Until he is caught or killed, I'll always be worried," Bevan said and looked at Ron and Zack.

"We still have work to do where Aaron Reece Caydon is concerned."

Jace and Taylor settled into their seats in first class for the long trip ahead of them. The attendant walked up. "Champagne?" she asked.

"Yes," Taylor answered.

Jace looked at the simple ring now surrounded on both sides by diamond bands. She reached and straightened the heart necklace.

When the glasses were brought back to them, Taylor gave Jace her glass.

"What shall we drink to?" Jace asked.

"To those whose love never died," Taylor said.

"To family," Jace responded.

"To our family," Taylor said and kissed her. He thought at that moment he could smell the lightest scent of lilacs, but he could be wrong.

Epilogue ❧

Eric looked out as the chartered plane he was sitting in began its descent to a small runway. He could see snow-capped mountains and shivered, knowing that it would be cold when he walked off the warm plane. He reached over and opened the bag next to him and pulled out the lined bomber-style jacket Zack had given him their last night together. He shook his head wondering how long she had known about the ring and this job. The pilot made a nice landing and once stopped, the co-pilot opened the door. Eric looked at the small man standing next to the Range Rover.

"Mr. Shaw, I'm Dan, your driver. Please get inside and I'll see to your belongings," he said.

"Thank you," Eric responded. He got inside the Rover and rubbed his hands together. The pilot and driver quickly placed all of Eric's luggage and equipment in the back.

"I hope you brought a lot of warm clothing," Dan said.

"I think what I brought should be sufficient, but I'll need to stop in town and pick up a few more things for outside work later," Eric said and sat back as the driver headed down the airport drive and out of town.

"We have a bit of a drive up the mountain," Dan said.

"No problem, and I like your tie. Not enough people these days show their patriotism," Eric said and pointed to Dan's American-flag tie.

An hour later, the Range Rover stopped in front of a house that sat over the edge of a cliff with a view of the Grand Tetons that was magnificent. Eric could see the lights inside and the beauty of the log built home. As he walked from the Rover to the front door he could smell the smoke coming from the chimney: all the things that made this job already worth the trip. Eric turned and looked as Dan began to take his equipment and luggage out.

"Go ahead, I'll get these," Dan told him.

Eric walked up to the door and knocked. A man about his height answered the door.

"Come in, I've been waiting for you, Mr. Shaw."

"Thank you; it's a bit chilly outside, but lovely here, and this is grand," Eric said.

"Drink?"

"Thank you, rum and coke, if you have it," Eric said. He looked at his employer who was heavyset, skin rather pale, and had dark eyes. Eric looked at the heavy beard, brushy eyebrows, bulbous nose, and long graying hair pulled back in a braid. He took his drink and sat down in front of the fireplace. He was having a difficult time imagining this man out in the wild doing any type of research.

"I'm excited to be here. Your offer was generous and a bit extravagant for the work you want done," Eric said and finished his drink.

"Not at all, Mr. Shaw. Your work is well known and I always get what I want."

"When do you want to start, Mr . . . ?" Eric asked.

"Now will be fine."

Eric looked perplexed.

The man walked over to Eric. "I would like to introduce you to the man financing all of this." He then pointed behind Eric.

Eric stood, turned, and dropped his glass on the floor. He knew the man now standing in front of him.

"I believe it's time we were properly introduced. My name is Caydon, Aaron Reece Caydon, and we have unfinished business." Aaron smiled and watched as Eric Shaw fell to the floor unconscious.

A.R.C.

Look for Me
Six-time award-winning.

A reporter, a healer, and a spy. In this gripping tale of Civil War–era romance and espionage, the lives of three people will be brought together with consequences that none of them could possibly foresee . . .

Samuel: a New York–based reporter who leaves the security and comfort of his home to report on the war. During the course of his assignment, his focus will shift dramatically from the men who are in combat to the efforts of the women who heal. Sarah: a Southern healer who also leaves the safety of her home to travel with nurses; she uses her relationship with nature to treat those in need. Mack: a teenage girl who disguises herself as a boy to infiltrate Union camps.

Mack and Sarah first meet when Mack delivers a letter to Sarah from her brother Ethan, and the two women forge a friendship—and a deception—that will be carried throughout the war. When Samuel encounters Sarah on the battlefield, he realizes that she is a friend from childhood that he has known for years. But when love blossoms between Samuel and Sarah, the war becomes a wedge between them, and they will be forced to make a promise to each other, for now and forever.

Wait for Me
Four-time award-winning.

December 7, 1941, America is at war. Many will go to fight, to heal, and to report. The Whites and Bowens will be there.

Susan Bowen, nurse and great-niece to Sarah Bowen, will answer the call of her country. She will become a task nurse and care for the wounded on battlefields far away from her hometown of Waynesboro, Georgia. In another part of the world she finds someone to care for, maybe to love. Is it chance or fate?

Larry White: young, handsome, and working his dream job as a reporter in Honolulu. Amidst the death and destruction at Pearl Harbor, he is saved by a beautiful woman. He's unsure if she was truly there, or was it just a dream? Larry is determined to make a difference in the war by reporting it, just like his great-uncle, Samuel White.

Deelyn Johns: pilot, mechanic, and dreamer. The sky is her playground. When the war begins, Deelyn searches for a place where she can be of the greatest help. After all, she can fly a plane!

They know the danger and face it; perhaps souls lost will find one another.

About the Author

Janet Shawgo has been a registered nurse for thirty years. She has spent twenty of those years as a travel nurse. She started writing in 2009, with her first novel being published in 2011. The *Look for Me* series has been awarded thirteen awards. She still works full time as a nurse and writes on her off-duty hours. She lives in Galveston, Texas.